Praise for
#1 *New York Times* and *USA TODAY* bestselling author

NORA ROBERTS

"When Roberts puts her expert fingers on the pulse of romance,
legions of fans feel the heartbeat."
—*Publishers Weekly*

"You can't bottle wish fulfillment,
but Nora Roberts certainly knows how to put it on the page."
—*New York Times*

"Roberts is indeed a word artist, painting her story
and her characters with vitality and verve."
—*Los Angeles Daily News*

"Characters that touch the heart, stories that intrigue,
romance that sizzles—Nora Roberts has mastered it all."
—*Rendezvous*

"Roberts is deservedly one of the best known
and most widely read of all romance writers."
—*Library Journal*

"Her stories have fueled the dreams of twenty-five million readers."
—*Entertainment Weekly*

"Roberts' bestselling novels are some of the best in the romance
genre. They are thoughtfully plotted, well-written stories
featuring fascinating characters."
—*USA TODAY*

Dear Reader,

There's nothing like a great movie to reenergize our spirits, or a magical night at the circus to make us believe anything is possible... including finding love. We at Silhouette Books are pleased to present a pair of stories about people who find themselves falling in love despite their greatest efforts not to. And who better to illustrate their romantic voyages than the master of romance, Nora Roberts!

In *Dual Image* Ariel Kirkwood is a beautiful actress playing the role of a lifetime, and Booth DeWitt is the man she's falling in love with. But the sexy screenwriter is doing everything in his power to fight his feelings for the captivating starlet—even though all he really wants is to be with her.

In *Untamed* lion trainer Jovilette Wilder had thought her sedate but sexy new boss was as meek as a lamb—until she felt his long, lingering kiss! Jo may tame lions for a living, but she had a feeling that facing off with the alarmingly charming Keane Prescott would be far more dangerous....

We hope these delightful classics inspire you to open your heart and dream a little dream—each and every day!

The Editors
Silhouette Books

NORA ROBERTS

Summer Dreams

Published by Silhouette Books

America's Publisher of Contemporary Romance

SILHOUETTE BOOKS

SUMMER DREAMS

ISBN-13: 978-0-373-28589-1

Copyright © 2010 by Harlequin Books S.A.

The publisher acknowledges the copyright holder
of the individual works as follows:

DUAL IMAGE
Copyright © 1985 by Nora Roberts

UNTAMED
Copyright © 1983 by Nora Roberts

Recycling programs
for this product may
not exist in your area.

This edition published by arrangement with Harlequin Books S.A.

For questions and comments about the quality of this book please contact us
at Customer_eCare@Harlequin.ca.

® and TM are trademarks of Harlequin Books S.A., used under
license. Trademarks indicated with ® are registered in the United States
Patent and Trademark Office, the Canadian Trade Marks Office and in
other countries.

Visit Silhouette Books at www.eHarlequin.com

Printed in U.S.A.

CONTENTS

Dual Image

Chapter One

Balancing a bag of groceries in one arm, Amanda let herself into the house. She radiated happiness. From outside came the sound of birds singing in the spring sunshine. The gold of her wedding ring caught the light. As a newlywed of three months, she was anxious to prepare a special, intimate dinner as a surprise for Cameron. Her demanding hours at the hospital and clinic often made it impossible for her to cook, and as a new bride she found pleasure in it. This afternoon, with two appointments unexpectedly canceled, she intended to fix something fancy, time-consuming and memorable. Something that went well with candlelight and wine.

As she entered the kitchen she was humming, a rare outward show of emotion for she was a reserved woman. With a satisfied smile, she drew a bottle of Cameron's favorite Bordeaux from the bag. As she studied the label, a smile lingered on her face while she remembered the first time they'd shared a bottle. He'd been so romantic, so attentive, so much what she'd needed at that point in her life.

A glance at her watch told her she had four full hours before her husband was expected home. Time enough to prepare an elaborate meal, light the candles and set out the crystal.

First, she decided, she was going upstairs to get out of her practical suit and shoes. There was a silk caftan upstairs, sheer, in misty shades of blue. Tonight, she wouldn't be a psychiatrist, but a woman, a woman very much in love.

The house was scrupulously neat and tastefully decorated. Such things came naturally to Amanda. As she walked toward the stairs, she glanced at a vase of Baccarat crystal and wished fleetingly she'd remembered fresh flowers. Perhaps she'd call the florist and have something extravagant delivered. Her hand trailed lightly over the polished banister as she started up. Her eyes, usually serious or intent, were dreamy. Carelessly, she pushed open the bedroom door.

Her smile froze. Utter shock replaced it. As she stood in the doorway, all color seemed to drain out of her cheeks. Her eyes grew huge before pain filled them. Out of her mouth came one anguished word.

"Cameron."

The couple in bed, locked in a passionate embrace, sprang apart. The man, smoothly handsome, his sleek hair disheveled, stared up in disbelief. The woman—feline, sultry, stunning— smiled very, very slowly. You could almost hear her purr.

"Vikki." Amanda looked at her sister with anguished eyes.

"You're home early." There was a hint, only a suspicion of a laugh in her sister's voice.

Cameron put a few more inches between himself and his sister-in-law. "Amanda, I…"

In one split second, Amanda's face contorted. With her eyes locked on the couple in bed, she reached in her jacket pocket and drew out a small, lethal revolver. The lovers stared at it in astonishment, and in silence. Coolly, she aimed and fired. A puff of confetti burst out.

"Ariel!"

Dr. Amanda Lane Jamison, better known as Ariel Kirkwood, turned to her harassed director as the couple in bed and members of the television crew dissolved into laughter.

"Sorry, Neal, I couldn't help myself. Amanda's *always* the victim," she said dramatically while her eyes danced. "Just think what it might do for the ratings if she lost her cool just once and murdered someone."

"Look, Ariel—"

"Or even just seriously injured them," she went on rapidly. "And who," she continued, flinging her hand toward the bed, "deserves it more than her spineless husband and scheming sister?"

At the hoots and applause of the crew, Ariel took a bow, then reluctantly turned over her weapon to her director when he held out his hand.

"You," he said with a long-suffering sigh, "are a certified loony, and have been since I've known you."

"I appreciate that, Neal."

"This time the tape's going to be running," he warned and tried not to grin. "Let's see if we can shoot this scene before lunch."

Agreeably, Ariel went down to the first floor of the set. She stood patiently while her hair and makeup were touched up. Amanda was always perfection. Organized, meticulous, calm— all the things Ariel herself wasn't. She'd played the character for just over five years on the popular daytime soap opera *Our Lives, Our Loves.*

In those five years, Amanda had graduated with honors from college, had earned her degree in psychiatric medicine and had gone on to become a respected therapist. Her recent marriage to Cameron Jamison appeared to be made in heaven. But, of course, he was a weak opportunist who'd married her for her money and social position, while lusting after her sister—and half the female population of the fictional town of Trader's Bend.

Amanda was about to be confronted with the truth. The story line had been leading up to this revelation for six weeks, and the letters from viewers had poured in. Both they and Ariel thought it was about time Amanda found out about her louse of a husband.

Ariel liked Amanda, respected her integrity and poise. When the cameras rolled, Ariel *was* Amanda. While in her personal life she would much prefer a day at an amusement park to an evening at the ballet, she understood all the nuances of the woman she portrayed.

When this scene was aired, viewers would see a neat, slender woman with pale blond hair sleeked back into a sophisticated knot. The face was porcelain, stunning, with an icy kind of beauty that sent out signals of restrained sexuality. Class. Style.

Lake-blue eyes, high curved cheekbones added to the look of polished elegance. A perfectly shaped mouth tended toward serious smiles. Finely arched brows that were shades darker than the delicate blond of her hair accented luxurious lashes. A flawless beauty, perfectly composed—that was Amanda.

Ariel waited for her cue and wondered vaguely if she'd turned off her coffeepot that morning.

They ran through the scene again, from cue to cut, then a second time when it was discovered that Vikki's strapless bathing suit could be seen when she shifted in bed. Then came reaction shots—the camera zoomed in close on Amanda's pale, shocked face and held for several long, dramatic seconds.

"Lunch."

Response was immediate. The lovers bounded out of either side of the bed. In his bathing trunks, J. T. Brown, Ariel's on-screen husband, took her by the shoulders and gave her a long hard kiss. "Look, sweetie," he began, staying in character, "I'll explain about all this later. Trust me. I gotta call my agent."

"Wimp," Ariel called after him with a very un-Amandalike grin before she hooked her arm through that of Stella Powell, her series sister. "Pull something over that suit, Stella. I can't face the commissary food today."

Stella tossed back her tousled mass of auburn hair. "You buying?"

"Always sponging off your sister," Ariel mumbled. "Okay, I'll spring, but hurry up. I'm starving."

On her way to her dressing room, Ariel walked off the set, then through two more—the fifth floor of Doctors Hospital and the living room of the Lanes, Trader Bend's leading family. It was tempting to shed her costume and take down her hair, but it would only mean fooling with wardrobe and makeup after lunch. Instead, she just grabbed her purse, an outsize hobo bag that looked a bit incongruous with Amanda's elegant business suit. She was already thinking about a thick slice of baklava soaked in honey.

"Come on, Stella." Ariel stuck her head in the adjoining dressing room as Stella zipped up a pair of snug jeans. "My stomach's on overtime."

"It always is," her coworker returned as she pulled on a bulky sweatshirt. "Where to?"

"The Greek deli around the corner." More than ready, Ariel started down the hall in her characteristically long, swinging gait while Stella hurried to keep up. It wasn't that Ariel rushed from place to place, but simply that she wanted to see what was next.

"My diet," Stella began.

"Have a salad," Ariel told her without mercy. She turned her head to give Stella a quick up-and-down glance. "You know, if you weren't always wearing those skimpy outfits on camera, you wouldn't have to starve yourself."

Stella grinned as they came to the street door. "Jealous."

"Yeah. I'm always elegant and *always* proper. You have all the fun." Stepping outside, Ariel took a deep breath of New York. She loved it—had always loved it in a way usually reserved for tourists. Ariel had lived on the long thin island of Manhattan all of her life, and yet it remained an adventure to her. The sights, the smells, the sounds.

It was brisk for mid-April, and threatening to rain. The air was damp and smelled of exhaust. The streets and sidewalks were clogged with lunchtime traffic—everyone hurrying, everyone with important business to attend to. A pedestrian swore and banged a fist on the hood of a cab that had clipped too close to the curb. A woman with spiked orange hair hustled by in black leather boots. Somone had written something un-complimentary on a poster for a hot Broadway play. But Ariel saw a street vendor selling daffodils.

She bought two bunches and handed one to Stella.

"You can never pass up anything, can you?" Stella mumbled, but buried her face in the yellow blooms.

"Think of all I'd miss," Ariel countered. "Besides, it's spring."

Stella shivered and looked up at the leaden sky. "Sure."

"Eat." Ariel grabbed her arm and pulled her along. "You always get cranky when you miss meals."

The deli was packed with people and aromas. Spices and honey. Beer and oil. Always a creature of the senses, Ariel drew in the mingled scents before she worked her way to the counter. She had an uncanny way of getting where she was going through a throng without using her elbows or stepping on toes. While she moved, she watched and listened. She wouldn't want to miss a scent, or the texture of a voice, or the clashing colors of food. As she looked behind the glass-fronted counter, she could already taste the things there.

"Cottage cheese, a slice of pineapple and coffee—black," Stella said with a sigh. Ariel sent her a brief, pitying look.

"Greek salad, a hunk of that lamb on a hard roll and a slice of baklava. Coffee, cream and sugar."

"You're disgusting," Stella told her. "You never gain an ounce."

"I know." Ariel moved down the counter to the cashier. "It's a matter of mental control and clean living." Ignoring Stella's rude snort she paid the bill then made her way through the crowded deli toward an empty table. She and a bull of a man reached it simultaneously. Ariel simply held her tray and sent him a stunning smile. The man straightened his shoulders, sucked in his stomach and gave way.

"Thanks," Stella acknowledged and dismissed him at the same time, knowing if she didn't Ariel would invite him to join them and upset any chance of a private conversation. The woman, Stella thought, needed a keeper.

Ariel did all the things a woman alone should know better than to do. She talked to strangers, walked alone at night and answered her door without the security chain attached. It wasn't that she was daring or careless, but simply that she believed in the best of people. And somehow, in a bit more than twenty-five years of living, she'd never been disillusioned. Stella marveled at her, even while she worried about her.

"The gun was one of your best stunts all season," Stella remarked as she poked at her cottage cheese. "I thought Neal was going to scream."

"He needs to relax," Ariel said with her mouth full. "He's been on edge ever since he broke up with that dancer. How about you? Are you still seeing Cliff?"

"Yeah." Stella lifted her shoulder. "I don't know why, it's not going anywhere."

"Where do you want it to go?" Ariel countered. "If you have a goal in mind, just go for it."

With a half laugh, Stella began to eat. "Not everyone plunges through life like you, Ariel. It always amazes me that you've never been seriously involved."

"Simple." Ariel speared a fork into her salad then chewed slowly. "I've never met anyone who made my knees tremble. As soon as I do, that'll be it."

"Just like that?"

"Why not? Life isn't as complicated as most people make it." She added a dash of pepper to the lamb. "Are you in love with Cliff?"

Stell frowned—not because of the question, she was used to Ariel's directness. But because of the answer. "I don't know. Maybe."

"Then you're not," Ariel said easily. "Love's a very definite emotion. Sure you don't want any of this lamb?"

Stella didn't bother to answer the question. "If you've never been in love, how do you know?"

"I've never been to Turkey, but I'm sure it's there."

With a laugh, Stella picked up her coffee. "Damn, Ariel, you've always got an answer. Tell me about the script."

"Oh, God." Ariel put down her fork, and leaning her elbows on the table, folded her hands. "It's the best thing I've ever read. I want that part. I'm going to get that part," she added with something that was apart from confidence. It was simple fact. "I swear, I've been waiting for the character of Rae to come along. She's heartless," Ariel continued, resting her chin on her folded hands. "Complex, selfish, cold, insecure. A part like that..." She trailed off with a shake of her head. "And the story," she added on a long breath as her mind jumped from one aspect to the next. "It's nearly as cold and heartless as she is, but it gets to you."

"Booth DeWitt," Stella mused. "It's rumored that he based the character of Rae on his ex-wife."

"He didn't gloss it over either. If he's telling it straight, she put him through hell. In any case," she said, as she began to eat again, "it's the best piece of work that's come my way. I'm going to read for it in a couple of days."

"TV movie," Stella said thoughtfully. "Quality television with DeWitt writing and Marshell producing. You'd have our own producer at your feet if you got it. Boy, what a boost for the ratings."

"He's already playing politics." With a small frown, Ariel broke off a chunk of baklava. "He got me an invitation to a party tonight at Marshell's condo. DeWitt's supposed to be there. From what I hear, he's got the last say on casting."

"He's got a reputation for wanting to push his own buttons," Stella agreed. "So why the frown?"

"Politics're like rain in April—you know it's got to happen, but it's messy and annoying." Then she shrugged the thought away as she did anything unavoidable. In the end, from what she knew of Booth DeWitt, she'd earn the part on her own merit. If there was one thing Ariel had an abundance of, it was confidence. She'd always needed it.

Unlike Amanda, the character she played on the soap, Ariel hadn't grown up financially secure. There'd been a great deal more love than money in her home. She'd never regretted it, or the struggle to make ends meet. She'd been sixteen when her mother had died and her father had gone into a state of shock that had lasted nearly a year. It had never occurred to her that she was too young to take on the responsibilities of running a home and raising two younger siblings. There'd been no one else to do it. She'd sold powder and perfume in a department store to pay her way through college, while managing the family home and taking any bit part that came her way.

They'd been busy, difficult years, and perhaps that in itself had given her the surplus of energy and drive she had today. And the sense that whatever had to be done, could be done.

"Amanda."

Ariel glanced up to see a small, middle-aged woman carrying a take-out bag that smelled strongly of garlic. Because she was called by her character's name almost as often as she was by her own, she smiled and held out her hand. "Hello."

"I'm Dorra Wineberger and I wanted to tell you you're just as beautiful as you are on TV."

"Thank you, Dorra. You enjoy the show?"

"I wouldn't miss it, not one single episode." She beamed at Ariel then leaned closer. "You're wonderful, dear, and so kind and patient. I just feel someone ought to tell you that

Cameron— He's not good for you. The best thing for you to do is send him packing before he gets his hands on your money. He's already pawned your diamond earrings. And this one…" Dorra folded her lips and glared at Stella. "Why you bother with this one, after all the trouble she's caused you… If it hadn't been for her, you and Griff would be married like you should be." She sent Stella an affronted glare. "I know you've got your eyes on your sister's husband, Vikki."

Stella struggled with a grin and, playing the role, tossed her head and slanted her eyes. "Men are interested in me," she drawled. "And why not?"

Dorra shook her head and turned back to Ariel. "Go back to Griff," she advised kindly. "He loves you, he always has."

Ariel returned the quick squeeze of her hand. "Thanks for caring."

Both women watched Dorra walk away before they turned back to each other. "Everyone loves Dr. Amanda," Vikki said with a grin. "She's practically sacred."

"And everyone loves to hate Vikki." With a chuckle, Ariel finished off her coffee. "You're so rotten."

"Yeah." Stella gave a contented sigh. "I know." She chewed her pineapple slowly, with a wistful look at Ariel's plate. "Anyway, it always strikes me as kind of weird when people get me confused with Vikki."

"It just means you're doing your job," Ariel corrected. "If you go into people's homes every day and don't draw emotion out of them, you better look for another line of work. Nuclear physics, log rolling. Speaking of work," she added with a glance at her watch.

"I know… Hey, are you going to eat the rest of that?"

Laughing, Ariel handed her the baklava as they rose.

★ ★ ★

It was well after nine when Ariel paid off the cab in front
of P. B. Marshell's building on Madison Avenue. She wasn't
concerned with being late because she wasn't aware of the time.
She'd never missed a cue or a call in her life, but when it wasn't
directly concerned with work, time was something to be
enjoyed or ignored.

She overtipped the cabbie, stuffed her change in her bag
without counting it, then walked through the light drizzle into
the lobby. She decided it smelled like a funeral parlor. Too many
flowers, too much polish. After giving her name at the security
desk, she slipped into an elevator and pushed the penthouse
button. It didn't occur to her to be nervous at the prospect of
entering P. B. Marshell's domain. A party to Ariel was a party.
She hoped he served champagne. She had a hankering for it.

The door was opened by a stiff-backed, stone-faced man in
a dark suit who asked Ariel's name in a discreet British accent.
When she smiled, he accepted her offered hand before he
realized it. Ariel walked past the butler, leaving him with the
impression of vitality and sex—a combination that left him disconcerted for several minutes. She lifted a glass of champagne
from a tray, and spotting her agent, crossed the room to her.

Booth saw Ariel's entrance. For an instant, he was reminded
of his ex-wife. The coloring, the bone structure. Then the impression was gone, and he was looking at a young woman with
casually curling hair that flowed past her shoulders. It seemed
misted with fine drops of rain. A stunning face, he decided. But
the look of an ice goddess vanished the moment she laughed.
Then there was energy and verve.

Unusual, he thought, as vaguely interested in her as he was
in the drink he held. He let his eyes skim down her and decided

she'd be slim under the casual pleated pants and boxy blouse. Then again, if she was, she would have exploited her figure rather than underplaying it. From what Booth knew of women, they accented whatever charms at their disposal and concealed the flaws. He'd come to accept this as a part of their innate dishonesty.

He gave Ariel one last glance as she rose on her toes to kiss the latest rage in an off-Broadway production. God, he hated these long, crowded pseudoparties.

"...If we cast the female lead."

Booth turned back to P. B. Marshell and lifted his glass. "Hmm?"

Too used to Booth's lapses of attention to be annoyed, Marshell backtracked. "We can get this into production and wrapped in time for the fall sweeps if we cast the female lead. That's virtually all that's holding us back now."

"I'm not worried about the fall sweeps," Booth returned dryly.

"The network is."

"Pat, we'll cast Rae when we find Rae."

Marshell frowned into his Scotch, then drank it. At two hundred and fifty pounds, he needed several glasses to feel any effect. "You've already turned down three top names."

"I turned down three actresses who weren't suitable," Booth corrected. He drank from his own glass as a man who knew liquor and maintained a cautious relationship with it. "I'll know Rae when I see her." His lips moved into a cool smile. "Who'd know better?"

A free, easy laugh had Marshell glancing across the room. For a moment his eyes narrowed in concentration. "Ariel Kirkwood," he told Booth, gesturing with his empty glass. "The network execs would like to push her your way."

"An actress." Booth studied Ariel again. He wouldn't have pegged her as such. Her entrance had caught his attention simply because it hadn't been an *entrance*. There was something completely unselfconscious about her that was rare in the profession. She'd been at the party long enough to have wangled an introduction to him and Marshell, yet she seemed content to stay across the room sipping champagne and flirting with an up-and-coming actor.

She stood easily, in a relaxed manner that wasn't a pose but would photograph beautifully. She made an unattractive face at the actor. The contrast of the ice-goddess looks and the free-wheeling manner piqued his curiosity.

"Introduce me," Booth said simply and started across the room.

Ariel couldn't fault Marshell's taste. The condo was stylishly decorated in elegant golds and creams. The carpet was thick, the walls lacquered. She recognized the signed lithograph behind her. It was a room she knew Amanda would understand and appreciate. Ariel enjoyed visiting it. She'd never have lived there. She laughed up at Tony as he reminisced about the improvisation class they'd taken together a few years before.

"And you started using gutter language to make sure everyone was awake," she reminded him and tugged on the goatee he wore for his current part.

"It worked. What cause is it this week, Ariel?"

Her brows lifted as she sipped her champagne. "I don't have weekly causes."

"Biweekly," he corrected. "Friends of Seals, Save the Mongoose. Come on, what are you into now?"

She shook her head. "There's something that's taking up a lot of my time right now. I can't really talk about it."

Tony's grin faded. He knew that tone. "Important?"

"Vital."

"Well, Tony." Marshell clapped the young actor on the back. "Glad to see you could make it."

Though it was very subtly done, Tony came to attention. "It was nice that you were having this on a night when the theater's dark, Mr. Marshell. Do you know Ariel Kirkwood?" He laid a hand on her shoulder. "We go back a long way."

"I've heard good things about you." Marshell extended his hand.

"Thank you." Ariel left her hand in his a moment as she sorted her impressions. Successful—fond of food from the bulk of him—amiable when he chose to be. Shrewd. She liked the combination. "You make excellent films, Mr. Marshell."

"Thank you," he returned and paused, expecting her to do some campaigning. When she left it at that, he turned to Booth. "Booth DeWitt, Ariel Kirkwood and Tony Lazarus."

"I've seen your play," Booth told Tony. "You know your character very well." He shifted his gaze to Ariel. "Ms. Kirkwood."

Disconcerting eyes, she thought, so clear and direct a green in such a remote face. He gave off signals of aloofness, traces of bitterness, waves of intelligence. Obviously he didn't concern himself overmuch with trends or fashion. His hair was thick and dark and a bit long for the current style. Yet she thought it suited his face. She thought the face belonged to the nineteenth century. Lean and scholarly with a touch of ruggedness and a harshness in the mouth that kept it from being smooth.

His voice was deep and appealing, but he spoke with a clipped quality that indicated impatience. He had the eyes of an observer, she thought. And the air of a man who wouldn't tolerate interference or intimacies. She wasn't certain she'd like him, but she did know she admired his work.

"Mr. DeWitt." Her palm touched his. Strength—she'd expected that. It was in his build, long, rangy—and in his face. Distance—she'd expected that as well. "I enjoyed *The Final Bell*. It was my favorite film of last year."

He passed this off as he studied her face. She exuded sex, in her scent, in her looks—not flagrant or elusive, but light and free. "I don't believe I'm familiar with your work."

"Ariel plays Dr. Amanda Lane Jamison on *Our Lives, Our Loves,*" Tony put in.

Good God, a soap opera, Booth thought. Ariel caught the faint disdain on his face. It was something else she'd expected. "Do you have a moral objection to entertainment, Mr. DeWitt?" she said easily as she sipped champagne. "Or are you just an artistic snob?" She smiled as she spoke, the quick, dashing smile that took any sting from the words.

Beside her, Tony cleared his throat. "Excuse me a minute," he said and exited stage left. Marshell mumbled something about freshening his drink.

When they were alone, Booth continued to study her face. She was laughing at him. He couldn't remember the last time anyone had had the courage, or the occasion, to do so. He wasn't certain if he was annoyed or intrigued. But at the moment he wasn't what he'd been for the past hour. Bored.

"I haven't any moral objections to soap operas, Ms. Kirkwood."

"Oh." She sipped her champagne. A sliver of sapphire on her finger winked in the light and seemed to reflect in her eyes. "A snob then. Well, everyone's entitled. Perhaps there's something else we can talk about. How do you feel about the current administration's foreign policy?"

"Ambivalent," he murmured. "What sort of character do you play?"

"A sterling one." Her eyes continued to dance. "How do you feel about the space program?"

"I'm more concerned about the planet I'm on. How long have you been on the show?"

"Five years." She beamed a smile at someone across the room and raised her hand.

He looked at her again, carefully, and for the first time since he'd come into the party, he smiled. It did something attractive to his face, though it didn't make him quite as approachable as it indicated. "You don't want to talk about your work, do you?"

"Not particularly." Ariel returned his smile with her own open one. Something stirred faintly in him that he'd thought safely dormant. "Not with someone who considers it garbage. In a moment, you'd ask me if I'd ever considered doing any serious work, then I'd probably get nasty. My agent tells me I'm supposed to charm you."

Booth could feel the friendliness radiating from her and distrusted it. "Is that what you're doing?"

"I'm on my own time," Ariel returned. "Besides—" she finished off her champagne "—you aren't the type to be charmed."

"You're perceptive," Booth acknowledged. "Are you a good actress?"

"Yes, I am. It would hardly be worth doing something if you weren't good at it. What about sports?" She twirled her empty glass. "Do you think the Yankees stand a chance this year?"

"If they tighten up the infield." Not your usual type, he decided. Any other actress up for a prime part in one of his scripts would've been flooding him with compliments and mentioning every job she'd ever had in front of the camera. "Ariel…" Booth plucked a fresh glass of champagne from a passing waiter and handed it to her. "The name suits you. A wise choice."

She felt a pull, a quick, definite pull, that seemed to come simply from the way he'd said her name. "I'll tell my mother you said so."

"It's not a stage name?"

"No. My mother was reading *The Tempest* when she went into labor. She was very superstitious. I could have been Prospero if I'd been a boy." With a little shudder, she sipped. "Well, Booth," she began, deciding she'd been formal long enough. "Shouldn't we just come out with the fact that we both know I'll be reading for the part of Rae in a couple of days? I intend to have it."

He nodded in acknowledgment. Though she was refreshingly direct, this was more what he'd expected. "Then I'll be frank enough to tell you that you're not the type I'm looking for."

She lifted a brow without any show of discomfort. "Oh? Why?"

"For one thing, you're too young."

She laughed—a free, breezy sound that seemed completely unaffected. He didn't trust that either. "I think my line is I can be older."

"Maybe. But Rae's a tough lady. Hard as a rock." He lifted his own drink but never took his eyes off her. "You've got too many soft points. They show in your face."

"Because this is me. And I've yet to play myself in front of a camera." She paused a moment as the idea worked around in her head. "I don't think I'd care to."

"Is any actress ever herself?"

Her eyes came back to his. He was watching her again with that steady intenseness most would have found unnerving.

Though the pull came again, Ariel accepted the look because it was part of him. "You don't care for us much as a breed, do you?"

"No." For some reason he didn't question, Booth felt compelled to test her. He lifted a strand of her hair. Soft— surprisingly soft. "You're a beautiful woman," he murmured.

Ariel tilted her head as she studied him. His eyes had lost nothing of their directness. She might have felt pleasure in the compliment if she hadn't recognized it as calculated. Instead she felt disappointment. "And?"

His brows drew together. "And?"

"That line usually leads to another. As a writer I'm sure you have several tucked away."

He let his fingers brush over her neck. She felt the strength in them, and the carelessness of the gesture. "Which one would you like?"

"I'd prefer one you meant," Ariel told him evenly. "But since I wouldn't get it, why don't we skip the whole thing? You know, your character, Phil, is narrow-minded, cool blooded and rude. I believe you portrayed yourself very well." She lifted her glass one last time and decided it was a shame that he thought so little of women, or perhaps of people in general. "Good night, Booth."

When she walked away, Booth stood looking after her for several moments before he started to laugh. At the time, it didn't occur to him that it was the first easy laugh he'd had in almost two years. It didn't even occur to him that he was laughing at himself.

No, she wasn't his Rae, he mused, but she was good. She was very, very good. He was going to remember Ariel Kirkwood.

Chapter Two

Booth stood by the wide expanse of window in Marshell's office and watched New York hustle by. From that height, he felt removed from it, and the rush and energy radiating up from the streets and sidewalks. He was satisfied to be separate. Connections equaled involvement.

None of the actresses they'd auditioned in the past two weeks came close to what he was after. He knew what he wanted for the part of Rae—who better?

When he'd first started the script it had been an impulse—therapy, he mused with a grim smile. Cheaper than a psychiatrist and a lot more satisfying. He'd never expected to do any more than finish it, purge his system and toss it in a drawer. That was before he'd realized it was the best work he'd ever done. Perhaps anger was the tenth Muse. In any case, he was first and foremost a writer. However painful it was to expose himself and his mistakes to the public, there was no tossing his finest work in a drawer. And since he was going to have it performed, he was going to have it performed well.

He'd thought it would be difficult to cast the part of Phil, the character who was essentially himself. And yet that had been surprisingly simple. The core of the story wasn't Phil, but Rae, a devastatingly accurate mirror of his ex-wife, Elizabeth Hunter. A superb actress, a gracious celebrity—a woman without a single genuine emotion.

Their marriage had started with a whirlwind and ended in disaster. Booth didn't consider himself blameless, though he placed most of the blame on his own gullibility. He'd believed in her image, fallen hard for the perfection of face and body. He could have forgiven the faults, the flaws soon discovered. But he could never, would never, forgive being used. And yet, Booth was still far from sure whether he blamed Liz for using him, or himself for allowing it to happen.

Either way, the tempestuous five-year marriage had given him grist for a clean, hard story that was going to be an elaborate television movie. And more, it had given him a firm distrust of women, particularly actresses. Two years before, when the break had finally come, he'd promised himself that he'd never become involved with another woman who could play roles that well. Honesty, if it truly existed, was what he'd look for when he was ready.

His thoughts came back to Ariel. Perhaps she was centered in his mind because of her surface resemblance to Liz, but he wasn't certain. There was no similarity in mannerisms, voice cadence or style of dress. And the biggest contrast seemed to be in personality. She hadn't put herself out to charm him or to hold his attention. And she'd done both. Perhaps she'd simply used a different angle on an old game.

While he hadn't trusted it, he'd enjoyed her lack of artifice. The breezy laugh, the unaffected gestures, the candid looks. It had been a long time since a woman had lingered in his mind.

A pity, Booth mused, that she was unsuitable for the part. He could have used the distraction. Instinct told him that Ariel Kirkwood would be nothing if she wasn't a distraction.

"I'm still leaning toward this Julie Newman." Chuck Tyler, the director, tossed an eight-by-ten glossy on Marshell's desk. "A lot of camera presence and her first reading was very good."

With the photo in one hand, Marshell tipped back in his deep leather chair. The sun at his back streamed over both the glossy and the gold he wore on either hand. "An impressive list of credits, too."

"No." Booth didn't bother to turn around, but stood watching the traffic stream. For some odd reason he visualized himself on his boat in Long Island Sound, sailing out to sea. "She lacks the elegance. Too much vulnerability."

"She can act, Booth," Marshell said with a now familiar show of impatience.

"She's not the one."

Marshell automatically reached in his pocket for the cigars he'd given up a month before. He swore lightly under his breath. "And we're running out of time and options."

Booth gave an unconcerned shrug. Yes, he'd like to be sailing, stripped to the waist with the sun on his back and the water so blue it hurt the eyes. He'd like to be alone.

When the buzzer on his desk rang, Marshell heaved a sigh and leaned forward to answer. "Ms. Kirkwood's here for her reading, Mr. Marshell."

With a grunt, Marshell flipped open the portfolio Ariel's agent had sent him, then passed it to Chuck. "Send her in."

"Kirkwood," Chuck mused, frowning over Ariel's publicity shot. "Kirkwood… Oh, yeah, I saw her last summer in an off-Broadway production of *Streetcar.*"

Vaguely interested, Booth looked over his shoulder. "Stella?"

"Blanche," Chuck corrected, skimming over her list of credits.

"Blanche DuBois?" Booth gave a short laugh as he turned completely around. "She's fifteen to twenty years too young for that part."

Chuck merely lifted his eyes. "She was good," he said simply. "Very good. And from what I'm told, she's very good on the soap. I don't have to tell you how many of our top stars started that way."

"No, you don't." Booth sat negligently on the arm of a chair. "But if she's stuck with the same part for five years, she's either not good enough for a major film or major theater, or she's completely without ambition. Because she's an actress, I'd have to go with the former."

"Keep sharpening your cynicism," Marshell said dryly. "It's good for you."

Booth's grin flashed—that rare one that came and went so quickly it left the onlooker dazzled and unsure why. Ariel caught a glimpse of it as she entered the room. It went a long way toward convincing her to change her initial opinion of him. It passed through her mind, almost as quickly as Booth's grin, that perhaps he had some redeeming personal qualities after all. She was always ready to believe it.

"Ms. Kirkwood." Marshell heaved his bulk from the chair and extended his hand.

"Mr. Marshell, nice to see you again." She took a brief scan of the room, her gaze lingering only fleetingly on Booth as he remained seated on the arm of the chair. "Your office is just as impressive as your home."

Booth waited while she was introduced to Chuck. She'd dressed very simply, he noticed. Deceptively so if you considered the bold scarves she'd twisted at the waist of the demure

blue dress. Violets and emeralds and wild pinks. A daring combination, and stunningly effective. Her hair was loose again,
giving her an air of youth and freedom he would never equate
with the character she wanted to portray. Absently, he took out
a cigarette and lit it.

"Booth." Ariel gave him an easy smile before her gaze flicked
over the cigarette. "They'll kill you."

He took a drag and let out a lazy stream of smoke. "Eventu-
ally." She wore the same carelessly sexy scent he'd noticed the
night of the party. Booth wondered why it was that it suited her
while contrasting at the same time. She fascinated. It seemed to
be something she did effortlessly. "I'm going to cue you," he
continued and reached for a copy of the script. "We'll use the
confrontation scene in the third act. You're familiar with it?"

All business, Ariel noted curiously. Does he ever relax? Does
he ever choose to? Though she was rarely tense herself, she recognized tension in him and wondered why he was nervous.
What nerves she felt herself were confined to a tiny roiling knot
in the center of her stomach. She always acknowledged it and
knew, if anything, it would help to push her through the reading.

"I'm familiar with it," she told him, accepting another copy
of the script.

Booth took a last drag on his cigarette then put it out. "Do
you want a lead-in?"

"No." Now her palms were damp. Good. Ariel knew better
than to want to be relaxed when twinges of emotions would
sharpen her skills. Taking deep, quiet breaths she flipped
through the bound script until she found the right scene. It
wasn't a simple one. It stabbed at the core of the character—
selfish ambition and icy sex. She took a minute.

Booth watched her. She looked more like the guileless

ingenue than the calculating leading lady, he mused and was almost sorry there wasn't a part for her in the film. Then she looked up and pinned him with a cold, bloodless smile that completely stunned him.

"You always were a fool, Phil, but a successful one and so rarely boring, it's hardly worth mentioning."

The tone, the mannerisms, even the expression was so accurate, he couldn't respond. For a moment, he completely lost Ariel in the character and the woman he'd fashioned her after. He felt a twist in his stomach, not of attraction or even admiration, but of anger—totally unexpected and vilely real. Booth didn't have to look at the script to remember the line.

"You're so transparent, Rae. It amazes me that you could deceive anyone into believing in you."

Ariel laughed, rather beautifully, so that all three men felt a chill race up their spine. "I make my living at deception. Everyone wants illusions, so did you. And that's what you got."

With a long, lazy stretch, she ran a hand through her hair, then let it fall, pale gold in the late-morning sunlight. It was one of Liz Hunter's patented gestures. "I acted my way out of that miserable backwater town in Missouri where I had the misfortune to be born, and I've acted my way right up to the top. You were a great help." She walked over to him with the small, cool smile still on her lips, in her eyes. With an eloquent gesture, she brushed her hand down his cheek. "And you were compensated. Very, very well."

Phil grabbed her wrist and tossed it aside. Ariel merely lifted a brow at the violence of the movement. "Sooner or later you're going to slip," he threatened.

She tilted her head and spoke very softly. "Darling, I never slip."

Slowly, Booth rose. The expression on his face might have

had any woman trembling, would have had any woman making some defensive move. Ariel merely looked up at him with the same coldly amused expression. It was he who had to force himself to calm.

"Very good, Ariel Kirkwood." Booth tossed the script aside.

She grinned, because every instinct told her she'd won. With the long expelled breath, she could almost feel Rae drain out of her. "Thanks. It's a tremendous part," she added as her stomach unknotted. "Really a tremendous part."

"You've done your research," Marshell murmured from behind his desk. Because he knew Elizabeth Hunter, Ariel's five-minute read had left him uncomfortable and impressed. And he knew Booth. There was little doubt in his mind as to what Rae's creator was feeling. "You'll be available for a callback?"

"Of course."

"I saw your Blanche DuBois, Ms. Kirkwood," Chuck put in. "I was very impressed then, and now."

She flashed him an unaffected smile though she was aware Booth was still staring at her. If he was moved, she thought, then the reading had gone better than she could have hoped. "It was my biggest challenge, up until now." She wanted to get out, walk, breathe the air, savor the almost-victory while she could. "Well, thank you." She pushed her hair from shoulder as she scanned the three men again. "I'll look forward to hearing from you."

Ariel walked toward the elevator too frightened to believe she was right, too terrified to believe she was wrong. Up until that moment, she hadn't let herself dwell on just how much she wanted the part, and just what it could mean in her life.

She wasn't without ambition, but she had chosen acting and had continued with it for the love of it. And the challenge.

Playing the part of Rae would hand her all three needs on a silver platter. As she stepped into the elevator, her palms were dry and her heart was pounding. She didn't hear Booth approach.

"I'd like to talk to you." He stepped in with her and punched the button for the lobby.

"Okay." A long sigh escaped as she leaned back against the side of the car. "God, I'm glad that's over. I'm starving. Nothing makes me hungrier than a reading."

He tried to relate the woman who was smiling at him with eyes warm and alive with the woman who had just exchanged lines with him. He couldn't. She was a better actress than he'd given her credit for, and therefore, more dangerous. "It was an excellent reading."

She eyed him curiously. "Why do I feel I've just been insulted?"

After the doors slid open Booth stood for a moment, then nodded. "I think I said before that you were perceptive."

Her slim heels clicked over the tile as she crossed the lobby with him. Booth noticed a few heads turn, both male and female, to look after her. She was either unaware or unconcerned. "Why are you on daytime TV?"

Ariel slanted him a look before she began to walk north. "Because it's a good part on a well-written, entertaining show. That's number one. Number two is that it's steady work. When actors are between jobs, they wait tables, wash cars, sell toasters and generally get depressed. While I might not mind the first three too much, I hate the fourth. Have you ever seen the show?"

"No."

"Then you shouldn't turn your nose up." She stopped by a sidewalk vendor and drew in the scent of hot pretzels. "Want one?"

"No," Booth said again and tucked his hands in his pockets.

Sexuality, sensuality—both seemed to pour out of her as she stood next to a portable pretzel stand on a crowded sidewalk. He continued to watch her as she took the first generous bite.

"I could live off them," she told him with her mouth full and her eyes laughing. "Good nutrition's so admirable and so hard to live with. I like to ignore it for long stretches of time. Let's walk," she suggested. "I have to when I'm keyed up. What do you do?"

"When?"

"When you're keyed up," Ariel explained.

"Write." He matched her casually swinging pace while the bulk of pedestrian traffic bustled by them.

"And when you're not keyed up you write," Ariel added as she took another bite of her pretzel. "Have you always been so serious?"

"It's steady work," he countered and she laughed.

"Very quick. I didn't think I'd like you, but you've got a nice sense of cautious humor." Ariel stopped at another vendor and bought a bunch of spring violets. She closed her eyes and breathed deep. "Wonderful," she murmured. "I always think spring's the best until summer. Then I'm in love with the heat until fall. Then fall's the best until winter." Laughing, she looked over the blooms into his eyes. "And I also tend to ramble when I'm keyed up."

When she lowered the flowers, Booth took her wrist, not with the same violence as he had during the reading, but with the same intensity. "Who are you?" he demanded. "Who the hell are you?"

Her smile faded but she didn't draw away. "Ariel Kirkwood. I can be a lot of other people when there's a stage or a camera, but when it's over, that's who I am. That's all I am. Are you looking for complications?"

"I don't have to look for them—they're always there."

"Strange, I rarely run into any." She studied him, all frank eyes and creamy beauty. Booth didn't care for the stir it brought him. "Come with me," she invited, then took his hand before he'd thought to object.

"Where?"

She threw back her head and pointed up the magnificently sheer surface of the Empire State Building. "To the top." Laughing, she pulled him inside. "All the way to the top."

Booth looked around impatiently as she bought tickets for the observation deck. "Why?"

"Does there always have to be a reason?" She slipped the violets into the twisted scarves at her waist, then tucked her arm through his. "I love things like this. Ellis Island, the Staten Island ferry, Central Park. What's the use of living in New York if you don't enjoy it? When's the last time you did this?" Her shoulder rested against his upper arm as they crowded into an elevator.

"I think I was ten." Even with the press of bodies and mingling scents he could smell her, wild and sweet.

"Oh." Ariel laughed up at him. "You grew up. Too bad."

Booth said nothing for a moment as he studied her. She seemed to always be laughing—at him or at some private joke she was content to keep to herself. Was she really that easy with herself and her life? Was anyone? Then he asked, "Don't we all?"

"Of course not. We all get older, but the rest is a personal choice." They herded off one elevator and onto another that would take them to the top.

This was a man she could enjoy, Ariel mused as she stood beside Booth. She could enjoy that serious, high-minded streak and the dry, almost reluctant humor. Still, there was the part in the film to think of. Ariel would have to be very careful to keep her feelings for one separate from her feelings for the other. But then, she'd never been a person who'd had any trouble separating the woman and the actress.

For now, the reading was over and the afternoon was free. Her mood was light, and there was a man with her who'd be fascinating to explore. The day could hardly offer anything more.

The souvenir stands were crowded with people—different countries, different voices. Ariel decided she'd buy something foolish on her way out. She caught Booth looking around him with his eyes slightly narrowed. An observer, she thought with a slight nod of approval. She was one herself, though perhaps on a different level. He'd dissect, analyze and file. She just enjoyed the show.

"Come on outside," she invited and took his hand in a characteristic gesture. "It's wonderful." Pushing open the heavy door, Ariel welcomed the first slap of wind with a laugh. With her hand still firmly gripping Booth's, she hurried to the wall to take in New York.

She never saw it as a toy board as many did from that height, but as something real enough to touch and smell from any distance. It never failed to excite and fascinate her. Ariel rarely asked more of anything or anyone. When she was here, she always believed she could accomplish whatever she needed to.

"I love heights." She leaned out as far as she could and felt the frantic current of air swirl around her. "Staggering heights. And wind. If I could, I'd come here every day. I'd never get tired of it."

Though it was normally an intimacy he would have shunned, Booth allowed his hand to stay in hers. Her skin was smooth and elegant; her face was flushed in the brisk air while her hair blew wildly. The eyes, he thought, the eyes were too alive, too full of everything. A woman like this would demand spectacular emotions from everyone she touched. The stir he felt wasn't as easily suppressed this time. Deliberately, he looked away from her and down.

"Why not the World Trade Center?" he asked and let his gaze skim over the island he lived on.

Ariel shook her head. "It doesn't have the same feeling as this, nothing does. Just like there's only one Eiffel Tower, one Grand Canyon and one Olivier." She didn't bother to brush her hair back from her face as she tilted toward him. "They're all spectacular and unique. What do you like, Booth?"

A family walked by laughing, the mother holding her skirts, the father carrying a toddler. He watched them pause nearby and look over the wall. "In what way?"

"In any way," Ariel told him. "If you could've spent today doing anything you wanted, what would you have done?"

"Gone sailing," he said, remembering that moment in Marshell's office. "I'd've been sailing on the sound."

Interest flickered in her eyes as it seemed every emotion or thought she had did. "You have a boat?"

"Yes. I don't have much time for it."

Don't take much time for it, she corrected silently. "A solitary pursuit. That's admirable." She turned, leaning back against the wall so that she could watch the people circle the deck. The wind plastered her dress against her, revealing the slenderness, the elegance of the woman. "I don't often like to be solitary," she murmured. "I need people, the contacts, the contrasts. I don't have to know them. I just like knowing they're there."

"Is that why you act?" They were face-to-face now, their bodies casually close—as if they were friends. It struck Booth as odd, but he had no desire to back away. "So you can have an audience?"

Her expression become thoughtful, but when she smiled, it was easy. "You're a very cynical man."

"That's the second time today that's been mentioned."

"It's all right. It probably comes in handy with your writing. Yes, I act for an audience," she continued. "I won't deny my own ego, but I think I act for myself first." She lifted her face so that the air could race over it. "It's a marvelous profession. How else can you be so many people? A princess, a tramp, a victim, a loser. You write to be read, but don't you first write to express yourself?"

"Yes." He felt something odd, almost unfamiliar—a loosening of muscles, an easing of thought. It took him a moment to realize he was relaxing, and only a moment longer to draw back. When you relaxed, you got burned. That much he was certain of. "But then writers have egos that nearly rival actors'."

Ariel made a sound that was somewhere between a sigh and an expulsion of air. "She really put you through the mill, didn't she?"

His eyes frosted, his voice chilled. "That's none of your business."

"You're wrong." Though she felt a twinge of regret when she sensed his withdrawal, Ariel went on. "If I'm going to play Rae, it's very much my business. Booth…" She laid a hand on his arm, wishing she understood him well enough to get past the wall of reserve, the waves of bitterness. "If you'd wanted to keep this part of your life private, you wouldn't have written it out."

"It's a story," he said flatly. "I don't put myself on display."

"In most cases, no," she agreed. "I've always felt a certain sense of distance in your work, though it's always excellent. And for someone so successful, you kept a fairly low profile, even when you were married to Liz Hunter. But you've let something out in this script. It's too late to pull it back now."

"I've written a story about two people who are totally unsuited to each other, who used each other. The man is a bit of an idealist, and just gullible enough to fall for an exquisite face. Before the story ends, he learns that appearances mean little and that trust and loyalty are illusions. The woman is cold, ambitious and gifted, but she'll never be satisfied with her own talents. She's a vampire in the pure sense of the word, and she sucks him dry. There may be similarities between the story and actuality, but my life is still my life."

"No trespassing." Ariel turned to look back down into the city, the world she understood. "All right, the signs are posted." She listened to the sound of the wind, the sound of voices. Someone reeked of a drugstore cologne. An empty bag of potato chips skimmed and rustled along the concrete. "I'm not a very good businesswoman. I won't apologize for my lifestyle or my personality, but I will do my best to keep our conversations very professional."

She took a deep breath and turned back to him. Some of the warmth had left her eyes, and he felt a momentary regret. "I'm a good actress, an excellent craftsman. I've known since the first moment I picked up the script that I could play Rae. And I'm astute enough to know how well my reading went."

"No, you're not a fool." Even with the regret, Booth felt more comfortable on this level. He understood her now—an actress in search of that prime part. "I wouldn't have said you were what I was looking for—until this afternoon. No one's come even close to the core of that character before you."

She felt the tickling dryness down in her throat, the sudden lurch of her heart rate. "And?" she managed.

"And I want you to come back and read with Jack Rohrer. He's cast as Phil. If the chemistry's there, you've got the part."

Ariel took a deep breath. She leaned against the sturdy observation glass and tried to take it calmly. She'd told him she'd be professional. No good, she realized as the pleasure bubbled up inside her. It simply wasn't any use. With a shout of laughter, she threw her arms around his neck and clung. The touching was vital, the sharing essential.

Ariel Kirkwood—the skinny dreamer from West 185th Street—was going to star in a DeWitt script, a P. B. Marshell production opposite Jack Rohrer. Would life never stop amazing her? As she clung to Booth, Ariel dearly hoped it wouldn't.

His hands had come to her waist in reflex, but he left them there as her laughter warmed his ear. He found it odd that he was sharply reminded of two things—his young niece's boundless pleasure when he'd given her an elaborate dollhouse one Christmas, and the first time, as a man, he'd ever held a woman. The softness was there—that unique strength and give only a woman's body has. The childlike pleasure was there—with the innocence only the young possess.

He could have held her. It moved in him to do so, just to hold something soft and sweet and without shadows. She fit so well against him. The curve of cheek against his, the alignment of bodies. She fit too well, so that he stood perfectly still and drew her no closer.

Something drifted through her pleasure and excitement. He smelt of soap—solid—as his body felt. There was nothing casual about him, nothing easy. He was all intensity and intellect. The strength drew her; his reserve drew her. He was a man who would be there to pick you up, however reluctantly, if you stumbled. Who would demand that you keep pace with him, and who would expect you to give him exactly the amount of room he wanted when he wanted it. He was a man whom a woman who ran on her emotions and her senses would do well to avoid. She wished almost painfully that his arms would come around her, even while she knew they wouldn't.

Ariel drew away but kept their faces close so that she might have a hint of what it would be like to have that serious, unsmiling mouth lowered to hers. She was breathless, and her eyes made no secret of her attraction or her surprise in feeling it.

"I'm sorry," she said quietly. "Physical displays come naturally to me. I have a feeling you don't care for them."

Had there ever been a woman he'd wanted to kiss more than this one? Almost, almost, he could taste the mouth inches from his own. Nearly, very nearly, he could feel its texture against his own. When he spoke, his voice was indifferent, his eyes remote. "There's a time and a place."

Ariel let out a long breath and decided she'd set herself up for a backhanded slap. "You're a tough man, Booth DeWitt," she murmured.

"I'm a realist, Ariel." He took out a cigarette, cupping his lighter against the wind with hands that amazed him because they weren't steady.

"What a hard thing to be." Consciously, she relaxed— shoulder muscles, stomach muscles, hands. A moment's awareness didn't equal trouble. She'd felt it before; it was a blessing and a curse in a woman like herself. Ariel didn't understand indifference to people or to things. Everything you saw, touched, heard, triggered some emotion. "But then, you're stuck with it." More at ease, she smiled at him. "I'm going to enjoy working with you, Booth, though I know it's not going to be a picnic. I'm going to give your script my very best shot, and we'll both benefit."

He nodded as the smoke whipped up and away. "I don't accept anything less than the best."

"Fine, you won't be disappointed." It was in her nature to reach out and touch, to add something personal. But one slap was enough for one day.

"Good."

With a laugh, she shook her head. "You're attractive, Booth. I haven't the least idea why because I don't think you're a very nice person."

He blew out another stream of smoke and watched her lazily. "I'm not," he agreed.

"In any case, we'll give each other what's needed professionally."

Then because she rarely resisted impulses of any kind, she kissed his cheek before thrusting the violets at him and walking away. Booth stood in the wind on top of New York with a handful of spring flowers and stared after her.

Chapter Three

Booth had been on and around sets most of his professional life. There were eighteenth-century drawing rooms, twentieth-century bedrooms, bars and restaurants and department stores. Spaceships and log cabins. With props and backdrops and ingenuity, anything could be created.

When you came to the bottom line, one set was the same as another—technicians, lights, cameras, booms, miles of cable. It was an industry of illusion and image. What looked glamorous outside the business was ultimately only a job, and often a tedious and exacting one. Long hours, lengthy delays, lights that made a studio into a furnace, bitter coffee.

From the outset of his career, he'd never been content to be isolated with his typewriter and ideas. He'd insisted from his very first screenplay on being involved with the production end. He understood the practicality and the creativity of the right camera angle, the proper lighting. It appealed to the realistic part of him. Still, he had the ability to see the set and the people while blocking out the crowding equipment. To watch as an outsider, to see as a viewer. This appealed to the dreamer he'd always kept under strict control.

Booth wasn't sure what had motivated him to visit the set of *Our Lives, Our Loves.* He knew that the script he was currently working on had hit a snag, and that he wanted to see Ariel again. Perhaps it was the scent of violets that continued to drift to him as he tried to work. Twice he'd started to throw them away…but he hadn't. Part of him, deep, long repressed, needed such things, however much he disliked acknowledging it.

So he had come to see Ariel, telling himself he simply wanted to watch her work before he committed himself to choosing her for the part of Rae. It was logical, practical. It was something he'd tried very hard to resist.

Ariel sat at the kitchen table with her bare feet propped in a chair while Jack Shapiro, who played Griff Martin, Amanda's college sweetheart, mulled over a hand of solitaire. On another part of the soundstage, her television parents were discussing their offspring. After they'd finished, she and Jack would tape their scene.

"Black six on the red seven," she mumbled, earning herself a glare from Jack.

"Solitaire," he reminded her. "As in alone."

"It's an antisocial game."

"You think headphones are antisocial."

"They are." Smiling sweetly, she moved the six herself.

"Why don't you go call the Committee for the Salvation of Three-legged Land Mammals? They probably want you at their next luncheon."

The timing wasn't quite right, she decided, to ask him to contribute to the Homes for Kittens fund she was currently involved with. "Don't get snotty," she said mildly. "You're supposed to adore me."

"Should've had my head examined after you threw me over for Cameron."

"It's your own fault for not explaining what you were doing alone in that hotel room with Vikki."

Jack sniffed and turned over another card. "You should've trusted me. A man has his pride."

"Now I'm stuck in a disastrous marriage *and* I might be pregnant."

Glancing up, he grinned. "Great for the ratings. Did you see them posted this week? We're up a whole point."

She leaned her elbows on the table. "Wait until things start heating up between Amanda and Griff again." She put a black ten on the jack of diamonds. "Sizzle, spark, smolder."

He smacked her hand. "You're a great smolderer." Unable to resist, he leered. "I haven't kissed you in six months."

"Then when you get your chance, big guy, make it good. Amanda's no pushover." Rising, she strolled away for a last-minute check with makeup.

The hospital set had already been prepared for the brief but intense meeting between the former lovers, Amanda and Griff. Some subtle dark smudges were added under her eyes to give the appearance of a sleepless night. The rest of her makeup gave her a slight pallor.

By the time the cameras rolled, Amanda was in her office, going through her patient files. She seemed very calm, very much in control. Her expression was totally serene. Abruptly, she slammed the drawer back in the cabinet and whirled around to pace. When the tape was edited, it would flash back to her discovery of her husband and sister. Amanda grabbed a china cup from her desk and hurled it against the wall. With the back of her hand to her mouth, she stared at the broken pieces. The knock at her office door had her balling her fists and making a visible struggle for control. Deliberately, she walked around her desk and sat down.

"Come in."

The camera focused on Jack as Dr. Griff Martin, rough-and-ready looks, rough-and-ready temper—Amanda's first and only lover before her marriage. Ariel knew what the director would edit in a reaction shot later, but now, with the tape running on Jack's entrance, she screwed up her face and stuck out her tongue. Jack gave her one of his character's patented lengthy looks designed to make the female heart flutter.

"Amanda, have you got a minute?"

When the lens was focused on her again, her face was properly composed with just a hint of strain beneath the serenity. "Of course, Griff." For a subtle sign of nerves, she gripped her hands together on the desktop.

"I've got a case of wife beating," he began in the clipped, almost surly tone of his character. Both Amanda and several million female viewers had found his diamond-in-the-rough style irresistible. "I need your help."

They went through the scene, laying the groundwork for a story line that would throw them together again and again over the next few weeks, building the sexual tension. When the camera was briefly at Jack's back he crossed his eyes at Ariel and bared his teeth. As she went back to her patient file, she made certain she walked over his foot. Neither of them lost the rhythm of the scene.

"You look tired." As Griff, Jack started to touch her shoulder, then stopped himself. Frustration radiated from his eyes. "Is everything all right?"

Amanda turned and gave him a soulful eye-locking look. Her mouth trembled open, then closed again. Slowly, she turned back to the file and shut the drawer quietly. "Everything's fine. I have a heavy workload right now. And I have a patient due in a few minutes."

"I'll get out of here then." He started for the door and paused. With his hand on the knob, he stared at her. "Mandy…"

Amanda kept her back to him. The camera came in close as she shut her eyes and fought for control. "I'll see your patient tomorrow, Griff." There was the faintest of tremors in her voice.

He waited five humming seconds. "Yeah, fine."

When she heard the door close, Amanda pressed her hands to her face.

"Cut."

"I'm going to get you for that," Jack said as he pushed the prop door open again. "I think you broke one of my toes."

Ariel fluttered her lashes at him. "You're such a baby."

"All right, children," the director said mildly. "Let's get the reaction shots."

Agreeably, Ariel moved behind Amanda's desk again. It was then she saw Booth. Surprise and pleasure showed on her face, though his expression wasn't welcoming. He was frowning at her, his arms crossed over a casual black sweater. He didn't return her smile, nor did she expect him to. Booth DeWitt wasn't a man who smiled often or easily. It only made her more determined to nudge him into it.

She'd thought about him—surprisingly often. At the moment, she had enough on her mind, both personally and professionally, yet she'd found herself wondering about Booth

DeWitt and what went on inside that aloof exterior. She'd seen flashes of something warm, something approachable. For Ariel, it was enough to make her dig for more.

And there'd been that pull—the pull she remembered with perfect clarity. She wanted to feel it again, to enjoy it, to understand it.

She finished the taping and had an hour before she and Stella would play out their confrontation scene on the Lane living-room set. "Jerry, I found a kitten for your daughter," she told one of the technicians as she rose. "It's a little calico, I can bring it in on Friday."

"Been to the pound again," Jack said with a sigh. Ignoring him, Ariel stepped over some cable and walked to Booth.

"Hi, want some coffee?"

"All right."

"I keep a Mr. Coffee in my dressing room. The stuff at the commissary's poison." She led the way, not bothering to ask why he was there. Her door was open, as she usually left it. Walking in, she went directly to the coffeemaker. "You have to make do with powdered milk."

"Black's fine."

Her dressing room was chaos. Clothes, magazines, pamphlets were tossed over all available space. Her dressing table was littered with jars and bottles and framed photographs of the cast. It smelled of fresh flowers, makeup and dust.

On the wall was a calendar that read February though it was midway through April. An electric clock was unplugged and stuck on 7:05. Booth counted three and one-half pairs of shoes on the floor.

In the midst of it, Ariel stood in a raw-silk suit the color of apricots with her hair pale and glowing in a sophisticated knot.

She smelled like a woman should at sunset—soft, with a hint of anticipation. As the coffee began to drip, she turned back to him.

"I'm glad to see you again."

The simplicity of the statement made Booth almost believe it. Cautiously, he kept half the room between them as he watched her. "The taping was interesting. You're very good, Ariel. You milked that five-minute scene for everything there was."

Again she had the impression more of criticism than flattery. "It's important in a soap. You're working in little capsules. Some people only tune in a couple times a week. Then there are those who turn it on as a whim. You hope to grab them."

"Your character." He eyed the suit, approving the subdued style. "I'd say she's a very controlled professional woman who's currently going through some personal crisis. There were a lot of sexual sparks bouncing around between her and the young doctor."

"Very good." With a smile, Ariel picked up two cups, mismatched. "That's neatly tied up. Want some M&M's? I keep a stash in my drawer."

"No. Do you always play around on set when you're not on camera?"

She stirred powdered milk into her coffee, added a generous spoon of sugar, then handed Booth his. "Jack and I have a running contest on who can make who blow their lines. Actually, it makes us sharper and lowers the tension level." Carelessly, she took magazines from a chair and left them stacked on the floor. "Sit down."

"How many pages of dialogue do you have to learn a week?"

"Varies," she said and sipped. "We run about eighty-five pages of script a day now that we've gone to an hour. Some days I might have twenty or thirty where my character's involved. But for the most part, I tape about three days a week—we don't do a lot of takes." Opening the drawer on her dressing table, she took a handful of candies and began to eat them one at a time. "I'm told it's the closest thing to live TV you can get."

Watching her, he drank. "You really enjoy it."

"Yes, I've been very comfortable with Amanda. Which is why I want to do other things as well. Ruts are monotonous places, but so easy to stay in."

He glanced around the room. "I can't imagine you in one."

Ariel laughed and sat on the edge of her dressing table. "A great compliment. You're frugal with them." Something in his aloof, cool expression made her smile. "Would you like to have dinner?" she asked on impulse.

For an instant surprise flickered over his face—the first time she'd seen it. "It's a bit early for dinner," he said mildly.

"I like the way you do that," she said with a nod. "Conversations with you are never boring. If you're free tonight, I could pick you up at seven."

She was asking him for a date, he thought, very simply, very smoothly, in a manner more friendly than flirtatious. As he had often since the first time he'd met her, Booth wondered what made her tick. "All right, seven." Reaching in his pocket, he pulled out a note pad and scrawled on it. "Here's the address."

Taking it, Ariel scanned the words with a small sound of approval. "Mmm, you've got a great view of the park." She looked up and grinned in the way that always made him think she'd just enjoyed a little private joke. "I'm a sucker for views."

"I've gathered that already."

Booth walked over to set down his mug and stood close enough so that his legs brushed hers. She didn't back away but watched him with clear, curious eyes. There was something deadly in that face, she thought. Something any woman would recognize and a wary one would retreat from. Fascinated, she counted the beat of her own rapid pulse.

"I'll let you get back to work."

With the slightest move on his part, the contact was broken. Ariel stayed exactly where she was. "I'm glad you stopped by," she said, though she was no longer sure it was precisely the truth.

With a nod, he was gone. Ariel sat on the edge of her cluttered dressing table and wondered if for the first time in her life she'd bitten off more than she could chew.

Because the sun was setting and it was a huge red ball, Ariel paid off the cab two blocks from Booth's apartment building. She wanted some time to think about a phone call she'd received about Scott, her brother's child.

Poor little guy, she thought. So vulnerable, so grown-up. She wondered how much longer it would be before the courts decided his fate. Because she wanted him with her so badly, Ariel refused to believe anything else would happen. Her brother's son, so suddenly orphaned, so miserably unhappy with his maternal grandparents.

They didn't want him, she reflected. Not really. There was such a world of difference between love and duty. Once everything was arranged, she'd be able to give him the kind of easy, unfettered childhood she'd had—with the financial advantages she hadn't known.

She wouldn't think of the complications now. To think of them would make her start doubting the outcome, and she couldn't bear it. She and her lawyers were taking all the possible steps.

Because she wanted no publicity to touch her nephew, Ariel had kept the entire matter to herself—something she rarely did.

Perhaps because she had no one to speak to about it, she worried. Every day she told herself Scott would be with her permanently before the end of summer. As long as she kept telling herself, she was able to believe it. Now it was evening, and there was no more she could do.

It was only a little past seven o'clock when she pushed the button of the elevator for Booth's floor in the sleek building on Park Avenue. She'd already set aside that one flash of nerves she felt about him and had decided to enjoy the evening. The idea that he'd been able to make her nervous at all was intriguing enough.

She liked men, the basic personality differences between them and women. Of her closest friends, many were men, in and out of the business. The key word remained *friends*—she was very cautious about lovers. She ran on emotion, and knowing it, had always been careful of physical relationships.

She was a romantic, unashamedly. Ariel had never doubted that there was one great love waiting for everyone. She had no intention of settling for less—with hearts and flowers and sky-rockets included. When she found the right man, she'd know. Whether it was tomorrow or twenty years from tomorrow didn't matter, as long as she found him. In the meantime, she filled her life with work, her friends and her causes. Ariel Kirkwood simply didn't believe in boredom.

She approved of the quiet, carpeted hallway as she strolled down to Booth's apartment. It was wainscoted and elegant. But as she lifted her hand to press the button on his door, she felt that odd flutter of nerves again.

Inside, Booth was standing by the high wide window that looked out over Central Park. He was thinking of her, had been thinking of her for most of the day. And he didn't care for it.

Twice, he'd nearly called to cancel the dinner, telling himself he had work to do. Telling himself he didn't have the time or the inclination to spend an evening with an actress he hardly knew. But he hadn't canceled because he could still see the way her eyes warmed, the way her whole face moved when she smiled.

A professional trick. Liz had had a bagful of them, and unless his perception was very, very wrong, this woman was as skilled an actress as Liz Hunter. That's what he told himself, and yet… And yet he hadn't canceled.

When the buzzer rang, Booth looked over his shoulder at the closed door. It was simply an evening, he decided. A few hours out of the day in which he could study the woman being considered for a major part in an important film. He had little doubt that she would make a pitch for the part before the night was over. With a shrug, Booth walked to the door. That was the business, and she was entitled.

Then, when he opened the door, she smiled at him. He realized he wanted her with an intensity he hadn't felt in years. "Hi. You look nice," she said.

The struggle with desire only made him more remote, made his voice more scrupulously polite. "Come in."

Ariel walked through the door then studied the room with open curiosity. Neat. Her first impression was one of meticulous order. Style. Who could fault a gleaming mix of Chippendale and Hepplewhite? The colors were muted, easy on the eyes. The furniture was arranged in such a way as to give a sense of balance. She could smell neither dust nor polish. It was as though the room was perpetually clean and rarely lived in. Somehow, she didn't think it really suited that harsh, nineteenth-century face. No, there was too much formality here for a man who looked like Booth, for a man who moved like him.

Though she felt no sense of welcome, she could appreciate the rather stationary beauty and respect the organized taste.

"A very fastidious man," she murmured, then walked over to study his view of the city.

She wore a dress with yards of skirt and whirls of color. Booth wondered if that was why he suddenly felt life jump into the room. He preferred the quiet, the settled, even the isolated. Yet somehow, for the first time, he felt the appeal of having warmth in his home.

"I was right about this," Ariel said and put her hands into the deep pockets of her skirt. "It's lovely. Where do you work?"

"I have an office set up in another room."

"I'd probably have put my desk right here." Laughing, she turned to him so that the mix of colors in her dress seemed to vibrate. "Then again, I wouldn't get much work done." His eyes were very dark and very steady, his face so expressionless he might have been thinking of anything or nothing. "Do you stare at everyone that way?"

"I suppose I do. Would you like a drink?"

"Yes, some dry vermouth if you have it." She wandered over to a cherrywood breakfront and studied his collection of Waterford. No one chose something so lovely, or so capable of catching light and fire if they lacked warmth. Where was his, she wondered. Buried so deep that he'd forgotten it, or simply dormant from lack of use?

Booth paused beside her and offered a glass. "You like crystal?"

"I like beautiful things."

What woman didn't? he thought brittlely. A Russian lynx, a pear-shaped diamond. Yes, women liked beautiful things, particularly when someone else was providing them. He'd already done more than his share of that.

"I watched your show today," Booth began, deciding to give her the opening for her pitch and see what she did with it. "You come across very well as the competent psychiatrist."

"I like Amanda." Ariel sipped her vermouth. "She's a very stable woman with little hints of vulnerability and passion. I like seeing how subtle I can make them without hiding them completely. What did you think of the show?"

"A mass of complication and intrigue. I was surprised that the bulk of the plots didn't concern fatal diseases and bed hopping."

"You're out of step." She smiled over the rim. "Of course, every soap has some of those elements, but we've done a lot of expanding. Murder, politics, social issues, even science fiction. We do quite a bit of location shooting now in the race for ratings." She drank again. This time it was an opal, milky blue, that gleamed on her hand. "Last year we shot in Greece and Venice. I've never eaten so much in my life. Griff and Amanda had a lovers' rendezvous in Venice that was sabotaged. You must've noticed Stella—she plays my sister Vikki."

"The barracuda." Booth nodded. "I recognized the type."

"Oh, Vikki's that all right. Plotting, scheming, being generally nasty. Stella has a marvelous time with her. Vikki's had a dozen affairs, broken up three marriages, destroyed a senator's career. Just last month she pawned our mother's emerald brooch to pay off gambling debts." With a sigh, Ariel drank again. "She has all the fun."

Booth's grin flashed, lingering in his eyes as they met Ariel's. "Are you talking about Stella or Vikki?"

"Both, I suppose. I wondered if I'd be able to do that."
"What?"
"Make you smile. You don't very often, you know."
"No?"

"No." She felt the tug again, sharp and very physical. Indulging herself, she let her gaze lower briefly to his mouth and enjoyed the sensation it brought to her own. "I guess you're too busy picking up parts of people and filing them away."

Finishing off his drink, he set the glass aside. "Is that what I do?"

"Always. It's natural, I suppose, in your line of work, but I decided I was going to pull one out of you before the evening was over." He was still watching her, and though the smile was only a hint now, it was still lurking. It suited him, she thought, that trace of amusement—a cautious, even reluctant amusement. And again, she felt the tug of attraction. With her brows slightly drawn together, she stepped closer. It wasn't something she could or would walk away from.

"Aren't you curious?" she asked quietly, then went on when he didn't answer. "The thing is, I'm not certain I can go through the evening wondering what it would be like."

She put one hand on his shoulder and leaned forward just until their lips touched. There was no pressure, no demand on either side, and yet she felt that slightest of contacts through her whole system. There was a twinge deep inside her, a soft rushing sound in her ears. The mouth against hers was warmer than she'd expected and its taste more potent. Their bodies weren't touching, and the kiss remained a mere meeting of lips. Ariel felt herself open and was mildly surprised. Then, she felt her knees tremble and was stunned.

Slowly, she backed up, unaware that her eyes were wide with shock. Desire had ripped through him at the taste of her mouth, but Booth knew how to conceal his emotions. He wanted her—in the part of Rae and in his bed. To his thinking it wouldn't be long before she offered him one to ensure the

other. He'd been much younger when Liz had lured him into
bed for a part. He was older now and knew the game. And
somehow, he felt Ariel would be more honest in her playing.

"Well…" Ariel let out a long breath while her mind raced.
She wished she had five minutes alone to think this through.
Somehow she'd always expected she'd fall in love in the blink
of an eye, but she wasn't idealistic enough to believe it would
be handed back to her. She needed to work out her next move.
"And now that the pressure's off—" she set her glass aside
"—why don't we go eat?"

Before she could step away, Booth took her arm. If they
were going to play out the scene, he wanted to do it then and
there. "What do you want?"

There was none of the quiet warmth in his voice that she'd
felt in the kiss. Ariel looked into his eyes and saw nothing but a
reflection of herself. An unwise man to love, she thought. And,
of course, she should have expected that was what would happen
to her when the time came. "To go to dinner," she told him.

"I've given you the opportunity to mention the part, you
haven't. Why?"

"That's business. This isn't."

He gave a quick laugh. "In this business, it's all business," he
countered. "You want to play Rae."

"I wouldn't have read for it if I didn't want it. And once I
finish the next reading I'll have it." It frustrated her that she
couldn't read him. "Booth, why don't you tell me what you're
getting at? It'd be easier for both of us."

He inclined his head, and with his hand on her arm drew her
an inch closer. "Just how much are you willing to do for it?"

His meaning was like a slap in the face. Outrage didn't come,
but a piercing hurt that made her face pale and her eyes darken.

"I'm willing to give the very best performance I'm capable of."
Jerking out of his hold, she started for the door.

"Ariel…" He hadn't expected to call her back, but the look
in her eyes had made him feel foul. When she didn't pause, he
was going across the room before he could stop himself.
"Ariel." Taking her arm again, he turned her around.

The hurt radiating from her was so sharp and real he couldn't
convince himself not to believe it. The strength of the need to
draw her against him was almost painful. "I'll apologize for that."

She stared at him, wishing it was in her to tell him to go to
hell. "I'll accept it," she said instead, "since I'm sure you don't
make a habit of apologizing for anything. She took a few pieces
out of you, didn't she?"

His hand dropped away from her arm. "I don't discuss my
private life."

"Maybe that's part of the problem. Is it women in general,
or just actresses you detest?"

His eyes narrowed so that she could only see a glint of the anger.
It wasn't necessary to see what you could feel. "Don't push me."

"I doubt anyone could." Though she felt the anger was a
promising sign, Ariel didn't feel capable of dealing with it, or
her own feelings at the moment. "It's a pity," she continued as
she turned for the door again. "When whatever's frozen inside
you thaws, I think you'll be a remarkable man. In the
meantime, I'll stay out of your way." She opened the door, then
turned back. "About the part, Booth, please deal with my
agent." Quietly, she closed the door behind her.

Chapter Four

"No, Scott, if you eat any more cotton candy your teeth're going to fall right out. And then—" Ariel hauled her nephew up for one fierce hug "—you'd be stuck with stuff like smashed bananas and strained spinach."

"Popcorn," he demanded, grinning at her.

"Bottomless pit." She nuzzled into his neck and let the love flow over her.

Sunday was precious, not only because of the sunshine and balmy spring temperatures, not only because there were hours and hours of leisure time left to her, but because she had the afternoon to spend with the most important person in her life.

He even smells like his father, Ariel thought and wondered if it were possible to inherit a scent. Still holding him, with his sturdy legs wrapped around her waist, she studied his face.

Essentially, it was like looking in a mirror. There'd only been ten months between Ariel and her brother, Jeremy, and they'd often been taken for twins. Scott had pale curling hair, clear blue eyes and a face that promised to be lean and rather elegant once it had fined down from childhood. At the moment, it was sticky with pink spun sugar. Ariel kissed him firmly and tasted the sweetness.

"Yum-yum," she murmured, kissing him again when he giggled.

"What about your teeth?"

Arching a brow, she shifted his weight to a more comfortable position. "It doesn't count when it's secondhand."

He gave her a crooked smile that promised to be a heartbreaker in another decade. "How come?"

"It's scientific," Ariel claimed. "Probably the sugar evaporates after being exposed to air and skin."

"You're making that up," he told her with great approval.

Struggling with a smile, she tossed her long smooth braid behind her back. "Who me?"

"You're the best at making up."

"That's my job," she answered primly. "Let's go look at the bears."

"They better have big ones," Scott stated as he wriggled down. "*Great* big ones."

"I hear they're enormous," she told him. "Maybe even big enough to climb right out of the cages."

"Yeah?" His eyes lit up at the idea. Ariel could almost see him writing out the scenario in his mind. The escape, the panic and screams of the crowd and his ultimate heroism in driving the giant, drooling bears back behind the bars. Then, of course, his humbleness in accepting the gratitude of the zookeepers. "Let's go!"

Ariel allowed herself to be dragged along at Scott's dashing pace, winding through the stream of people who'd come to spend their day at the Bronx Zoo. This she could give him, she thought. The fun, the preciousness of childhood. It was such a short time, so concentrated. So many years were passed as an adult—with obligations, responsibilities, worries, timetables. She wanted to give him the freedom, to show him what boundaries you could leap over and the ones you had to respect. Most of all, she wanted to give him love.

She loved and wanted him, not only for the memories he brought back of her brother, but for himself—his uniqueness and odd stability. Though she was a woman who ran her life on a staggered routine that wasn't a routine at all, who enjoyed coming and going on the impulse of the moment, she'd always needed stability—someone to care for, to nurture, to give her back some portion of the emotion she spent. There was nothing like a child, with its innocence and lack of restrictions, to give and take of love. Even now, while he raced and laughed and pointed, caught up in the day and the animals, Scott was feeding her.

If Ariel had believed Scott was happy living with his grandparents, she could have accepted it. But she knew that they were smothering all the specialness that radiated from him.

They weren't unkind people, she mused, but simply set in their thinking. A child was to be formed along certain lines, and that was that. A child was a duty, a solemn one. While she understood the duty, it was joy that came first. They would raise him to be responsible, polite and well-read. And they'd forget the wonder of it.

Perhaps it would have been easier if Scott's grandparents hadn't disapproved of Ariel's brother so strongly or if Scott hadn't been conceived in youthful defiance and passion...and out of wedlock. Marriage and Scott's birth hadn't eased over the strain in the relationship, nor had the tragic and sudden accident that had taken her brother and young sister-in-law.

Scott's grandparents would look at the boy and be reminded that their daughter had married against their wishes and was dead. Ariel looked at him and saw life at its best.

He needs me, she thought, and ruffled his hair as he stood staring wide-eyed at a lumbering bear. Even when her heart wasn't involved, she'd never been able to resist a need. With Scott, her heart had been lost the first time she'd seen him—red and scrawny behind a hospital glass wall.

And she understood that she needed him. To have someone receive her love was vital. She thought of Booth.

He needed her, too, she thought, as a small secret smile touched her lips. Though he didn't know it. A man like that needed the ease that love could bring to his life, and the laughter. And she wanted to give it to him.

Why? Leaning against the barrier, Ariel shook her head. She had no solid reason, and that was enough to convince her it was right. When you could dissect something and find all the answers, you could find all the wrong ones. She trusted instincts and emotions much more than she trusted the intellect. She loved—quickly, unwisely and completely. When she thought about it, Ariel decided she should never have expected it to be otherwise.

If she told him now, he'd think she was lying or insane. She could hardly blame him. It wouldn't be easy to win the confidence of a man as wary or as cynical as Booth DeWitt. With a smile, Ariel nibbled on some of Scott's popcorn. Challenges kept the excitement in life, after all. Whether Booth realized it or not, she was about to add some excitement to his.

"Why're you laughing, Ariel?"

She grinned down at Scott, then scooped him up. He laughed as he always did at her quick, physical shows of affection. "Because I'm happy. Aren't you? It's a happy day."

"I'm always happy with you." His arms went tight around her neck. "Can't I stay with you? Can't I live at your house—all the time?"

She buried her face in the curve of his shoulder—a tender place—knowing she couldn't tell him how hard she was trying to give him that. "We have today," she said instead. "All day."

Holding him, she could smell the scent of his soap and shampoo, the scent of roasted popcorn, the hot, pungent scent of the sun. With another laugh, she set her nephew down. Today, she told herself, that was what she'd show him.

"Let's go see the snakes. I like to watch them slither."

Booth couldn't understand why she kept crowding his mind. He should have been able to push Ariel into a corner of his brain and keep her there while he worked. Instead, she kept filling it.

He could have accepted it if he'd been able to keep her in her slot—the actress he was all but certain would play his Rae. He could have rationalized his obsession if it had remained a professional one. But Booth kept seeing her as she'd been on top of New York, with her hair blowing frantically and her eyes filled with the wonder of it. That woman had nothing in common with the character of Rae.

And he could see her as she'd looked in his apartment. Vital, fresh—with energy and integrity shimmering from her. He could remember her hurt when he'd been deliberately cruel, and his own guilt—a sensation he'd sworn he'd never feel again. He hardly knew her, and yet she was drawing things out of him he'd promised himself he wouldn't feel again. He was perceptive enough to know she was a woman who could draw out more. For that reason, he'd decided to keep a safe, professional distance between them.

Still, as Booth watched Ariel talk with Jack Rohrer before the reading, he couldn't keep the established lines firmly in place. Was it because she was beautiful and he had always been susceptible to beauty? Was it because she was just unique enough to catch the attention and hold it?

As a writer he couldn't suppress his fascination with the unusual. But he got something from her—some feeling of absolute stability despite the fact that she dressed somewhere between a Gypsy and a teenager. He'd already asked her who she was and had been far from satisfied with her answer. Perhaps, just perhaps he should find out for himself.

"They look good together," Marshell murmured.

The sound Booth made might have been agreement or disinterest, but he didn't take his eyes from Ariel. If he hadn't remembered her first reading so well, he'd have sworn he was making a mistake even considering her for the part. Her smile was much too open, her gestures too fluid. You could look at her and feel the warmth. He found it disconcerting to realize she made him nervous.

Desire. Yes, he felt desire. Booth weighed and measured it. Strong, hard and very nearly urgent—and that with only a look. Of course, she was a woman a man had to want. He wasn't worried about the desire, or even his interest, but about the niggling sensation that something was being slipped out of him without his knowledge and against his will.

Pulling out a cigarette, he watched her through the blue-tinted smoke. It might be worth his while, both as a man and as a writer, to see how many faces she could wear, and how easily she wore them. He sat on the edge of Marshell's desk.

"Let's get started."

At the brief, quiet order, Ariel turned her head and met

Booth's gaze. *He's different today,* she thought, but couldn't quite pigeonhole the reason. He still looked at her with that intrusive, serious stare that bordered on the brooding. The distance was still there; she was sensitive enough to recognize the wall he kept erected between himself and the rest of the world. But there was something…

Ariel smiled at him. When he didn't respond, she picked up her copy of the script. She was going to give the best damn reading of her career. For herself and—for some odd reason—for Booth.

"All right, I'd like you to start at the top of the scene where they've come home from the party." Absently Booth tapped his cigarette in a gold-etched ashtray. Behind him, Marshell nibbled on a stomach mint. "Do you want to read it over first?"

Ariel glanced up from the script. *He still thinks I'm going to blow it,* she realized, and was grateful for the hard knot in her stomach. "It isn't necessary," she told him, then turned to Jack.

For the second time, Booth witnessed the transformation. How was it that even her eyes seemed to go paler, icier when she spoke as Rae? He could feel the old sexual pull and intellecutal abhorrence his ex-wife had always brought to him. With the cigarette smoldering between his fingertips, Booth listened to Rae's scorn and Phil's anger—and remembered all too clearly.

A vampire. He'd called her that and accurately. Bloodless, heartless, alluring. Ariel slipped into the character as if it were a second skin. Booth knew he should admire her for it, even be grateful that she'd made his search for the right actress end. But her chameleon skill annoyed him.

The chemistry was right. Ariel and Jack hurled their lines at each other while the anger and sexual sparks flew. There wasn't any escaping it and no logical reason to try. Without knowing why, Booth was certain that giving Ariel the part was good professional judgment and a serious personal error. He'd just have to deal with the latter as he went.

"That'll do."

The moment Booth cut the scene, Ariel threw her head back and let out breathless laughter. The release—the sudden absence of tension—was tremendous. It would always be that way, she realized, with a part as tough and as cold as this one.

"Oh God, she's so utterly hateful, so completely self-consumed." Eyes alight, face flushed, she whirled to Booth. "You despise her, and yet she pulls you in. Even when you see the knife she's going to slide under your ribs, it's hard to step away."

"Yes." Watching the scene had disturbed him more than he'd expected. Rising, Booth left his hands in his pockets. "I want you for the part. We'll contact your agent and negotiate the details."

She sighed, but the smile lingered around her mouth. "I can see I've overwhelmed you," Ariel said dryly. "But the bottom line is the part. You won't regret it. Mr. Marshell, Jack, it'll be a pleasure working with you."

"Ariel…" Marshell rose and accepted her offered hand. It had been a long time since he'd watched a scene that had left him as shaken as this one. "Unless I miss my guess—and I never do—you're going to hit it big with this."

She flashed him a grin and felt like flying. "I don't suppose I'll complain. Thank you."

Booth had her elbow before she could turn around, and before he'd realized he intended to touch her. He wanted to vent fury on something, someone, but reasoned it away. "I'll walk you out."

Feeling the tension in his fingers, she had to resist the urge to soothe it. This wasn't a man who'd appreciate stroking. "All right."

They followed the same route they'd taken the week before, but this time in silence. Ariel sensed he needed it. When they came to the street door, she waited for him to say whatever he intended to say.

"Are you free?" he asked her.

A bit puzzled, she tilted her head.

"For an early dinner," he elaborated. "I feel I owe you a meal."

"Well." She brushed the hair back from her face. His invitation, such as it was, pleased her—something she took no trouble to hide. "Technically that's the other way around. Why do you want to have dinner with me?"

Just looking at her—the laughing eyes, the generous mouth—pulled him in two directions. Get closer before you lose it. Back off before it's too late. "I'm not completely sure."

"Good enough." She took his hand and lifted her free one for a cab. "Do you like grilled pork chops?"

"Yes."

She laughed over her shoulder before pulling him into the cab. "An excellent start." After giving the driver an address in Greenwich Village, she settled back. "I think the next move is to have a conversation without a word, one single word, that has to do with business. We might just make it in each other's company for more than an hour."

"All right." Booth nodded. He'd made the decision to get to know her and get to know her he would. "But we'll steer away from politics, too."

"Deal."

"How long have you lived in New York?"

"I was born here. A native." She grinned and crossed her

legs. "You're not. I read somewhere that you're from Philadelphia and very top-drawer. Lots of influential relatives." She didn't even glance around when the cab skidded and swerved. "Are you happy in New York?"

He'd never thought about equating it with happiness, but now that he did, the answer came easily. "Yes. I need the demands and the movement for long periods of time."

"And then you need to go away," she finished. "And be alone—on your boat."

Before he could be uncomfortable with her accuracy, he'd accepted it. "That's right. I relax when I'm sailing and I like to relax alone."

"I paint," she told him. "Terrible paintings." With a laugh, she rolled her eyes. "But it helps me work the kinks out when I get them. I keep threatening people with an original Kirkwood as a Christmas present, but I haven't the heart to do it."

"I'd like to see one," he murmured.

"The problem seems to be that I splatter my mood on the canvas. Here we are." Ariel hopped out of the cab and stood on the curb.

Booth glanced around at the tiny storefronts. "Where're we going?"

"To the market." In her easy manner, she hooked her arm through his. "I don't have any pork chops at home."

He looked down at her. "Home?"

"Most of the time I'd rather cook than eat out. And tonight I'm too wired to deal with a restaurant. I have to be busy."

"Wired?" After studying her profile, Booth shook his head. His hair was dark in the lowering sun, and the movement sent it settling carelessly around his face. A contrast, Ariel mused, to the rather formal exterior. "I'd have said you look remarkably calm."

"Uh-uh. But I'm trying to save the full explosion until after my agent calls and tells me everything's carved in granite. Don't worry—" she smiled up at him "—I'm a fair cook."

If a man judged only by that porcelain face, he'd never have believed she'd know one end of the stove from the other. But Booth knew about surfaces. Maybe, just maybe, there'd be a surprise under hers. Despite all the warnings he'd given himself, he smiled. "Only fair?"

Her eyes lit in appreciation. "I hate to brag, but actually, I'm terrific." She steered him into a small, cluttered market that smelled heavily of garlic and pepper, and began a haphazard selection for the evening meal. "How're the avocados today, Mr. Stanislowski?"

"The best." The grocer looked over her head to study Booth out of the corner of his eye. "Only the best for you, Ariel."

"I'll have two then, but you pick them out." She poked at a head of romaine. "How did Monica do on her history quiz?"

"Ninety-two percent." His chest swelled a bit under his apron, but he continued to speculate on the dark, brooding man who'd come in with Ariel.

"Terrific. I need four really nice center-cut chops." While he selected them, she studied the mushrooms, well aware that he was bursting with curiosity over Booth. "You know, Mr. Stanislowski, Monica would love a kitten."

As he started to weigh the meat, the grocer sent her an exasperated glance. "Now, Ariel…"

"She's certainly old enough to care for one on her own," Ariel continued and pinched a tomato. "It'd be company for her, and a responsibility. And she did get ninety-two on that quiz." Looking over, she sent him a dashing, irresistible smile. He flushed and shifted his feet.

"Maybe if you were to bring one by, we could think about it."

"I will." Still smiling, she reached for her wallet. "How much do I owe you?"

"That was smoothly done," Booth murmured when they stepped outside. "And it's the second time I've heard you palming off a kitten. Did your cat have a litter?"

"No, I just happen to know about a number of homeless kittens." She tilted her face toward him. "If you're interested…"

"No." The answer was firm and brief as he took the bag from her.

Ariel merely smiled and decided she could work on him later. Now, she breathed in the scent of spices and baking from the open doorways. Some children raced along the sidewalk, laughing. A few old men sat out on the stoops to gossip. After the dinner hour, Ariel knew other members of the family would come out to talk and exchange news and enjoy the spring weather. Through a screened window she heard some muted snatches of Beethoven's Ninth, and farther down the pulse of top forty rock.

Two years before, Ariel had moved to the Village for the neighborhood feel, and had never been disappointed. She could sit outside and listen to the elderly reminisce, watch the children play, hear about the latest teenage heartthrob or the newest baby. It had been exactly what she'd needed when her family had gone its separate ways.

"Hi, Mr. Miller, Mr. Zimmerman."

The two old men who sat on the steps of the converted brownstone eyed Booth before they looked at Ariel. "Don't think you should give that Cameron another chance," Mr. Miller told her.

"Boot him out." Mr. Zimmerman gave a wheeze that might have been a chuckle. "Get yourself a man with backbone."

"Is that an offer?" She kissed his cheek before climbing the rest of the steps.

"I'll have a dance at the block party," he called after her.

Ariel winked over her shoulder. "Mr. Zimmerman, you can have as many as you want." As they started up the inside steps, Ariel began to fish in her bag for her keys. "I'm crazy about him," she told Booth. "He's a retired music instructor and still teaches a few kids on the side. He sits on the stoop so he can watch the women go by." She located the keys attached to a large, plastic, grinning sun. "He's a leg man."

Automatically, Booth glanced over his shoulder. "He told you?"

"You just have to watch the direction his eyes take when a skirt passes."

"Yours included?"

Her eyes danced. "I fit into the category of niece. He thinks I should be married and raising large quantities of babies."

She fit a single key into a single lock, something Booth thought almost unprecedented for New York, then pushed open the door. He'd been expecting the unusual. And he wasn't disappointed.

The focal point of the living room was a long oversize hammock swinging from brass ceiling hooks. One end of it was piled with pillows and beside it was a washstand holding one thick candle, three-quarters burned down. There was color—he'd known there'd be an abundance of it—and a style that was undefinable.

The sofa was a long, curved French antique upholstered with faded rose brocade, while a long wicker trunk served as a coffee table. As in Ariel's dressing room, the entire area was cluttered with books, papers and scents. He caught the fragrance of candle wax, potpourri and fresh flowers. Bunches of spring blossoms were spilling from a collection of vases that ran from dime-store pottery to Meissen.

There was an umbrella stand in the shape of a stork that was filled with ostrich and peacock feathers. A pair of boxing gloves hung in the corner behind the door.

"I guess you'd class as a featherweight," Booth mused.

Ariel followed his gaze and smiled. "They were my brother's. He boxed in high school. Want a drink?" Before he could answer, she took the bag from him, then headed down a hallway.

"A little Scotch and water." When he turned, his attention and his senses were struck by a wall of paintings. They were hers, of course. Who else would paint with that kind of kinetic energy, verve and disregard for rules? There were splotches of color, lines of it, zigzags. Moving closer, Booth decided that while he wouldn't call them terrible, he wasn't quite sure what he'd call them. Vivid, eccentric, disturbing. Certainly they weren't paintings to relax by. They showed both flair and heedlessness, and whether she'd intended them to or not they suited the room to perfection.

As he continued to study the paintings, three cats came into the room. Two were hardly more than kittens, coal black and amber eyed. They dashed around his legs once before they made a beeline for the kitchen. The other was a huge tiger who managed to walk with stiff dignity on three legs. Booth could hear Ariel laugh and say something to the two cats who had found her. The tiger watched Booth with quiet patience.

"Scotch and water." Ariel came back in, barefoot, carrying two glasses.

Booth accepted the glass, then gestured with it. "Those must be some kinks you work out."

Ariel glanced toward her paintings. "Looks like it, doesn't it? Saves money on a therapist—though I shouldn't say that since I play the role of one."

"You've quite a place here."

"I learned I thrive on confusion." Laughing up at him, she sipped. "You've met Butch, I see." She bent and slid one hand over the tiger's back. He arched, letting out a grumble of a purr. "Keats and Shelley were the rude ones. They're having their dinner."

"I see." Booth glanced down to see Butch rub against Ariel's leg before he waddled over to the sofa and leaped onto a cushion. "Don't you find it difficult tending three cats in a city apartment while dealing with a demanding profession?"

She only smiled. "No. I'm going to start the grill."

Booth lifted a brow. "Where?"

"Why, on the terrace." Ariel walked over and slid open a door. Outside was a postage-stamp balcony more along the lines of a window ledge. On it she'd crammed pots of geraniums and a tiny charcoal grill.

"The terrace," Booth murmured over her shoulder. Only an incurable optimist or a hopeless dreamer would have termed it so. He found himself grateful she had. Laughing, he leaned against the doorjamb.

After straightening from the grill, Ariel stared at him. The sound of his laughter whispered along her skin and eased her mind. "Well, well. That's very nice. Do you know that's the first time since I've met you that you've laughed and meant it?"

Booth shrugged and sipped at his Scotch. "I suppose I'm out of practice."

"We'll soon fix that," Ariel said. She smiled, holding her hand out, palm up. "Got a match?"

Booth reached in his pocket, but something—perhaps the humor in her eyes—changed his mind. Stepping forward, he took her shoulders and lowered his mouth to hers.

He'd caught her off guard. Ariel hadn't expected him to do anything on impulse, and he'd given no sign of his intention. Before she had time to prepare, the power of the kiss whipped through her, touching the emotions, the senses, then taking over.

It wasn't a mere touching of lips this time, but a hard, thorough demand that had her wrapped in his arms and trapped against the side of the door. She reached up to take his face in her hands as she gave, unquestioningly, what he sought from her.

There was no gradual smoldering, no experimentation, but a leap of flame so intense and quick it seemed they were already lovers. She felt the instant intimacy and understood it. Her heart was already his, she couldn't deny him her body.

He felt the need churn and was relieved. It had been long, too long, since he'd more than indifferently wanted a woman. There was nothing indifferent about the passion he felt now. It was hard and clear, like the wind that buffeted him when he sailed. It spelled freedom. Drawing her closer, Booth absorbed it.

He could smell her—that warm, teasing fragrance that seemed to pulse out of her skin. How often had that scent come to him when he'd only thought of her? He remembered her taste. Alluring, giving and again warm. And the feel of her body— slender, soft, with still more warmth. It was that that touched every aspect of her, that promised to fill him. He needed it, though he'd gone for years without knowing it. Perhaps he needed her.

And it was that that had him pulling back when he wanted more and more of what she had an abundance of.

Her eyes opened slowly when her mouth was free. Ariel looked directly, unblinkingly at him. This time she saw more than a reflection of self. She saw longings and caution and a glimpse of emotion that stirred her.

"I've wanted you to do that," she murmured.

Booth forced himself to level, forced himself to think past the senses she sent swimming. "I haven't got anything for you."

That hurt, but Ariel knew love wasn't painless. "I think you're wrong. But then, I have a tendency to rush into things. You don't." She took a deep breath and a step back. "Why don't you light this and I'll go make a salad?" Without waiting for his answer she turned and walked into the kitchen.

Steady, she ordered herself. She knew she had to be steady to deal with Booth and the feelings he brought to her. He wasn't a man who would accept a flood of emotion all at once, or the demands that went with it. If she wanted him in her life, she'd have to tread carefully, and at his pace.

He wasn't nearly as hard and cool as he tried to be, Ariel mused. With a half smile, she began to wash the fresh vegetables. She could tell from his laugh, and from those flickers of amusement in his eyes. And, of course, she was certain she couldn't have fallen in love with a man without a sense of humor. It pleased her to be able to draw it out of him. The more they were together, the easier it was. She wondered if he knew. Humming, she began to slice an avocado.

Booth watched her from the doorway. A smile lingered on her lips, and her eyes held that light he was growing too used to. She used the kitchen knife with the careless confidence of one who was accustomed to domestic chores. In one easy movement she tossed her hair behind her back.

Why should such a simple scene hold so much appeal for

him, he wondered. Just looking at her standing at the sink, her hands full, the water running, he could feel himself relaxing. What was it about her that made him want to put his feet up and his head back? At that moment, he could see himself going to her to wrap his arms around her waist and nuzzle. He must be going mad.

She knew he was there. Her senses were keen, and sharper still where Booth was involved. Keeping her back to him, she continued preparing the salad. "Have any trouble lighting it?"

He lifted a brow. "No."

"Well, it doesn't take long to heat up. Hungry?"

"A bit." He crossed the room to her. He wouldn't touch her, but he'd get just a little closer.

Smiling, she held up a thin slice of avocado, offering him a bite. Ariel could see the wariness in his eyes as he allowed her to feed him. "I'm never a bit hungry," she told him, finishing off the slice herself. "I'm always starving."

He'd told himself he wouldn't touch her, yet he found that the back of his hand was sliding over the side of her face. "Your skin," he murmured. "It's beautiful. It looks like porcelain, feels like satin." His gaze skimmed over her face, over her mouth before it locked on hers. "I should never have touched you."

Her heart was pounding. Gentleness. That was unexpected and would undermine her completely. "Why?"

"It leads to more." His fingers ran slowly down the length of her hair before he dropped his hands. "I haven't any more. You want something from me," he murmured.

Her breath trembled out. She'd never realized what a strain it was to hold in your emotions. She'd never tried. "Yes, I do. For now, just some companionship at dinner. That should be easy."

When she started to turn back to the sink, Booth stopped

her. "Nothing about this is going to be easy. If I continue to see you, like this, I'm going to take you to bed."

It would be easy, so easy, just to go into his arms. But he'd never accept the generosity, and she'd never survive the emptiness. "Booth, I'm a grown woman. If I go to bed with you, it's my choice."

He nodded. "Perhaps. I just want to make sure I have one." He turned and left her alone in the room.

Ariel took a deep breath. She wasn't going to have it, she decided. No, not any of it. He'd simply have to learn how to cope without the moodiness and tension. Lifting the platter of chops, she went back into the living room.

"Lighten up, DeWitt," she ordered and caught a glimpse of surprise on his face as she went to the grill. "I have to deal with melodrama and misery in every episode. I don't let it into my personal life. Fix yourself another drink, sit down and relax." Ariel set the chops on the grill, added some freshly ground pepper, then walked to the stereo. She switched on jazz, bluesy and mellow.

When she turned around he was still standing, looking at her. "I mean it," she told him. "I have a firm policy about worrying about what complications might come up. They're going to happen if you think about it or if you don't. So why waste your time?"

"Is it that easy for you?"

"Not always. Sometimes I have to work at it."

Thoughtfully, he drew out a cigarette. "We won't be good together," he said after he'd lit it. "I don't want anyone in my life."

"Anyone?" She shook her head. "You're too intelligent to believe a person can live without anyone. Don't you need friendship, companionship, love?"

Blowing out a stream of smoke, he tried to ignore the twinge the question brought him. He'd spent more than two years convincing himself he didn't. Why should he just now, so suddenly, realize the fruitlessness of it? "Each one of those things requires something in return that I no longer want to give."

"Want to give." Her gaze was thoughtful, her mouth unsmiling. "At least you're honest in your phrasing. The more I'm around you, the more I realize you never lie to anyone—but yourself."

"You haven't been around me enough to know who or what I am." He crushed out his cigarette and thrust his hands in his pockets. "And you're much better off that way."

"I or you?" she countered, then shook her head when he didn't answer. "You're letting her make a victim out of you," Ariel murmured. "I'm surprised."

His eyes narrowed; the green frosted. "Don't open closets unless you know what's inside, Ariel."

"Too safe." She preferred the simple anger she felt from him now. With a half laugh, she crossed to him and put her hands on his upper arms. "There's no fun in life without risks. I can't function without fun." Her fingers squeezed, gently. "Look, I enjoy being with you. Is that all right?"

"I'm not sure." She was pulling him in again, with the lightest of touches. "I'm not sure it is for either of us."

"Do yourself a favor," she suggested. "Don't worry about it for a few days and see what happens." Rising on her toes, she brushed his mouth in a gesture that was both friendly and intimate. "Why don't you fix that drink?" she added, grinning. "Because I'm burning the chops."

Chapter Five

"No, Griff, I won't discuss my marriage." Amanda picked up a delft-blue watering can and meticulously tended the plants in her office window. The sun, a product of the sweltering stage lights, poured through the glass.

"Amanda, you can't keep secrets in small towns. It's already common knowledge that you and Cameron aren't living together any longer."

Beneath the trim, tailored jacket, her shoulders stiffened. "Common knowledge or not, it's my business." Keeping her back to him, she examined a bloom on an African violet.

"You're losing weight, there are shadows under your eyes. Damn it, Mandy, I can't stand to see you this way."

She waited a beat, then turned slowly. "I'm fine. I'm capable of handling what needs to be handled."

Griff gave a short laugh. "Who'd know that better than I do?"

Something flared in her eyes, but her voice was cool and final. "I'm busy, Griff."

"Let me help you," he said with sudden, characteristic passion. "It's all I've ever wanted to do."

"Help?" Her voice chilled as she set down the can. "I don't need any help. Do you think I should confide in you, trust you after what you did to me?" As she tilted her head, the tiny sapphires in her ears glinted. She shifted on her mark. "The only difference between you and Cameron is that I let you tear up my life. I won't make the same mistake again."

Fury burst from him as he grabbed her arm. "You never asked me what Vikki was doing in my room. Not then, and not in all these months. You bounced back quick, Mandy, and ended up with another man's ring on your finger."

"It's still there," she said quietly. "So you'd better take your hands off me."

"Do you think that's going to stop me now that I know you don't love him?" Passion, rage, desire—all emanated from his eyes, his voice, his body. "I can look at you and see it," he went on before she could deny it. "I know what's inside you like no one else does. So handle it." He dragged his hands through her hair and dislodged pins. The camera dollied closer. "And handle this."

Pulling her against him, Griff crushed her mouth with his. She nearly tore away. Nearly. For a heartbeat, she was still. Amanda lifted her hands to his shoulders to push away, but clung instead. A soft, muffled moan escaped as passion flared. For a moment, they were locked together as they'd once been. Then, he dragged her away, keeping his hands tight on her arms. Desire and anger sparked between them. His tangible, hers restrained.

"You're not going to back away from me this time," he told her. "I'll wait, but I won't wait long. You come to me, Mandy. That's where you belong."

Releasing her, Griff stormed out of the office. Amanda lifted an unsteady hand to her lips and stared at the closed door.

"Cut."

Ariel marched around the prop wall of her office. "You ate those onions on purpose."

Jack tugged on her disheveled hair. "Just for you, sweetie."

"Swine."

"God, I love it when you call me names." Dramatically, Jack gathered her in his arms and bent her backward in an exaggerated dip. "Let me take you to bed and show you the true meaning of passion."

"Not until you chew a roll of breath mints, fella." Giving him a firm push, Ariel freed herself, then turned to her director. The furnace of stage lights had already been dimmed. "Neal, if that's it for today, I've got an appointment across town."

"Take off. See you at seven on Monday."

In the dressing room, Ariel stripped Amanda's elegant facade away and replaced it with slim cotton pants and a billowy, tailored man's shirt. After slipping on flat shoes she left the studio and went outside. There was a small group of fans waiting, hoping that someone recognizable would appear. They clustered around Amanda, autograph books in hand, as they chattered about the show and tossed questions.

"Are you going to go back with Griff?"

Ariel looked over at the sparkling-eyed teenager and grinned. "I don't know…he's awfully hard to resist."

"He's super! I mean, his eyes are just so *green*." She tucked her gum into the corner of her mouth and sighed. "I'd die if he looked at me the way he looks at you."

Ariel thought of another pair of green eyes and nearly sighed herself. "We'll have to wait to see what develops, won't we? I'm glad you like the show." Easing away from the crowd, she hailed a cab. The minute she gave the address, she slumped back against the seat.

She wasn't sure why she felt so tired. She supposed it was the prospect of the meeting that made her so bone weary. True, she hadn't been sleeping as well as was her habit, but she'd gone through wakeful phases before without any strain.

Booth. If Booth were the only thing on her mind, she could have dealt with it well enough. She hoped she would. But there was Scott.

The idea of confronting his grandparents didn't frighten her, but it did weary her. Ariel had spoken with them before. There was no reason to believe this session would be any different.

She remembered the way Scott had beamed and glowed at the zoo. Such a simple thing. Such a vital thing. The way he'd clung to her—it tore at her heart. If there were just some other way…

Closing her eyes, she sighed. She didn't believe there would be another way, not even with all her natural optimism. In the end, they'd come to a complicated, painful custody suit with Scott caught in the middle.

What was best? What was right? Ariel wanted someone to tell her, to advise and comfort her. But for the first time in her life she felt it impossible to confide in anyone. The more private she kept this affair, the less chance there was of Scott being hurt by it. She would just have to follow her instincts, and hope.

With her mind on a dozen other things, Ariel paid the cabbie and walked into the sleek steel building that housed her lawyer's offices. On the way from the lobby to the thirtieth floor, she gathered all her confidence together. This would be perhaps the last time she'd have the opportunity to speak with Scott's grandparents on an informal basis. She needed to give it her best shot.

The little tremor in her stomach wasn't so different from stage fright. Comfortable with it, Ariel walked into Bigby, Liebowitz and Feirson.

"Good afternoon, Ms. Kirkwood." The receptionist beamed a smile at Ariel and wondered if she could get away with a similar outfit. Not slim enough, she decided wistfully. Instead of looking dashing, she'd just look frumpy. "Mr. Bigby's expecting you."

"Hello, Marlene. How's the puppy working out?"

"Oh, he's so smart. My husband couldn't believe that a mutt could learn so many tricks. I really want to thank you for arranging it for me."

"I'm glad he's got a good home." She caught herself lacing her fingers together—a rare outward sign of tension. Deliberately Ariel dropped her hands to her sides as the receptionist rang through.

"Ms. Kirkwood's here, Mr. Bigby. Yes, sir." She rose as she replaced the receiver. "I'll take you back. If you have time before you leave, Ms. Kirkwood, my sister'd love your autograph. She never misses your show."

"I'd be happy to." Ariel's fingers groped for each other and she restrained them. *Save the nerves for later,* she told herself, *when you can afford them.* For once, she'd apply some of Amanda's steady calm to her personal life.

"Well, Ariel." The spindly, bearded man behind the massive desk rose as she entered. The room carried a vague scent of peppermint and polish. "Right on time."

"I never miss a cue." Ariel crossed the plush carpet with both hands extended. "You look good, Charlie."

"I feel good since you talked me into giving up smoking. Six months," he said with a grin. "Three days and—" he checked his watch "—four and a half hours."

She squeezed his hands. "Keep counting."

"We've got about fifteen minutes before the Andersons are due. Want some coffee?"

"Oh, yeah." On the words, Ariel sunk into a creamy leather chair.

Bigby pushed his intercom. "Would you bring some coffee back, Marlene? So…" He set down the receiver and folded his neat, ringless hands. "How're you holding up?"

"I'm a wreck, Charlie." She stretched out her legs and ordered herself to relax. First the toes, then the ankles, then all the way up. "You're practically the only one I can talk to about this. I'm not used to holding things in."

"If things go well you won't have to much longer."

She sent him a level look. "What chance do we have?"

"A fair one."

With a small sigh, Ariel shook her head. "Not good enough."

After a brief knock, Marlene entered with the coffee tray. "Cream and sugar, Ms. Kirkwood?"

"Yes, thank you." Ariel accepted the cup then immediately rose and began to pace. Maybe if she could turn some of the nerves to energy she wouldn't burst. Maybe. "Charlie, Scott needs me."

And you need him, he thought as he watched her. "Ariel, you're a responsible member of your community with a good reputation. You have a steady job with an excellent income, though it can and will be argued that it's not necessarily stable. You put your brother through college and have some sort of an involvement with every charity known to man." He saw her smile at that and was pleased. "You're young, but not a child. The Andersons are both in their midsixties. That should have some bearing on the outcome, and you'll have the emotion on your side."

"God, I hate to think of there being sides," she murmured. "There're sides in arguments, in wars. This can't be a war, Charlie. He's just a child."

"As difficult as it is, you're going to have to think practically about this."

With a nod, she sipped uninterestedly at her coffee. Practical. "But I'm single, and I'm an actress."

"There're pros and cons. This last-ditch meeting was your idea," he continued. "I don't like to see you get churned up this way."

"I have to try just once more before we find ourselves in court. The idea that Scotty might have to testify…"

"Just an easy talk with the judge in chambers, Ariel. It's not traumatic, I promise you."

"Not to you, maybe not to him, but to me…" She whirled around, her eyes dark with passion. "I'd give it up, Charlie. I swear I'd give it up this minute if I could believe he'd be happy with them. But when he looks at me…" Breaking off, she shook her head. Both hands were clenched on the coffee cup and she concentrated on relaxing them. "I know I'm being emotional about this, but it's the only way I've ever been able to judge what was right and what was wrong. If I look at it practically, I know they'll feed him and shelter him and educate him. But nurturing…" She turned to stare out of the window. "I keep coming back to the nurturing. Am I doing the best for him, Charlie? I just want to be sure."

For a moment, he sat fondling the gold pen on his desk. She asked hard questions. In the law, it wasn't a matter of best, but of justice. The two weren't always synonymous. "Ariel, you know the boy. At the risk of sounding very unlawyerlike, I say you have to do what your heart tells you."

Smiling, she turned back. "You say the right things. That's all I've ever been able to do." For a moment, she hesitated, then plunged. Since she was here for advice, she'd go all the way with it. "Charlie, if I told you I'd fallen in love with a man who thinks relationships are to be avoided at all costs and actresses are the least trustworthy individuals on the planet, what would you say?"

"I'd say it was typical of you. How long do you figure it'll take you to change his mind?"

Laughing, she dragged a hand through her hair. "Always the right thing," she said again.

"Sit down and drink your coffee, Ariel," he advised. "You're the one who says if something's meant to happen, it happens."

"When have I ever said anything so trite?" she demanded but did as he said. "All right, Charlie." She heaved a long sigh. "Do you want to give me the lecture on what I should expect and what I shouldn't say?"

"For what good it'll do." He toyed with the edge of Ariel's file. "You'll meet the Andersons' lawyer, Basil Ford. He's very painstaking and very conservative. I've dealt with him before."

"Did you win?"

Bigby grinned at her as he leaned back in his chair. "I'd say we're about even. Since this is a voluntary, informal meeting, there won't be that much for either Ford or me to do. But if he asks you a question you shouldn't answer, I'll take care of it." Meticulously, Bigby settled the English bone-china cup back in its saucer. "Otherwise, say what you want, but don't elaborate more than necessary. Above all, don't lose your temper or your grip. If you want to yell or cry, wait until they've gone."

"You've gotten to know me very well," she murmured. "All right, I'll be calm and lucid." When the buzzer sounded on his desk, Ariel balled her hands into fists.

"Yes, Marlene, bring them in. And we'll need more coffee." He looked across at Ariel, measuring the strain in her eyes against the strength. "It's a discussion," he reminded her. "It's doubtful anything will be decided here today."

She nodded and concentrated on relaxing her hands.

When the door opened, Bigby rose, all joviality. "Basil, good to see you." He stretched his hand out to meet that of the erect, gray-suited man with thinning hair. "Mr. and Ms. Anderson, please have a seat. We'll have coffee in a moment. Basil Ford, Ariel Kirkwood."

Ariel nearly let out a tense giggle at the cocktail introduction. "Hello, Mr. Ford." She found his handshake firm and his gaze formidable.

"Ms. Kirkwood." He sat smoothly with his briefcase by his side.

"Hello, Mr. Anderson, Ms. Anderson."

Ariel received a nod from the woman and a brief formal handshake from her husband. Attractive people. Solid people. She'd always felt that from them—along with their rigidity. Both stood straight, a product of their military training. Anderson had retired from active service as a full colonel ten years before, and in her youth, his wife had been an Army nurse.

They'd met during the war, had served together and married. You could sense their closeness—the intimacy of thoughts and values. Perhaps, Ariel mused, that was why they had trouble seeing anyone else's viewpoint.

Together, the Andersons sat on a cushy two-seater sofa. Both were conservatively dressed: her iron-gray hair was skimmed back and his snowy white was cropped close. Feeling the waves of their disapproval, Ariel bit back a sigh. Instinct and experience told her she'd never get through to them on an emotional level.

While coffee was served, Bigby steered the conversation into generalities. The Andersons answered politely and ignored Ariel as much as possible. Because they spoke around her, she took care not to ask them any direct questions. She'd antagonize them soon enough.

She recognized the signal when Bigby sat behind his desk and folded his hands on the surface.

"I believe we can all agree that we have one mutual concern," he began. "Scott's welfare."

"That's why we're here," Ford said easily.

Bigby skimmed his gaze over Ford and concentrated on the Andersons. "Since that's the case, an informal meeting like this where we can exchange points of view and options should be to everyone's benefit."

"Naturally, my clients' main concern is their grandchild's well-being." Ford spoke in his beautiful orator's voice before he sipped his coffee. "Ms. Kirkwood's interest is understood, of course. As to the matter of custody, there's no question as to the rights and capability of Mr. and Ms. Anderson."

"Nor of Ms. Kirkwood's," Bigby put in mildly. "But it isn't rights and capabilities we're discussing today. It's the child himself. I'd like to make it clear that, at this point, we're not questioning your intentions or your ability to raise the child." He spoke to the Andersons again, skillfully bypassing his colleague. "The issue is what's best for Scott as an individual."

"My grandson," Anderson began in his deep, raspy voice, "belongs where he is. He's well fed, well dressed and well disciplined. His upbringing will have a sense of order. He'll be sent to the best schools available."

"What about well loved?" Ariel blurted out before she could stop herself. "What money can't buy…" Leaning forward she focused her attention on Scott's grandmother. "Will he be well loved?"

"An abstract question, Ms. Kirkwood," Ford put in briskly. "If we could—"

"No, it isn't," Ariel interrupted, sparing him a glance before she turned back to the Andersons. "There's nothing more solid than love. Nothing more easily given or withheld. Will you hold him at night if he's frightened of shadows? Will you understand how important it is to pretend that he's protecting you? Will you always listen when he needs to talk?"

"He won't be coddled if that's what you mean." Anderson set down his coffee and rested a hand on one knee. "A child's values are molded early. These fantasies—that you encourage—aren't healthy. I have no intention of allowing my grandson to live in a dreamworld."

"A dreamworld." Ariel stared at him and saw a solid rock wall of resistance. "Mr. Anderson, Scott has a beautiful imagination. He's full of life, and visions."

"Visions." Anderson's lips thinned. "Visions will do nothing but make him look for what isn't there, expect what he can't have. The boy needs a firm basis in reality. In what *is*. You make your living from pretending, Ms. Kirkwood. My grandson won't live his life in a storybook."

"There're twenty-four hours in every day, Mr. Anderson. Isn't there enough reality in that so we can put a small portion of time aside for wishing? All children need to believe in wishes, especially Scott after so much has been taken away from him. Please…" Her gaze shifted to the stiff-backed woman on the sofa. "You've known grief. Scott lost the two people in the world who meant love and security and normality. All of those things have to be given back to him."

"By you?" Ms. Anderson sat very still, her eyes remained very level. In them Ariel saw remnants of pain. "My daughter's child will be raised by me."

"Ms. Kirkwood." Ford interrupted smoothly, then crossed his legs. "To touch on more practical matters, I'm aware that you currently have a key role in a— Daytime drama, I believe is the word. This equals a regular job with a steady income. But to be down-to-earth for a moment, it's habitual for these things to change. How would you support a child if your income was interrupted?"

"My income won't be interrupted." Bigby caught her eye, so with an effort Ariel held on to her temper. "I'm under contract. I'm also signed to do a film with P. B. Marshell." Noticing the flicker of speculation, Ariel blessed fate for throwing the part her way.

"That's very impressive," Ford told her. "However, I'm sure you'd be the first to admit that your profession is renowned for its ups and downs."

"If we're talking financial stablity, Mr. Ford, I assure you that I'm capable of giving Scott all the material requirements necessary. If my career should take a downswing, I'd simply supplement it. I've experience in both the retail and the restaurant business." A half smile teased her mouth as she thought of her days selling perfume and powder, and waiting tables. Oh, yes, *experience* was the right word. "But I can't believe any of us would put a bank statement first when we're discussing a child." It was said calmly, with only a hint of disdain.

"I'm sure we all agree that the child's monetary well-being is of primary importance," Bigby put in. The subtle tone of his voice was his warning to Ariel. "There's no question that both the Andersons and my client are capable of providing Scott with food, shelter, education, etc."

"There's also the matter of marital status." Ford stroked a long finger down the side of his nose. "As a single woman, a single professional woman, Ms. Kirkwood, just how much time would you be able to spare for Scott?"

"Whatever he needs," Ariel said simply. "I recognize my priorities, Mr. Ford."

"Perhaps." He nodded, resting a hand on the arm of his chair. "And perhaps you haven't thought this through completely. Having never raised a child, you might not be fully aware of the time involved. You have an active social life, Ms. Kirkwood."

His words and tone were mild, his meaning clear. Any other time, in any other place, she would have been amused. "Not as active as it reads in print, Mr. Ford."

Again, he nodded. "You're also a young woman, attractive. I'm sure it's reasonable to assume that marriage is highly likely at some time in the future. Have you considered how a potential husband might feel about the responsibility of raising someone else's child?"

"No." Her fingers laced together. "If I loved a man enough to marry him, he'd accept Scott as part of me, of my life. Otherwise, he wouldn't be the kind of man I'd love."

"If you had to make a choice—"

"Basil." Bigby held up a hand, and though he smiled, his eyes were hard. "We shouldn't get bogged down in this sort of speculation. No one expects us to solve this custody issue here today. What we want is to get a clear picture of everyone's feelings. What your clients and mine want for Scott."

"His well-being," Anderson said tersely.

"His happiness," Ariel murmured. "I want to believe they're the same thing."

"You're no different from your brother." Anderson's voice

was sharp and low, like the final snap of a whip. "Happiness. He preached happiness at all costs to my daughter until she tossed aside all her responsibilities, her education, her values. Pregnant at eighteen, married to a penniless student who put more effort into flying a kite than keeping a decent job."

Ariel's mouth trembled open as the pain struck. No, she wouldn't waste her breath defending her brother. He needed no defense. "They loved each other," she said instead.

"Loved each other." Color rose in Anderson's cheeks, the first and only sign of emotion Ariel had seen from him. "Can you honestly believe that's enough?"

"Yes. They were happy together. They had a beautiful child together. They had dreams together." Ariel swallowed as the urge to weep pounded at her. "Some people never have that much."

"Barbara would still be alive if we'd kept her away from him."

Ariel looked over at the older woman and saw more than pain now. The strong, bony hands shook slightly, the voice broke. It was a combination of grief and fury that Ariel recognized and understood. "Jeremy's gone, too, Ms. Anderson," she said quietly. "But Scott's here."

"He killed my daughter." The woman's eyes glowed against a skin gone abruptly pale.

"Oh, no." Ariel reached out, shocked by the words, drawn by the pain. "Ms. Anderson, Jeremy adored Barbara. He'd never have done anything to hurt her."

"He took her up in that plane. Barbara had no business being up in one of those small planes. She wouldn't have been if he hadn't taken her."

"Ms. Anderson, I know how you feel—"

She jerked away from Ariel's offer of comfort, her breath

suddenly coming fast and shallow. "Don't you tell me you know how I feel. She was my only child. My only child." Rising, she sent Ariel an icy stare that shimmered with tears. "I won't discuss Barbara with you, or Barbara's son." She walked from the office in quick, controlled steps that were silent on the carpet.

"I won't have you upsetting my wife." Mr. Anderson stood, erect and unyielding. "We've known nothing but misery since the first time we heard the name Kirkwood."

Though her knees had begun to shake, Ariel rose to face him. "Scott's name is Kirkwood, Mr. Anderson."

Without a word, he turned and strode out of the room.

"My clients are understandably emotional on this issue." Ford's voice was so calm Ariel barely heard it. With the slightest nod of agreement, she wandered to stare out the window.

She didn't register the subdued conversation the attorneys carried on behind her. Instead, she concentrated on the flow of traffic she could see but not quite hear from thirty floors below. She wanted to be down there, surrounded by cars and buses and people.

Strange how she'd nearly convinced herself she was resigned to her brother's death. Now, the helpless anger washed over her again until she could have screamed with it. Screamed just one word. *Why?*

"Ariel." Bigby put a hand on her shoulder and repeated her name before Ariel turned her head. Ford and his clients had left. "Come sit down."

She lifted a hand to his. "No, I'm all right."

"Like hell you are."

With a half laugh, she rested her forehead against the glass. "I will be in a minute. Why is it, Charlie, I never believe how hard or how ugly things can be until they happen? And even then— Even then I can't quite understand it."

"Because you look for the best. It's a beautiful talent of yours."

"Or an escape mechanism," she murmured.

"Don't start coming down on yourself, Ariel." His voice was sharper then he'd intended, but he had the satisfaction of seeing her shoulders straighten. "Another of your talents is being able to pull in other people's emotions. Don't do it with the Andersons."

Letting out a long sigh, she continued to stare down to the street. "They're hurting. I wish there was a way we could share the grief instead of hurling it at one other. But there's nothing I can do about them," she whispered and closed her eyes briefly, tightly. "Charlie, Scott doesn't belong with them. He's all I care about. Not once, not one single time did either of them call him by name. He was always the boy, or my grandchild, never Scott. It's as though they can't give him his own identity, maybe because it's too close to Jeremy's." For an extra moment she rested her palms against the window ledge. "I only want what's right for Scott—even if it's not me."

"It's going to go to court, Ariel, and it's going to be very, very hard on you."

"You've explained all that before. It doesn't matter."

"I can't give you any guarantees on the outcome."

She moistened her lips and turned to face him. "I understand that, too. I have to believe that whatever happens will be what's best for Scott. If I lose, I was meant to lose."

"At the risk of being completely unprofessional—" he touched the tips of her hair "—what about what's best for you?"

With a smile, she cupped his face in her hand and kissed his cheek. "I'm a survivor, Charlie, and a whole hell of a lot tougher than I look. Let's worry about Scott."

He was capable of worrying about more than one thing at a time, and she was still pale, her eyes still a bit too bright. "Let me buy you a drink."

Ariel rubbed her knuckles against his beard. "I'm fine," she said definitely. "And you're busy." Turning, she picked up her purse. Her stomach was quivering. All she wanted to do was to get out in the air and clear her head. "I just need to walk for a bit," she said half to herself. "After I think it all the way through again I'll feel better."

At the door she paused and looked back. Bigby was still standing by the window, a frown of concern on his face. "Can you tell me we have a chance of winning?"

"Yes, I can tell you that. I wish I could tell you more."

Shaking her head, Ariel pulled open the door. "It's enough. It has to be enough."

Chapter Six

Booth considered taking everything he'd written that day and ditching it. That's what sensible people did with garbage. Leaning back in his chair, he scowled at the half-typed sheet staring back at him, and at the stack of completed pages beside his machine. Then again, tomorrow it might not seem quite so much like garbage and he could salvage something.

He couldn't remember the last time he'd hit a wall like this in his work. It was like carving words into granite—slow, laborious, and the finished product was never perfectly clear and sharp. You got sweaty, your muscles and eyes ached, and you barely made a dent. He'd given the script ten hours that day, and perhaps half of that with his full concentration. It was out of character. It was frustrating.

It was Ariel.

What the hell was he going to do about it? Booth ran his hands over his face with a weariness that came from lack of production rather than lack of energy. There'd never been a woman he couldn't block out of his mind for long periods of time—even Liz at the height of their disastrous marriage. But this woman… With a sound of annoyance, Booth pushed away from the typewriter. This woman was breaking all the rules. His rules—the ones he'd formed for personal survival.

The worst of it was he just wanted to be with her. Just to see her smile, hear her laugh, listen to her talk about something that didn't have to make sense.

And the hardest of it was the desire. It shifted and rippled continually under the surface of his thoughts. He had the blessing-curse of a writer's imagination. No effort was needed for Booth to feel the way her skin would heat under his hands, the way her mouth would give and take. And it took no effort to project mentally how she could foul up his life.

Because they'd be working together, he could only avoid her so much. Making love with her was inevitable—so inevitable he knew he'd have to weigh the consequences. But for now, with his rooms quiet around him and thoughts of Ariel crowding his mind, Booth couldn't think beyond having her. Prices always had to be paid…. Who would know that better than he?

Glancing down at his work, Booth admitted that he was already paying. His writing was suffering because he couldn't control his concentration. His pace, usually smooth, was erratic and choppy. What he was producing lacked the polish so integral to his style.

Too often, he caught himself staring into space—something writers do habitually. But it wasn't his characters who worked in his mind. Too often, he found himself awake before dawn after a restless night. But it wasn't his plot that kept him from sleep.

It was Ariel.

He thought of her too much, too exclusively for comfort. And he was a man who hoarded his comfort. His work was always, had always been, of paramount importance to him. He intended it to continue to be. Yet he was allowing someone to interfere, intrude.

Allowing? Booth shook his head as he lit a cigarette. He was a man of words, of shades of meanings, and knew that wasn't the proper one. He hadn't allowed Ariel into his mind—she'd invaded it.

The smoke seared his throat. Too many cigarettes, he admitted as he took another drag. Too many long days and nights. He was pushing it—and there were moments, a few scattered moments when he took the time to wonder why.

Ambition wasn't the issue. Not if ambition equaled the quest for glory and money. Glory had never concerned him, and money had never been a prime motivation. Success perhaps, in that he had always sought then insisted on quality when anything was associated with his name. But it was more a matter of obsession—that was what his writing had been since he'd first put pen to paper.

When a man had one obsession, it was easy to have two. Booth stared at the half-typed page and thought of Ariel.

The doorbell rang twice before he roused himself to answer it. If his work had been flowing at all, he would have ignored it completely. Interruptions, he thought ruefully as he left the littered desk behind, sometimes had their advantages.

"Hi." Ariel smiled at him and kept her hands in her pockets. It was the only way she could keep them from lacing together. "I know I should've called, but I was walking and took the chance that you wouldn't be frantically writing some monumental scene." *You're babbling,* she warned herself and clenched both hands.

"I haven't written a monumental scene in hours." He studied her a moment, perceptive enough to know that beneath the smile and animated voice there was trouble. A week before, perhaps even days before, he'd have made an excuse and shut her out. "Come in."

"I must've caught you at a good time," Ariel commented as she crossed the threshold. "Otherwise you'd've growled at me. Were you working?"

"No, I'd stopped." She looked ready to burst, he mused. The casualness, the glib remarks didn't mask the outpouring of emotion. It showed in her eyes, in her movements. A quick glance showed him that her hands were fists in her pockets. Tension? One didn't associate the word with her. He wanted to touch her, to soothe, and had to remind himself that he didn't need anyone else's problems. "Want a drink?"

"No— Yes," she amended. Perhaps it would calm her more than the two-hour walk had done. "Whatever's handy. It's a beautiful day." Ariel paced to the window and found herself reminded too much of standing in Bigby's office. She turned her back on the view. "Warm. Flowers are everywhere. Have you been out?"

"No." He handed her a dry vermouth without offering her a chair. In this mood he knew she'd never sit still.

"Oh, you shouldn't miss it. Perfect days're rare." She drank, then waited for her muscles to loosen. "I was going to walk through the park, then found myself here."

He waited a moment as she stared down into her glass. "Why?"

Slowly, Ariel lifted her eyes to his. "I needed to be with someone—it turned out to be you. Do you mind?"

He should have. God knows he wanted to. "No." Without thinking, Booth took a step closer—physically, emotionally. "Do you want to tell me about it?"

"Yes." The word came out on a sigh. "But I can't." Turning

away, she set down her glass. She wasn't going to level. Why had she been so sure she would? "Booth, it isn't often I can't handle things or find myself so scared that running away looks like the best out. When it happens, I need someone."

He was touching her hair before he could stop himself, was turning her to face him before he'd weighed the pros and cons. And he was holding her before either of them could be surprised by the simplicity of it.

Ariel clung as relief flowed over her. He was strong—strong enough to accept her strength and understand the moments of weakness. She needed that very basic human support, without question, without demands. His chest was hard and firm against her. Over her back his hands ran gently. He said nothing. For the first time in hours, Ariel felt her balance return. Kindness gave her hope; she was a woman who'd always been able to survive on that alone.

What's troubling her, Booth wondered. He could feel the panic in the way her hands gripped him. Even when he felt her begin to relax he remembered that first frantic grip. Her work, he thought. Or something more personal? Either way, it had nothing to do with him. And yet… While she was soft and vulnerable in his arms he felt it had everything to do with him.

He should step back. His lips brushed through her hair as he breathed in her fragrance. It was never safe to lower the wall. His lips skimmed along her temple.

"I want to help you." The words ran through his mind and spilled out before he was aware of them.

Ariel's arms tightened around him. That phrase meant more, infinitely more, than I love you. Without knowing it, he'd just given her everything she needed. "You have." She tilted her head back so that she could see his face. "You are."

Lifting a hand, she ran her fingers over the long firm bones in his face, over the taut skin roughened by a day's growth of beard. Love was something that moved in her too strongly to be ignored. She needed to share it, if not verbally, then by touch.

Softly, slowly, she closed the distance and brushed his lips with hers. Her lids lowered, but through her lashes she watched his eyes as he watched hers. The intensity in his never altered. Ariel knew he was absorbing her mood, and testing it.

It was he who shifted the angle, without increasing the pressure. Easily he toyed with her mouth, nipping into the softness of her bottom lip, tracing the shape with just the tip of his tongue until the flutter in her stomach spread to her chest. He needed to draw in the sensation of her as a woman, as an individual. He wanted to know her physically; he needed to understand the subtleties of her mind. As she felt her body give, her mind yield, Ariel wondered how it was he didn't hear the love shouting out of her.

He was struck by the emotion that raced from her. He'd never held a woman capable of such feeling, or one who, by possessing it, demanded it in return. It wasn't a simple matter of response. Even as his senses began to swim, Booth understood that. He wanted to give to her. And though he wanted, he knew he couldn't. Risks were for the foolish, and he couldn't afford to play the fool a second time.

Compassion, however, touched off compassion. If nothing else, he could give her a few hours' relief from whatever plagued her mind. He ran his hands up her arms for the sheer pleasure of it. "How nice a day is it?" he asked.

Ariel smiled. Her fingers were still on his face, her lips only inches from his. "It's spectacular."

"Let's go out." Booth paused only long enough to take her hand before he headed for the door.

"Thank you." Ariel touched her head briefly to his shoulder in one more simple show of affection he wasn't accustomed to. It warmed him—and cautioned him.

"What for?"

"For not asking questions." Ariel stepped into the elevator, leaned back against the wall and sighed.

"I generally stay out of other people's business."

"Do you?" She opened her eyes and the smile lingered. "I don't. I'm an inveterate meddler—most of us are. We all like to get inside other people. You just do it more subtly than most."

Booth shrugged as the elevator reached lobby level. "It's not personal."

Ariel laughed as she stepped out. Swinging her purse over her shoulder, she moved in her habitual quick step. "Oh, yes, it is."

He stopped a moment and met the humor in her eyes. "Yes," he admitted. "It is. But then, as a writer I can observe, dissect, steal other people's thoughts and feelings without having to get involved enough to advise or comfort or even sympathize."

"You're too hard on yourself, Booth," Ariel murmured. "Much too hard."

His brow quirked in puzzlement. Of all the things he'd ever been accused of, that wasn't one of them. "I'm a realist."

"On one level. On another you're a dreamer. All writers are dreamers on some level—the same way all actors are children on one. It has nothing to do with how clever you are, how practical, how smart. It goes with the job." She stepped out into the warmth and the sun. "I like being a child, and you like being a dreamer. You just don't like to admit it."

Annoyance. He should've felt annoyance but felt pleasure instead. As long as he could remember, no one else had ever understood him. As long as he could remember, he'd never cared. "You've convinced yourself you know me very well."

"No, but I've made a few scratches in the surface." She sent him a saucy look. "And you've a very tough surface."

"And yours is very thin." Unexpectedly he cupped her face in his hand for a thorough study. His fingers were firm, as if he expected resistance and would ignore it. "Or seems to be." How could he be sure, he wondered. How could one person ever be sure of another?

Ariel was too used to being examined, and already too used to Booth to be disconcerted. "There's little underneath that doesn't show through."

"Perhaps that's why you're a good actress," he mused. "You absorb the character easily. How much is you, and how much is the role?"

He was far from ready to trust, she realized when he dropped his hand. "I can't answer that. Maybe when the film's over, you'll be able to."

He inclined his head in acknowledgment. It was a good answer—perhaps the best answer. "You wanted to walk in the park."

Ariel tucked her arm companionably through his. "Yeah. I'll buy you an ice cream."

Booth turned his head as they walked. "What flavor?"

"Anything but vanilla," Ariel said expansively. "There's nothing remotely vanilla about today."

She was right, Booth decided. It was a spectacular day. The grass was green, the flowers vivid and pungent. He could smell the park smells. Peanuts and pigeons. Enthusiastic joggers pumped by in colorful sweatbands and running shorts, streaks of sweat down their backs.

Spring would soon give way to early summer. The trees were full, the leaves a hardy shade rather than the tender hue they'd been only weeks before. Shade spread in invitation while the sun baked the benches and paths. He knew Ariel would choose the sun. And he wondered, as he strolled along beside her, why he'd gone so long without seeking it himself.

As Ariel bit into an ice cream confection coated with chocolate and nuts, she thought of Scott. But this time, the apprehension was gone. She'd only needed to lean on someone for a moment, draw on someone else's emotional strength, to have her faith return. Her head was clear again, her nerves gone. With a laugh, she turned into Booth's arms and kissed him hard.

"Ice cream does that to me." She was still laughing as she dropped onto a swing. "And sunshine." She leaned way back and kicked her feet to give herself momentum. The tips of her hair nearly skimmed the ground. It was pale, exquisitely pale in the slanting sun. As it fell back, it left her face unframed and stunning. Her skin was flushed with color as she pushed off again and let herself glide.

"You seem to be an expert." Booth leaned against the frame of the swing as her legs flashed by him.

"Absolutely. Want to join me?"

"I'll just watch."

"It's one of your best things." Ariel threw out her legs again for more height and enjoyed the thrill that swept through her stomach. "When's the last time you were on one of these?"

A memory surged through his mind—of himself at five or six and his primly uniformed, round-faced nanny. She'd pushed him on a swing while he'd squealed and demanded to go higher. At the time he hadn't believed there was any more to life than that rushing pendulum ride. Abruptly, he appreciated Ariel's claim that she enjoyed being a child.

"A hundred years ago," he murmured.

"Too long." Skimming her feet on the ground, she slowed the swing. "Get on with me." She blew the hair out of her eyes and grinned at his blank expression. "You can stand, one foot on either side of me. It's sturdy enough—if you are," she added with just enough of a challenge in the tone to earn a scowl.

"Practicing your psychiatry?"

Her grin only widened. "Is it working?"

She was laughing at him again, and knowing it, Booth took the bait. "Apparently." He stepped behind her to grab the chain with his hands. "How high do you want to go?"

Ariel tipped back her head to give him an upside-down smile. "As high as I can."

"No crying uncle," Booth warned as he began to push her.

"Ha." Ariel tossed back her hair and shifted her grip. "Fat chance, DeWitt."

She felt him jump nimbly onto the swing as they began to fly, then threw her body into it until the rhythm steadied. The sky tilted over her, blue and dusted with clouds. The ground swayed, brown and green. She rested her head against a firm, muscled thigh and let the sensations carry her.

Grass. She could smell it, sun drenched and trampled, mixed with the dusty scent of dry earth. Children's laughter, cooing pigeons, traffic—Ariel could hear each separate sound individually and as a mixture.

The air tasted of spring—sweet, light. An image of a watermelon ran through her mind. Yes, that was what she thought of as the breeze fluttered over her cheeks. But overall, most of all, it was Booth who played with her senses. It was him she felt firmly against her back, his quiet breathing she heard beneath all the other sounds. She could smell him—salt and soap and tobacco. She had only to shift the angle of her head to see his strong, capable hands around the chain of the child's swing. Ariel closed her eyes and absorbed it all. It was like coming home. Content, she slid her hands higher on the chain so that they brushed his. The contact, warm flesh to warm flesh, was enough.

He'd forgotten what it was like to do something for no reason. And by forgetting it, Booth had forgotten the purity of pleasure. He felt it now, without the intellectual justifications he so often restricted himself with. Because he understood that freedom brought vulnerability, he'd doled it out to himself miserly. Only on those rare occasions when he was completely alone, away from responsibilities and his work, had he allowed his heart and mind to drift. Now, it happened so spontaneously he hardly realized it. Bypassing the dangers of relaxation, Booth enjoyed the ride.

"Higher!" Ariel demanded on a breathless laugh as she leaned into the arch. "Much higher!"

"Much higher and you'll land on your nose."

Her sound of pleasure rippled over the air. "Not me. I land on my feet. Higher, Booth!"

When she turned her head up to laugh into his face, he lost himself in her. Beauty—it was there, but not the cool, distant beauty he saw on camera. Looking at her now, he saw nothing of his Rae, nothing of her Amanda. There was only Ariel. For the first time in longer than he cared to remember, he felt a twinge of hope. It scared the hell out of him.

"Faster!" she shouted, not giving him any time to dwell on what was happening inside him. Her laughter was infectious, as was her enthusiasm. They soared together until his arms ached. When the swing began to slow, she leaped from it and left him wobbling.

"Oh, that was wonderful." Still laughing, Ariel turned in a circle, arms wide. "Now I'm starving. Absolutely starving."

"You just had ice cream." Booth leaped off the swing to find himself breathless and his blood pumping.

"Not good enough." Ariel whirled around to him and linked her hands behind his head. "I need a hot dog—really need a hot dog with everything."

"A hot dog." Because it seemed so natural, he bent to kiss her. Her mouth was warm, the lips curved. "Do you know what they put in those things?"

"No. And I don't want to. I want to stuff myself with whatever nasty stuff it has in it and feel wonderful."

Booth ran his hands down her sides. "You do feel wonderful."

Her smile changed, softened. "That's about the nicest thing you've ever said to me. Kiss me again, right here, while I'm still flying."

Booth drew her closer as his lips tasted hers. Fleetingly he wondered why the gentle kiss moved him equally as much as the passion had yet somehow differently. He wanted her. And along with her body he wanted that energy, that verve, the joie de vivre. He wanted to explore and measure it, and to test it for its genuineness. Booth was still far from sure that anyone in the world he knew could be quite so real. And yet, he was beginning to want to believe it.

Drawing her away he watched her lashes flutter up, her lips curve. But he remembered that sense of panic he'd felt from her when he'd first opened his door. If her emotions were as vibrant as they seemed, she wouldn't be limited to joy and vivacity.

"A hot dog," he repeated and speculated on how much he would learn of her and how long it would take. "It's your stomach, but I'll spring for it."

"I knew you could be a sport, Booth." She slipped her arm around his waist as they walked. "I just might have two."

"Masochistic tendencies run in your family?"

"No, just gluttony. Tell me about yours."

"I don't have masochistic tendencies."

"Your family," she corrected, chuckling. "They must be very proud of you."

His brow lifted while a ghost of a smile played around his mouth. "That depends on your point of view. I was supposed to follow family tradition and go into law. Throughout most of my twenties I was the black sheep."

"Is that so?" Tilting her head, she studied him with fresh interest. "I can't imagine it. I've always had a fondness for black sheep."

"I would've made book on it," Booth said dryly. "But one might say I've been accepted back into the fold in the past few years."

"It was the Pulitzer that did it."

"The Oscar didn't hurt," Booth admitted, seeing the humor in something he'd barely noticed before. "But the Pulitzer had more clout with the DeWitts of Philadelphia."

Ariel scented the hot dog stand and guided him toward it. "You'll be adding an Emmy to the list next year."

He pulled out his wallet as Ariel leaned over the stand and breathed deeply. "You're very confident."

"It's the best way to be. Are you having one?"

The scent was too good to resist. When had he eaten last? What had he eaten? Booth shrugged the thoughts way. "I suppose."

Ariel grinned and held up two fingers to the concessionaire. When hers was in its bun she began to go through the condiments one at a time. "You know, Booth—" she piled on relish "—*The Rebellion* was brilliant, clean, hard-hitting, exquisite characterizations, but it wasn't as entertaining as your *Misty Tuesday.*"

Booth watched her take the first hefty bite. "My purpose in writing isn't always to entertain."

"No, I understand that." Ariel chewed thoughtfully, then accepted the soda Booth offered her. "It's just my personal preference. That's why I'm in the profession. I want to be entertained, and I need to entertain."

He added a conservative line of mustard to his hot dog. "That's why you've been satisfied with daytime drama."

She shot him a look as they began to walk again. "Don't get snide. Quality entertainment's the core of it. If I was handy juggling plates and riding a unicycle, that's what I'd do."

After the first bite, Booth realized the hot dog was the best thing he'd eaten in a week, perhaps in months. "You have a tremendous talent," he told her, but didn't notice the surprised lift of her brow at the ease of the compliment. "It's difficult for me to understand why you aren't doing major films or theater. A series, even a weekly series is dragging, backbreaking work. Being a major character in a show that airs five days a week has to be exhausting, impossible and frustrating."

"Exactly why I do it." She licked mustard from her thumb. "I was raised right here in Manhattan. The pace's in my blood. Have you ever considered why L.A. and New York are on opposite ends of the continent?"

"A lucky geographical accident."

"Fate," Ariel corrected. "Both might be towns where show business is of top importance, but no two cities could have more opposing paces. I'd go crazy in California—mellow isn't my speed. I like doing the soap because it's a daily challenge, it keeps me sharp. And when there's the time and the opportunity, I like doing things like *Streetcar*. But…" She finished off her hot dog with a sigh. "Doing the same play night after night becomes too easy, and you get too comfortable."

He drank down cola—a flavor he'd nearly forgotten. "You've been playing the same character for five years."

"Not the same thing." She crunched an ice cube and enjoyed the shock of cold. "Soaps're full of surprises. You never know what kind of angle they're going to throw at you to pump up ratings or lead in a fresh story line." She scooted around a middle-aged matron walking a poodle. "Right now Amanda's facing a crumbling marriage and a personal betrayal, the possibility of an abortion and a rekindling of an old affair. Not dull stuff. And though it's top secret, I'll tell you she's going to work with the police on a profile of the Trader's Bend Ripper."

"The what?"

"As in Son of Jack the Ripper," she said mildly. "Her former lover Griff's the number-one suspect."

"Doesn't it ever bother you that so much melodrama goes on in a small town with four or five connecting families?"

She stopped to look at him. "Do you know your Coleridge?"

"Passably."

"'The willing suspension of disbelief.'" Ariel crumbled her napkin, then tossed both it and her empty cup into a trash can. "It's all that's necessary to get along in this world. Believe it might happen, it could happen. Plausibility's all that's necessary. As a writer, you should know that."

"Perhaps I should. I've always leaned more toward reality."

"If it works for you." The lift of her shoulders seemed to

indicate that all was accepted. "But sometimes it's easier to believe in coincidence, or magic or simple luck. Straight reality without any detours is a very hard road."

"I've had a few detours," he murmured. It occurred to him that Ariel Kirkwood had already led him off the paved road he'd adhered to for years. Booth began to wonder just where her twisting direction would lead them. Lost in thought, he didn't notice that they were in front of his building until she stopped. His work was waiting, his privacy, his solitude. He wanted none of it.

"Come up with me."

The request was simple, the meaning clear. And her need was huge. Shaking her head, Ariel touched the hair that had fallen over his forehead. "No, it's best that I don't."

He took her hand before she could drop it back to her side. "Why? I want you, you want me."

If it were only so simple, she thought as the desire to love him grew and grew. But she knew, instinctively, that it wouldn't be simple, not for either of them once begun. For him there was too much distrust, for her too many vulnerabilities.

"Yes, I want you." Ariel saw the change in his eyes and knew it would be much more difficult to walk away than to go with him. "And if I came upstairs, we'd make love. Neither of us is ready for that, Booth, not with each other."

"If it's a game you're playing to make me want you more, it's hardly necessary."

She drew her hand from his and stood on her own. "I like to play games," she said quietly. "And I'm very good at most of them. Not this kind."

Pulling out a cigarette, he lit it with a snap of his lighter. "I've no patience for the wine and candlelight routine, Ariel."

He saw the humor light in her eyes and could have cursed her. "How lucky that I don't have a need for them." Putting her hands on his shoulders, she leaned forward and kissed him. "Think of me," she requested and turned quickly to walk away.

As he stared after her, Booth knew he'd think of little else.

Chapter Seven

It was going to be hard work, with long days, short nights and constant demands on both the body and the mind. Ariel was going to love every minute of it.

The producers of the soap were cooperating fully with Marshell; the network strategy was to everyone's advantage. The word, the big word, was always *ratings*. But it was Ariel who had to squeeze in the time for both projects, and Ariel who had to learn hundreds of pages of script as Amanda and as Rae.

Under different circumstances they might have simply written around her for a few weeks on *Our Lives, Our Loves,* but with Amanda and Griff's relationship heating up and the Ripper on the prowl, it wasn't possible. Amanda had a key role in too many vital scenes. So instead, Ariel had to shoot a backbreaking number of those scenes in a short period of time. This would give her three straight weeks to concentrate exclusively on the film. If that project ran behind schedule, she'd have to compensate by dividing her time and energies between Amanda and Rae.

The idea of eighteen-hour days and 5:00 a.m. calls couldn't dull her enthusiasm. The pace, merciless as it was, was almost natural to her in any case. And it helped keep her mind off the custody trial, which was set for the following month.

And there was Booth. Even the idea of working with him excited her. The daily contact would be stimulating. The professional competition and cooperation would keep her sharp. The preproduction stages had shown her that Booth would be as intimately involved with the film as any member of the cast and crew—and that he had unquestioned authority.

Throughout the sometimes hysterical meetings, he'd remained calm and had said little. But when he spoke, he was rarely questioned. It wasn't a matter of arrogance or overbearing, as Ariel saw it. Booth DeWitt simply didn't comment unless he knew he was right.

Perhaps, if it was meant to be, they'd move closer to each other as the film progressed. Emotion. It was what she wanted to give him, and what she needed from him. Time. She knew it was a major factor in whatever happened between them. Trust. This above all was needed—and this, above all, was missing.

There were times during the preproduction stages of the filming that Ariel felt Booth watching her too objectively, and distancing himself from her too successfully.

Ariel found herself at an impasse. The more skillfully she played Rae, the more firmly Booth stepped back from her. She understood it, and was helpless to change it.

The set was elegant, the lighting low and seductive. Across a small rococo table, Rae and Phil shared lobster bisque and champagne. Ariel's costume was clinging midnight silk. Diamonds and sapphires winked at her ears and throat. An armed guard in the studio attested to the fact that paste wasn't used on a Marshell production.

The intimate late-night supper was actually taking place at

8:00 a.m. in the presence of a full crew. Sipping lukewarm ginger ale from a tulip glass, Ariel gave a husky laugh and leaned closer to Jack.

She knew what was needed here—sex, raw and primitive under a thin sheen of sophistication. It would have to leap onto the screen with a gesture, a look, a smile, rather than through dialogue. She was playing a role within a role. Rae was her character, and Rae was never without a mask. Tonight, she would project a warmth, a soft femininity that was no more than a facade. It was Ariel's job to show both this, and the skill with which Rae played the part. If the actress Ariel portrayed wasn't clever, the impact on the character of Phil would waver. The connection between the two was vital. They fed each other, and by doing so, the entire story.

Rae wanted Phil, and the viewer had to know that she wanted him physically nearly as much as she wanted the connections he could bring her professionally. To win him, she had to be what he wanted. Ambition and skill were a deadly combination when added to beauty. Rae had all three and the capacity to use them. It was Ariel's job to show the duality of her nature, but to show it subtly.

The scene would end in the bedroom; that portion of the film would be shot at a different time. Now, the tension and the sexuality had to be heightened to a point where both Phil and the audience were completely seduced.

"Cut!"

Chuck ran a hand over the back of his neck and lapsed into silence. Both the actors and crew recognized the gesture from their director and remained silent and alert. The scene wasn't pleasing him, and he was working out why. Keyed up, Ariel didn't allow the tension to drain out of her. She needed the nerves to maintain the image of Rae. The sight of the ginger ale and the scent of the food in front of her made her stomach roll uneasily. They were already on the fourth take. Objectively, she watched her glass being refilled, her plate replaced. When this was over, she thought, she'd never even look at a glass of ginger ale again.

"Disgusting, isn't it?"

Glancing over, Ariel saw Jack Rohrer grimace at her. She locked Rae in a compartment of her brain before she grinned at him. "I've never wanted a cup of coffee and a bagel so much in my life."

"Please." He leaned back from the table. "Don't mention real food."

"More feline," Chuck said abruptly and focused on Ariel. "That's how I see Rae—a sleek black cat with manicured claws."

Ariel smiled at the image. Yes, that was Rae.

"When you say the line, 'One night won't be enough, you make me greedy,' you should practically purr it."

Ariel nodded while she flexed her hands. Yes, Rae would purr that line, while she calculated every angle. Ariel had a mental image of a cat—glossy, seductive and just this side of evil.

Just before the clapper was struck for the next take, Ariel caught Booth's eye. He was frowning at her while he stood off camera. Though his hands were casually in his pockets and his expression was still and calm, she sensed the wall of tension around him. Unable to break it down, she used it and the eye contact to pull herself back into character.

As the scene unfolded, she forgot the flat, warm taste of the ginger ale, forgot the intrusion of cameras and crew. Her attention was completely focused on the man across from her, who was no longer a fellow actor but an intended victim. She smiled at something he said, a smile Booth recognized too well. Seductive as black lace, cold as ice. There wasn't a man alive who'd be immune to it.

When she reached the line Chuck had focused on, Ariel paused a beat, dipping her fingertip into Jack's glass, then slowly touched the dampened skin to her mouth, then his. The seductive ad lib had the temperature on the set soaring. Even while he mentally approved the gesture and Ariel's intuition, Booth felt his stomach muscles tighten.

She knew her character, he mused, almost as well as he did himself. So well, it was always an effort to separate them in his mind. This attraction that plagued him—at whom was it directed? That surge of jealousy he felt unexpectedly when the woman on set melted into another man's arms—for whom did he really feel it? He'd entwined reality and fiction so tightly in this script, then had chosen an actress skilled enough to blur those lines. Now, he found himself trapped between fiction and fact. Was the woman he wanted the shadow or the light?

"Cut! Cut and print! Fantastic." Grinning from ear to ear, Chuck walked over and kissed both Ariel and Jack. "We're lucky the camera didn't overload on that scene."

Jack flashed a white-toothed smile. "You're lucky I didn't. You're damn good." Jack laid a hand on Ariel's shoulder. "So damn good I'm going to have a cup of coffee and call my wife."

"Ten minutes," Chuck announced. "Set up for reaction shots. Booth, what'd you think?"

"Excellent." With his eyes on Ariel, Booth walked toward them. There was nothing of the cat about her now. If anything, she looked a bit weary. He found that while the knot in his stomach had loosened, he had to fight the urge to stroke her cheek. Booth was more accustomed to the first sensation. "You look like you could use some coffee yourself."

"Yeah." Again, Ariel forced herself to lock Rae's personality away. She wanted nothing more than to relax completely, but knew she could only allow herself a few degrees. "You buying?"

Nodding, he led her off set where a catering table was already set up with coffee, doughnuts and Danishes. Ariel's stomach revolted at the thought of food, but she took the steaming Styrofoam cup in both hands.

"This schedule's difficult," Booth commented.

"Mmm." She shrugged that off and let the coffee wash away the aftertaste of ginger ale. "No, the schedule's no tighter than the soap's—lighter in some ways. The scene was difficult."

He lifted a brow. "Why?"

The scent of the coffee was real and solid. Ariel could almost forget the spongy food she'd had to nibble on for the past two hours. "Because Phil's smart and cautious—not an easy man to seduce or to fool. Rae has to do both, and she's in a hurry." She glanced over the rim of her cup. "But then, you know that."

"Yes." He took her wrist before she could drink again. "You look tired."

"Only between takes." She smiled, touched by the reluctant concern. "Don't worry about me, Booth. Frantic's my natural pace."

"There's something else."

She thought of Scott. It's not supposed to show, she reminded herself. The minute you walk into the studio, it's not supposed to show. "You're perceptive," she murmured. "A writer's first tool."

"You're stalling."

Ariel shook her head. If she thought about it now, too

deeply, her control would begin to slip. "It's something I have to deal with. It won't interfere with my work."

He took her chin firmly into his hand. "Does anything?"

For the first time, Ariel felt a threat of pure anger run through her. "Don't confuse me with a role, Booth—or another woman." She pushed his hand away, then turning her back on him, walked back onto the set.

The temper pleased him, perhaps because it was easier to trust negative emotions. Leaning back against the wall, Booth made a decision. He was going to have her—tonight. It would ease a portion of the tension in him and alleviate the wondering. Then both of them, in their own way, would have to deal with the consequences.

Ariel found the anger was an advantage. Rae, she mused, was a woman who had anger simmering just below the surface at all times. It added to the discontent, and the ambition. Instead of trying to rid herself of it—something she wasn't certain she could do in any case—Ariel used it to add more depth to an already complicated character. As long as she clung to Rae's mercurial, demanding personality, she didn't feel her own weariness or frustrations.

True, her senses were keen enough so that she knew exactly where Booth was and where his attention was focused even when she was in the middle of a scene. That was something to be dealt with later. The more he pushed at her—mentally, emotionally— the more she was determined to give a stellar performance.

By six and wrap time, Ariel discovered that Rae had drained her. Her body ached from the hours of standing under the lights. Her mind reeled from the repetition of lines, the drawing and releasing of emotions. It was only the first week of filming, and already she felt the strain of the marathon.

Nobody said it'd be easy, Ariel reminded herself as she slipped into her dressing room to change into her street clothes. And it wouldn't be nearly so important if it were. The trouble was, she was beginning to equate her success in the part with her success in her relationship with Booth. If she could pull one off, she could do the same with the other.

Shaking her head, Ariel stripped out of her costume, shedding Rae as eagerly as she did the silk. An idea like that, she reminded herself, had a very large trapdoor. Rae was a part to be acted, no matter how entangled it was with reality. Booth was real life—her life. No matter how willing she was to take risks or accept a challenge, that was something she couldn't afford to forget.

Gratefully, Ariel creamed off her stage makeup and let her skin breathe. She sat, propping her feet on her dressing table so that the short kimono she wore skimmed her thighs. Taking her time, letting herself come down, she undid the sleek knot the hairdresser had arranged and let her hair fall free. With a contented sigh, Ariel tipped her head back, shut her eyes and fell into a half doze.

That was how Booth found her.

The room was cluttered in her usual fashion so that she seemed to be a single island of calm. The air was assaulted with scents—powder, face cream, the same potpourri just hinting of lilac that she kept at home. The lights around her mirror were glaring. Her breathing was soft and even.

As he shut the door behind him, Booth let his gaze run up the long slender length of her legs, exposed from toe to thigh. The kimono was loosely, almost carelessly knotted, so that it gaped intriguingly down the center of her body nearly to the waist. Her hair fell behind the chair, mussed from her own hands so that the curve of neck and shoulder made an elegant contrast.

Her face seemed a bit pale without the color needed for the camera...fragile. Without it, the faintest of shadows could be seen under her eyes.

Booth wanted almost painfully to possess her, just as she was at that moment. With hardly a thought as to what he was doing, he turned the lock on the door. He sat on the arm of a chair, lit a cigarette and waited.

Ariel woke slowly. She tended to sleep quickly and wake gradually. Even before she'd drifted from that twilight world to consciousness, she knew she was refreshed. The nap had been no more than ten minutes. Any longer and she'd have been groggy, any shorter, tense. With a sigh, she started to stretch. Then she sensed she wasn't alone. Curious, she turned her head and looked at Booth.

"Hello."

He saw no remnants of the anger in her eyes, nor was there any coolness, that sign of resentment, in her voice. Even the weariness he'd sensed in her briefly had vanished. "You didn't sleep long." His cigarette had burned down nearly to the filter without his noticing. He crushed it out. "Though I don't know anyone who could've slept at all in that position."

"For a ten-minute session, I can sleep anywhere." She pointed her toes, tensing all her muscles, then released them. "I had to recharge."

"A decent meal would help."

Ariel put a hand to her stomach. "It wouldn't hurt."

"You barely touched anything at lunch."

It didn't surprise her that he'd noticed, only that he'd commented on it. "Normally I'd have gorged myself. Eating lobster bisque at dawn threw my whole system out of whack. A bagel's more my style. Or a bowl of Krispie Krinkies."

"Of what?"

"Eight essential vitamins," she said with a half grin. Reluctantly, she slid her feet to the floor. The gap in her robe shifted, and absently she tugged at the lapels. "We are wrapped for the day, aren't we? There isn't a problem?"

"We wrapped," he agreed. "And there's a problem."

The brush she'd lifted paused halfway to her hair. "What kind?"

"Personal." He rose and took the brush from her hand. "Every day this week I've watched you, listened to you, smelled you. And every day this week, I've wanted you." He took the brush through her hair in one long, smooth stroke while in the lighted mirror, his eyes met hers. When she didn't move, he drew the brush down again, cupping the curve of her shoulder with his free hand. "You asked me to think of you. I have."

Too close to the surface, Ariel warned herself. Her emotions were always too close to the surface. There was nothing she could do about it. "Every day this week," she began in a voice that was already husky, "you've watched me and listened to me be someone else. You might be wanting someone else."

His eyes remained on hers as he lowered his mouth to her ear. "I'm not watching anyone else now."

Her heart lurched. Ariel would have sworn she felt the jerk of movement inside her breast. "Tomorrow—"

"The hell with tomorrow." Booth let the brush drop as he drew her to her feet. "And yesterday." His gaze was intense, a hot, hot green that had her throat going dry. She'd wondered what it would be like if he allowed any emotion freedom. This was his passion, and it was going to sweep her away.

If she hadn't loved him… But, of course, she did. All caution whipped away as her mouth met his. There was a time for thinking, and a time for feeling. There was a time for withholding, and a time for giving freely. There was a time for reason, and a time for romance.

All that Ariel had, all that she felt, thought, wished, went into the touch of mouth to mouth. And as her body followed her heart, she wrapped herself around him and offered unconditionally. She felt the floor tilt and the air freeze before she became lost in her own longings. Her lips parted, inviting; her tongue touched, arousing. Her breath fluttered, answering.

She was firm, as he was, yet softer. Feeling the hard length of man against her, she became completely, utterly feminine. The pleasure was liquid, passing through her as warmed wine. As his grip tightened, she melted further until she was as pliant as any man's fantasy. But she was very real.

He'd never known another woman like her, so utterly free with emotions that flowed and crested until he was drowning in them. Passion had been expected and was there, but… More, infinitely more, was a range of feeling so intense, so sweet, it was irresistible.

As he'd watched her on the set, he'd wanted her. When he'd come into the room to see her sleeping, desire had assaulted him. Now, with her yielding, vibrating with emotions he could hardly name, Booth needed her as he'd never needed anyone. And had never wanted to.

Too late. The thought ran through his mind that it was too late for her—too late for him. Then his hands were buried in her hair, his thoughts a kaleidoscope of sensations.

She smelled faintly of lemon from the cream she'd used on her face, while her hair carried the familiar fragrance of light sexuality. The thin material of her kimono swished as his hands parted it to find her. And she was softer than a dream, but so small he had a moment's fear that he would hurt her. Then her body arched, pressing against his hand so that it was her strength that aroused him. With a sound that was more of surrender than triumph, he buried his face against her throat.

Even while her mind was floating, Ariel knew she had to feel the texture of his flesh against hers. Slowly, her hands ran up his sides, drawing up his sweater. She followed the movement, over his shoulders, until there was nothing barring her exploration—and nothing to stop her sensitized skin from meeting his.

When he drew her down she went willingly. As her back rested against the littered sofa, she cupped her hands behind his head and brought his mouth back to hers. The taste of his passion rippled through her and lit the next spark.

Not so passive now, not so pliant, she moved under him, sending off twinges of excitement to pulse through both of them. The sudden aggression of her lips was welcome. The kiss went on and on, deeper, moister, while two pairs of hands began to test and appreciate.

He could feel the frantic beat of her heart under his palm. When he pressed his lips against her breast, he felt her shudder. The outrageous desire to absorb her ran through him as he began to draw in her variety of tastes, now with his lips, now with the tip of his tongue. Sometimes, some places, it was hot, others sweet, but always it was Ariel.

The lights glared into the room, reflecting from the mirror as he began a thorough, intense journey over her. The curve of her shoulder held fascinations he'd never known before. The skin at the inside of her wrist was so delicate he almost thought he could hear the blood run through the veins. Everywhere he touched, he felt her pulse. She was so giving. That alone was enough to make his head swim.

And as he touched, tasted, took, so did she. If he became more demanding, she responded in kind, keeping pace with him. Or perhaps it was he who kept pace with her. She stroked with those long, elegant fingers so that he knew what it was to be on the verge of madness, and within sight of heaven.

She wanted nothing more than what she could find in him. Touches of tenderness that moved her. Flares of fires that tormented her. His hair brushed over her skin and that alone excited her. Flesh grew damp with passion and the struggle to control—the struggle to prolong. Ariel learned that pleasure alone was a shallow thing; but pleasure, when combined with love, was all.

Together, they understood that there could be no more waiting. The final barriers of clothing were tugged impatiently away. She opened for him. Madness and heaven became one.

Ariel felt as though she could run for miles. Her body was alive with so many sensations. Her mind leaped with them. She lay beneath Booth, tingling with an awareness that radiated down to her toes and fingertips. With her eyes closed, her body still aligned with his, she counted his heartbeats as they thudded against her. In that private, liquid world they'd gone to, Booth hadn't been calm, he hadn't been detached. Letting her lashes flutter up, she smiled. His hand was laced with hers. She wondered if he were aware of it. He'd wanted her. Just her.

Contentment. Was that what he was feeling? Booth lay sated, drained, aware only of Ariel's warm, slim form beneath him. As far as he could remember, he'd never experienced anything remotely like this. Total relaxation…a complete lack of tension. He didn't even have the energy to dissect the feeling, and instead enjoyed it. With a sound of pure pleasure, he turned his face in to her throat. He felt as well as heard her gurgle of laughter.

"Funny?" he murmured.

Ariel ran her hands up the length of his back, then down again to his waist. "I feel good. So good." Her fingertips skimmed over his hips. "So do you."

Shifting slightly, Booth raised himself on one elbow so that he could look at her. Her eyes were laughing. With a fingertip he traced the spot just below her jaw where he'd discovered delectable, sensitive skin. "I still don't know what I'm doing with you."

She brushed the hair from his forehead and watched it fall back again. "Do you always have to have an intellectual reason?"

He frowned, but his fingers spread over her face as if he were blind and memorizing it. "I always have."

She wanted to sigh but smiled instead. Taking his face in her hands, Ariel brought him down for a hard kiss. "I defy the intellect."

That made him laugh, and because he was off balance, she was able to roll him over. With her body slanted across his, she stretched and nuzzled into his shoulder. Booth felt the crinkle of paper and the rumple of cloth beneath him. "What am I lying on?"

"Mmm. This and that."

Arching, he pulled a crumpled pamphlet from under his left hip. "Anyone ever mention that you're sloppy?"

"From time to time."

Absently, Booth glanced at the pamphlet about the plight of baby seals before he dropped it to the floor. He tugged at another paper stuck to his right shoulder. A halfway house for battered wives. Curiosity piqued, he twisted a bit and found another. ASPCA literature.

"Ariel, what is all this?"

She gave his shoulder a last nibble before she rested her cheek on it. He held several wrinkled leaflets. "I suppose you might call it my hobby."

"Hobby?" He put his free hand under her chin to lift it. "Which one?"

"All of them."

"All?" Booth looked at the leaflets in his hand again and wondered how many others were squashed beneath him. "You mean you're actively involved in all these organizations?"

"Yeah. More or less."

"Ariel, no one person would have the time."

"Oh, no." She shifted, folding her arms across his chest for support. "That's a cop-out. You make time." She tilted her head toward the papers he held. "Those baby seals, do you know what's done to them, how it's done?"

"Yes, but—"

"And those abused women. Most of them come into that shelter without any self-esteem, without any emotional or financial support. Then there's—"

"Wait a minute." He let the papers slide to the floor so he could take her shoulders. How slim they were, he realized abruptly. And how easily she could make him forget just how delicately she was formed. "I understand all that, but how can you be involved in all these causes, run your life and pursue your career?"

She smiled. "There're twenty-four hours in every day. I don't like to waste any of them."

Seeing that she was perfectly serious, Booth shook his head. "You're a remarkable woman."

"No." Ariel bent her head and kissed his chin. It dipped slightly in the center—not quite a cleft. "I just have a lot of energy. I need to put it somewhere."

"You could put all of it into furthering your career," he pointed out. "You'd be top box office within six months. There'd be no question of your success."

"Maybe. But I wouldn't be happy with it."

"Why?"

It was back; she felt it. The doubts, the distrust. With a sigh, Ariel sat up. In silence, she picked up her kimono and pulled it on. How quickly warmth could turn to chill. "Because I need more."

Dissatisfied, Booth took her arm. "More what?"

"More everything!" she said with a sudden passion that stunned him. "I need to know I've done my best, and not just in one area of my life. Do you really think I'm so limited?"

The fire in her eyes intrigued him. "I believe what I said indicated your lack of limitations."

"Professionally," she snapped. "I'm a person first. I need to know I touched someone, helped somehow." She dragged both hands through her hair in frustration. "I need to know I cared. Success isn't just a little gold statue for my trophy case, Booth." Whirling, she yanked open the door of her closet and pulled out her street clothes.

As Booth sat up, the papers beneath him rustled. "You're angry."

"Yes, yes, yes!" With her back to him, Ariel wriggled into her briefs. In the mirror, Booth could see the reflected temper on her face.

"Why?"

"Your favorite question." Ariel flung the kimono to the

floor, then dragged a short-sleeved sweatshirt over her head. "Well, I'll give you the answer, and you're not going to like it. You still equate me with her." She flung the words at him; as they hit, he too began to dress. "Still," she continued, "even after what just happened between us, you still measure me by her."

"Maybe." He rose and drew his sweater over his head. "Maybe I do."

Ariel stared at him a moment, then stepped into her jeans. "It hurts."

Booth stood very still as the two words sliced into him. He hadn't expected them—their simplicity, their honesty. He hadn't expected his own reaction to them. "I'm sorry," he murmured.

Stepping closer, he touched her arm and waited for her to look up at him. The hurt was in her eyes, and he knew it was the second time he'd put it there. "I've never been a particularly fair man, Ariel."

"No," she agreed. "But it's hard for me to believe that someone so intelligent could be so narrow-minded."

He waited for his own anger to rise, and when it didn't, shook his head. "Maybe it's simplest to say you weren't in my plans."

"I think that's clear." Turning away, she began to brush her hair methodically. Hurt pulsed from her still, laced with anger. It never occurred to her to rely on pride and conceal them both. "I told you before that I tend to rush into things. I also understand that not everyone keeps the same pace. But I'd think by this time you'd see that I'm not the character you created—or the woman who inspired her."

"Ariel." She stiffened when he took her shoulders. He could see her fingers flex on the brush handle. "Ariel," he said again and lowered his brow to the top of her head. Why did he want so much what he'd cut himself off from? "I'll hurt you again," he said quietly. "I'm bound to hurt you if I continue to see you."

Her body relaxed on a sigh. Why was she fighting the inevitable? "Yes, I know."

"And knowing that, knowing what you could do to my own life, I don't want to stop seeing you."

She reached up to cover the hand on her shoulder with her own. "But you don't know why."

"No, I don't know why."

Ariel turned in his arms and held him. For a moment they stood close, her head on his shoulder, his hands at her waist. "Buy me dinner," she requested, then tipped back her head and smiled at him. "I'm starving. I want to be with you. Those are two definite facts. We'll just take the rest as it comes."

He'd been right to call her remarkable, Booth thought. He pressed his lips to her brow. "All right. What would you like to eat?"

"Pizza with mushrooms," she answered immediately. "And a cheap bottle of Chianti."

"Pizza."

"A huge one—with mushrooms."

With a half laugh he tightened his hold. He was no longer sure he could let go. "It sounds like a good start."

Chapter Eight

At 7:00 a.m., Ariel sat in a makeup chair, with a huge white drop cloth covering her costume, going over her lines while a short, fussy-handed man with thinning hair slanted blusher over her cheekbones. She could hear, but paid no attention to, the buzz of activity around her. Someone shouted for gel for the lights. A coil of cable was dropped to the floor with a thud. Ariel continued to read.

The upcoming scene was a difficult one, with something perilously close to a soliloquy in the middle. If she didn't get the rhythm just right, the pitch perfect, the entire mood would be spoiled.

And her own mood wasn't helping her concentration.

She'd had another lovely Sunday with Scott, which had ended with a tense and tearful departure. Though she'd long ago resigned herself to the fact that she was a creature of emotional highs and lows, Ariel couldn't rid herself of the despondency or the nagging sense of guilt.

Scott had clung to her, with great, silent tears running down his cheeks, when she'd returned him to the Andersons' home in Larchmont. It was the first time in all the months since his parents' death that he'd created a scene at the end of their weekly visit. The Andersons had met his tears with grim, tight-lipped impatience while both had cast accusing glares at Ariel.

After she'd soothed him, Ariel had wondered all during the lengthy train ride home if she'd unconsciously brought on the scene. By wanting him so badly, was she encouraging him to want her? Did she spoil him? Was she overcompensating because of her love for his father and her pain in the loss?

She'd spent a sleepless night over it, and the questions had built and pressed on her. But there'd been no firm answers in the morning. Within a few weeks, she'd have to live with the decision of a judge who would see Scott as a minor rather than as a little boy who liked to play pretend games. Could a judge, however experienced, however fair, see the heart of a child? It was one more question that kept her awake at night.

Now, Ariel knew she had to put her personal business aside. Her part in the film was more than a job; it was a responsibility. Both the cast and the crew depended on her to do her best. Her name on the contract guaranteed she would give all her skill. And, she reminded herself as she rubbed an aching temple, worrying wasn't going to help Scott.

"My dear, if you continue to fidget, you'll spoil what I've already done."

Bringing herself back, Ariel smiled at the makeup man. "Sorry, Harry. Am I beautiful?"

"Almost exquisite." He pursed his lips as he touched up her brows. The natural arch, he thought with professional admiration, needed very little assistance from him. "For this scene, you should look like Dresden. Just a little more here…." Ariel sat obediently while he smoothed more color into her lips. "And I'll have to insist that there be no more frowning. You'll spoil my work."

Surprised, Ariel met his eyes. She'd been sure she'd had her expression, if not her thoughts, under control. Foolish, she decided, then reminded herself that problems were to be left on the other side of the studio door. That was the first rule of showmanship.

"No more frowns," she promised. "I can't be responsible for spoiling a masterpiece."

"Well, nothing changes. Still cramming before zero hour."

"Stella!" Ariel glanced up and broke into the first true smile of the day. "What're you doing here?"

"Taking a busman's holiday." Stella dropped into the chair beside Ariel, pulling up her legs, then folding them under her. "I used your name—and some charm," she added with a sweep of her lashes, "to get in. You don't mind if I watch the morning's shooting, do you?"

"Of course not. How're things at Trader's Bend?"

"Heating up, love, heating up." With a wicked smile, Stella tossed her thick mane of hair behind her shoulder. "Now that Cameron's trying to blackmail Vikki over her gambling debts, and the Ripper's claimed his third victim, *and* Amanda and Griff are starting to simmer, they can't keep up with the mail or the phone calls. Rumor is *Tube* wants to do a two-part spread on the cast. That's big time."

Ariel's brow quirked. "Cover story?"

"That's what I hear through the grapevine. Hey, I got stopped in the market the other day. A woman named Ethel Bitterman gave me a lecture on moral standing and family loyalty over the cucumbers."

Laughing, Ariel drew off her protective drape to reveal a

frothy, raspberry-colored sundress. This was what she'd needed, she realized. That sense of camaraderie and family. "I've missed you, Stella."

"Me, too. But tell me…." Stella's gaze skimmed up the dress that, while demure and feminine, reeked of sex. "How does it feel to be playing the bad girl for a change?"

Ariel's eyes lit up. "It's wonderful, but it's tough. It's the toughest part I've ever played."

Stella smiled and buffed her nails on her sleeve. "You always claimed I had all the fun."

"I might've been right," Ariel countered. "And I may've over-simplified. But I don't remember ever working harder than this."

Stella rested her chin on her hand. "Why?"

"I guess because Rae's always playing a part. It's like trying to get inside a half dozen personalities and make them one person."

"And you're eating it up," Stella observed.

"I guess I am." With a quick laugh she settled back. "Yeah, I am. One day I'll feel absolutely drained, and the next so wired…" She shrugged and set her script aside. If she didn't know her lines by now, she never would. "In any case, I know if I have a choice, when this is over, I'd like to do a comedy. A Judy Holliday type. Something full of fun and wackiness."

"What about Jack Rohrer?" Stella dug in her purse and found a dietary lemon drop. "What's he like to work with?"

"I like him." Ariel smiled ruefully. "But he doesn't make it a picnic. He's a perfectionist—like everyone else on this film."

"And the illustrious Booth DeWitt?"

"Watches everything," Ariel murmured.

"Including you." Moving only her eyes, Stella changed the focus of her attention. "At least he has been for the past ten minutes."

Ariel didn't have to turn her head. She already knew. In her mind's eye she could see him, standing a bit apart from the grips and gaffers as they checked the lighting and the set. He'd remove himself from the activity so as not to interfere with the flow, but his presence would be felt by everyone. And that presence alone would make everyone just tense enough to be sharp.

She knew he'd be watching her, half-wary, half-accepting. More than anything else, she wanted to merge the two into trust. And trust into love.

Booth watched her laugh at something Stella said. He watched the animated hand movements, the slight tilt of her head that meant she was avidly interested. Then again, Ariel rarely did anything that wasn't done avidly. Whatever had been clouding her mood when she'd come in earlier had been smoothed over. As he remembered the trouble in her eyes, Booth wondered what problem plagued her and why, when she seemed so willing to share everything, she was unwilling to share that.

Lighting a cigarette, Booth told himself he should be grateful she kept it to herself. Why should he want to be involved? He knew very well that one of the quickest ways to become vulnerable to someone else was to become concerned with their problems.

Beside him a stagehand thoroughly sprayed an elegant arrangement of fresh flowers. The lighting director called for a final check on the candlepower. A mike boom was lowered into place. Booth wondered what Ariel had done over the weekend.

He'd wanted to spend it with her, but she'd put him off and he hadn't insisted. He wouldn't box her in, because by doing so he set limits on himself. That was a trap he wouldn't fall into. But he remembered the utter peace he'd felt lying with her in her dressing room after passion was spent.

He couldn't say she was a calming influence—too much energy crackled from her. Yet she had a talent for soothing the tension from his mind.

He wanted to talk to her again. He wanted to touch her again. He wanted to make love with her again. And he wanted to escape from his own needs.

"Places!" The assistant director called out as he paced the set, rechecking the blocking.

Booth leaned back against the wall, his thumbs hooked absently in his pockets. It never occurred to him, as it often had to Ariel, how seldom he sat.

They would shoot a section of an extensive scene that morning. The other parts would be filmed later on the lawns of a Long Island estate. The elegant lawn party they'd shoot on location was to be Rae's first full-scale attempt at entertaining since marrying Phil. And afterward, indoors and in private, would come their first full-scale argument.

She looked like something made of spun-sugar icing. Her words were as vicious as snake venom. And all the while, with the fury and the poison oozing from her, she hadn't a hair out of place. The fragile color in her cheeks never fluctuated. It was Ariel's job to keep the character cold-blooded, and the words smoldering.

She knew it was all in the eyes. Rae's gestures were a facade. Her smile was a lie. Both the ice and the fire had to come from the eyes. The scene had to be underplayed, understated from her end. It was a constant strain to keep her own emotions from bubbling out. If *she* were to fight with words, she'd shout them, hurl them—and fling off the ones tossed back at her. Rae drawled them, almost lazily. And Ariel ached.

This was Booth's life, she thought. Or a mirror image of what had been his life. This was his pain, his mistakes, his misery. She was caught up in it. If she hurt, how did he feel watching?

Rae gave Phil a bored look as he grabbed both her arms.

"I won't have it," he raged at her, eyes blazing while hers remained cool as a lake.

"Won't have it?" Rae repeated, transmitting utter disdain with the tone, with the movement of an eyebrow. "What is it you won't have?"

"I will not have you raying the pole." Jack closed his eyes and made a gargling sound.

"Raying the pole?" Ariel repeated. "Having a little trouble with your tongue?"

She felt the tension snap as the scene was cut, but wasn't certain if she was grateful or not. She wanted this one over.

"Playing the role," Jack enunciated carefully. "I will not have you *playing* the *role*. I got it." He held up both hands, mocking himself and his flubbed line.

"Fine, as long as you understand that I can and will ray the pole whenever I choose."

He grinned at Ariel. "Smart mouth."

She patted his cheek. "Aw, yours'll wise up, Jack. Give yourself a chance."

"Places. Take it from the entrance."

For the third time that morning, Ariel swung through the French doors with her skirts billowing behind her.

They moved through the scene again, immersing themselves in the characters even with the starts and stops and changes of camera angles.

To end the scene, Rae was to laugh, take the glass of Scotch from Phil's hand, sip, then toss the contents into his face.

Caught up in character, Ariel took the glass, tasted the warm, weak tea, then with an icy smile, poured the contents over the elegant floral arrangement. Without missing a beat in the change of staging, Jack ripped the glass out of her hand and hurled it across the room.

"Cut!"

Snapping back, Ariel stared at her director. "Oh, God, Chuck, I don't know where that came from. I'm sorry." With a hand pressed to her brow, she looked down at the now drenched mixture of fragile hothouse blooms.

"No, no. Damn!" Laughing, he gave her a bear hug. "That was perfect. Better than perfect. I wish I'd thought of it myself." He laughed again and squeezed Ariel until she thought her bones might crack. "She'd have done that. She *would* have done just that." With his arm slung around Ariel's shoulder, Chuck turned to Booth. "Booth?"

"Yes." Without moving, Booth indicated a nod. "Leave it as it stands." He pinned Ariel with cool, green eyes. He should have written it that way, he realized. Throwing a drink in Phil's face was too obvious for Rae. Even too human. "You seem to know her better than I do now."

She let out an uneven breath, giving Chuck's hand a squeeze before she walked toward Booth. "Is that a compliment?"

"An observation. They're setting up for the close-ups," he murmured, then brought his attention back to her. "I won't give you carte blanche, Ariel, but I'm willing to feed you quite a bit of rope in your characterization. And obviously so is Chuck. You understand Rae."

She could have been amused or annoyed. As always when she had a choice, Ariel chose amusement. "Booth, if I were playing a mushroom, I'd understand that mushroom. It's my job."

He smiled because she made it easy. "I believe you would."

"Didn't you catch the commercial where I played the ripe, juicy plum?"

"Must've been out of town."

"It was a classic. Over and above my shower scene for Fresh Wave shampoo—though, of course, sensuality was the basis in both spots."

"I want to come home with you tonight," he said quietly. "I want to stay with you tonight."

"Oh." When would she get used to the simple ways he had of saying monumental things?

"And when we're alone," Booth murmured as he watched the pulse in her throat begin to flutter, "I want to take off your clothes, little by little, so that I can touch every inch of you. Then I want to watch your face while we make love."

"Ariel, let's get these close-ups!"

"What?" A bit dazed, she mumbled the word while she continued to stare at Booth. Already she could feel his hands on her, taste his breath as it mixed with her own.

"They can have your face—for now," Booth told her, more aroused by her reaction to his words than he would have thought possible. "Tonight, it's mine."

"Ariel!"

Flung back to the present, she turned to go back to the set. With a look that was amused and puzzled, she glanced back over her shoulder. "You're not predictable, Booth."

"Is that a compliment?" he countered.

She grinned. "My very best one."

Hour after hour, line after line, scene after scene, the morning progressed. Though the film was naturally shot out of sequence, Ariel could feel it beginning to jell. Because it was

television, the pace was fast. Her pace. Because it was DeWitt
and Marshall, the expectations were high. As were hers.

You sweltered under the lights; changed moods, costumes;
were powdered, dusted and glossed. Again and again. You sat
and waited during scene changes or equipment malfunctions.
And somewhere between the tension and the tedium was
your vocation.

Ariel understood all that, and she wanted all of that. She
never lost the basic pleasure in performing, even after ten
retakes of a scene where Rae rode an exercise bike while discussing a new script with her agent.

Muscles aching, she eased herself off the bike and dabbed
at the sweat, which didn't have to be simulated, on her face.

"Poor baby." Stella grinned as a stagehand offered Ariel a
towel. "Just remember, Ariel, we never work you this hard on
Our Lives."

"Rae *would* have to be a fitness fanatic," she muttered, stretching her shoulders. "Body conscious. I'm conscious now." With
a little moan, Ariel bent to ease a cramp in her leg. "Conscious
of every muscle in my body that hasn't been used in five years."

"It's a wrap." Chuck gave her a companionable slap on the
flank as he passed. "Go soak in a hot tub."

Ariel barely suppressed a less kind suggestion. She slung the
towel over her shoulder, gripped both damp ends and stuck out
her tongue.

"You never did have any respect for directors," Stella commented. "Come on, kid, I'll keep you company while you
change. Then I've got a hot date."

"Oh, really?"

"Yeah. My new dentist. I went in for a checkup and ended
up having a discussion on dental hygiene over linguine."

"Good God." Not bothering to hide a grin, Ariel pushed open her dressing-room door. "He works fast."

"Uh-uh, I do." With a laugh that held both pleasure and nerves, Stella walked into the room. "Oh, Ariel, he's so sweet—so serious about his work. And..." Stella broke off and dropped onto Ariel's cluttered sofa. "I remember something you said a few weeks ago about love—it being a definite emotion or something." She lifted her hands as if to wave away the exact phrase and grip the essence. "Anyway, I haven't come down to earth since I sat in that tilt-back chair and looked up into those baby-blue eyes of his."

"That's nice." For the moment Ariel forgot her sore muscles and the line of sweat dripping down her back. "That's really nice, Stella."

Stella searched for another lemon drop and found her supply depleted. Knowing Ariel, she walked to the dressing table, pulled open a drawer and succumbed to the stash of candy-coated chocolate. "I heard somewhere that people in love can spot other people in love." She slanted her friend a look as Ariel stripped out of her leotard. "To test a theory, my guess is that you've fallen for Booth DeWitt."

"Right the first time." Ariel pulled on the baggy sweatpants and shirt she'd worn to the studio.

With a frown, Stella crunched candy between her teeth. "You always liked the tough roles."

"I seem to lean toward them."

"How's he feel about you?"

"I don't know." Gratefully, Ariel creamed off the last of her makeup. With a flourish, she dumped one more part of Rae into the waste can. "I don't think he does, either."

"Ariel..." Reluctance to give advice warred with affection and loyalty. "Do you know what you're doing?"

"No," she answered immediately, both brows lifting. "Why would I want to?"

Stella laughed as she headed for the door. "Stupid question. By the way—" she stopped with her hand on the knob "—I just thought I'd mention that you were brilliant today. I've worked with you week after week for five years, and today you blew me away. When this thing hits the screen, you're going to take off so fast even you won't be able to keep up."

Astonished, pleased and, perhaps for the first time, a bit frightened, Ariel sat on the edge of her dressing table. "Thanks—I think."

"Don't mention it." Slipping into the character of Vikki, Stella blew Ariel a cool kiss. "See you in a couple of weeks, big sister."

For several moments after the door shut, Ariel sat in silence. Did she, when push came to shove, want to take off and take off fast? She remembered that P. B. Marshell had said something similiar to her after her second reading for the part, but Ariel had seen that more as an overall view of the project itself. She knew Stella, and understood that the praise from her had been directed personally and individually. For the first time the ripple effect of the role of Rae struck her fully. However much a cliché it sounded, it could make her a star.

Wearing her baggy sweats, one hip leaning on her jumbled dressing table, Ariel explored the idea.

Money—she shrugged that away. Her upbringing had taught her to view money for what it was, a means to an end. In any case, her financial status for the past three years had been more than adequate for both her needs and her taste.

Fame. She grinned at that. No, she couldn't claim she was immune to fame. It still brought her a thrill to sign her name in an autograph book or talk to a fan. That was something she hoped would never change. But fame had degrees, and with each rise in height, the payment for it became greater. The more fans, the less privacy. That was something she'd have to think about carefully.

Artistic freedom. It was that, Ariel admitted on a deep breath, that was the clincher. To be able to *choose* a part rather than be chosen. Glory and a big bank account were nothing in comparison. If Rae could bring her that…

With a shake of her head, she rose. Daydreaming about the future couldn't change anything. For now, her career, and her life, would simply have to go a day at a time. Still, she was a woman who liked to expect everything. Ariel would much rather be disappointed than pessimistic. She was grinning when she opened the door and nearly collided with Booth.

"You look happy," he commented as he took her arms to balance her.

"I am happy." Ariel kissed him hard and firm on the mouth. "It's been a good day."

The kiss, casual as it was, shot straight through him. "You should be exhausted."

"No, you should be exhausted after running the New York Marathon. How do you feel about a giant hamburger and a glutton's portion of fries?"

He'd had a quiet restaurant in mind—something French and dimly lit. After a glance at her sweat suit and glowing face, Booth shook his head. "Sounds perfect. It's your turn to buy."

Ariel tucked her arm through his. "You got it. Do you like banana milk shakes?"

His expression stated his opinion clearly. "I don't believe I've ever had one."

"You're going to love it," Ariel promised.

It wasn't as bad as he'd imagined—and the hamburger had been hefty and satisfying. Dusk was settling over the city when they returned to Ariel's apartment. The moment she opened the door, the kittens dashed for her feet.

"Good grief, you'd think they hadn't been fed in a week." Bending, she scooped up both of them and nuzzled. "Did you miss me, you little pigs, or just your evening meal?"

Before Booth realized what she was up to, Ariel had thrust both kittens into his arms. "Hang on to them for me, will you?" she said easily. "I have to feed Butch, too." She sauntered toward the kitchen, with the three-legged Butch waddling behind. Booth was left with two mewing kittens and no choice but to follow. One—Keats or Shelley—climbed onto his shoulder as he went after Ariel.

"I'm surprised you don't have a litter of puppies, as well." He lifted a brow as the kitten sniffed at his ear.

Ariel laughed as the kitten batted playfully at Booth's hair. "I would if the landlord wasn't so strict. But I'm working on him. Meanwhile—" she set out three generous bowls of food "—it's chow time."

Chuckling, she took the kitten from Booth's shoulder while the other leaped to the floor. Within seconds all three cats were thoroughly involved. "See?" She brushed a few traces of cat hair from his shirt. "They're no trouble at all, hardly any expense and wonderful companions, especially for someone who works most often at home."

Booth gave her a steady look, cupped her face in his hands, then grinned despite himself. "No."

"No what?"

"No, I don't want a cat."

"Well, you can't have one of mine," she said amiably. "Besides, you look more like the dog type."

"Oh, really?" He slipped his arms around her waist.

"Mmm. A nice cocker spaniel that would sleep by your fire at night."

"I don't have a fireplace."

"You should have. But until you take care of that, the puppy could curl right up on a little braided rug by the window."

He caught her bottom lip between his teeth and nipped lightly. "No."

"No one should live alone, Booth. It's depressing."

He could feel her response in the quickening of her heartbeat, the quiet shudder of breath. "I'm used to living alone. I like it that way."

She liked the feel of his roughened cheek against hers. "You must've had a pet when you were a child," Ariel murmured.

Booth remembered the golden Labrador with the lolling tongue that he'd adored—and that he hadn't thought of in years. Oh, no, he thought as he felt himself begin to weaken. She wasn't going to get to him on this. "As a child, I had the time and the temperament for a pet." Slowly, he slipped his hands under her sweatshirt and up her back. "Now I prefer other ways of spending my free time."

But she'd laid the groundwork, Ariel thought with a small smile. Advance and retreat was the secret of a successful campaign. "I have to shower," she told him, drawing back far enough to smile again. "I'm still sticky from that last scene."

"I enjoyed watching it. You've fascinating thigh muscles, Ariel."

Amused, she lifted both brows. "I have *aching* thigh muscles. And I'll tell you something, if I were to ride a bike for the three or four miles I did today, it wouldn't be anchored to the floor."

"No." He gathered her hair in his hand to draw her head back. "You wouldn't be content to stay in the same place." He touched his mouth teasingly to hers, retreating when she would have deepened the touch to a kiss. "I'll wash your back."

Thrills raced up her spine as if he already were. "Hmm, what a nice idea. I suppose I should warn you," she continued as they walked out of the kitchen, "I like the water in my shower hot—very hot."

When they stepped into the bathroom, he slipped his hands under the baggy sweatshirt. She was slim and warm beneath. "Don't you think I can take it?"

"I figure you're pretty tough." Eyes laughing up at him, Ariel began to unbutton his shirt. "For a screenwriter."

In one surprising move, Booth whipped the sweatshirt over her head and bit down on her shoulder. "I'd say you're pretty soft." He ran his hands down her rib cage, then banded her waist. "For an actress."

"Touché," Ariel murmured breathlessly as he tugged loose the drawstring of her pants.

"I like to feel you," he said, stroking his hands over her as she continued to undress him. "Though there isn't much of you. An elegant little body. Long boned, hipless." His hands journeyed down her back, and farther. "Very smooth."

By the time they were both naked, Ariel was shivering. But not from cold. Drawing away, she turned the taps. Water rushed from the showerhead, striking porcelain and steaming toward the ceiling. Stepping in, Ariel closed her eyes to let her body soak up the heat and the sensuality.

That was one of the things that continued to fascinate him about her—her capacity for experiencing. Nothing was ever ordinary to her, Booth decided as he stepped behind her and drew the curtain closed. She wouldn't know the meaning of boredom. Everything she did or thought was unique, and being unique, exciting.

As the water coursed over them both, he wrapped his arms around her and drew her back against his chest. This was affection, he realized, the sort he'd felt very rarely in his life. Yet he felt it for her.

Ariel lifted her face to the spray. So many sensations buffeted her at that moment, she couldn't keep up. So she stopped trying. It was enough to be close, to be held. And to love. Perhaps some people needed more—security, words, promises. Perhaps one day, she would, too. But now, just for now, she had all she wanted. Turning, she caught Booth close and fastened her mouth to his.

Passion flared in her quickly this time, as if it had been waiting for hours, days. Maybe years. It built so fast that the kiss alone had her gasping for air and fretting for more. Without being aware of it, she stood on her toes so that the curve of their bodies would be aligned. With desperate fingers, she combed through his hair and gripped, as if he might try to break away. But his arms were tight around her, and his mouth was as seeking as hers.

Reeling toward the crest, Ariel clung, and Ariel offered.

God, he'd never known anyone so giving. As he drank in all the flavors of her mouth, Booth wondered if it were possible for a woman to be so confident, so comfortable with herself that she could be this generous. Without any hesitation, her body was there for him. Her mind was tuned to him. Instinctively, Booth knew she thought more of his needs, his pleasures, than her own. And by doing so, she touched off a long dormant tenderness.

"Ariel…" Murmuring her name, he ran kisses over her face, which the water made incredibly soft, incredibly sweet. "You make me want things I'd forgotten—and almost believe in them again."

"Don't think." She rubbed her lips over his to soothe, to entice. "This time don't think at all."

But he would, Booth told himself. Or he'd take her too quickly, and perhaps too roughly. This time, he'd give her back a portion of what she'd already given him. Cupping the soap in his hand, he ran it over her back. He thought he heard her purr like one of her cats. It made him smile.

Her senses began to sharpen. She could hear the hiss of the spray as it struck tile, and feel the steam as it billowed in puffy clouds. Soapy hands slid over her—slick, soft, sensitive. His flesh was wet and warm where her mouth pressed. Through half-closed eyes she could see the lather cling to her, then him, before it was sluiced away.

His hand moved once between their slippery bodies to find her—stunningly—so that she cried out in surprise and rippling pleasure. Then it journeyed elsewhere while his lips traced hot and damp over her shoulder. The tang of citrus from the soap made her head reel.

"Do they still ache?" Booth asked her as his fingers kneaded the backs of her thighs.

"What?" Floating, Ariel leaned against him, her arms curved over his back, her hands firm on his shoulders. Water struck her back in soft, hissing spurts, then seemed to slither away. "No, no, nothing aches now."

With a laugh, Booth dipped his tongue into her ear and felt her shiver. "Your hair goes to gold when it's wet."

She smelled the shampoo, felt its cool touch on her scalp

before he began to massage. Nothing, Ariel thought, had ever aroused her more.

Slowly, lingeringly, he washed her hair while the frothy bubbles of shampoo ran down his arms. The scent was familiar to him now, that fresh, inviting fragrance that caught at him every time he was near her. He enjoyed the intimacy of having the scent spill over him and cling—to her skin, to his. Shifting his weight, he moved them both under the gush of the shower so that water and lather raced down their bodies and away.

And while they stood, hot and wet and entangled, he slipped into her. It seemed natural, as if he'd been her lover for years. It was thrilling, as though he'd never touched her before.

He felt Ariel's nails dig into his shoulders, heard her moan of surrender and demand. He took her there, with more care than he'd ever shown a woman. And he felt a rush of freedom.

Chapter Nine

Ariel rode a roller coaster for two weeks. Her time with Booth seemed like a ride with dips and curves and speed and surprises. Of course, she'd always loved them—the faster and wilder the better.

She'd been right when she'd told Booth he was unpredictable. Neither was he a simple man to deal with. Ariel decided she wanted it no other way.

There were times he was incredibly tender, showing her flashes of romance and affection that she'd never expected from him. A box of wildflowers delivered before an early studio call. A rainy-day picnic in his apartment with champagne in paper cups while thunder raged.

Then there were the times he pulled away, drew into himself so intensely that she couldn't reach him. And when she knew, instinctively, not to try.

The anger and impatience in him were ingrained. Perhaps it was that, contrasting with the glimpses of humor and gentleness, that had caused her to lose her heart. It was the whole man she loved, no matter how difficult. And it was the whole man she wanted to belong to. This man—brooding, angry, reluctantly sweet—was the man she'd been waiting for.

As the film progressed, their relationship grew closer, despite Booth's occasional stretches of isolation. Closer, yes, but without the simplicity she looked for. For love, in Ariel's mind, was a simple thing.

If he was resisting love, so much the better, Ariel told herself. When he accepted it—she wouldn't allow herself to doubt he would—it would be that much stronger. For she needed absolute love, the unconditional giving of heart and mind. She could wait a little longer to have it all.

If she had one regret, it was that she wasn't free to confide in him about Scott. The closer the trial came, the more she felt the need to talk to Booth about it, seek comfort, gain reassurance. Though it was tempting, Ariel never even considered it. This problem was hers, and hers alone. As Scott was hers to protect and defend.

When she thought of the future, it was still in sections. Booth, Scott, her career. She needed her own brand of absolute faith to believe that they'd all come together in the end.

After a long, hectic morning, Ariel considered the lengthy delay anticipated because of equipment breakdown a reward. It was the first time in weeks she'd be able to watch *Our Lives, Our Loves,* and catch up on Amanda's life with the people of Trader's Bend.

"You're not really going to watch television for the next hour," Booth protested as Ariel pulled him down the corridor.

"Yes, I am. It's like visiting home." She shook the bag of pretzels in her hand. "And I've got provisions."

"When they get the sound board fixed, you're going to have a hell of an afternoon ahead of you." He kneaded her shoulder as they walked. Though it didn't often show, he'd seen brief glimpses of strain in her eyes, isolated moments when she looked a bit lost. "You'd be better off putting your feet up and catching a nap."

"I never nap." When she pushed open her dressing room door, she upended a stack of magazines. Hardly sparing them a glance, she walked over to the small portable television set in the corner.

"I seem to recall coming in here one day and finding you with your feet up on the table and your eyes closed."

"That's different." She fiddled with a dial until she was satisfied with the color. "That was recharging. I'm not ready for recharging, Booth." Eyes wide and excited, she whirled around. "It's really going well, isn't it? I can feel it. Even after all these weeks, the edge is still on. That's a sure sign we're doing something special."

"I was a bit leery about doing a film for television." He took a few pamphlets from the sofa and dropped them onto a table. "Not anymore. Yes, it's going to be very special." He held out a hand to her. "You're very special."

As always, the subtle unexpected statement went straight to her heart. Ariel took the offered hand and brought it to her lips. "I'm going to enjoy watching you accept that Emmy."

He lifted a brow. "And what about yours?"

"Maybe," she said and laughed. "Just maybe." The lead-in music for the soap distracted her. "Ah, here we go. Back to Trader's Bend." Dropping onto the sofa, she pulled Booth with her. After ripping open the bag of pretzels, Ariel became totally absorbed.

She didn't watch as an actress or as a critic, but as a viewer. Relaxing her mind, she let herself become caught up in the connecting plot lines and problems. Even when she saw herself on the screen, she didn't look for flaws or perfection. She didn't consider she was looking at Ariel, but at Amanda.

"Don't tell me what I want," Amanda told Griff in a low, vibrating voice. "You have no business offering me unsolicited advice on my life, much less coming into my house uninvited."

"Now, you look." Griff took her arm when she would have turned away. "You're pushing yourself right to the edge. I can see it."

"I'm doing my job," she corrected coolly. "Why don't you concentrate on yours and leave me alone?"

"Leaving you alone's the last thing I'm going to do." As the camera zoomed in, the viewer was witness to his struggle for control. When Griff continued, his voice was calmer but edged with his familiar passion. "Damn it, Mandy, you're almost as close to this Ripper thing as the cops. You know better than to stay in this house by yourself. If you won't let me help you, at least go stay with your parents for a while."

"With my parents." Her composure began to crack as she dragged a hand through her hair. "Stay with my parents, while Vikki's there? Just how much do you think I can take?"

"All right, all right." Frustrated, he tried to draw her against him, only to have her jerk away. "Mandy, please, I'm worried about you."

"Don't be. And if you really want to help, leave me alone. I need to go over the psychiatric profile before I meet with Lieutenant Reiffler in the morning."

Fisted hands were shoved in his pockets. "Okay, look, I'll sleep down here on the couch. I swear I won't touch you. I just can't leave you out here alone."

"I don't want you here!" she shouted, losing her tenuous

grip on control. "I don't want anyone, can't you understand that? Can't you understand that I need to be alone?"

He stared at her while she fought back tears, shoulders heaving. "I love you, Mandy," he said so quietly it could barely be heard. But his eyes had already said it.

As the camera zoomed in on her, a single tear spilled out and rolled down Amanda's cheek. "No," she whispered, turning away. But Griff's arms came around her, drawing her back against him.

"Yes, you know I do. There's never been anyone for me but you. It killed me when you left me, Mandy. I need you in my life. I need what we'd planned to have together. We've got a second chance. All we have to do is take it."

Staring into nowhere, Amanda pressed a hand to her stomach where she knew Cameron's baby was sleeping—a baby Griff would never accept, and one she had to. "No, there aren't any second chances, Griff. Please leave me alone."

"We belong together," he murmured, burying his face in her hair. "Oh, God, Mandy, we've always belonged together."

For his sake, for her own, she had to make him leave. Pain flashed into her eyes before she controlled her expression. "You're wrong," she said flatly. "That was yesterday. Today I don't want you to touch me."

"I can't crawl anymore." Ripping himself away from her, Griff headed for the door. "I won't crawl anymore."

As the door slammed behind him, Amanda slumped down on the couch. Curling on her side, she buried her face in a pillow and wept. The camera panned slowly to the window to show a shadowy silhouette behind the closed curtains.

"Well, well," Booth murmured at the commercial break. "The lady has her problems."

"And then some." Ariel stretched and leaned back against the cushions. "That's the thing about soaps—one problem gets resolved and three more crop up."

"So, is she going to give Griff a break and take him back?"

Ariel grinned at the casualness of the question. He really wants to know, she mused, pleased. "Tune in tomorrow."

His eyes narrowed. "You know the story line."

"My lips are sealed," she said primly.

"Really?" Booth caught her chin in his hand. "Let's see." He pressed his to them firmly, and though hers curved, they remained shut. Challenged, he shifted closer and his fingers spread over her jawline, lightly stroking. With the barest of touches, he traced the shape of her mouth, wetting her lips, using no pressure. When he nibbled at one corner, then the other, he felt the telltale melting of her bones, heard the quiet sigh. Effortlessly, his tongue slipped between her lips to tease hers.

"Cheat," Ariel managed.

"Yeah." God, she made him feel so good. He'd almost stopped wondering how long it would last. The end, what he considered the inevitable end to what they brought each other, was becoming more blurred every day. "I've never believed in playing fair."

"No?" Her sudden aggression caught him off balance. Before he knew it, Booth was on his back, with her body pressed into his. "In that case, no holds barred."

The greedy kiss left him stunned, so that by the time he'd gripped some control again, she'd unbuttoned his shirt for her seeking hands. "Ariel…" Half-amused, half-protesting, he took her wrist, but her free hand skimmed down the center of his body to spread over his stomach.

Amusement, protests, reason, slipped away.

"I never get enough of you." He gripped her hair, destroying the sleek knot the hairdresser had tended so carefully hours before.

"I plan to see that you don't." With quick, open mouthed kisses she moved over his shoulder, drawing away the shirt as she went.

She took him over hills and into valleys with such speed and fury he could only follow. For as long as he could remember, Booth had led in every aspect of his life—not trusting enough to let another guide. But now he could barely keep pace with her. The energy, the verve he'd so long admired in her was in complete control. As he was swept along, Booth wondered why it was suddenly so easy to break yet another rule. Then, as she had once requested, he didn't think at all.

Feelings. Ariel drew them in as they radiated from him. This was what she'd been so patiently, so desperately waiting for. Emotions were finally overtaking him. As they merged with her own, she felt the bond, the link, and nearly wept with the wonder of it.

He loves me, she thought. Maybe he doesn't know it yet, maybe he won't for days and weeks to come. But it's there. The urge to weep altered to an urge to laugh. And it was with laughter and with joy that she took him into her.

Winded, Booth lay still while Ariel curled like a cat on his chest. "Was all that just to keep me from learning the story line?"

Her chuckle was muffled against his skin. "There're no lengths I won't go to to protect security." She snuggled against him. "No sacrifice too great."

"With that in mind, I think I'll ask about the identity of the Ripper—tonight." Drawing her up, he examined her. The silk blouse she'd been wearing was unbuttoned and trailing over one shoulder. The thin slacks lay in a heap on the floor. Her hair was a provocative tangle. "You're going to catch hell from wardrobe and makeup."

"It was worth it." Straightening her blouse, Ariel began to do up the buttons. "I'll tell them I took a nap."

With a laugh, he sat up and tugged on her tumbled hair. "There's no mistaking what you've been up to. Your eyes always give you away."

"Do they?" Carefully, she stepped into her slacks. "I wonder." Absently smoothing out the creases, she turned to him. "You haven't seen it in all these weeks." As she watched, his brows drew together. "You're a perceptive man, and I've never had a strong talent or a strong desire to hide my feelings." She smiled as he continued to frown at her. "I love you."

His face, his body—Ariel thought even his mind—went very still. He said nothing. "Booth, you don't have to look as though I've just pulled a gun on you." Stepping closer, she touched the back of her hand to his cheek. "Taking love's easy—giving it's a bit harder, for some people anyway. Please, take it as it's offered. It's free."

He wasn't at all certain what he was feeling—only that he'd never felt anything like it before. The very novelty made him wary. "It's not wise to give things away, Ariel, especially to someone who isn't ready for them."

"And holding on to something when it needs to be given's even more foolish. Booth, can't you trust me even now, just enough to accept my feelings?"

"I don't know," he murmured. As he rose, conflicting emotions, conflicting desires tore at him. He wanted to distance himself as quickly and as completely as possible. He wanted to hold her and never let go. Panic, he felt the stab of it. Pleasure, the sweetness of it.

"They're there whether you can or can't. I've never been good at controlling my emotions, Booth. I'm not sorry for it."

Before he could speak there was a brisk knock on the door. "Ariel, you're needed on the set in fifteen minutes."

"Thank you."

He had to think, Booth told himself. Be logical.... Be careful. "I'll send the hairdresser in."

"Okay." She smiled, and it almost reached her eyes. When he'd gone, Ariel stared at her reflection in the mirror. The lights around it were dull and dark. "So who expected it'd be easy?" she asked herself.

In just under fifteen minutes, Ariel walked back toward the set. She looked every bit as cool and as sleek as she had when she'd walked off over an hour before. Despite Booth's reaction, which she'd half expected, she felt lighter, easier, after telling Booth of her feelings. It was, after all, merely stating aloud what was, sharing what couldn't be changed. As a general rule, Ariel considered concealments a waste of time, and consequences a by-product of living. Her gait was free and easy as she crossed the studio.

She knew something was happening before she saw the thicket of people or heard the excited voices. Tension in the air. She felt it and thought instantly of Booth. But it wasn't Booth she saw when she passed the false wall of the living-room set.

Elizabeth Hunter.

Elegance. Ice. Smooth, smooth femininity. Outrageous beauty. Ariel saw her laugh lightly and lift a slender cigarette to her lips. She posed effortlessly, as if the cameras were on and focused on her. Her hair shimmered, pale, frosty. Her skin was so exquisite it might have been carved from marble.

On the screen, she was larger than life, desirable, unattainable. Ariel saw little difference in the flesh. There couldn't be a man alive who wouldn't dream of peeling off that layer of frost and finding something molten and wild inside. If she were truly like Rae, Ariel thought, that man—any man—would be disappointed. Curious, she walked closer.

"Pat, how could I stay away?" Liz lifted one graceful hand and touched Marshell's check. A fantasy of diamonds and sapphires winked on her ring finger. "After all, one might say I have a…vested interest in this film." The provocative pout—a Hunter trademark—touched her mouth. "Don't tell me you're going to chase me away."

"Of course not, Liz." Marshell looked uncomfortable and resigned. "None of us knew you were in town."

"I just wrapped the Simmeon film in Greece." She drew on the slender cigarette again and carelessly flicked ashes on the floor. "I flew right in." She shot a look over Marshell's shoulder. Not hostile, not grim, but simply predatory. It was then Ariel saw Booth.

He stood slightly apart from the circle of people around Liz, as if he again sought distance without wholly removing himself. He met the look his ex-wife sent him without a flicker of expression. Even if Ariel had chosen to intrude, she doubted if she could have gauged his thoughts.

"I wasn't allowed to read the screenplay." Liz continued to talk to Marshell though her eyes remained on Booth. "But little dribbles leaked through to me. I must say, I'm fascinated. And a bit miffed that you didn't ask me to do the film."

Marshell's eyes hardened, but he stuck with diplomacy. "You were unavailable, Liz."

"And inappropriate," Booth added mildly.

"Ah, Booth, always the clever last word." Liz blew smoke in his direction and smiled.

It was a smile Ariel recognized. She'd seen it on the screen in countless Hunter movies. She'd mimicked it herself as Rae. It was the smile a witch wore before she cut the wings off a bat. Without realizing it, Ariel moved forward in direct defense of Booth. Liz's gaze shifted and locked.

It wasn't a pleasant survey. Again, not hostile but simply and essentially cold. Ariel studied Liz in turn and absorbed impressions. She was left with a sensation of emptiness. And what she felt was pity.

"Well…" Liz held out her cigarette for disposal. A small woman with a wrinkled face plucked it from her fingers. "It's easy to deduce that this is Rae."

"No." Unconsciously, Ariel smiled with the same cold glitter as Liz. "I'm Ariel Kirkwood. Rae's a character."

"Indeed." The haughty lift of brow had been used in a dozen scenes. "I always try to absorb the character I portray."

"And it works brilliantly for you," Ariel acknowledged with complete sincerity. "I limit that to when the lights are on, Miss Hunter."

Only the barest flicker in her eyes betrayed annoyance. "Would I have seen you do anything else, dear?"

There was no mistaking the patronizing tone. Again, Ariel felt a flash of sympathy. "Possibly."

He didn't like seeing them together. No, Booth thought violently, by God, he didn't. It had given him a wave of sheer pleasure to see Liz again and feel nothing. Absolutely nothing. No anger, no frustration. Not even disgust. The lack of feeling had been like a balm. Until Ariel had come on set.

Face-to-face, they could have been sisters. The resemblance was heightened by the fact that Ariel's hair, makeup and wardrobe were styled to Liz's taste. He saw too many similarities. And as he looked closer, too many contrasts. Booth wasn't sure which annoyed him more.

No matter how she was dressed, warmth flowed from Ariel. The inner softness edged through. He could feel the emotion from her even three feet away. And he saw…pity? Yes, it was pity in her eyes. Directed at Liz. Booth lit a cigarette with a jerk of his wrist. God, he'd rid himself of one and was being reeled in by another. Standing there, he could feel the quicksand sucking at his legs. Was there any closer analogy for love?

"Let's get started," he ordered briefly. Liz shot him another look.

"Don't let me hold things up. I'll stay out of the way." She glided to the edge of the set, sat in a director's chair and crossed her legs. A burly man, the small woman and what was hardly more than a boy settled behind her.

The audience had Ariel's adrenaline pumping. The scene they were to shoot was the same one she'd auditioned with. More than any other, Ariel felt it encapsulated Rae's personality, her motives, her essence. She didn't think Liz Hunter would enjoy it, but…Ariel felt she'd be able to gauge just how successful her performance was by Liz's reaction to it.

With a faintly bored expression on her face, Liz sat back and watched the scene unfold. The dialogue was not precisely a verbatim account of what had occurred between her and Booth years before, but she recognized the tenor. Damn him, she thought with a flicker of anger that showed nowhere on her sculpted face. Damn him for his memory and his talent. So this was his revenge.

While she hoped the film fell flat, she was too shrewd to believe it would. She could shrug that off. Liz was clever enough, experienced enough to make the film work for her rather than against her. With the right angle, she could get miles and miles of publicity from Booth's work. That balanced things...to a point.

She was a woman of few emotions, but the most finely tuned of these was jealousy. It was this that ate at her as she sat, silent, watching. Ariel Kirkwood, she thought as one rose-tipped nail began to tap on the arm of the chair. Liz was vain enough to consider herself more beautiful, but there was no denying the difference in age. Years were something that haunted her.

And talent. Her teeth scraped against each other because she wanted to scream. Her own skill, the accolades and awards she'd received for it were never enough. Especially when she was faced with a beautiful, younger woman of equal ability. Damn them both. Her finger began to tap harder, staccato. The young man put a soothing hand on her shoulder and was shrugged away.

Liz could taste the envy that edged toward fury. The part should have been hers, she thought as her lips tightened. If she had played Rae, she'd have added a dozen dimensions to the part—such as it was. She had more talent in the palm of her hand than this Ariel Kirkwood had in her whole body. More beauty, more fame, more sexuality. Her head began to pound as she watched Ariel skillfully weave sex and ice into the scene.

Then her eyes met Booth's, and she nearly choked on an oath. He was laughing at her, Liz realized. Laughing, though his mouth was sober and his expression calm. He'd pay for that, she told herself as her lids lowered fractionally. For that and for everything else. She'd see that he and this no-talent actress from nowhere both paid.

Booth knew his ex-wife well enough to know what was

going on in her mind. It should have pleased him; perhaps it would have only a few weeks before. Now, it did little more than slightly disgust him.

Shifting his gaze from her, he focused his attention on Ariel. Of all the scenes in the screenplay, this was the hardest for him. He'd crystallized himself too well as Phil in these few sharp, hard lines. And his Rae was too real here. Ariel made her too real, he thought as he wished for a cigarette. In this short, seven-minute scene, which would take much, much longer to complete, it was almost impossible to separate Ariel from Rae—and Rae from Liz.

Ariel had said she loved him. Fighting discomfort that was laced with panic, Booth watched her. Was it possible? Once before he'd believed a woman who'd whispered those words to him. But Ariel…there was no one and nothing quite like Ariel.

Did he love her? Once before he'd believed himself in love. But whatever emotion it had been, it hadn't been love. And it had been smeared with a fascination for great beauty, great talent, cool, cool sex. No, he didn't understand love—if it existed in the way he believed Ariel thought of it. No, he didn't understand it, and he told himself he didn't want it. What he wanted was his privacy, his peace.

And while he stood there, watching his own scene being painstakingly reproduced on film, he had neither.

"Cut. Cut and print." Chuck ran a hand along the back of his neck to ease the tension. "Hell of a job." Letting out a long breath, he walked toward Ariel and Jack. "Hell of a job, both of you. We'll wrap for today. Nothing's going to top that."

Relieved, Ariel let her stomach relax, muscle by muscle. She glanced over idly at the sound of quiet applause.

Liz rose gracefully from her chair. "Marvelous job." She

gave Jack her dazzling, practiced smile before she turned to Ariel. "You have potential, dear," Liz told her. "I'm sure this part will open a few doors for you."

Ariel recognized the swipe and took it on the chin. "Thank you, Liz." Deliberately, she drew the pins from her hair and let it fall free. She wanted badly to shed Rae. "It's a challenging part."

"You did your best with it." Smiling, Liz touched her lightly on the shoulder.

I must've been on the money, Ariel thought and grinned. *I must've been right on the money.*

Liz wanted to rip the thick, tumbled hair out by the roots. She turned to Marshell. "Pat, I'd love to have dinner. We've a lot to catch up on." She slipped her arm through his and patted his hand. "My treat, darling."

Mentally swearing, Marshell acquiesced. The best way to get her out without a scene was simply to get her out. "My pleasure, Liz. Chuck, I'll want a look at the dailies first thing in the morning."

"Oh, by the way." Liz paused beside Booth. "I really don't think this little film will do much harm to your career, darling." With an icy laugh she skimmed a finger down his shirt. "And I must say, I'm rather flattered, all in all. No hard feelings, Booth."

He looked down at the beautiful, heartless smile. "No feelings, Liz. No feelings at all."

Her fingers tightened briefly on Marshell's arm before she swept away. "Oh, Pat, I must tell you about this marvelous young actor I met in Athens…."

"Exit stage left," Jack murmured, then shrugged when Ariel raised a brow at him. "Must still be functioning as Phil. But let me tell you, that's one lady I wouldn't turn my back on."

"She's rather sad," Ariel said half to herself.

Jack gave a snort of laughter. "She's a tarantula." With another snort he cupped a hand on Ariel's shoulder. "Let me tell you something, kid. I've been in the business a lot of years, worked with lots of actresses. You're first class. And that just gripped her cookies."

"And that's sad," Ariel repeated.

"Better put a layer of something over that compassion, babe," he warned. "You'll get burned." Giving her shoulder a last squeeze, he walked off the set.

Gratefully, Ariel dropped into a chair. The lights were off now, the temperature cooling. Most of the stagehands were gone, except for three who huddled in a corner discussing a poker game. Tipping her head back, she waited as Booth approached.

"That was a tough one," she commented. "How do you feel?"

"I'm fine. You?"

"A little drained. I've only a few scenes left, none of them on this scale. Next week, I'll be back to Amanda."

"How do you feel about that?"

"The people on the soap are like family. I miss them."

"Children leave home," he reminded her.

"I know. So will I when the time's right."

"We both know you won't be signing another contract with the soap." He drew out a cigarette, lighting it automatically, drawing in smoke without tasting it. "Whether you're ready to admit it or not."

Feeling his tension, she tensed in turn. "You're mixing us again," she said quietly. "Just how much longer is it going to take you to see me for who I am, without the shadows?"

"I know who you are," Booth corrected. "I'm not sure what to do about it."

She rose. Maybe it was the lingering strain from the scene,

or perhaps her sadness from watching Liz Hunter suffer in her own way. "I'll tell you what you don't want," she said with an edge to her voice he hadn't heard before. "You don't want me to love you. You don't want the responsibility of my emotions or of your own."

He could deal with this, Booth thought as he took another drag. A fight was something he could handle effortlessly. "Maybe I don't. I told you what I thought right up front."

"So you did." With a half laugh, she turned away. "Funny that you're the one who's always preaching change at me, and you're the one so unable to do so yourself. Let me tell you something, Booth." She whirled back, vibrantly glowing Ariel. "My feelings are mine. You can't dictate them to me. The only thing it's possible for you to do is dictate to yourself."

"It isn't a matter of dictating." He found he didn't want the cigarette after all. It tasted foul. Booth left it smoldering, half-crushed, in an ashtray. "It's a matter of not being able to give you what you want."

"I haven't asked you for anything."

"You don't have to ask." He was angry, really angry, without being aware when he'd crossed the line. "You've pulled at me from the start—pulled at things I want left alone. I made a commitment once, I'll be damned if I'll do it again. I don't want to change my lifestyle. I don't want—"

"To risk failure again," Ariel finished.

His eyes blazed at her, but his voice was very, very calm. "You're going to have to learn to watch your step, Ariel. Fragile bones are easily broken."

"And they mend." Abruptly, she was too weary to argue, too weary to think. "You'll have to work out your own solution, Booth. The same as I'll work out mine. I'm not sorry

I love you, or that I've told you. But I am sorry that you can't accept a gift."

When he'd watched her walk away, Booth slipped his hands in his pockets and stared at the darkened set. No, he couldn't accept it. Yet he felt as though he'd just tossed away something he'd searched for all of his life.

Chapter Ten

The water was a bit choppy. Small whitecaps bounced up, were swallowed, then bounced back again. Directly overhead the sky was a hard diamond blue, but to the east, dark clouds were boiling and building. There was the threat of rain in the wind that blew in from the Atlantic. Booth estimated he had two hours before the storm caught up with him—an hour before he'd be forced to tack to shore to avoid it.

And on shore the heat would be staggering, the humidity thick enough to slice. On the water, the breeze smelled of summer and salt and storms. He could taste it as it whipped by him and billowed his sail. Exhilaration—he knew it for the sensation that could clear the mind and chill the skin. Holding lightly to the rigging, he let the wind take him.

Booth wore nothing but cutoffs and deck shoes. He hadn't bothered to shave for two days. His eyes had grown accustomed to squinting against the sun reflecting off the water, and his hands to the feel of rough rope against the palm. Both were harsh, both were challenging.

Exhilaration? This time it hadn't come with the force he'd

expected. For days he'd sailed as long as the sun and the weather allowed. He'd worked at night until his mind was drained.

Escape? Was that a better word for what he'd come for? Perhaps, Booth mused as he sailed over the choppy water. Lifting a beer to his lips he let the taste race over his tongue. Perhaps he was escaping, but he was no longer needed on the set, and he had finally had to admit that he couldn't work in the city. He needed a few days away from the filming, from the pressure to produce, from his own standards of perfection.

That was all a lie.

None of those things had driven him out of Manhattan and onto Long Island. He'd needed to get away from Ariel—from what Ariel was doing to him. And perhaps most of all from his feelings for her. Yet the miles didn't erase her from his thoughts. It took no effort to think of her, and every effort not to. Though she haunted him, Booth was certain he'd been right to come away. If thinking of her ate at him, seeing her, touching her would have driven him mad.

He didn't want her love, he told himself savagely. He couldn't—wouldn't—be responsible for the range of emotions Ariel was capable of. Booth took another long pull from the beer can, then scowled at the water. He wasn't capable of loving her in return. He didn't possess those kinds of feelings. Whatever emotions he had were directed exclusively toward his work. He'd promised himself that. Inside, in the compartment that held the brighter feelings one person had for another, he was empty. He was void.

He ached for her—body, mind, soul.

Damn her, he thought as he jerked at the rigging. Damn her for pulling at him, for crowding him…for asking nothing of him. If she'd asked, demanded, pleaded, he could have refused.

It was so simple to say no to an obligation. All she did was give until he was so full of her, he was losing himself.

He'd work, Booth told himself as he began to tack methodically back toward shore. The boat bucked beneath him as the wind kicked up. Adjusting the sails, he concentrated on the pure physicality of the task. Use your muscles, your back, not your brain. Don't think, he warned himself, until it's time to write again.

He'd bury himself in work for the rest of the afternoon. He'd pour himself into his writing through the evening, late into the night, until his mind was too jumbled to think of anything—anyone. He'd stay away from her physically until he could stay away from her mentally. Then he'd go back to New York and pick up his life as he'd left it. Before Ariel.

Thunder rumbled ominously as he docked the boat.

Ariel watched the lightning snake across the sky and burst. The night sky was like a dark mirror abruptly cracked then made whole again. Still no rain. The heat storm had been threatening all evening, building up in the east and traveling toward Manhattan. She'd looked forward to it. Wearing a long shirt and nothing else, she stood at the window to watch it come.

Earlier, her neighbors had been sitting on their stoops, fanning and sweating and complaining of the heat. She didn't mind it. Before the night was over the rain would wash away the stickiness. But at the moment, though her thin shirt was clinging damply to her back and thighs, she enjoyed the enervating quality of the heat, and the violence in the sky.

The storm was coming from the east, she thought again. Perhaps Booth was already watching the rain she still anticipated. She wondered if he was working, oblivious to the booming thunder. Or if, like her, he stood and watched the fury in the sky. She wondered when he'd come back—to her.

He would, Ariel affirmed staunchly. She only hoped he'd come back with an easy mind. She'd thrown him a curve. With a half smile, Ariel felt the first rippling breeze pass through the screen and over her skin. She wasn't sorry, though his reaction had hurt, then angered her. That was over. Perhaps, for a moment, she'd forgotten that to Booth love wasn't the open-ended gift it was to her. He'd see the restrictions, the risks, the pains.

The pains, she thought, resting her palms on the window-sill. Why was she always so surprised to find out she could hurt just as intensely as she could be happy? She wanted him, physically, but he was miles from her reach, emotionally, but he'd distanced himself from her feelings.

She hadn't been surprised when Booth had absented himself from the last few days of shooting. All the key scenes had been done. Nor was she surprised when Marshell had mentioned idly that Booth had gone to his secluded Long Island home to write and to sail. She missed him, she felt the emptiness; but Ariel was too independent to mourn the loss of him for a few days. He needed his solitude. A part of her understood that, enough to keep her from misery.

Hadn't she herself painted almost through the night after Liz Hunter had visited the set?

Ariel glanced around at the frantic canvas slashed with cobalt and scarlets. It wasn't a painting she'd keep in the living room for long. Too angry, too disturbing. As soon as she'd fully coped with those feelings, she'd stick the canvas in a closet.

Everyone had his or her own means of dealing with the darker emotions. Booth's was to draw into himself; hers was to let them lash out. Either way, any way, the resolution would come. She had only to hang on a little while longer.

And so she told herself when she thought of Scott. The hearing would begin at the end of the week. That, too, would be resolved, but Ariel refused to look at any more than one solution. Scott had to come to her. The doubts she'd once harbored about her right to claim him, his need to be with her, were gone. As time went on, he became more and more unhappy with the Andersons. His visits were punctuated by desperate hugs, and more and more by pleas that he be allowed to stay with her.

It wasn't a matter of abuse or neglect. It was a simple matter of love, unconditional love that came naturally from her, and didn't come at all from his grandparents. Whatever hardships she and Scott were facing now would be a thing of the past before long. It was a time to concentrate on whens instead of nows. That was how she got through the slowly moving days between the filming and the hearing. Without Booth.

Ariel closed her eyes as the rain began to gush out of the sky. Oh God, if only the night were over.

The rain was just tapering off as Booth pushed away from his computer. He'd gotten more accomplished than he'd anticipated, but the juices were drying up. He knew better than to push himself when he got to this point. In another hour he'd try again perhaps, or maybe not for a day or two. But it would come back, and the story would flow again.

No, he couldn't write anything now, but it was still this side of midnight and he was restless. The storm had cleared the air, making him wish he were on the water again, under the burgeoning moonlight. He should eat. As he rubbed the stiffness from his neck, he remembered he hadn't bothered with dinner. A meal and an early night.

As he walked through the house into the kitchen, silence drummed around him. Strange, he'd never noticed just how thick silence could be, just how empty a house could be when it had only one occupant. And stranger still, how only a few months before he'd have appreciated both, even expected both. Again, before Ariel. His life seemed to have come down to two stages. Before Ariel and after Ariel. It wasn't an easy admission for a man to make.

Booth pulled a tray of cold cuts out of the refrigerator without any real interest. Mechanically, he fixed a sandwich, found a ripe peach and poured a glass of milk. The solitary meal had never seemed less appealing—so much so he considered tipping the entire mess down the sink.

Shaking off the feeling, he carried it into his bedroom and set the plate on the dresser. What he needed was some noise, he decided. Something to occupy his mind without straining the brain. Booth switched on the television, then flipped the channel selector without any particular goal in mind.

Normally he would have bypassed the late-night talk show in favor of an old movie. When Liz's laughter flowed out at him, he paused. He might still have passed it by, but his curiosity was piqued. Thinking it might be an interesting diversion, Booth picked up his plate, set it on the bedside table and stretched out.

He'd been on the show himself a number of times. Though he wasn't overly fond of the format or the exposure, he knew the game well enough to understand the need to reach the public through the form. The show was popular, slickly run, and the host knew his trade. With boyish charm he could draw the unexpected out of celebrities and keep the audience from turning the channel or just flicking off the switch.

"Of course I was terribly excited to film on location in Greece, Bob." Liz leaned just a bit closer to her host while her ice-blue gown glistened coolly in the lights. "And working with Ross Simmeon was a tremendous experience."

"Didn't I hear you and Simmeon had a feud going?" Robert MacAllister tossed off the question with a grin. It said, come on, relax, you can tell me. It was a well-practiced weapon.

"A feud?" Liz fluttered her lashes ingenuously. She was much too sharp to be caught in that trap. She crossed her legs so that the gown shimmered over her body. "Why, no. I can't imagine where anyone would get that idea."

"It must have something to do with the three days you refused to come on set." With a little deprecating shrug, MacAllister leaned back in his chair. "A disagreement over the number of lines in a key scene."

"That's nonsense." *Damn Simmeon and all the rumormongers.* "I'd had too much sun. My physician put me on medication for a couple of days and recommended a rest." She glittered a smile right back at him. "Of course there were a few tense moments, as there will be on any major film, but I'd work with Ross tomorrow...." or the devil himself, her tone seemed to say. "If the right script came along."

"So, what're you up to now, Liz? You've had an unbroken string of successes. It must be getting tough to find just the right property."

"It's always hard to put together the right touch of magic." She gestured gracefully so that the ring on her hand caught the light and glittered. "The right script, the right director, the right leading man. I've been so lucky—particularly since *To Meet at Midnight.*"

Booth set his half-eaten sandwich aside and nearly laughed. *He'd* written it for her and had made her a major star. Top box office. Luck had had nothing to do with it.

"Your Oscar-winning performance," Bob acknowledged. "And of course a brilliant screenplay." He sent her an off-center smile. "You'd agree with that?"

It was the opening she'd been waiting for. And maneuvering toward. "Oh, yes. Booth DeWitt is possibly—no, assuredly the finest screenwriter of the eighties. Regardless of our, well, personal problems, we've always respected each other professionally."

"I know all about personal problems," Bob said ruefully and got the laugh. His three marriages had been well publicized. And so had his alimony figures. "How do you feel about his latest work?"

"Oh." Liz smiled and let one hand flutter to her throat before it fell into her lap. "I don't suppose the content's much of a secret, is it?"

Again the expected laugh, a bit more restrained.

"I'm sure Booth's script is wonderful, they all are. If it's, ah, one-sided," she said carefully, "it's only natural. From what I'm told it's common for a writer to reflect some parts of his personal life...and in his own way," she added. "As a matter of fact, I visited the set just last week. Pat Marshell's producing, you know, and Chuck Tyler's directing."

"But..." Bob prompted, noting her obvious reluctance.

"As I said, it's so difficult to find that right brand of magic." She tossed out the first seeds with a smile. "And Booth's never done anything for the small screen before. A difficult transition for anyone."

"Jack Rohrer's starring." Obligingly, Bob fed her the next line.

"Yes, excellent casting there. I thought Jack was absolutely brilliant in *Of Two Minds*. That was a script he could really sink his teeth into."

"But this one…"

"Well, I happen to be a big Jack Rohrer fan," Liz said, apparently sidestepping the question. "I doubt there's any part he can't find some meat on."

"And his costar?" Bob folded his hands on his desk. Liz was out for the jugular, he decided. It wouldn't hurt his ratings.

"The female lead's a lovely girl. I can't quite think of her name, but I believe she has a part on a soap opera. Booth often likes to experiment rather than to go with experienced actors."

"As he did with you."

Her eyes narrowed fractionally. She didn't quite like that tone, or that direction. "You could put it that way." The haughtiness in her voice indicated otherwise. "But really, when one has the production rate this project has, one should shoot for the best talent available. Naturally, that's a personal opinion. I've always thought actors should pay their dues—God knows, I paid mine—rather than be cast in a major production because of a…shall we say personal whim?"

"Do you think Booth DeWitt has a personal whim going with Ariel Kirkwood? That's her name, isn't it?"

"Why, yes, I think it is. As to the other, I could hardly say." She smiled again, charmingly. "Especially on the air, Bob."

"Her physical resemblance to you is striking."

"Really?" Liz's eyes frosted. "I much prefer being one of a kind, though of course it's flattering to have someone attempt to emulate me. Naturally, I wish the girl the best of luck."

"That's gracious of you, Liz, particularly since the plot line's rumored to be less than kind to the character that some say mirrors you."

"Those that know me will pay little attention to a slanted view, Bob. All in all, I'll be fascinated to see the finished product." The statement was laced with boredom, almost as if she'd yawned. "That is, of course, if it's ever actually aired."

"Ever aired? You see some problem there?"

"Nothing I can talk about," she said with obvious reluctance. "But you and I know how many things can happen between filming and airing, Bob."

"No plans to sue, huh, Liz?"

She laughed, but it came off hollow. "That would give the film entirely too much importance."

Bob mugged at the camera. "Well, with that we'll take a little break here. When we come back, James R. Lemont will be joining us to tell us about his new book, *Hollywood Secrets*. We know about those, too, don't we, Liz?" After his wink, the screen switched to the first commercial.

Leaning back against the pillows, his meal forgotten, Booth drew on his cigarette and sent the smoke to the ceiling. He was angry. He could feel it in the hard knot in his stomach. The swipes she'd taken at the film hadn't even been subtle, he reflected. Oh, perhaps she'd fool a certain percentage of people, but no one remotely connected with the business, and no one with any perception. She'd done her best to toss a few poison darts and had ended up, in Booth's opinion, by making a fool of herself.

But he was angry. And the anger, he discovered, came from the slices she'd taken at Ariel. Quite deliberate, quite calculated, and unfortunately for Liz, quite obvious. She was a cat, and normally a clever one. Jealousy was essentially the only thing that could make her lose that edge.

Naturally she'd be jealous of Ariel, Booth mused. Of anyone

young, beautiful and talented. Add that to the bile she'd have to swallow over the film itself, and Liz would be as close to rage as her limited range of emotions would allow. And this was her way of paying back.

Rising, Booth slammed off the set before he paced the room. She'd bring up the film—and Ariel—in every interview she gave, at every party she attended, in the hope to sabotage both. Of course, she wouldn't do any appreciable damage, but knowing that didn't ease his temper. No one had the right to take potshots at Ariel, and the fact that they were being taken through him, because of him, made it worse.

He could, if he chose, book himself on the circuit to promote the film and to counter Liz's campaign. That would only add fuel to the fire. He knew the best way to make the storm Liz was trying to brew fizzle was to keep silent. Frustrated, he walked to the window. He could hear the water from there. Just barely. He wondered if Ariel had watched the late-night talk show. And how she was dealing with it.

Stretched out in the hammock, plumped by pillows, with a bowl of fresh popcorn resting on her stomach, Ariel listened to Liz Hunter. Her brow lifted once as a reference was made to herself. Ariel crunched on popcorn and smiled as Robert Mac-Allister reminded Liz that *the girl's* name was Ariel Kirkwood.

Poor Liz, she thought. She was only making it worse for herself. Perhaps because Ariel had been inside Rae's skin for so many weeks, she noticed small things. The tapping of a fingertip on the arm of the chair, the brief tightening of the lips, the flash in the eyes that was a bit of anger, a bit of desperation. The more Liz talked, the shakier her support became.

She'd have been much better off if she'd said nothing, Ariel mused. A no-comment, a shrug of that haughty shoulder. Miscalculation, Ariel thought with a sigh. A foolish one.

I can't hurt her. Ariel shifted her gaze from the screen to the ceiling. No one can take her talent away from her. A pity she doesn't realize that. It's Booth she really wants to hurt, Ariel decided. She'd want to make him pay for using Rae to strip off a few masks. Yet didn't Liz realize he was just as bitterly honest with his own character?

Ariel glanced back at the television screen as Liz's face dominated the screen. There was a line of dissatisfaction between her brows, very faint. Ariel wondered if she were the only one who noticed it, because she was so intimately involved. I know you, Ariel told the image on the screen, I know you inside and out. And that made her swallow hard. It was just a little scary.

Ariel lay back, tuning out the sound of the set and tuning back into the rain. It was nearly over, only a patter now against the windowpane. Booth had probably seen it, she decided. And if he hadn't caught the show, he'd know of the content very soon. He'd be angry. Ariel could almost see his hard-eyed, grim-mouthed reaction. She herself had been fighting an edge of temper that threatened to dominate her other feelings.

Anger was useless; she wished she could tell him. He had to know that he'd opened the door for this when he'd written the script. She'd opened it a bit further when she'd taken the part. She hoped, when he'd calmed, that he'd see Liz Hunter had done the film more good than harm.

When the phone rang, Ariel leaned over. Years of experience kept her balanced rather than tumbling out of the hammock and onto the floor. Swinging a bit dangerously, she gripped the phone and hauled it up to her. "Hello."

"That witch."

With a half laugh, Ariel lay back on the pillows. "Hi, Stella."

"Did you catch the MacAllister show?"

"Yeah, I've got it on."

"Listen, Ariel, she's making a joke out of herself. Anyone with two brain cells will see that."

"Then why're you angry?"

She could hear Stella take a deep breath. "I've been sitting here listening to that woman talk, wishing you the *best* of luck." Stella muttered something under her breath, then began to talk so fast the words tumbled into each other. "The best of luck my foot. She'd like to see you drop off the face of the earth. She'd like to stick a knife in you."

"A nail file, maybe."

"How can you joke about it?" Stella demanded.

Because if I don't I might just start screaming. "How can you take it so seriously?" Ariel said instead.

"Listen, Ariel…" Stella's voice was barely controlled. "I know that kind of woman. I've been playing the type for the past five years. There's nothing she wouldn't do, nothing, if she thought she could get to you. Damn it, you trust everyone."

"Some less than others." Though the concern and the loyalty touched her, she laughed. "Stella, I'm not a complete fool."

"You're not a fool at all," Stella shot back, outraged. "But you're naive. You actually believe the kid who stops you on the street asking for a donation is really collecting for a foundling home."

"He might be," Ariel mumbled. "Besides, what does that have to do with—"

"Everything!" Stella cut her off with something close to a roar. "I care about you. I worry about you every time I think about you walking blithely down the street without a thought to the crazies in the world."

"Come on, Stella, if I thought about it too much I'd never go out at all."

"Well think about this: Liz Hunter's a powerful, vindictive woman who'd like to ruin you. You watch your back, Ariel."

Who'd know that better than I? Ariel thought with a quick shudder. I've been playing her character for weeks. "If I promise, will you stop worrying?"

"No." Slightly mollified, Stella sighed. "Promise anyway."

"You got it. Are you calm now?"

Stella made a quiet sound in her throat. "I don't understand why you're not angry."

"Why should I be when you're doing it for me—and so well?"

Stella heaved a long breath. "Good night, Ariel."

"Night, Stella… Thanks."

Ariel replaced the receiver and swung gently to and fro in the hammock. As she stared up at the ceiling, she marveled over how fortunate she was. Friendship was a precious thing. To have someone ready to leap to your defense, claws bared, was a comforting sensation. She had friends like that, and a job that paid her well for doing what she would gleefully have done for nothing. She had the unquestioning love of a little boy, and God willing, would have him to care for within a few weeks. She had so much.

As Ariel lay back, struggling to count her blessings, she thought of Booth. And ached for him.

Two days later, Ariel received a surprise visit. It was her first free day since resuming her role of Amanda. She was spending it doing something she rarely started, and more rarely finished. Housecleaning.

In tattered shorts and a halter, she sat on her windowsill two stories up, and leaning out, washed the outside of her windows. The volume on her radio was turned up so that the sinuous violins of *Scheherazade* all but shook the panes. Occasionally someone from the neighborhood would shout up at her. Ariel would stop working—something that took no effort at all— and shout back down.

The important thing was to keep busy, to keep occupied. If she gave herself more than a brief moment of spare time, time to think, she might go mad. The next day marked the beginning of the custody hearing. And a full two weeks since she'd last seen Booth. Ariel polished window glass until it shone.

She felt something like an itch between the shoulder blades, like a fingertip on the back of the neck. Twisting her head, she looked down and saw Booth on the sidewalk below. Relief came in waves. Even if she'd tried, even if she'd thought to try, she couldn't have stopped the smile that illuminated her whole face.

"Hi."

Looking up at her, he felt a need so great it buckled his knees. "What the hell are you doing?"

"Washing the windows."

"You could break your neck."

"No, I'm anchored." One of the kittens brushed against her ankles so that she jolted and braced herself with her knees. "Are you coming up?"

"Yeah." Without another word, he disappeared from view.

As he climbed the stairs Booth reminded himself of his promise. He wasn't going to touch her—not once. He would say what he'd come to say, do what he'd come to do, then leave. He wouldn't touch her and start that endless cycle of longings and desires and dreams all over again. Over the past two weeks he'd purged himself of her.

As he reached the landing he nearly believed it. Then she opened the door.

She still held a damp rag in one hand. She wore no makeup; the flush of color in her cheeks came from pleasure and exertion. Her hair was scooped back and tied with a bit of yarn. The scent of ammonia was strong.

His fingers itched for just one touch, just one. Booth curled them into his palms and stuck them in his pockets.

"It's good to see you." Ariel leaned against the door and studied him. People didn't change in two weeks, she reminded herself as she compared every angle and plane in his face with the memory she'd been carrying with her. He looked the same, a bit browner perhaps from the sun, but the same. Love washed over her.

"You've been sailing."

"Yes, quite a bit."

"It's good for you. I can see it." She stepped back, knowing from the tense way he was standing that he wouldn't accept her hand if she offered. "Come in."

He stepped into chaos. When Ariel cleaned, it was from the bottom up and nothing was safe. Drawers had been turned out, tables cleared off. Furniture and windows gleamed. There wasn't a clear place to stand, much less sit.

"Sorry," she said as she followed his survey. "I'm a bit behind on my spring cleaning." The pressure in her chest was increasing with every second they stood beside each other, and miles apart. "Want a drink?"

"No, nothing. I'll make this quick because you're busy." He'd make it quick because it hurt, physically, painfully, not to touch what he still wanted…and to still want what he'd convinced himself he couldn't have. "I'm assuming you saw the MacAllister show the other night."

"That's old news," Ariel countered. She sat on the hammock, legs dangling free, fingers locked tightly.

With his hands still in his pockets, Booth rocked back on his heels. "How'd you feel about it?"

With a shrug, Ariel crossed her ankles. "She took a couple stabs at the film, but—"

"She took a couple stabs at you," he corrected. His voice had tightened, his eyes narrowed.

Gauging his mood, Ariel decided to play it light. She smiled. "I'm not bleeding."

Booth frowned at her a moment, then judged she was a great deal less concerned than he. That was something he had to change. "She hasn't stopped there, Ariel." He walked closer, the better to study her face, the better to perhaps catch the drift of her scent. "She had quite a little session with the producer of your show, then with a few network executives."

"With my producer?" Puzzled, she tilted her head and tried to reason it out. "Why?"

"She wants them to fire you—or, ah, to let your contract lapse."

Stunned, she said nothing. But her face went pale. The rag slipped silently from her hand to the floor.

"She'd agree to do a series of guest spots for the show, if you were no longer on it. Your producer politely turned her down. So she went upstairs."

Ariel swallowed the panic. All she could think, all that drummed in her mind was, *not now, not during the hearing.* She needed the stability of that contract for Scott. "And?"

He hadn't expected this white-lipped, wide-eyed reaction. A woman with her temperament should have been angry, angry enough to rage, throw things, explode. He could even have understood amusement, a burst of laughter, a shake of the head and a shrug. She was confident enough for that. He'd thought she was. What he saw in her eyes was basic fear.

"Ariel, just how important do you think you are to the show?"

She found she had to swallow before she could form the first word. "Amanda's a popular character. I get the lion's share of mail, a lot of it addressed to Amanda rather than me. In my last contract, my scale was upgraded with the minimum amount of negotiation." She swallowed again and gripped her hands together. That was all very logical, all very practical. She wanted to scream. "Anyone can be replaced. On a soap, that's the number-one rule. Are they going to let me go?"

"No." Frowning at her, he stepped closer. "I'm surprised you'd think they would. You're already their biggest reason for the ratings lead. And with the film due in the fall, the show's bound to cash in on it. In a strictly practical way of thinking, you—day after day—are worth a great deal more to the network than Liz in a one-shot deal." When Ariel let out a long breath he had to fight the urge to take her into his arms. "Does the show mean that much to you?"

"Yes, it means that much to me."

"Why?"

"It's my show," she said simply. "My character." As the panic faded, the anger seeped in. "If I leave it, it'll be because it's what I want, or because I'm not good enough anymore." Giving in to rage she plucked up a little yellow vase from the table beside her and flung it and the baby's breath it held at the wall. Glass shattered, flowers spilled. "I've given five years of my life to that show." As her breathing calmed again, she stared at the shards of vase and broken blooms. "It's important to me," she continued, looking back up at Booth. "At the moment, for a lot of reasons, it's essential." Ariel gripped the side of the hammock and struggled to relax. "How did you hear about this?"

"From Pat. There's been quite a meeting of the minds as concerns you. We decided you should hear about this latest move privately."

"I appreciate it." The anger was fading. Relief made her light-headed. "Well, I'm sorry she feels so pressured that she'd try to do me out of a job, but I imagine she'll back off now."

"You're smarter than that."

"There's nothing she can do to me, not really. And every time she tries, she only makes it worse for herself." Slowly, deliberately, she relaxed her hands. "Every interview she gives is free publicity for the film."

"If there's any way she can hurt you, she will. I should've thought of that before I cast you as Rae."

Smiling, Ariel lifted her hands to his arms. "Are you worried about me? I'd like you to be...just a little."

He should have backed off right then. But he needed, badly needed to absorb that contact. Just her hands on his arms. If he were careful, very careful, it might be enough. "Whatever trouble she causes you I'm responsible for."

"That's a remarkably ridiculous statement—arrogant, egotistical." She grinned. "And exactly like you. I've missed you, Booth. I've missed everything about you."

She was drawing him closer, but more, she was drawing him in. Even as her hand reached for his face, he was lowering his mouth to hers. And the first taste was enough to make him forget every promise he'd made during this absence.

Ariel moaned as her lips met his. It seemed she'd been waiting for years to feel that melting thrill again. More. The greed flashed through her. She pulled him down so that the hammock swayed under their combined weight.

There was no gentleness in either of them now. Impatience shimmered. Without words they told each other to hurry—hurry and touch me; it's been too long. And as clothes were tugged away and flesh met flesh, they both took hungrily from the other.

The movement of the hammock was like the sea, and he felt the freedom. There was freedom simply in being near her again. And from freedom sprang the madness. He couldn't stop his hands from racing over her. He couldn't prevent his mouth from trying to devour every inch. He was starving for her and no longer cared that he had vowed to abstain. Her skin flowed warm and soft under his hands. Her mouth was hot and silky. The generosity he could never quite measure simply poured from her.

She'd stopped thinking the moment he'd kissed her again. Ariel didn't need the intellect now, only the senses. She could taste the salt on his skin as they clung together in the moist heat of the afternoon; the dark male flavor along his throat enticed her back, again and again. There was a fury of desire in him, more than she'd ever known in him before. It made her skin tremble to be wanted with such savagery.

But with the trembling came a mirroring desire in herself. The top of the hammock scraped against her back as his body pressed against hers. For one isolated moment, she thought she could feel the individual strands, then that sensation faded into another.

His hands were in her hair, holding her head back so that he could plunder her mouth. She heard his breath shudder, and saw, as her lashes fluttered up, that he was watching her. Always watching.

His eyes stayed open and on hers when he plunged into her.

He wanted to see her, needed to know that her need for him was as great as his for her. And he could see it—in the trembling mouth. His name came from there in a breathy whisper. In the stunned pleasure in her eyes. He could bring her that. He could bring her that, Booth thought as he buried his face in her hair. He wanted to bring her everything.

"Ariel…" In the last sane corner of his mind he knew they were both near the edge. He took her face in his hands and crushed his mouth to hers so that they crested, swallowing each other's cry of pleasure.

The movement of the hammock eased, soothing now, like a cradle. They were wrapped together, facing, with her head in the curve of his shoulder. Their bodies were damp from the heat in the air, and from the heat within. A length of her hair fell over her and onto his chest.

"I thought of you," Booth murmured. His eyes were closed. His heartbeat was slowing, but the arms around her didn't loosen. "I could never stop thinking about you."

Ariel's eyes were open, and she smiled. She'd needed no other words but those. "Sleep with me awhile." Turning her head she kissed his shoulder before settling again. "Just for a little while."

For days and nights she'd thought only of tomorrows. The time had come again to think only of now. Long after he slept, she lay awake, feeling the hammock move gently.

Chapter Eleven

Ariel sat on a small wooden bench outside the courtroom. It was a busy hallway with people coming and going, but no one paid much attention to a solitary woman in a cream-colored suit who stared straight ahead.

The first day of the hearing was over, and she felt a curious mixture of relief and tension. It had begun; there was no going back. A door opened down the hall, and a flood of people poured out. She'd never felt more alone in her life.

Bigby had outlined it for her. There'd been no surprises. Despite the legal jargon, the first day had dealt basically with establishing the groundwork. Still, to Ariel's mind the preliminary questions had been terribly cut-and-dried. But the wheels had begun to turn, and now that they had, maybe the pace would pick up.

Just let it be over with quickly, she thought and closed her eyes briefly. *Just let it be done.* The tension came from the thought of tomorrow. The relief came from the absolute certainty that she was doing the right thing.

Bigby came out of the courtroom with his slim briefcase in

his hand. With his other, he reached out to her. "Let me buy you a drink."

Ariel smiled, linking her hand with his as she rose. "Deal. But make it coffee."

"You did well in there today."

"I didn't do much of anything."

He started to speak, then changed his mind. Maybe it was best not to point out how much she'd done by simply being. Her freshness, the concern in her eyes, the tone of her voice— all of that had been a vital contrast to the stiff backs and stone faces of the Andersons. A judge in a custody suit, a good one, was influenced by more than facts and figures.

"Just keep doing it," he advised, then gave her hand a squeeze as they walked down the hall. Neither of them noticed the dark-suited man in horn rims who followed. "Tell me how the rest of your life's going," he requested. In his unobtrusive way, Bigby guided her through the doors as he guided her thoughts. "It isn't every day I represent a rising celebrity."

She laughed even as the first wave of heat rose off the sidewalk and struck her. New York in midsummer was hot and humid and sweaty. "Is that what I am?"

"Your picture was in *Tube*—and your name was brought up on the MacAllister show." He grinned as she arched a brow. "I'm impressed."

"Read *Tube,* do you, Charlie?" He was trying to keep her calm, she realized. And he was doing it expertly. She slid a companionable arm through his. "I have to admit, the publicity isn't going to hurt the soap, the film or me."

"In that order?"

Ariel smiled and shrugged. "Depends on my mood." No, she wasn't without ambition. The *Tube* spread had given her

a great deal of self-satisfaction. "It's been a long time between shampoo commercials, and I won't be sorry if I don't
have to stand, lathered up, for three hours again anytime
soon."

They entered a coffee shop where the temperature dropped by
twenty-five degrees. Ariel gave a quick shiver and a sigh of relief.
"So professionally, everything's rolling along?" Charlie asked.

"No complaints." Ariel slipped into the little vinyl booth and
pushed off her shoes. "They're casting for *Chapter Two* next
week. I haven't done live theater in too long."

Bigby clucked his tongue as he picked up a menu. The man
in the dark suit took the booth behind them, settling with his
back to Ariel's. "You don't sit still, do you?"

"Not any longer than I can help it. I have good feelings about
the custody suit, maybe because I'm on a professional roll. It's
all going to work out, Charlie. I'm going to have Scott with
me, and Booth's film's going to be a smash."

He eyed her over his glasses, then grinned. "The power of
positive thinking."

"If it works." She leaned her elbows on the table, then rested
her chin on her fists. "All my life I've been moving toward
certain goals, without really understanding that I was setting
them for myself. They're almost within reach."

Bigby glanced up at the waitress before he turned back to
Ariel. "How about some pie with the coffee?"

"You twisted my arm. Blueberry." She touched the tip of
her tongue to her lip because she could almost taste it.

"Two of each," Bigby told the waitress. "Speaking of Booth
DeWitt..." he went on.

"Were we?"

He caught the gleam of amusement in Ariel's eye. "I think

you mentioned him to me a few weeks ago. A man who didn't think much of relationships or actresses?"

"You've quite a memory—and very sharp deductive skills."

"It was easy enough to put two and two together, particularly after Liz Hunter's performance on the MacAllister show the other night."

"Performance?" Ariel repeated with a half smile.

"An actor can usually see through another, I'd think. A lawyer's got a lot of actor in him." He paused and folded his hands on the chipped Formica much as he did on his desk. "She put DeWitt through the wringer a couple of years ago."

"They damaged each other. You know, sometimes I think people can be attracted to the specific persons who are the worst for them."

"Is that from personal experience?"

Her eyes became very sober, her mouth very soft. "Booth is right for me. In a lot of ways he'll make my life difficult, but he's right for me."

"What makes you so sure?"

"I'm in love with him." When the pie was brought over, Ariel ignored the coffee and concentrated on it. "Bless you, Charlie," she said after the first bite.

He lifted a brow at the sliver of pie she was in raptures over. "You're easily impressed."

"Cynic. Eat it."

He picked up a fork and polished it absently with a paper napkin. "At the risk of putting my foot in it, DeWitt isn't the type of man I'd've matched you with."

Ariel swallowed the next mouthful. "Oh?"

"He's very intense, serious-minded. His scripts have certainly indicated that. And you're…"

"Flaky?" she suggested, breaking off the next piece of pie.

"No." Bigby opened one of the little plastic containers of cream that were heaped in a bowl on the table. "You're anything but that. But you're full of life—the joy of it. It's not that you don't face the hard side when it comes up, but you don't look for it. It seems to me DeWitt does."

"Maybe—maybe he expects it. If you expect it and it happens, you aren't as staggered by it. For some people, it's a defensive move." A small frown creased her brow before she smoothed it away. "I think Booth and I can learn a lot from each other."

"And what does Booth think—or am I out of line?"

"You're not out of line, Charlie," she said absently as she remembered how grim Booth had been when he'd come to her door, how intensely he'd made love to her. He'd relaxed, degree by slow degree. Then he'd slept, with his arms tightly around her, as if he'd just needed to hold on. To her, she'd wondered, or to the peace? Perhaps it didn't matter. "It's hard for Booth," she murmured. "He wanted to be left alone, wanted his life to go on a certain way. I've interfered with that. He needs more time, more space."

"And what do you need?"

She looked over and saw her answer hadn't pleased him. *He's thinking of me,* Ariel realized, touched. Reaching over, she laid a hand on his. "I love him, Charlie. That's enough, for now. I do know it's not enough for always, but people can't put a control switch on emotions. I can't," she corrected.

"Does that mean he can?"

"To a certain extent." Ariel opened her mouth again, then shook her head. "No, I don't want to change him, even in that way. Not change. I need the balance he brings me, and I need to be able to lighten some of those shadows he carries around. It's the same with Scott, in a way. I need the stability he brings to my life—the way Scott, maybe children in general, can center it. Basically, I have an outrageous need to be needed."

"Have you told Booth about Scott? About the custody hearing?"

"No." Ariel stirred sugar into her coffee but didn't drink it. "It doesn't seem fair to saddle him with a problem that was already in full swing when we met. Instinct tells me to handle it myself, then when it's resolved, to tell Booth in my own way."

"He might not like it," Bigby pointed out. "The one thing Ford brought up in our last meeting that I have to agree with is that some men can't or won't be responsible for another man's child."

Ariel shook her head. "I don't believe that of Booth. But if it's true, it's something I'll have to deal with."

"If you did have to make a choice?"

She said nothing at first, as she dealt with the ache even the possibility brought her. "When you make a choice between two people you love," Ariel said quietly, "you choose the one who needs you the most." She lifted her eyes again. "Scott's only a child, Charlie."

He leaned across to pat her hand. "I just wanted to hear you say it. To be completely unprofessional again," he said with a grin, "there isn't a man in the world who'd turn down either you or Scott."

"That's why I'm crazy about you." She paused a moment, then touched her fork to her tongue. "Charlie, would you think I was really a hedonist if I ordered another piece of this pie?"

"Yes."

"Good." Ariel lifted a hand and gestured for the waitress. "Once in a while I just have to be decadent."

★ ★ ★

Amanda's life was a pressure cooker. As she went over the pacing of her lines one last time, Ariel decided she was grateful for the tension. It helped her deal with reality just a little better. She'd spent the morning in court, and the following day she was scheduled to take the stand. That was one part she couldn't rehearse for. But the good feeling she'd experienced the first day of the hearing hadn't faded, nor had her optimism. It was poor Amanda, Ariel mused, who'd continue to have problems that would never completely be resolved. That was life in a soap opera.

The rest of the cast had yet to return from the lunch break. Ariel sat alone in the studio—lounged, that is, on the rumpled bed she would rise from when Amanda was awakened by the sound of breaking glass. Alone and defenseless, she'd face the Trader's Bend Ripper. She'd have only her wits and professional skill to protect her from a psychotic killer.

Already in costume, a plain nightshirt in periwinkle-blue, she continued to murmur her lines out loud while doing a few lazy leg lifts. She'd had some vague twinges of guilt about the second piece of blueberry pie.

"Well, well, so this is the lightning pace of daytime television."

Immersed in the gripping scene between Amanda and a psychopath, Ariel dropped the script and gasped. The pages fluttered back down to her stomach while her hand flew to her throat. "Good God, Booth. I hope you're up on your CPR, because my heart just stopped."

"I'll get it started again." Placing a hand on either side of her head, he leaned down and kissed her—softly, slowly, thoroughly. As surprised by the texture of the kiss as she'd been by his sudden appearance, Ariel lay still and absorbed. She knew only that something was different; but with her mind spinning and her blood pumping she couldn't grab on to it.

He knew. As he eased down to sit on the bed and prolonged the kiss, Booth understood precisely what was different. He loved her. He'd awakened alone in his own bed that morning, reaching for her. He'd read something foolish in the paper and had automatically thought how she'd have laughed. He'd seen a young girl with a balloon giggling as she'd dragged her mother toward the park. And he'd thought of Ariel.

And thinking of her, he'd seen that the sky was beautiful and blue, that the city was frantic and full of surprises, that life was a joy. How foolish he'd been to resist her, and all she offered.

She was his second chance…. No, if he were honest, he'd admit that Ariel was his first chance at real happiness— complete happiness. He was no longer going to allow memories of ugliness to bar him from that, or from her.

"How's your heart rate?" he murmured.

Ariel let out a long breath, let her eyes open slowly. "You can cancel the ambulance."

He glanced at the tumbled bed, then down her very sedate, very appealing costume. "Were you having a nap?"

"I," she countered primly, "was working. The rest of the cast is at lunch, I wasn't due in till one." She pushed at the hair that fell dark and disordered over his brow. No tension, she thought immediately, and smiled. "What're you doing here? You're usually knee-deep in brilliant phrases this time of day."

"I wanted to see you."

"That's nice." Sitting up, she threw her arms around his neck. "That's very nice."

It would take so little, Booth mused as he held her close. What would her reaction be when he told her that he'd stopped resisting, and that nothing had ever made him happier than having her in his life? Tonight, he thought, nuzzling into her neck. Tonight when they were alone, when there was no one to disturb them, he'd tell her. And he'd ask her.

"Can you stay awhile?" Ariel didn't know why she felt so wonderful, nor did she want to explore the reasons.

"I'll stay until you wrap, then I'm going to steal you and take you home with me."

She laughed, and as she shifted her weight, the script crumpled beneath her.

"Your lines," Booth warned.

"I know them. This—" she flung back her head so that her eyes glittered "—is a climactic scene full of danger and drama."

He looked back at the bed. "And sex?"

"No!" Shoving him away she scrambled onto her knees. "Amanda's tossing and turning in bed, her dreams were disturbed. Fade out—soft focus—she's wandering through a mist, lost, alone. She hears footsteps behind her. Close-up. Fear. And then…" While her voice took on a dramatic pitch, she tossed her hair behind her back. "Up ahead, she sees a figure in the fog." Ariel lifted a hand as if to brush away a curtain of mist. "Should she run toward it—away from it? The footsteps behind her come faster, her breathing quickens. A sliver of moonlight—pale, eerie—cuts through. It's Griff up ahead holding out a hand to her, calling her name in an echoing, disembodied voice. He loves her, she wants to go to him. But the footsteps are closing in. And as she begins to run, there's the sharp, cruel glimmer of a knife."

Ariel grabbed both of his shoulders then did a mock faint into his lap. Booth grinned. A quick tug of her hair had her eyes opening. "And then?"

"The man wants more." Scrambling up again, Ariel pushed the script aside. "The scream's caught in her throat, and before she can free it, there's a crash, a splinter of glass. Amanda jerks up in bed, her face glistening with sweat, her breath heaving." When she demonstrated, Booth wondered if she knew just how clever she was. "Did she dream it, or did she really hear it? Frightened, but impatient with herself, she gets out of bed."

Swinging her feet to the floor, Ariel got out of bed, frowning at the door as Amanda would do, absently pushing back her hair and reaching for the low light beside the bed. "Perhaps it was the wind," she continued. "Perhaps it was the dream, but she knows she'll never get back to sleep unless she takes a look. Music builds—lots of bass—as she opens the bedroom door. Cut to commercial."

"Come on, Ariel." Exasperated, he grabbed her hand and pulled her back toward the bed.

Obligingly she circled his neck with her arms as she stood in front of him. "Now you'll learn the best way to keep that shine on your no-wax floor."

He pinched her, hard. "It's the Ripper."

"Maybe," she said with a flutter of her lashes. "Maybe not."

"It's the Ripper," he said decisively. "And our intrepid Amanda goes downstairs. How does she get out of being victim number five?"

"Six," Ariel corrected. "The saying goes, that's for me to know and you to find out." With a jerk of his wrist, he'd whipped her around so that she tumbled into his lap, laughing. "Go ahead, torture me, do your worst. I'll never talk." Linking her hands around his neck, she looked up at him and smiled. And she was so beautiful, so full of life at its best that she took his breath away.

"I love you, Ariel."

He felt the fingers at his neck go limp, saw the smile fade, her eyes widen. Inside, Ariel felt as though someone had just cut off the flow of blood from her heart. "That's a tough way to find out a plotline," she managed after a moment. She would have sat up if she'd had the strength to resist the gentle pressure of his hand on her shoulder.

"I love you, Ariel," he repeated, forgetting all his plans for telling her with finesse and with intimacy. "I think I always have. I know I always will." He cupped her face in his hand as her eyes filled. "You're everything I've ever wanted and was afraid to hope for. Stay with me." He touched his lips to hers and felt the tremor. "Marry me."

When he would have drawn back, she clutched at his shirt. Burying her face in his shoulder she took a deep breath. "Be sure," she whispered. "Booth, be absolutely sure because I'll never give you a moment's peace. I'll never let you get away. Before you ask me again, remember that. I don't believe in mutual disagreements or irreconcilable differences. With me, it's forever, Booth. It's for always."

He forced her head back. In his eyes she saw the fire and the passion. And the love. "You're damn right." Her breathless laugh was muffled against his mouth. "I want to get married quickly." He punctuated the words with another kiss. "And quietly. Just how soon can they shoot around Amanda so we can have more than a weekend honeymoon?"

Ariel hadn't known anyone could outpace her. Now, her thoughts jumbled as she struggled to keep up. Marriage—he was already talking of marriage and honeymoons. "Well, I, let's see… After Griff saves Amanda from the Ripper, she loses the baby and goes into a coma. The hospital scenes could be—"

"Aha." With a self-satisfied smile, Booth kissed her nose. "So Griff saves her from the Ripper, which removes him from the list of suspects."

Ariel's eyes narrowed. "You rat."

"Just be glad I'm not a spy for another network. You're a pushover."

"I'll show you a pushover," Ariel claimed, and overbalanced him so that he landed on his back. He loved her. The thought brought on such giddiness, she collapsed against him, laughing. Before he could retaliate, they heard someone rushing up the stairs.

"Ariel! Ariel, you'd better take a look at—" Stella skidded to a halt when she saw Ariel and Booth laughing and half lying on the bed. She whipped the paper she held behind her back and swore under her breath. "Whoops!" With the aid of an embarrassed smile she called on all her skill to keep either of them from noticing that she felt slightly ill inside and desperately worried. "Well, I'd've knocked if you'd bothered to close the door." She gestured with her free hand toward the false wall. "Suppose I go out and come in again?" *Right after I burn this paper,* she thought grimly, and grinning, backed up.

"Don't go." Ariel struggled all the way up, but kept one hand tucked into Booth's. "I'm about to bestow a singularly great honor on you." She squeezed Booth's fingers. "My sister, however rotten, should be the first to know."

"By all means."

"Stella…" Ariel stopped because she caught a glimpse of something in her friend's eyes. A glimpse was enough. "What is it?"

"Nothing. I remembered I have to talk to Neal about something, that's all. Look, I'd better catch him before he—"

But Ariel was already rising from the bed. "What was it you wanted me to see, Stella?"

"Oh, nothing." There was a warning, a deliberate one, in her eyes. "It can wait."

Unsmiling, Ariel held out her hand, palm up.

Stella's fingers curled tighter around the paper. "Ariel, it's not a good time. I think you'd better—"

"I think I'd better see it now."

"Damn it." With a glance over Ariel's shoulder at Booth, Stella passed her the paper.

Celebrity Explorer, Ariel noted with a slight flicker of annoyance. As tabloids went it was bottom of the barrel. Half-amused, she glanced over the exploitive headlines. "Really, Stella, if this is the best you can do for lunchtime reading, I'm disillusioned." Absently, she turned it over and scanned under the fold. From behind her Booth saw the tension shoot into her body.

SOAP OPERA QUEEN'S DESPERATE BATTLE

FOR LOVE CHILD

Below the bold print headline was a grainy picture of Ariel sitting on the grass in Central Park with Scott's face caught in her hands. In one part of her mind she remembered that frozen moment from their last Sunday afternoon. As she stared at it, appalled, sickened, she didn't hear Booth rise and come to her.

Something slammed into his stomach—not a hammer but a fist that thrust then ground deep. Even the poor quality of the photo didn't disguise the stunning resemblance between Ariel and the child that laughed into her face. There was no mistaking the tie of blood. As the headline shouted out at him, Booth wanted to murder.

"Just what the hell is this?"

Shaken, Ariel looked up. Scott was not to see it, she thought over and over. This was not to touch him. How? How had it leaked? The Andersons? No, she rejected that thought instantly. They wanted publicity less than she did.

The picture…who'd taken it? Someone had followed her, she decided. Someone had followed her and found out about Scott, the custody hearing. Then they'd twisted it into an ugly headline and an exploitive article. But who…?

Liz Hunter. Ariel's fingers tightened on the newspaper. Of course, it had to be. There were few women who knew better than Ariel what that type of person was capable of. Liz hadn't been able to get to her professionally, so she'd taken the next step.

"Ariel, I asked you what the hell this is."

Ariel focused on Booth abruptly. *Oh God,* she thought, *now I have to work my way through the ugliness before I can explain.* Already, she saw the anger, the distrust. "I'd like to talk to you privately," she said calmly enough. "Down in my dressing room."

As Ariel turned to go, Stella reached out, then dropped her hand helplessly back to her side. "Ariel, I'm sorry."

She only shook her head. "No, it's all right. We'll talk later."

As they wound their way through the studio, down the corridors, she tried to think logically. All she could see was that nasty headline and grainy picture. When she walked into the dressing room she went directly to the coffeepot, needing to do something with her hands. She heard the door close and the lock click.

"This isn't the way I wanted to handle this, Booth." She pulled in a deep breath as she fumbled with the coffee. "I didn't expect any publicity…I've been so careful."

"Yes, careful." He jammed his hands into his pockets.

She pressed her lips together as the tone of his voice pricked along her skin. "I know you must have questions. If I…"

"Yes, I have questions." He snatched the paper from her

dressing table. He, too, needed to occupy his hands. "Are you involved in a custody suit?"

"Yes."

He felt the grinding in his stomach again. "So much for trust."

"No, Booth." She whirled around, then stopped as a hundred conflicting emotions, a hundred opposing answers hammered at her. Would this be the time of choice? Would she have to choose after all, when she almost had everything she needed? "Please, let me explain. Let me think how to explain."

"You're involved in a custody suit." He remembered those brief flashes of strain he'd seen in her from time to time. He wanted to tear the paper to shreds. "You have this child, and you didn't tell me. What does that say about trust?"

Confused, she dragged a hand through her hair. "Booth, I was already deeply involved in this before we even met. I couldn't drag you into it."

Bitterness seeped into him. Booth hated to taste it…again. "Oh, I see. You were already involved, so it was none of my business. It appears that you have two separate standards for your trust, Ariel. The one for yourself, and the one for everyone else."

"That's not true," she began, then fumbled to a halt. Was it? "I don't mean for it to be." Her voice began to shake, then her hands. "Booth, I've been frightened. Part of the fear was that something would leak out. The most important thing to me was that none of this touch Scott."

He waited, trying to be impassive as she brushed away the first tear. "That's the boy's name?"

"Yes. He's only four years old."

He turned away because the grief on her face was destroying him. "And his father?"

"His father's name was Jeremy. He's dead."

Booth didn't ask if she'd loved him. He didn't have to. She'd loved another man, he thought. Had borne another man's child. Could he deal with that, accept it? Resting his palms on her dressing table he let the emotion run through him. Yes, he thought so. It didn't change her, or him. And yet…and yet she hadn't told him. It was that that brought the change.

"Who has the boy now?" he asked stiffly.

"His grandparents. He's not…he's not happy with them. He needs me, Booth, and I need him. I need both of you. Please…" Her voice lowered to a whisper. "Don't ask me to choose. I love you. I love you so much but he's just a little boy."

"Choose?" Booth flicked on his lighter, then tossed it onto her cluttered dressing table as he took the first drag from his cigarette. "Damn it, Ariel, just how insensitive do you think I am?"

She waited until she could control the throb of her heart at the base of her throat. "Would you take both of us?"

Booth blew out smoke. Fury was just below the surface. "You kept it from me. That's the issue now. I could hardly turn away from a child that's part of you."

She reached for him. "Booth—"

"You kept it from me," he repeated, watching her hand drop away. "Why?"

"Please understand, if I kept it from you it was only because I wanted to protect him. He's had a difficult time already, and I was afraid that if I talked about the hearing to anyone, anyone at all, there was a risk of something like that." She gestured to the paper, then turned away.

"There's nothing you don't know about my life, Ariel. I can't help but resent that there was something so vital to yours that you kept from me. All this time, almost from the first minute, you've asked me to trust you. Now that I've given that to you, I find you haven't trusted me."

"I put Scott first. He needed someone to put him first."

"I might be able to understand that, if you could explain to me why you ever gave him up."

"Gave him up?" Ariel stared, but tears blurred her vision. "I don't know what you mean."

"I thought I knew you!" Booth exploded. "I believed that, and believing it fell in love with you when I'd sworn I'd never get emotionally involved again. How could you give up your child? How could you have a child and say nothing to me?"

"Give up my child?" she repeated dumbly. "But no, no! It's nothing like that."

"Damn it, Ariel, you've let someone else raise your child. And now that you want him back, now that you're involved in something as serious as a custody battle, you do it alone. How could you love me, how could you preach trust at me and say nothing?"

"I was afraid to tell you or anyone. You don't understand how it might affect Scott if he knew—"

"Or how it might affect you?" He swung his arm toward the discarded paper.

Ariel sucked in her breath and barely controlled a raging denial. Perhaps she'd deserved that. "My concern was for Scott," she said evenly. "A custody suit would hardly damage my reputation. Any more than an illegitimate child would— though he's not my child. Jeremy was my brother."

It was Booth's turn to stare. Nothing made sense. Underlying his confusion was the thought that tears didn't belong in Ariel's eyes. Her eyes were for laughter. "The boy's your nephew?"

"Jeremy and his wife died late last winter." She couldn't go to him now; she could see he wasn't ready. And neither was she. "His grandparents, the Andersons, were appointed guardians. He's not happy with them."

Not her child, Booth thought again, but her brother's child. He waited to gauge his own reaction and found he was still hurt, still angry. Whether the boy was her son or not hadn't been the issue. She'd blocked that part of her life from him.

"I think," Booth said slowly, "that you'd better start at the beginning."

Ariel opened her mouth, but before she could speak, someone pounded on her door. "Phone for you, Ariel, in Neal's office. Urgent."

Banking back frustration, she left the room, heading for Neal's office. So much to explain, she thought. To Booth and to herself. She rubbed her temple with two fingers as she picked up the phone. "Hello."

"Ms. Kirkwood."

"Yes, this is Ariel Kirkwood." Her frown deepened. "Mr. Anderson?"

"Scott's missing."

Chapter Twelve

She said nothing. Only seconds passed, but a hundred thoughts raced through her mind, tumbling over each other one at a time so that none was clear. Every nerve in her stomach froze. Vaguely she felt the ache in her hand where she gripped the receiver.

"Ms. Kirkwood, I said that Scott is missing."

"Missing?" she repeated in a whisper. The word itself brought up too many visions. Terrifying ones. She wanted to panic, but forced herself, by digging her nails into her palm, to talk, and to listen carefully. But even the whisper she forced out shook. "How long?"

"Apparently since around eleven o'clock. My wife thought he was next door, playing with a neighbor's child. When she called him home for lunch, she learned he'd never been there."

Eleven… With a sick kind of dread Ariel looked at her watch. It was nearly two. Three hours. Where could a small boy go in three hours? Anywhere. It was an eternity. "You've called the police?"

"Of course." His voice was brisk but through it ran a thread of fear Ariel was too dazed to hear. "The neighborhood's been searched, people questioned. Everything possible's being done."

Everything possible? What did that mean? She repeated the phrase over in her mind, but it still didn't make sense. "Yes, of course." She heard her own words come hollowly through the rushing noise in her head. "I'll be there right away."

"No, the police suggest that you go home and stay there, in case Scott contacts you."

Home, she thought. They wanted her to go home and do nothing while Scott was missing. "I want to come. I could be there in thirty minutes." The whisper shattered into a desperate plea. "I could help look for him. I could—"

"Ms. Kirkwood," Anderson cut her off, then breathed deeply before he continued. "Scott's an intelligent boy. He knows where you live, he knows your phone number. At a time like this it's best to admit that it's you he wants to be with. If he— If it's possible for him to contact anyone, it would be you. Please, go home. If he's found here, I'll call you immediately."

The single phrase ran through her mind three times. *If it's possible for him to contact anyone...*

"All right. I'll go home. I'll wait there." Dazed, she stared at the phone, not even aware that she'd replaced the receiver herself. Marveling that she could walk at all, she moved to the door.

Of course she could walk, Ariel told herself as she pressed a hand to the wall for support. She could function—she had to function. Scott was going to want her when he was found. He'd be full of stories and adventures—especially if he had the chance to ride in a police car. He'd want to tell her about all of it. The phone would probably be ringing when she opened her front door. He'd probably just been daydreaming and wandered a few blocks away, that was all. They'd be calling, so she should get home quickly. Her legs felt like rubber and would hardly move at all.

Booth was brooding at the picture of Ariel and Scott when he heard the door open. He turned, the paper still in his hand, but the questions that had been pressing at him faded the moment he saw her. Her skin was like parchment. He'd never seen her eyes look vacant, nor had he expected to.

"Ariel…" He was crossing to her before he'd finished speaking her name. "What is it?"

"Booth." She put her hand on his chest. Warm, solid. She could feel the beat of his heart. No, none of it was a dream. Or a nightmare. "Scott's missing. They don't know where he is. He's missing."

He took a firm hold on her shoulders. "How long, Ariel?"

"Three hours." The first wave of fear rammed through the shock. "Oh God, no one's seen him in three hours. Nobody knows where he is!"

He only tightened his hold on her shoulders when her body began to shake. "The police?"

"Yes, yes, they're looking." Her fingers curled, digging at his shirt. "They don't want me to come, they want me to go home and wait in case he…Booth."

"I'll take you home." He brushed the hair away from her face. His touch, his voice, was meant to soothe. "We'll go home and wait for the call. They're going to find him, Ariel. Little boys wander off all the time."

"Yes." She grabbed on to that, and to his hand. Of course that was true. Didn't she have to watch him like a hawk when they went to the park or the zoo? "Scott daydreams a lot. He could've just walked farther than he should. They're going to call me…I should be home."

"I'm going to take you." Booth kept hold of her as she took a disoriented study of the room. "You change, and I'll let them know you can't tape this afternoon."

"Change?" Puzzled she looked down and saw she still wore Amanda's nightshirt. "All right, I'll hurry. They could call any minute."

She tried to hurry, but her fingers kept fumbling with the most basic task. She needed her jeans, but her mind seemed to fade in and out as she pulled them on. Then her fingers slid over the snap. She tried to think logically but the pounding at the side of her head made it impossible. Holding off the nausea helped. It gave her something tangible to concentrate on while she fought with the laces of her shoes.

Booth was back within moments. When she turned to look at him he could feel her panic. "Ready?"

"Yes." She nodded and walked out with him, one foot in front of the other, while images of Scott, lost, frightened, streamed through her head. Or worse, much worse—Scott getting into a car with a stranger, a stranger whose face was only a shadow. She wanted to scream. She climbed into a cab.

Booth took her icy hand in his. "Ariel, it isn't like you to anticipate the worst. Think." He put his other hand over hers and tried to warm it. "There're a hundred harmless reasons for his being out of touch for a few hours. He might've found a dog, or chased a ball. He might've found some fascinating rock and taken it to a secret place to study it."

"Yes." She tried to picture those things. It would be typical of Scott. The image of the car and the stranger kept intruding. He had no basic fear of people, something she'd always admired in him. Now it filled her with fear. Turning her face in to Booth's shoulder she tried to convince herself that the phone would be ringing when she opened the front door.

When the cab stopped, she jerked upright and scrambled for the handle. She was dashing up the steps before Booth had paid the driver.

Silence. It greeted her like an accusation. Ariel stared at the phone and willed it to ring. When she looked at her watch, she saw it had been less than thirty minutes since Anderson's call. Not enough time, she told herself as she began to pace. *Too much time.* Too much time for a little boy to be alone.

Do something! The words ran through her mind as she struggled to find something solid to grip on to. She'd always been able to do something in any situation. There were answers, and if not answers, choices. But to wait. To have no answer, no choice but to wait… She heard the door close and turned. Her hands lifted, then fell helplessly.

"Booth. Oh God, I don't know what to do. There must be something—anything."

Without a word he crossed to her, wrapped his arms around her and let her cling to him. Strange that it would have taken this—something so frightening for her—to make him realize she needed him every bit as much as he needed her. Whatever doubts he'd had, and whatever anger had lingered that she'd kept part of her life from him, dropped away. Love was simpler than he'd ever imagined.

"Sit down, Ariel." As he spoke, he eased her toward a chair. "I'm going to fix you a drink."

"No, I—"

"Sit down," he repeated with a firmness he knew she needed. "I'll make coffee, or I'll see about getting you a sedative."

"I don't need a sedative."

He nodded, rewarded by the sharp, quick answer. If she was angry, just a little angry, she wouldn't fall apart. "Then I'll make coffee."

The moment he went into the kitchen she was up again. Sitting was impossible, calm out of the question. She should never have agreed to come back and wait, Ariel told herself. She should have insisted on going out and looking for Scott herself. It was useless here—she was useless here. But if he called and she wasn't there to answer... Oh, God. She pressed her hands to her face and tried not to crumble. What time was it?

This time when she looked at her watch she felt the first hysterical sob build.

"Ariel." Booth carried two cups of coffee, hot and strong. He watched as she shuddered, swallowing sobs, but the tears ran freely.

"Booth, where could he be? He's hardly more than a baby. He doesn't have any fear of strangers. It's my fault because—"

"Stop." He said the word softly, but it had the effect of cutting off the rapidly tumbling words. He held out the cup, waiting for her to take it in both hands. It shook, nearly spilling the coffee over the rim. As it depleted, she sat again. "Tell me about him."

For a moment she stared at the coffee, as if she had no idea what it was or how she'd come to be holding it. "He's four...almost five. He wants a wagon, a yellow one, for his birthday. He likes to pretend." Lifting the cup, she swallowed coffee, and as it scalded her mouth, she calmed a bit. "Scott has a wonderful imagination. You can give him a cardboard box and he'll see a spaceship, a submarine, an Egyptian tomb. Really see it, do you know what I mean?"

"Yes." He laid a hand on hers as he sat beside her.

"When Jeremy and Barbara died, he was so lost. They were beautiful together, the three of them. So happy."

Her eyes were drawn to the boxing gloves that hung behind the door. Jeremy's gloves. They'd be Scott's one day. Something ripped inside her stomach. Ariel began to talk faster. "He's a lot like his father, the same charm and curiosity. The Andersons, Barbara's parents, never approved of Jeremy. They didn't want Barbara to marry him, and rarely saw her after she did. After...after the accident, they were appointed Scott's guardians. I wanted him, but it seemed natural that he go with them. A house, a yard, a family. But..." Breaking off, she cast a desperate look at the phone.

"But?" Booth prompted.

"They just aren't capable of understanding the kind of person Scott is. He'll pretend he's an archeologist and dig a hole in their yard."

"That might annoy anyone," Booth said and drew a wan smile from her.

"But he wouldn't dig up the yard if he had a sand dump and someone told him it could be a desert. Instead, he's punished for his imagination rather than having it redirected."

"So you decided to fight for him."

"Yes." Ariel moistened her lips. Had she waited too long? "Even if that were all, I might not have started proceedings. They don't love him." Her eyes shimmered as she looked up again. "They just feel responsible for him. I can't bear thinking he could grow up without all the love he should have."

Where is he, where is he, where is he?

"He won't." Booth drew her against him to kiss the tears at the corners of her eyes. "After you get custody, we'll see that he doesn't."

Cautiously, she pulled back, though her fingers were still tight on his shoulders. "We?"

Booth lifted a brow. "Is Scott part of your life?"

"Yes, he—"

"Then he's part of mine."

Her mouth trembled open twice before she could speak. "No questions?"

"I've wasted a lot of time with questions. Sometimes there's no need for them." He pressed her fingers to his lips. "I love you."

"Booth, I'm so afraid." Her head dropped against him. The dam burst.

He let her weep, those harsh sobs that were edged with grief and fear. He let her hold on and pull out whatever strength she could find in him. He lived by words, but knew when clever phrases were of no use. So in silence, Booth held her.

Crying would help, he thought, smoothing her hair. It would allow her to give in to fear without putting a name on it. While she was vulnerable to tears, it was he who willed the phone to ring. And he was denied.

The passion exhausted her. Ariel lay against Booth, light-headed, disoriented, only aware of that hollow ache inside that meant something vital was wrong. Her mind groped for the reason. *Scott.* He was missing. The phone hadn't rung. He was still missing.

"Time," she murmured, staring over his shoulder at the phone through eyes that were swollen and abused by tears. "What time is it now?"

"It's nearly four," he answered, hating to tell her, hating the convulsive jerk he felt because her body was pressed so close to his. There were a dozen things he could say to offer comfort. All useless. "I'll make more coffee."

At the knock on the door, she looked around listlessly. She wanted no company now. Ignoring the knock, she turned her back to the door. It was the phone that was important. "I'll get the coffee." Forcing herself to move, she rose. "I don't want to see anyone, please."

"I'll send them away." Booth walked to the door, already prepared to position himself in front of it to shield her. When he opened it, he saw a young woman wearing a bandanna and paint-smeared overalls. Then he saw the boy.

"Excuse me. This little boy was wandering a couple blocks from here. He gave this address. I wonder if—"

"Who are you?" Scott demanded of Booth. "This is Ariel's house."

"I'm Booth. Ariel's been waiting for you, Scott."

Scott grinned, showing small white teeth. Baby teeth, Booth realized. He's hardly more than a baby. "I would've been here sooner, but I got a little lost. Bobbi was painting her porch and said she'd walk me over."

Booth laid a hand on Scott's head and felt the softness of hair—like Ariel's. "We're very grateful to you, Miss…"

"Freeman, Bobbi Freeman." She grinned and jerked her head toward Scott. "No trouble. He might've lost his way a bit, but he sure knows what he wants. It seems to be Ariel and a peanut butter sandwich. Well, hey, I've got to get back to my porch. See you later, Scott."

"Bye, Bobbi." He yawned hugely. "Is Ariel home now?"

"I'll get her." Leaving Scott to climb onto the hammock, Booth walked toward the kitchen. He stopped Ariel in the doorway then took the two cups from her hands. "There's someone here to see you."

She shut her eyes. "Oh, please, Booth. Not now."

"I don't think he'll take no for an answer."

Something in his tone had her opening her eyes again, had

her heart drumming against her ribs. Skirting passed him, she hurried into the living room. A small blond boy swung happily in her hammock with two kittens in his lap. "Oh, God, Scott!"

His arms were already reaching for her as she dashed across the room and yanked him against her. Warmth. She could feel the warmth of his small body and moaned from the joy of it. His rumpled hair brushed against her face. She could smell the faintest memory of soap from his morning wash, mixed with the sweat of the day and the gumdrops he was forever secreting in his pockets. Weeping, laughing, she sank to the floor holding him.

"Scott, oh, Scott. You're not hurt?" The quick fear struck at her again and she pulled him away to examine his face, his hands, his arms. "Are you hurt anywhere?"

"Uh-uh." A bit miffed at the question, Scott squirmed. "I didn't see Butch yet. Where's Butch?"

"How did you get here?" Ariel grabbed him again and gave in to the need to kiss his face—the rounded cheeks, the straight little nose, the small mouth. "Scott, where've you been?"

"On the train." His whole face lit. "I rode on the train all by myself. For a surprise."

"You…" Incredulous, Ariel stared at him. "You came from your grandparents', all alone?"

"I saved up my money." With no little pride he reached in his pocket and pulled out what he had left—a few pennies, two quarters and some gumdrops. "I walked to the station, but it took lots longer than a cab does. It isn't as far in a cab," he decided with a small boy's logic. "And I paid for the ticket all by myself—just like you showed me. I'm hungry, Ariel."

"In a minute." Appalled at the idea of his traveling alone and defenseless, she took both his arms. "You walked all the way to the train station, then rode the train here?"

"And I only got a little bit lost once, when Bobbi helped me. And I was hardly scared at all." His lip trembled. Screwing up his face, he buried it against her. "I wasn't."

All the things that might have happened to him flashed hideously through her mind. Ariel tightened her hold and thanked God. "Of course you weren't," she murmured, struggling to hold on to her emotions until she'd both schooled and scolded. "You're so brave, and so smart to remember the way. But Scott—" she tilted his face to hers "—it was wrong for you to come here all alone."

"But I wanted to see you."

"I know, and I always want to see you." Again she kissed him, just to feel the warmth of his cheek. "But you left without telling your grandparents, and they're so worried. And I've been worried," she added, brushing the hair from his temple. "You have to promise you won't ever do it again."

"I don't want to do it again." With his mouth trembling again, he rubbed his fists against his eyes. "It took a long time and I got hungry, and then I got lost and my legs were so tired. But I wasn't scared."

"It's all right now, baby." Still holding him, she rose. "We'll fix you something to eat, then you can rest in the hammock. Okay?"

Scott sniffled, snuggling closer. "Can I have peanut butter?"

"Absolutely." Booth came back into the room and watched as both heads turned toward him. He might be her own child, he thought, wonderingly. Surprised, he felt a yearning to hold the boy himself. "I just saw a peanut butter sandwich in the kitchen. I think it's yours."

"Okay!" Scott scrambled out of Ariel's arms and bounced away.

Getting unsteadily to her feet, Ariel pressed the heel of her hand to her brow. "I could skin him alive. Oh, Booth," she whispered as she felt his arms go around her. "Isn't he wonderful?"

By dusk, Scott was asleep, with a tattered stuffed dog that had been his father's gripped in one hand. The three-legged Butch kept guard on the pillow beside him. Ariel sat on the sofa next to Booth and faced Scott's grandfather. Coffee grew cold on the table between them. As always, Mr. Anderson sat erect; his clothes were impeccable. But there was a weariness in his eyes Ariel had never seen before.

"Anything might've happened to the boy on a jaunt like that."

"I know." Ariel slipped her hand into Booth's, grateful for the support. "I've made him promise he won't ever do anything like it again. You and your wife must've been sick with worry. I'm sorry, Mr. Anderson. I feel partially to blame because I've let Scott buy the train tickets before."

He shook his head, not speaking for a moment. "An intrepid boy," he managed at length. "Sharp enough to know which train to take, when to get off." His eyes focused on Ariel's again. "He wanted badly to be with you."

Normally the statement would have warmed her. Now, it tightened the already sensitive muscles of her stomach. "Yes. Children often don't understand the consequences of their actions, Mr. Anderson. Scott only thought about coming, not about the hours of panic in between or about the dangers. He was tired and frightened when he got here. I hope you won't punish him too severely."

Anderson took a deep breath and rested a hand on either thigh. "I realized something today, Ms. Kirkwood. I resent that boy."

"Oh, no, Mr. Anderson—"

"Please, let me finish. I resent him, and I don't like knowing that about myself." His voice was clipped, unapologetic and, Ariel realized, old. Not so much in years, she thought, but in attitude. "And more, I've realized that his presence in the house is a constant strain on my wife. He's a reminder of something we lost. I'm not going to justify my feelings to you," he added briskly. "The boy is my grandchild, and therefore, I'm responsible for him. However, I'm an old man, and not inclined to change. I don't want the boy, and you do." He rose while Ariel could only stare at him. "I'll notify my attorney of my feelings on the matter."

"Mr. Anderson." Shaken, Ariel rose. "You know I want Scott, but—"

"I don't, Ms. Kirkwood." With his shoulders straight, Anderson gave her a level look. "It's as basic as that."

And as sad. "I'm sorry" was all she could say.

With a nod only, he left.

"How," Ariel began after a stretch of silence, "could anyone feel that way about a child?"

"About the child?" Booth countered. "Or about themselves?"

She turned to him, puzzled only for a moment. "Yes, that's it, isn't it?"

"I'm an expert on the subject. The difference is—" he drew her down to him again, circling her with his arm so that her head rested against his shoulder "—someone pushed her way into my life and made me see it."

"Is that what I did?" She laughed, riding the next curve on the roller coaster the day had been. Scott was sleeping on her bed, with kittens curled at his feet. He could stay there now. No more tearful goodbyes. "Pushed my way into your life?"

"You can be very tenacious." He gave her hair a sharp tug then captured her mouth as she gasped. "Thank God."

"Should I warn you that once I push my way in, I won't ever get out?"

"No." He shifted so that she could sit across his lap, and he could watch her face. "Let me find out for myself."

"It won't be easy for you, you know."

"What?"

"Dealing with me if you decide to marry me."

His brow rose, and unable to resist, she traced it with a fingertip. "If?"

"I'm giving you your last chance for escape." Half-serious, Ariel pressed her palm to his cheek. "I do most things on impulse—eating, spending, sleeping. I much prefer living in chaos to living in order. The fact is I can't function in order at all. I'll get you involved, one way or the other, in any number of organizations."

"That one remains to be seen," Booth muttered.

Ariel only smiled. "I haven't scared you off yet?"

"No." He kissed her, and as the shadows in the room lengthened, neither of them noticed. "And you won't. I can also be tenacious."

"Remember, you'll be taking on a four-year-old child. An active one."

"You've a poor opinion of my stamina."

"Oh, no." This time when she laughed, it held a husky quality. "I'll drive you crazy with my disorganization."

"As long as you stay out of my office," he countered, "you can turn everything else into a building lot."

She tightened her arms around his neck and clung for a moment. He meant it, she told herself, giddy. He meant it all.

She had Booth, and Scott. And with them, her life was taking the next turning point. She could hardly wait to find what waited around the corner.

"I'll spoil Scott," she murmured into Booth's neck. "And the rest of our children."

He drew her back slowly, a half smile on his mouth. "How many is implied by *the rest?*"

Her laughter was free and breezy. "Pick a number."

★ ★ ★ ★ ★

Untamed

❧

For my sons,
Life's a circus.
Go for it!

Chapter One

At the crack of the whip, twelve lions stood on their haunches and pawed the air. On command, they began to leap from pedestal to pedestal in a quick, close-formation, figure-eight pattern. This required split-second timing. With voice and hand commands the trainer kept the tawny, springing bodies moving.

"Well done, Pandora."

At her name and the signal, the muscular lioness leaped to the ground and lay down on her side. One by one the others followed suit, until, snarling and baring their teeth, they stretched across the tanbark. A male was positioned beside each female; at a sharp reproof from the trainer, Merlin ceased nibbling on Ophelia's ear.

"Heads up!" They obeyed as the trainer walked briskly in front of them. The whip was tossed aside with a flourish, then, with apparent nonchalance, the trainer reclined lengthwise across the warm bodies. The center cat, a full-maned African, let out a great, echoing bellow. As a reward for his response to the cue, his ear was given a good scratching. The trainer rose from the feline couch, clapped hands and brought the lions to their feet. Then, with a hand signal, each was called by name and sent through the chute and into their cages. One stayed behind, a huge, black-maned cat who, like an ordinary tabby, circled and rubbed up against his trainer's legs.

Deftly, a rope was attached to a chain that was hidden under his mane. Then, with swift agility, the trainer mounted the lion's back. As the door of the big cage opened, lion and rider passed through for a tour of the practice ring. When they reached the back door of the ring barn, Merlin, the obliging lion, was transferred to a wheel cage.

"Well, Duffy." Jo turned after the cage was secured. "Are we ready for the road?"

Duffy was a small, round man with a monk's fringe of chestnut hair and a face that exploded with ginger freckles. His open smile and Irish blue eyes gave him the look of an aging choirboy. His mind was sharp, shrewd and scrappy. He was the best manager Prescott's Circus Colossus could have had.

"Since we open in Ocala tomorrow," he replied in a raspy voice, "you'd better be ready." He shifted his fat cigar stump from the right side of his mouth to the left.

Jo merely smiled, then stretched to loosen muscles grown taut during the thirty minutes in the cage. "My cats are ready, Duffy. It's been a long winter. They need to get back on the road as much as the rest of us."

Duffy frowned. As circumstances had it, he stood only inches higher than his animal trainer. Widely spaced, almond-shaped eyes stared back at him. They were as sharp and green as emeralds, surrounded by thick, inky lashes. At the moment they were fearless and amused, but Duffy had seen them frightened, vulnerable and lost. He shifted his cigar again and took two quick puffs as Jo gave a cage hand instructions.

He remembered Steve Wilder, Jo's father. He had been one

of the best cat men in the business. Jo was as good with the cats as Wilder had been. In some ways, Duffy acknowledged, even better. But she had the traits of her mother: delicate build; dark, passionate looks. Jolivette Wilder was as slender as her aerialist mother had been, with bold green eyes and straight, raven black hair that fell to just below her waist. Her brows were delicately arched, her nose small and straight, her cheekbones high and elegant, while her mouth was full and soft. Her skin was tawny from the Florida sun; it added to her gypsy-like appearance. Confidence added spark to the beauty.

Finishing her instructions, Jo tucked her arm through Duffy's. She had seen that frown before. "Somebody quit?" she asked as they began to walk toward Duffy's office.

"Nope."

His monosyllabic reply caused Jo to lift a brow. It was not often Duffy answered any question briefly. Years of experience told her to hold her tongue as they moved across the compound.

Rehearsals were going on everywhere. Vito the wire walker informally sharpened his act on a cable stretched between two trees. The Mendalsons called out to each other as they tossed their juggling pins high in the air, while the equestrian act led their horses into the ring barn. She saw one of the Stevenson girls walking on stilts. She'd be six now, Jo mused, tossing the hair from her eyes as she watched the young girl's wavering progress. Jo remembered the year she had been born. It had been that same year that she had been allowed to work the big cage alone. She had been sixteen, and it had been another full year before she had been permitted to work an audience.

For Jo, there had never been any home but the circus. She had been born during the winter break, had been tucked into her parents' trailer the following spring to spend her first year and each subsequent one of her life thereafter on the road. She had inherited both her fascination and her flair with animals from her father, her style and grace of movement from her mother. Though she had lost both parents fifteen years before, they continued to influence her. Their legacy to her had been a world of restlessness, a world of fantasies. She had grown up playing with lion cubs, riding elephants, wearing spangles and traveling like a gypsy.

Jo glanced down at a cluster of daffodils growing by the side of Prescott's winter office and smiled. She remembered planting them when she had been thirteen and in love with a tumbler. She remembered, too, the man who had stooped beside her, offering advice on bulb planting and broken hearts. As Jo thought of Frank Prescott, her smile grew sad.

"I still can't believe he's gone," she murmured as she and Duffy moved inside.

Duffy's office was sparsely furnished with a wooden desk, metal filing cabinets and two spindly chairs. A collage of posters adorned the walls. They promised the amazing, the astounding, the incredible: elephants that danced, men who flew through the air, beautiful girls who spun by their teeth, raging tigers that rode horseback. Tumblers, clowns, lions, strong men, fat ladies, boys who could balance on their forefingers; they brought the magic of the circus into the drab little room.

As Jo glanced over at a narrow pine door, Duffy followed her gaze. "I keep expecting him to come busting through there with some crazy new idea," he mumbled as he began to fiddle with his prize possession, an automatic coffeemaker.

"Do you?" With a sigh Jo straddled a chair, then rested her chin on its back. "We all miss him. It's not going to seem the same without him this year." She looked up suddenly, and her eyes were angry. "He wasn't an old man, Duffy. Heart attacks should be for old men." She brooded into space, touched again with the injustice of Frank Prescott's death.

He had been barely into his fifties and full of laughter and simple kindness. Jo had loved him and trusted him without reservation. At his death she had grieved for him more acutely than she had for her own parents. In her longest memory he had been the core of her life.

"It's been nearly six months," Duffy said gruffly as he studied her face. When Jo glanced up, he stuck out a mug of coffee.

"I know." She took the mug, letting it warm her hands in the chilly March morning. Resolutely, she shook off the mood. Frank would not have wanted to leave sadness behind. Jo studied the coffee, then sipped. It was predictably dreadful. "Rumor has it we're following last year's route to the letter. Thirteen states." Jo smiled, watching Duffy wince over his coffee before he downed it. "Not superstitious, are you?" She grinned, knowing he kept a four-leaf clover in his billfold.

"Pah!" he said indignantly, coloring under his freckles. He set down his empty cup, then moved around his desk and sat behind it. When he folded his hands on the yellow blotter, Jo knew he was getting down to business. Through the open window she could hear the band rehearsing. "We should be in Ocala by six tomorrow," he began. Dutifully, Jo nodded. "Should have the tents up before nine."

"The parade should be over by ten, and the matinee will start at two," Jo finished with a smile. "Duffy, you're not going to ask me to work the menagerie in the sideshow again, are you?"

"Should be a good crowd," he replied, adroitly skirting her question. "Bonzo predicts clear skies."

"Bonzo should stick with pratfalls and unicycles." She watched as Duffy chewed on the stub of a now dead cigar. "Okay," she said firmly, "let's have it."

"Someone's going to be joining us in Ocala, at least temporarily." He pursed his lips as his eyes met Jo's. His were blue, faded with age. "I don't know if he'll finish out the season with us."

"Oh, Duffy, not some first of mayer we have to break in this late?" Jo demanded, using the circus term for novice. "What is he, some energetic writer who wants an epic on the vanishing tent circus? He'll spend a few weeks as a roustabout and swear he knows all there is to know about it."

"I don't think he'll be working as a roustabout," Duffy muttered. Striking a match, he coaxed the cigar back to life. Jo frowned, watching the smoke struggle toward the ceiling.

"It's a bit late to work in a new act now, isn't it?"

"He's not a performer." Duffy swore lightly under his breath, then met Jo's eyes again. "He owns us."

For a moment Jo said nothing. She sat unmoving, as Duffy had seen her from time to time when she trained a young cat. "No!" She rose suddenly, shaking her head. "Not him. Not now. Why does he have to come? What does he want here?"

"It's his circus," Duffy reminded her. His voice was both rough and sympathetic.

"It'll never be his circus," Jo retorted passionately. Her eyes lit and glowed with a temper she rarely let have sway. "It's Frank's circus."

"Frank's dead," Duffy stated in a quiet, final tone. "Now the circus belongs to his son."

"Son?" Jo countered. She lifted her fingers to press them against her temple. Slowly, she moved to the window. Outside, the sun was pouring over the heads of troupers. She watched the members of the trapeze act, in thick robes worn over their tights, head toward the ring barn. The chatter of mixed languages was so familiar she failed to notice it. She placed her palms on the window sill and with a little sigh, steadied her temper. "What sort of son is it who never bothers to visit his father? In thirty years he never came to see Frank. He never wrote. He didn't even come to the funeral." Jo swallowed the tears of anger that rose to her throat and thickened her voice. "Why should he come now?"

"You've got to learn that life's a two-sided coin, kiddo," Duffy said briskly. "You weren't even alive thirty years ago. You don't know why Frank's wife up and left him or why the boy never visited."

"He's not a boy, Duffy, he's a man." Jo turned back, and he saw that she again had herself under control. "He's thirty-one, thirty-two years old now, a very successful attorney with a fancy Chicago office. He's very wealthy, did you know?" A small smile played on her lips but failed to reach her eyes. "And not just from court cases and legal fees; there's quite a lot of money on his mother's side. Nice, quiet, old money. I can't understand what a rich city lawyer would want with a tent circus."

Duffy shrugged his broad, round shoulders. "Could be he wants a tax shelter. Could be he wants to ride an elephant. Could be anything. He might want to take inventory and sell us off, piece by piece."

"Oh, Duffy, no!" Emotion flew back into Jo's face. "He couldn't do that."

"The heck he couldn't," Duffy muttered as he stubbed out his cigar. "He can do as he pleases. If he wants to liquidate, he liquidates."

"But we have contracts through October...."

"You're too smart for that, Jo." Duffy frowned, scratching his rim of hair. "He can buy them off or let them play through. He's a lawyer. He can figure the way out of a contract if he wants to. He can wait till August when we start to negotiate again and let them all lapse." Seeing Jo's distress, he backpedaled. "Listen, kiddo, I didn't say he was going to sell, I said he *could.*"

Jo ran a hand through her hair. "There must be something we can do."

"We can show a profit by the end of the season," Duffy said wryly. "We can show the new owner what we have to offer. I think it's important that he sees we're not just a mud show but a profitable three-ring circus with class acts. He should see what Frank built, how he lived, what he wanted to do. I think," Duffy added, watching Jo's face, "that you should be in charge of his education."

"Me?" Jo was too incredulous to be angry. "Why? You're better qualified in the public relations department than I am. I train lions, not lawyers." She could not keep the hint of scorn from her voice.

"You were closer to Frank than anyone. And there isn't anyone here who knows this circus better than you." Again he frowned. "And you've got brains. Never thought much use would come of all those fancy books you read, but maybe I was wrong."

"Duffy." Her lips curved into a smile. "Just because I like to read Shakespeare doesn't mean I can deal with Keane Prescott. Even thinking about him makes me furious. How will I act when I meet him face to face?"

"Well." Duffy shrugged before he pursed his lips. "If you don't think you can handle it…"

"I didn't say I *couldn't* handle it," Jo muttered.

"Of course, if you're afraid…"

"I'm not afraid of anything, and I'm certainly not afraid of some Chicago lawyer who doesn't know sawdust from tanbark." Sticking her hands in her pockets, she paced the length of the small room. "If Keane Prescott, attorney-at-law, wants to spend his summer with the circus, I'll do my best to make it a memorable one."

"Nicely," Duffy cautioned as Jo moved to the door.

"Duffy," she paused and gave him an innocent smile. "You know what a gentle touch I have." To prove it, Jo slammed the door behind her.

Dawn was hovering over the horizon as the circus caravan drew up in a large, grassy field. Colors were just a promise in a pale gray sky. In the distance was grove upon grove of orange trees. As Jo stepped from the cab of her truck, the fragrance met her. It's a perfect day, she decided, then took a long, greedy breath. To her, there was no more beautiful sight than dawn struggling to life.

The air was vaguely chilly. She zipped up her gray sweat jacket as she watched the rest of the circus troupe pouring out of their trucks and cars and trailers. The morning quiet was soon shattered by voices. Work began immediately. As the Big Top canvas was being unrolled out of the spool truck, Jo went to see how her lions had fared the fifty-mile journey.

Three handlers unloaded the traveling cages. Buck had been with Jo the longest. He had worked for her father, and during the interim between his death and Jo's professional debut, he had worked up a small act with four male lions. His shyness had made his retirement from performing a relief. To Buck, two people were a crowd. He stood six-feet-four, and his build was powerful enough for him to pad the sideshow from time to time as Hercules the Strong Man. He had an impressive head of wild blond hair and a full, curling beard. His hands were wide, with thick, strong fingers, but Jo remembered their gentleness when the two of them had delivered a lioness of a pair of cubs.

Pete's small frame seemed puny beside Buck's. He was of indeterminable age. Jo guessed between forty and fifty, but she was never certain. He was a quiet man with skin like polished mahogany and a rich, low-pitched voice. He had come to Jo five years before, asking for a job. She had never asked where he had come from, and he had never told her. He wore a fielder's cap and was never seen without a wad of gum moving gently in his teeth. He read Jo's books and was the undisputed king of the poker table.

Gerry was nineteen and eager. He was nearly six feet and still carried the lankiness of his youth. His mother sewed, and his father was a souvenir salesman, or a candy butcher, as circus jargon had it. Working the big cage was Gerry's dream, and because it had been hers, Jo had finally agreed to tutor him.

"How are my babies?" she demanded as she approached. At each cage she paused and soothed a nervous cat, calling each by name until they had settled. "They've traveled well. Hamlet's still edgy, but it's his first year on the road."

"He's a mean one," Buck muttered, watching Jo move from cage to cage.

"Yes, I know," she replied absently. "He's smart, too." She had twisted her hair into one thick braid and now tossed it to her back. "Look, here come some towners." A few cars and a smattering of bikes drew into the field.

These were the people from the outlying towns who wanted to see a Big Top raised, who wanted to see the circus, if only for a moment, from the other side. Some would watch while others would lend a hand with tent poles, stretching canvas and rigging. They would earn a show pass and an unforgettable experience.

"Keep them clear of the cages," Jo ordered, nodding to Pete before she moved toward the still flaccid canvas. Buck lumbered beside her.

The field was alive with ropes and wire and people. Six elephants were harnessed but idle, with their handlers standing by the stake line. As workers pulled on guy ropes, the dusky brown canvas billowed up like a giant mushroom.

The poles were positioned—side, quarter, center—while the canvas muffled the sounds of scrambling workers. In the east the sun was rising fast, streaking the sky with pink. There were shouted instructions from the head canvas man, laughter from adventuresome boys and an occasional oath. As the quarter poles were driven into the sag of canvas, Jo signaled Maggie, the large African elephant. Obligingly, Maggie lowered her trunk. Jo stepped nimbly into the *u,* then scrambled onto the wide, gray back.

The sun grew higher by the second, shooting the first streams of light onto the field. The scent of orange blossoms mingled with the odor of leather harnesses. Jo had watched the canvas rise under a lightening sky countless times. Each time it was special, and the first raising each season was the most special of all. Maggie lifted her head and trumpeted as if pleased to be around for another season. With a laugh Jo reached back and swatted her rough, wrinkled rump. She felt free and fresh and incredibly alive. If there were a moment, she thought suddenly, that I could capture and bottle, it would be this one. Then, when I'm very old, I could take it out and feel young again. Smiling, she glanced down at the people swarming below her.

Her attention was caught by a man who stood by a coil of cable. Typically, she noted his build first. A well-proportioned body was essential to a performer. He was lean and stood straight. She noted he had good shoulders but doubted if there was much muscle in his arms. Though he was dressed casually in jeans, *city* stood out all over him. His hair was a dark, rich blond, and the early breeze had disturbed it so that it teased his forehead. He was clean-shaven, with a narrow, firm-jawed face. It was an attractive face. It was not, Jo mused, smoothly handsome like Vito the wire walker's but more aware, more demanding. Jo liked the face, liked the shape of the long, unsmiling mouth, liked the hint of bone beneath his tawny skin. Most of all she liked the directness of the amber eyes that stared back at her. They're like Ari's, she observed, thinking of her favorite lion. She was certain that he had been watching her long before she had looked down. Knowing this, Jo was impressed with his unselfconsciousness. He continued to stare, making no effort to camouflage his interest. She laughed, unperturbed, and tossed her braid from her shoulder.

"Want a ride?" she called out. Too many strangers had walked in and out of her world for her to be aloof. She watched his brow lift in acknowledgment of her offer. She would see if it was only his eyes that were like Ari's. "Maggie won't hurt you. She's gentle as a lamb, just bigger." Instantly, she saw he had understood the challenge. He walked across the grass until he stood beside her. He moved well, she noted. Jo tapped Maggie's side with the bull hook she carried. Wearily, the elephant knelt down on her trunklike front legs. Jo held out her hand. With an agility that surprised her, the man mounted the elephant and slid into place behind her.

For a moment she said nothing, a bit stunned by the trembling that had coursed up her arm as her palm had met his. The contact had been brief. Jo decided she had imagined it. "Up, Maggie," she said, giving her mount another tap. With an ele- phantine sigh, Maggie obeyed, rocking her passengers gently from side to side.

"Do you always pick up strange men?" the voice behind her inquired. It was a smooth, well-keyed voice, a good pitchman's voice.

Jo grinned over her shoulder. "Maggie's doing the picking up."

"So she is. Are you aware that she's remarkably uncomfort- able?"

Jo laughed with genuine enjoyment. "You should try riding her a few miles in a street parade while keeping a smile on your face."

"I'll pass. Are you in charge of her?"

"Maggie? No, but I know how to handle her. You have eyes like one of my cats," she told him. "I like them. And since you seemed to be interested in Maggie and me, I asked you up."

This time it was he who laughed. Jo twisted her head, wanting to see his face. There was humor in his eyes now, and his teeth were white and straight. Liking his smile, she answered with one of her own. "Fascinating. You asked me to take a ride on an elephant because I have eyes like your cat's. And no offense to the lady beneath me, but I was looking at you."

"Oh?" Jo pursed her lips in thought. "Why?"

For several seconds he studied her in silence. "Strange, I believe you really don't know."

"I wouldn't ask if I did," she returned, shifting her weight slightly. "It would be a waste of time to ask a question if I knew the answer." She shifted again and turned away from him. "Hold on now. Maggie's got to earn her bale of hay."

The poles hung between the canvas and the ground at forty-five degree angles. Quickly the elephant's chains were hooked to the metal rings at the base of the quarter poles. Jo urged Maggie forward in unison with her coworkers. Poles skidded along the ground, then up into place, pushing the canvas with it. The Big Top billowed to life under the early morning sky.

Her job done, Maggie moved through the flaps and into the light. "Beautiful, isn't it?" Jo murmured. "It's born fresh every day."

Vito walked by, calling out to Jo in Italian. Sending him a wave, she called back in his own language, then signaled to Maggie to kneel again. Jo waited until her passenger had dismounted before she slid off. It surprised her, when they stood face to face, that he was so tall. Tilting back her head, she judged him to be only two inches shy of Buck.

"You looked shorter when I was up on Maggie," she told him with her usual candor.

"You looked taller."

Jo chuckled, patting Maggie behind the ear. "Will you see the show?" She knew that she wanted him to, knew as well that she wanted to see him again. She found this both strange and intriguing. Men had always taken a second place to her cats, and towners had never interested her.

"Yes, I'm going to see the show." There was a slight smile on his face, but he was studying her thoughtfully. "Do you perform?"

"I have an act with my cats."

"I see. Somehow I pictured you in an aerial act, flying from the trapeze."

She sent him an easy smile. "My mother was an aerialist." Someone called her name, and looking, Jo saw Maggie was needed for raising the sideshow tent. "I have to go. I hope you like the show."

He took her hand before she could lead Maggie away. Jo stood still, again surprised by a trembling up her arm. "I'd like to see you tonight."

Glancing up, she met his eyes. They were direct and unself-conscious. "Why?" The question was sincere. Jo knew she wanted to see him as well but was unsure why.

This time he did not laugh. Gently, he ran a finger down the length of her braid. "Because you're beautiful, and you intrigue me."

"Oh." Jo considered. She had never thought of herself as beautiful. Striking, perhaps, in her costume, surrounded by her cats, but in jeans, without makeup, she doubted it. Still, it was an interesting thought. "All right, if there's no trouble with the cats. Ari hasn't been well."

A smile played at the corners of his mouth. "I'm sorry to hear that."

There was another loud summons for Jo, and both looked toward it. "I see you're needed," he said with a nod. "Perhaps you could point out Bill Duffy for me before you go."

"Duffy?" Jo repeated, surprised. "You can't be looking for a job?" There was incredulity in her voice, and he grinned.

"Why can't I?"

"Because you don't fit any of the types."

"Are there types?" he asked, both interested and amused. Jo shook her head in annoyance.

"Yes, of course, and you don't fit into any of them."

"Actually, I'm not looking for a job, so to speak," he told her, still smiling. "But I am looking for Bill Duffy."

It was against Jo's nature to probe. Privacy was both guarded and respected in the circus. Shielding her eyes with her hand, Jo looked around until she spotted Duffy supervising the raising of the cookhouse tent. "There," she said, pointing. "Duffy's the one with the red checked jacket. He still dresses like an outside talker."

"A what?"

"You'd call it a barker, I imagine." With easy grace she mounted the patient Maggie. "That's a towner's term, not a circus one." She smiled at him, then urged Maggie into a walk. "Tell Duffy Jo said to give you a pass," she called over her shoulder, then waved and turned away.

Dawn was over, and it was morning.

Chapter Two

Jo stood at the back door of the Big Top waiting for her cue. Beside her was Jamie Carter, alias Topo. He was a third generation clown and wore his bright face and orange wig naturally. He was young and limber and used these traits as well as his makeup to bring enthusiasm to his craft. To Jo, Jamie was more brother than friend. He was tall and thin, and under his greasepaint his face was mobile and pleasant. He and Jo had grown up together.

"Did she say anything?" Jamie demanded for the third time. With a sigh, Jo tossed closed the flap of the tent. Inside, clowns were performing around the hippodrome track while hands set up the big cage.

"Carmen said nothing. I don't know why you waste your time." Her voice was sharp, and Jamie bristled.

"I don't expect you to understand," he said with great dignity. His thin shoulders drew straight under his red polka dot shirt. "After all, Ari's the closest you've come to being involved with the opposite sex."

"That's very cute," Jo replied, unoffended by the jibe. Her annoyance stemmed from seeing Jamie make a fool of himself

over Carmen Gribalti, the middle sister of the flying Gribal-
tis. She was darkly beautiful, graceful, talented, selfish and sub-
limely indifferent to Jamie. Looking into his happy, painted face
and moody eyes, Jo's irritation dissipated. "She probably hasn't
had a chance to answer the note you sent her," she soothed.
"The first day of a new season's always wild."

"I suppose," Jamie muttered with a grudging shrug. "I don't
know what she sees in Vito."

Jo thought of the wire walker's dark, cocky looks and
rippling muscles. Wisely, she refrained from mentioning them.
"Who can account for taste?" She gave him a smacking kiss
on his round, red nose. "Personally, I get all wobbly when I see
a man with thick, orange hair."

Jamie grinned. "Proves you know what to look for in a man."

Turning, Jo lifted the flap again, noting Jamie's cue was
nearly upon them. "Did you happen to notice a towner
hanging around today?"

"Only a couple dozen of them," Jamie answered dryly as he
lifted the pail of confetti he used to finish the gag now being
performed inside.

Jo shot him a half-hearted glare. "Not the usual type. About
thirty, I think," she continued. "Wearing jeans and a T-shirt.
He was tall, six-one, six-two," she went on as laughter poured
out of the open flap to drown out her words. "He had dark
blond straight hair."

"Yeah, I saw him." Jamie nudged her out of his way and
prepared to make his entrance. "He was going into the red
wagon with Duffy." With a wild, high-pitched scream, Topo
the clown bounded into the Big Top in size fifteen tennis
shoes, brandishing his bucket of confetti.

Thoughtfully, Jo watched Jamie chase three other clowns

around the track. It was odd, she thought, for Duffy to take a towner into the administration trailer. He had said he wasn't looking for a job. He wasn't a drifter; there was an unmistakable air of stability about him. He wasn't a circus hand from another show, either. His palm had been too smooth. And, her mind added as she vaulted onto Babette, a pure white mare, there had been an undeniable aura of urbanity about him. Success, as well, she thought. And authority. No, he had not been looking for a job.

Jo shrugged, annoyed that a stranger was crowding into her thoughts. It irritated her further that she had scanned the crowds for him during the parade and that even now she wondered if he sat somewhere in the circular arena. He hadn't been at the matinee. Jo patted the mare's neck absently, then straightened as she heard the ringmaster's whistle.

"Ladies and gentlemen," he called in deep, musical tones. "Presenting the most spectacular exhibition of animal subjugation under the Big Top. Jovilette, Queen of the Jungle Cats!"

Jo nudged Babette with her heels and raced into the arena. The applause rose to meet her as the audience appreciated the dashing figure she cut. Swathed in a black cape, raven hair flying free under a glittering tiara, she galloped bareback on the snow white mare. In each hand she held a long, thin whip, which she cracked alternately overhead. At the entrance to the big cage she leaped from the still racing horse. While Babette galloped out of the back door and into the care of a handler, Jo shifted both whips into one hand, then removed the cape with a flourish. Her costume was a close-fitting, one-piece jumpsuit, dazzling in white and spangled with gold sequins. In dramatic contrast, her hair hung straight and severe down her back.

Make an entrance, Frank had always said. And Jovilette made an entrance.

The twelve cats were already in the cage, banding its inside edge as they perched on blue and white pedestals. Entering the main cage appeared routine to the audience, but Jo knew it was one of the most dangerous moments of the act. To enter, she had to pass directly between two cats as she moved from the safety cage to the main arena. She always stationed her best behaved cats there, but if one was irritated, or even playful, he could easily strike out with a powerful paw. Even with sharp claws retracted, the damage could be deadly.

She entered swiftly and was surrounded by cats on all sides. Her spangles and tiara caught the lights and played with them as she began to move around the cage, cracking the whip for showmanship while using her voice to command the cats to rise on their haunches. She moved them through their routine, adjusting the timing to compensate for any feline reluctance, letting one trick begin where the last ended.

Jo disliked overdone propping, preferring action and movement. The contrast of the big, tawny cats and the small white and gold woman were the best props available to her. She used them well. Hers was a *picture act,* relying on style and flash, rather than a *fighting act,* which emphasized the ferocity of the big cats by employing blank-bulleted guns and rehearsed charges, or *bounces.* Her confidence transmitted itself to the audience, making her handling of the cats appear effortless. In truth, her body was coiled for any danger, and her mind was focused so intently on her cats, there might have been no audience at all.

She stood between two high pedestals as the cats leaped over her head from both directions. They set up a light breeze, which stirred her hair. They roared when she cued them, setting up an echoing din. Now and then one reached out to paw at the stock of her whip, and she stopped him with a quick command. She sent her best leaper through a hoop of flame and coaxed her best balancer to walk on a glistening silver ball. She ended to waves of applause by trotting Merlin around the hippodrome track.

At the back door Merlin jumped into a wheel cage and was turned over to Pete. "Nice show," he said as he handed her a long chenille robe. "Smooth as silk."

"Thanks." Cold, she bundled into the robe. The spring night was frigid in contrast to the hot lights and heat in the big cage. "Listen, Pete, tell Gerry he can feed the cats tonight. They're behaving themselves."

Pete snapped his gum and chuckled. "Won't he be riding high tonight." As he moved to the truck that would pull the cage to the cat area, Jo called after him.

"Pete." She bit her lip, then shrugged when he twisted his head. "You'll keep an eye on him, won't you?"

Pete grinned and climbed into the cab of the truck. "Who you worried about, Jo? Those big cats or that skinny boy?"

"Both," she answered. The rhinestones in her tiara sparkled as she tossed her head and laughed. Knowing she had nearly an hour before the finale parade, Jo walked away from the Big Top. She thought of wandering to the cookhouse for some coffee. Mentally, she began replaying every segment of her act. It had gone well, she thought, pleased with the timing and the flow. If Pete had said it had been smooth, Jo knew it had. She had heard his criticisms more than once over the past five years. True, Hamlet had tested her once or twice, but no one knew that but Jo and the cat. She doubted if anyone but Buck would have seen that he had given her trouble. Closing her eyes a moment, Jo rolled her shoulders, loosening tight, tensed muscles.

"That's quite an act you have."

Jo whirled around at the sound of the voice. She could feel her heart rate accelerate. Though she wondered at her interest in a man she barely knew, Jo was aware that she had been waiting for him. There was a quick surge of pleasure as she watched him approach, and she allowed it to show on her face.

"Hello." She saw that he smoked a cigar, but unlike Duffy's, his was long and slim. Again she admired the elegance of his hands. "Did you like the show?"

He stopped in front of her, then studied her face with a thoroughness that made her wonder if her makeup had smeared. Then he gave a small, surprised laugh and shook his head. "Do you know," he began, "when you told me this morning that you did an act with cats, I had Siamese in mind rather than African."

"Siamese?" Jo repeated blankly, then laughed. "House cats?" He brushed her hair behind her back while Jo giggled at the thought of coaxing a Siamese to jump through a flaming hoop.

"From my point of view," he told her as he let a strand of her hair linger between his fingers, "it made more sense than a little thing like you walking into a cage with a dozen lions."

"I'm not little," Jo corrected good-naturedly. "Besides, size hardly matters to twelve lions."

"No, I suppose it doesn't." He lifted his eyes from her hair and met hers. Jo continued to smile, enjoying looking at him. "Why do you do it?" he asked suddenly.

Jo gave him a curious look. "Why? Because it's my job."

By the way he studied her, Jo could see that he was not satisfied with the simplicity of her answer. "Perhaps I should ask *how* you became a lion tamer."

"Trainer," Jo corrected automatically. To her left, she could hear the audience's muffled applause. "The Beirots are starting," she said with a glance toward the sound. "You shouldn't miss their act. They're first-rate acrobats."

"Don't you want to tell me?" His voice was soft.

She lifted a brow, seeing that he truly wanted to know. "Why, it's not a secret. My father was a trainer, and I have a knack for working with cats. It just followed." Jo had never thought about her career past this point, and she shrugged it aside. "You shouldn't waste your ticket standing out here. You can stand by the back door and watch the rest of the act." Jo turned to lead the way to the performer's entrance but stopped when his hand took hers.

He stepped forward until their bodies were nearly touching. Jo could feel the heat from his as she watched his face. Her heart was thudding in a quick, steady rhythm. She could hear it vibrate through her the same way it did when she approached a new cat for the first time. Here was something new, something untested. She tingled with the excitement of the unknown when he lifted his hand to touch her cheek. She did not move but let the warmth spread while she watched him carefully, gauging him. Her eyes were wide, curious and unafraid.

"Are you going to kiss me?" she asked in a tone that expressed more interest than desire.

His eyes lit with humor and glittered in the dim light. "I had given it some thought," he answered. "Do you have any objections?"

Jo considered a moment, dropping her eyes to his mouth. She liked its shape and wondered how it would feel against hers. He brought her no closer. One hand still held hers while the other slid around to cradle her neck. Jo shifted her gaze until their eyes met again. "No," she decided. "I haven't any objections."

The corners of his mouth twitched as he tightened his hold slightly on the base of her neck. Slowly, he lowered his head toward hers. Curious and a bit wary, Jo kept her eyes open, watching his. She knew from experience that you could tell more about people and about cats from the eyes. To her surprise, his remained open as well, even as their lips met.

It was a gentle kiss, without pressure, only a whisper of a touch. Amazed, Jo thought she felt the ground tremble under her feet. Dimly, she wondered if the elephants were being led by. But it can't be time, she thought in confusion. His lips moved lightly over hers, and his eyes remained steady. Jo's pulse drummed under her skin. They stood, barely touching, as the Big Top throbbed with noise behind them. Lazily, he traced her lips with the tip of his tongue, teasing them open. Still there was no demand in the kiss, only testing. Unhurried, confident, he explored her mouth while Jo felt her breath accelerating. A soft moan escaped her as her lids fluttered down.

For an instant she surrendered utterly to him, to the new sensations swimming through her. She leaned against him, straining toward pleasure, sighing with it as the kiss lingered.

He drew her away, but their faces remained close. Dizzily, Jo realized that she had risen to her toes to compensate for their difference in height. His hand was still light on the back of her neck. His eyes were gold in the darkening night.

"What an incredible female you are, Jovilette," he murmured. "One surprise after another."

Jo felt stunningly alive. Her skin seemed to tingle with new feelings. She smiled. "I don't know your name."

He laughed, releasing her neck to take her other hand in his. Before he could speak, Duffy called out from the direction of the Big Top. Jo turned to watch as he moved toward them in his quick, rolling walk.

"Well, well, well," he said in his jolly, rough voice. "I didn't know you two had met. Has Jo been showing you around already?" Reaching them, he squeezed Jo's shoulder. "Knew I could count on you, kiddo." Jo glanced at him in puzzlement, but he continued before she could form a question. "Yes, sir, this little girl puts on quite a show, doesn't she? Always a grabber. And she knows this circus like the back of her hand. Born and raised to it," he continued. Jo relaxed. She recognized that Duffy was into one of his spiels, and there was no stopping him. "Yessiree, any questions you got, you just ask our Jo, and she'll tell you. 'Course, I'm always at your disposal, too. Anything I can tell you about the books or accounts or contracts and the like, you just let me know." Duffy puffed twice on his cigar as Jo felt her first hint of unease.

Why was Duffy rambling about books and contracts? Jo glanced at the man who still held her hands in his. He was watching Duffy with an easy, amused smile.

"Are you a bookkeeper?" Jo asked, perplexed. Duffy laughed and patted her head.

"You know Mr. Prescott's a lawyer, Jo. Don't miss your cue." He gave them both a friendly nod and toddled off.

Jo had stiffened almost imperceptibly at Duffy's offhand information, but Keane had felt it. His brows lowered as he studied her. "Now you know my name."

"Yes." All warmth fled from Jo. Her voice was as cool as her blood. "Would you let go of my hands, Mr. Prescott?"

After a brief hesitation Keane inclined his head and obliged. Jo stuffed her hands quickly into the pockets of her robe.

"Don't you think we've progressed to the first name stage of our relationship, Jo?"

"I assure you, Mr. Prescott, if I had known who you were, we wouldn't have progressed at all." Jo's words were stiff with dignity. Inside, though she tried to ignore it, she felt betrayal, anger, humiliation. All pleasure had died from the evening. Now the kiss that had left her feeling clean and alive seemed cheap and shabby. No, she would not use his first name, she vowed. She would never use it. "If you'll excuse me, I have some things to do before my cue."

"Why the turnaround?" he asked, halting her with a hand on her arm. "Don't you like lawyers?"

Coldly, Jo studied him. She wondered how it was possible that she had completely misjudged the man she had met that morning. "I don't categorize people, Mr. Prescott."

"I see." Keane's tone became detached, his eyes assessing. "Then it would appear that you have an aversion to my name. Should I assume you hold a grudge against my father?"

Jo's eyes glittered with quick fury. She jerked her arm from his hold. "Frank Prescott was the most generous, the kindest, most unselfish man I've ever known. I don't even associate you with Frank, Mr. Prescott. You have no right to him." Though it was nearly impossible, Jo forced herself to speak in a normal tone of voice. She would not shout and draw anyone's attention. This would be kept strictly between Keane Prescott and herself. "It would have been much better if you had told me who you were right away, then there would have been no mix-up."

"Is that what we've had?" he countered mildly. "A mix-up?"

His cool tone was nearly Jo's undoing. He watched her with a dispassionate curiosity that tempted her to slap him. She fought to keep her fury from spilling over into her voice. "You have no right to Frank's circus, Mr. Prescott," she managed quietly. "Leaving it to you is the only thing I've ever faulted him for." Knowing her control was slipping, Jo whirled, running across the grass until she merged with the darkness.

Chapter Three

The morning was surprisingly warm. There were no trees to block the sun, and the smell of the earth was strong. The circus had moved north in the early hours. All the usual scents merged into the aroma of circus: canvas, leather, sweating horses, greasepaint and powder, coffee and oilcloth. The trailers and trucks sat in the accustomed spots, forming the "back yard" that would always take the same formation each time the circus made a stop along the thousands of miles it traveled. The flag over the cookhouse tent signaled that lunch was being served. The Big Top stood waiting for the matinee.

Rose hurried along the midway toward the animal cages. Her dark hair was pinned neatly in a bun at the back of her neck. Her big brown eyes darted about searchingly, while her mouth sat softly in a pout. She was wrapped in a terry cloth robe and wore tennis shoes over her tights. When she saw Jo standing in front of Ari's cage, she waved and broke into a half-run. Watching her, Jo shifted her attention from Ari. Rose was always a diversion, and Jo felt in need of one.

"Jo!" She waved again as if Jo had not seen her the first time, then came to a breathless halt. "Jo, I only have a few minutes. Hello, Ari," she added out of politeness. "I was looking for Jamie."

"Yes, I gathered." Jo smiled, knowing Rose had set her heart on capturing Topo's alter ego. And if he had any sense, she thought, he'd let himself be caught instead of pining over Carmen. Silly, she decided, dismissing all affairs of the heart. Lions were easier to understand. "I haven't seen him all morning, Rose. Maybe he's rehearsing."

"Drooling over Carmen, more likely," Rose muttered, sending a sulky glare in the direction of the Gribalti trailer. "He makes a fool of himself."

"That's what he's paid for," Jo reminded her, but Rose did not respond to the humor. Jo sighed. She had a true affection for Rose. She was bright and fun and without pretentions. "Rose," she said, keeping her voice both light and kind. "Don't give up on him. He's a little slow, you know," she explained. "He's just a bit dazzled by Carmen right now. It'll pass."

"I don't know why I bother," she grumbled, but Jo saw the dark mood was already passing. Rose was a creature of quick passions that flared and soon died. "He's not so very handsome, you know."

"No," Jo agreed. "But he has a cute nose."

"Lucky for him I like red," Rose returned and grinned. "Ah, now we're speaking of handsome," she murmured as her eyes drifted from Jo. "Who is this?"

At the question, Jo glanced over her shoulder. The humor fled from her eyes. "That's the owner," she said colorlessly.

"Keane Prescott? No one told me he was so handsome. Or so tall," she added, admiring him openly as he crossed the back yard. Jo noted that Rose always became more Mexican around men. "Such shoulders. Lucky for Jamie I'm a one-man woman."

"Lucky for you your mama can't hear you," Jo muttered, earning an elbow in the ribs.

"But he comes here, *amiga,* and he looks at you. La, la, my papa would have Jamie to the altar *pronto* if he looked at me that way."

"You're an idiot," Jo snapped, annoyed.

"Ah, Jo," Rose said with mock despair. "I am a romantic."

Jo was helpless against the smile that tugged at her lips. Her eyes were laughing when she glanced up and met Keane's. Hastily, she struggled to dampen their brilliance, turning her mouth into a sober line.

"Good morning, Jovilette." He spoke her name too easily, she thought, as if he had been saying it for years.

"Good morning, Mr. Prescott," she returned. Rose gave a loud, none-too-subtle cough. "This is Rose Sanches."

"It's a pleasure, Mr. Prescott." Rose extended a hand, trying out a smile she had been saving for Jamie. "I heard you were traveling with us."

Keane accepted the hand and smiled in return. Jo noticed with annoyance that it was the same easy, disarming smile of the stranger she had met the morning before. "Hello, Rose, it's nice to meet you."

Seeing her friend's Mexican blood heat her cheeks, Jo intervened. She would not permit Keane Prescott to make a conquest here. "Rose, you only have ten minutes to get back and into makeup."

"Holy cow!" she said, forgetting her attempt at sophistication. "I've got to run." She began to do so, then called over her shoulder, "Don't tell Jamie I was looking for him, the pig!" She ran a little further, then turned and ran backwards. "I'll look for him later," she said with a laugh, then turned back and streaked toward the midway.

Keane watched her dart across the compound while holding up the long skirts of her robe in one hand. "Charming."

"She's only eighteen," Jo offered before she could stop herself.

When Keane turned to her, his look was one of amusement. "I see," he said. "I'll take that information under advisement. And what does the eighteen-year-old Rose do?" he asked, slipping his thumbs into the front pockets of his jeans. "Wrestle alligators?"

"No," Jo returned without batting an eye. "Rose is Serpentina, your premier sideshow attraction. The snake charmer." She was pleased with the incredulous look that passed over his face. It was replaced quickly, however, with one of genuine humor.

"Perfect." He brushed Jo's hair from her cheek before she could protest by word or action. "Cobras?" he asked, ignoring the flash in her eyes.

"And boa constrictors," she returned sweetly. Jo brushed the dust from the knees of her faded jeans. "Now, if you'll excuse me..."

"No, I don't think so." Keane's voice was cool, but she recognized the underlying authority. She did her best not to struggle against it. He *was* the owner, she reminded herself.

"Mr. Prescott," she began, banking down hard on the urge to mutiny. "I'm very busy. I have to get ready for the afternoon show."

"You've got an hour and a half until you're on," he countered smoothly. "I think you might spare me a portion of that time. You've been assigned to show me around. Why don't we start now?" The tone of the question left room for only one answer. Jo's mind fidgeted in search of a way out.

Tilting her head back, she met his eyes. He won't be easy to beat, she concluded, studying his steady, measuring gaze. I'd better study his moves more carefully before I start a battle. "Where would you like to begin?" she asked aloud.

"With you."

Keane's easy answer brought a deep frown to Jo's brows. "I don't understand what you mean."

For a moment Keane watched her. There was no coyness or guile in her eyes as they looked into his. "No, I can see you don't," he agreed with a nod. "Let's start with your cats."

"Oh." Jo's frown cleared instantly. "All right." She watched as he pulled out a thin cigar, waiting until the flame of his lighter licked the tip before speaking. "I have thirteen—seven males, six females. They're all African lions between four-and-a-half and twenty-two years."

"I thought you worked with twelve," Keane commented as he dropped his lighter into his pocket.

"That's right, but Ari's retired." Turning, Jo indicated the large male lion dozing in a cage. "He travels with me because he always has, but I don't work him anymore. He's twenty-two, the oldest. My father kept him, even though he was born in captivity, because he was born the same day I was." Jo sighed, and her voice became softer. "He's the last of my father's stock. I couldn't sell him to a zoo. It seemed like shoving an old relative into a home and abandoning him. He's been with this circus every day of his life, just as I have. His name is Hebrew for *lion*." Jo laughed, forgetting the man beside her as she sifted through memories. "My father always gave his cats names that meant lion somehow or other. Leo, Leonard, Leonara. Ari was a first-class leaper in his prime. He could climb, too; some cats won't. I could teach Ari anything. Smart cat, aren't you, Ari?" The altered tone of her voice caused the big cat to stir. Opening his eyes, he stared back at Jo. The sound he made was more grumble than roar before he dozed again. "He's tired," Jo murmured, fighting a shaft of gloom. "Twenty-two's old for a lion."

"What is it?" Keane demanded, touching her shoulder before she could turn away. Her eyes were drenched with sadness.

"He's dying," she said unsteadily. "And I can't stop it." Stuffing her hands in her pockets, Jo moved away to the main group of cages. To steady herself, she took two deep breaths while waiting for Keane to join her. Regaining her composure, she began again. "I work with these twelve," she told him, making a sweeping gesture. "They're fed once a day, raw meat six days a week and eggs and milk on the seventh. They were all imported directly from Africa and were cage broken when I got them."

The faint sound of a calliope reached them, signaling the opening of the midway. "This is Merlin, the one I ride out on at the finish. He's ten, and the most even-tempered cat I've ever worked with. Heathcliff," she continued as she moved down the line of cages, "he's six, my best leaper. And this is Faust, the baby at four and a half." The lions paced their cages as Jo walked Keane down the line. Unable to prevent herself, Jo gave Faust a signal by raising her hand. Obediently, he sent out a huge, deafening roar. To Jo's disappointment, Keane did not scramble for cover.

"Very impressive," he said mildly. "You put him in the center when you lie down on them, don't you?"

"Yes." She frowned, then spoke her thoughts candidly. "You're very observant—and you've got steady nerves."

"My profession requires them, too, to an extent," he returned.

Jo considered this a moment, then turned back to the lions. "Lazareth, he's twelve and a natural ham. Bolingbroke, he's ten, from the same lioness as Merlin. Hamlet," she said stopping again, "he's five. I bought him to replace Ari in the act." Jo stared into the tawny eyes. "He has potential, but he's arrogant. Patient, too. He's just waiting for me to make a mistake."

"Why?" Keane glanced over at Jo. Her eyes were cool and steady on Hamlet's.

"So he can get a good clean swipe at me," she told him without altering her expression. "It's his first season in the big cage. Pandora," Jo continued, pointing out the females. "A very classy lady. She's six. Hester, at seven, my best all-around. And Portia; it's her first year, too. She's mostly a seat-warmer."

"Seat-warmer?"

"Just what it sounds like," Jo explained. "She hasn't mastered any complicated tricks yet. She evens out the act, does a few basics and warms the seat." Jo moved on. "Dulcinea, the prettiest of the ladies. Ophelia, who had a litter last year; and Abra, eight, a bit bad-tempered but a good balancer."

Hearing her name, the cat rose, stretched her long, golden body, then began to rub it against the bars of the cage. A deep sound rumbled in her throat. Jo scowled and jammed her hands into her pockets. "She likes you," she muttered.

"Oh?" Lifting a brow, Keane studied the three-hundred-pound Abra more carefully. "How do you know?"

"When a lion likes you, it does exactly what a house cat does. It rubs against you. Abra's rubbing against the bars because she can't get any closer."

"I see." Humor touched his mouth. "I must admit, I'm at a loss on how to return the compliment." He drew on his cigar, then regarded Jo through a haze of smoke. "Your choice of names is fascinating."

"I like to read," she stated, leaving it at that. "Is there anything else you'd like to know about the cats?" Jo was determined to keep their conversation on a professional level. His smile had reminded her all too clearly of their encounter the night before.

"Do you drug them before a performance?"

Fury sparked Jo's eyes. "Certainly not."

"Was that an unreasonable question?" Keane countered. He dropped his cigar to the ground, then crushed it out with his heel.

"Not for a first of mayer," Jo decided with a sigh. She tossed her hair carelessly behind her back. "Drugging is not only cruel, it's stupid. A drugged animal won't perform."

"You don't touch the lions with that whip," Keane commented. He watched the light breeze tease a few strands of her hair. "Why do you use it?"

"To get their attention and to keep the audience awake." She smiled reluctantly.

Keane took her arm. Instantly, Jo stiffened. "Let's walk," he suggested. He began to lead her away from the cages. Spotting several people roaming the back yard, Jo refrained from pulling away. The last thing she wanted was the story spreading that she was having a tiff with the owner. "How do you tame them?" he asked her.

"I don't. They're not tame, they're trained." A tall blond woman walked by carrying a tiny white poodle. "Merlin's hungry today," Jo called out with a grin.

The woman bundled the dog closer to her breast in mock alarm and began a rapid scolding in French. Jo laughed, telling her in the same language that Fifi was too tough a mouthful for Merlin.

"Fifi can do a double somersault on the back of a moving horse," Jo explained as they began to walk again. "She's trained just as my cats are trained, but she's also domesticated.

The cats are wild." Jo turned her face up to Keane's. The sun cast a sheen over her hair and threw gold flecks into her eyes. "A wild thing can never be tamed, and anyone who tries is foolish. If you take something wild and turn it into a pet, you've stolen its character, blanked out its spark. And still, there's always an essence of the wild that can come back to life. When a dog turns on his master, it's ugly. When a lion turns, it's lethal." She was beginning to become accustomed to his hand on her arm, finding it easy to talk to him because he listened. "A full-grown male stands three feet at the shoulder and weighs over five hundred pounds. One well-directed swipe can break a man's neck, not to mention what teeth and claws can do." Jo gave a smile and a shrug. "Those aren't the virtues of a pet."

"Yet you go into a cage with twelve of them, armed with a whip?"

"The whip's window dressing." Jo discounted it with a gesture of her hand. "It would hardly be a defense against even one cat at full charge. A lion is a very tenacious enemy. A tiger is more bloodthirsty, but it normally strikes only once. If it misses, it takes it philosophically. A lion charges again and again. Do you know the line Byron wrote about a tiger's spring? 'Deadly, quick and crushing.'" Jo had completely forgotten her animosity and began to enjoy her walk and conversation with this handsome stranger. "It's a true description, but a lion is totally fearless when he charges, and stubborn. He's not the razzle-dazzle fighter the tiger is, just accurate. I'd bet on a lion against a tiger any day. And a man simply hasn't a prayer against one."

"Then how do you manage to stay in one piece?"

The calliope music was just a hint in the air now. Jo turned, noting with surprise that they had walked a good distance from camp. She could see the trailers and tents, hear occasional shouts and laughter, but she felt oddly separated from it all. She sat down cross-legged on the grass and plucked a blade. "I'm smarter than they are. At least I make them think so. And I dominate them, partly by a force of will. In training, you have to develop a rapport, a mutual respect, and if you're lucky, a certain affection. But you can't trust them to the point where you grow careless. And above all," she added, glancing over as he sat down beside her, "you have to remember the basic rule of poker. Bluff." Jo grinned, leaning back on her elbows. "Do you play poker?"

"I've been known to." Her hair trailed out along the grass, and he lifted a strand. "Do you?"

"Sometimes. My assistant handler, Pete…" Jo scanned the back yard, then smiled and pointed. "There he is, by the second trailer, sitting with Mac Stevenson, the one with the fielder's cap. Pete organizes a game now and then."

"Who's the little girl on stilts?"

"That's Mac's youngest, Katie. She wants to walk on them in the street parade. She's getting pretty good. There's Jamie," she said, then laughed as he did a pratfall and landed at Katie's wooden stilts.

"Rose's Jamie?" Keane asked, watching the impromptu show in the back yard.

"If she has her way. He's currently dazzled by Carmen Gribalti. Carmen won't give Jamie the time of day. She bats her lashes at Vito, the wire walker. He bats his at everyone."

"A complicated state of affairs," Keane commented. He twisted Jo's hair around his fingers. "Romance seems to be very popular in circus life."

"From what I read," she countered, "it's popular everywhere."

"Who dazzles you, Jovilette?" He gave her hair a tug to bring her face around to his.

Jo hadn't realized he was so close. She need do no more than sway for her mouth to touch his. Her eyes measured his while she waited for her pulse to calm. It was odd, she thought, that he had such an effect on her. With sudden clarity, she could smell the grass, a clean, sweet scent, and feel the sun. The sounds of the circus were muted in the background. She could hear birds call out with an occasional high-pitched trill. She remembered the taste of his mouth and wondered if it would be the same.

"I've been too busy to be dazzled," she replied. Her voice was steady, but her eyes were curious.

For the first time, Jo truly *wanted* to be kissed by a man. She wanted to feel again what she had felt the night before. She wanted to be held, not lightly as he had held her before, but close, with his arms tight around her. She wanted to renew the feeling of weightlessness. She had never experienced a strong physical desire, and for a moment she explored the sensation. There was a quiver in her stomach which was both pleasant and disturbing. Throughout her silent contemplations Keane watched her, intrigued by the intensity of her eyes.

"What are you thinking of?"

"I'm wondering why you make me feel so odd," she told him with simple frankness. He smiled, and she noticed that it grew in his eyes seconds before it grew on his mouth.

"Do I?" He appeared to enjoy the information. "Did you know your hair catches the sunlight?" Keane took a handful, letting it spill from between his fingers. "I've never seen another woman with hair like this. It's a temptation all in itself. In what way do I make you feel odd, Jovilette?" he asked as his eyes trailed back up to hers.

"I'm not sure yet." Jo found her voice husky. Abruptly, she decided it would not do to go on feeling odd or to go on wanting to be kissed by Keane Prescott. She scrambled up and brushed off the seat of her pants.

"Running away?" As Keane rose, Jo's head snapped up.

"I never run away from anything, Mr. Prescott." Ice sharpened her voice. She was annoyed that she had allowed herself to fall under his charm again. "I certainly won't run from a city-bred lawyer." Her words were laced with scorn. "Why don't you go back to Chicago and get someone thrown in jail?"

"I'm a defense attorney," Keane countered easily. "I get people out of jail."

"Fine. Go put a criminal back on the streets, then."

Keane laughed, bringing Jo's temper even closer to the surface. "That covers both sides of the issue, doesn't it? You dazzle me, Jovilette."

"Well, it's strictly unintentional." She took a step back from the amusement in his eyes. She would not tolerate him making fun of her. "You don't belong here," she blurted out. "You have no business here."

"On the contrary," he disagreed in a cool, untroubled voice. "I have every business here. I own this circus."

"Why?" she demanded, throwing out her hands as if to push his words aside. "Because it says so on a piece of paper? That's all lawyers understand, I imagine—pieces of paper with strange little words. Why did you come? To look us over and calculate the profit and loss? What's the liquidation value of a dream, Mr. Prescott? What price do you put on the human spirit? Look at it!" she demanded, swinging her arm to encompass the lot behind them. "You only see tents and a huddle of trailers. You can't possibly understand what it all means. But Frank understood. He loved it."

"I'm aware of that." Keane's voice was still calm but had taken on a thin edge of steel. Jo saw that his eyes had grown dark and guarded. "He also left it to me."

"I don't understand why." In frustration, Jo stuffed her hands in her pockets and turned away.

"Neither do I, I assure you, but the fact remains that he did."

"Not once in thirty years did you visit him." Jo whirled back around. Her hair followed in a passionate arch. "Not once."

"Quite true," Keane agreed. He stood with his weight even on both legs and watched her. "Of course, some might look at it differently. Not once in thirty years did he visit me."

"Your mother left him and took you to Chicago—"

"I won't discuss my mother," Keane interrupted in a tone of clipped finality.

Jo bit off a retort, spinning away from him again. Still she could not find the reins to her control. "What are you going to do with it?" she demanded.

"That's my business."

"Oh!" Jo spun back, then shut her eyes and muttered in a language he failed to understand. "Can you be so arrogant? Can you be so dispassionate?" Her lashes fluttered up, revealing eyes dark with anger. "Do the lives of all those people mean nothing to you? Does Frank's dream mean nothing? Haven't you enough money already without hurting people to get more? Greed isn't something you inherited from Frank."

"I'll only be pushed so far," Keane warned.

"I'd push you all the way back to Chicago if I could manage it," she snapped.

"I wondered how much of a temper there was behind those sharp green eyes," Keane commented, watching her passion pour color into her cheeks. "It appears it's a full-grown one." Jo started to retort, but Keane cut her off. "Just hold on a minute," he ordered. "With or without your approval, I own this circus. It might be easier for you if you adjusted to that. Be quiet," he added when her mouth opened again. "Legally, I can do with my—" he hesitated a moment, then continued in a mordant tone "—inheritance as I choose. I have no obligation or intention of justifying my decision to you."

Jo dug her nails into her palms to help keep her voice from shaking. "I never knew I could grow to dislike someone so quickly."

"Jovilette." Keane dipped his hands into his pockets, then rocked back on his heels. "You disliked me before you ever saw me."

"That's true," she replied evenly. "But I've learned to dislike you in person in less than twenty-four hours. I have a show to do," she said, turning back toward the lot. Though he did not follow, she felt his eyes on her until she reached her trailer and closed the door behind her.

Thirty minutes later Jamie sprang through the back door of the Big Top. He was breathless after a lengthy routine and hooked one hand through his purple suspenders as he took in gulps of air. He spotted Jo standing beside the white mare. Her eyes were dark and stormy, her shoulders set and rigid. Jamie recognized the signs. Something or someone had put Jo in a temper, and she had barely ten minutes to work her way out of it before her cue.

He crossed to her and gave a tug on her hair. "Hey."

"Hello, Jamie." Jo struggled to keep her voice pleasant, but he heard the traces of emotion.

"Hello, Jo," he replied in precisely the same tone.

"Cut it out," she ordered before taking a few steps away. The mare followed docilely. Jo had been trying for some time to put her emotions back into some semblance of order. She was not succeeding.

"What happened?" Jamie asked from directly behind her.

"Nothing," Jo snapped, then hated herself for the short nastiness of the word.

Jamie persisted, knowing her too well to be offended. "Nothing is one of my favorite topics of conversation." He put his hands on her shoulders, ignoring her quick, bad-tempered jerk. "Let's talk about it."

"There's nothing to talk about."

"Exactly." He began massaging the tension in her shoulders with his white gloved hands.

"Oh, Jamie." His good-heartedness was irresistible. Sighing, she allowed herself to be soothed. "You're an idiot."

"I'm not here to be flattered."

"I had an argument with the owner." Jo let out a long breath and shut her eyes.

"What're you doing having arguments with the owner?"

"He infuriates me." Jo whirled around. Her cape whipped and snapped with the movement. "He shouldn't be here. If he were back in Chicago…"

"Hold it." With a slight shake of her shoulders, Jamie halted Jo's outburst. "You know better than to get yourself worked up like this right before a show. You can't afford to have your mind on anything but what you're doing when you're in that cage."

"I'll be all right," she mumbled.

"Jo." There was censure in his voice mixed with affection and exasperation.

Reluctantly, Jo brought her gaze up to his. It was impossible to resist the grave eyes in the brightly painted face. With something between a sigh and a moan, she dropped her forehead to his chest. "Jamie, he makes me so mad! He could ruin everything."

"Let's worry about it when the time comes," Jamie suggested, patting her hair.

"But he doesn't understand us. He doesn't understand anything."

"Well, then it's up to us to make him understand, isn't it?"

Jo looked up and wrinkled her nose. "You're so logical."

"Of course I am," he agreed and struck a pose. As he wiggled his orange eyebrows, Jo laughed. "Okay?" he asked, then picked up his prop bucket.

"Okay," she agreed and smiled.

"Good, 'cause there's my cue."

When he disappeared behind the flap, Jo leaned her cheek against the mare and nuzzled a moment. "I don't think I'm the one to make him understand, though."

I wish he'd never come, she added silently as she vaulted onto the mare's back. *I wish I'd never noticed how his eyes are like Ari's and how nice his mouth is when he smiles,* she thought. Jo ran the tip of her tongue gingerly over her lips. *I wish he'd never kissed me. Liar.* Her conscience spoke softly in her ear: *Admit it, you're glad he kissed you. You've never felt anything like that before, and no matter what, you're glad he kissed you last night. You even wanted him to kiss you again today.*

She forced her mind clear, taking deep, even breaths until she heard the ringmaster announce her. With a flick of her heels, she sent the mare sprinting into the tent.

It did not go well. The audience cheered her, oblivious to any problem, but Jo was aware that the routine was far from smooth. And the cats sensed her preoccupation. Again and again they tested her, and again and again Jo was forced to alter her timing to compensate. When the act was over, her head throbbed from the strain of concentration. Her hands were clammy as she turned Merlin over to Buck.

The big man came back to her after securing the cage. "What's the matter with you?" he demanded without preamble. By the underlying and very rare anger in his voice, Jo knew he had observed at least a portion of her act. Unlike the audience, Buck would note any deviation. "You go in the cage like that again, one of those cats is going to find out what you taste like."

"My timing was a little off, that's all." Jo fought against the trembling in her stomach and tried to sound casual.

"A little?" Buck glowered, looking formidable behind the mass of blond beard. "Who do you think you're fooling? I've been around these ugly cats since before you were born. When you go in the cage, you've got to take your brain in with you."

Only too aware that he was right, Jo conceded. "I know, Buck. You're right." With a weary hand she pushed back her hair. "It won't happen again. I guess I was tired and a little off-balance." She sent him an apologetic smile.

Buck frowned and shuffled. Never in his forty-five years had he managed to resist feminine smiles. "All right," he muttered, then sniffed and made his voice firm. "But you go take a nap right after the finale. No coffee. I don't want to see you around again until dinner time."

"Okay, Buck." Jo kept her voice humble, though she was tempted to grin. The weakness was going out of her legs, and the dull buzz of fear was fading from between her temples. Still she felt exhausted and agreeable to Buck's uncharacteristic tone of command. A nap, she decided as Buck drove Merlin away, was just what she needed, not to mention that it was as good a way as any to avoid Keane Prescott for the rest of the day. Shooing this thought aside, Jo decided to while away the time until the finale in casual conversation with Vito the wire walker.

Chapter Four

It rained for three days. It was a solid downpour, not heavy but insistent. As the circus wound its way north, the rain followed. Nevertheless, canvas men pitched the tents in soggy fields and muddy lots while straw was laid on the hippodrome track and performers scurried from trailers to tents under dripping umbrellas.

The lot near Waycross, Georgia, was scattered with puddles under a thick, gray sky. Jo could only be grateful that no evening show had been scheduled. By six, it was nearly dark, with a chill teasing the damp air. She hustled from the cookhouse after an early supper. She would check on the cats, she decided, then closet herself in her trailer, draw the curtains against the rain and curl up with a book. Shivering, she concluded that the idea was inspired.

She carried no umbrella but sought questionable shelter under a gray rolled-brimmed hat and thin windbreaker. Keeping her head lowered, she jogged across the mud, skimming around or hopping over puddles. She hummed lightly, anticipating the simple pleasures of an idle evening. Her humming ended in a muffled gasp as she ran into a solid object.

Fingers wrapped around her upper arms. Even before she lifted her head, Jo knew it was Keane who held her. She recognized his touch. Through some clever maneuvering, she had managed to avoid being alone with him since they had walked together and looked back on the circus.

"Excuse me, Mr. Prescott. I'm afraid I wasn't looking where I was going."

"Perhaps the weather's dampened your radar, Jovilette." He made no move to release her. Annoyed, Jo was forced to hold her hat steady with one hand as she tilted her head to meet his eyes. Rain fell cool on her face.

"I don't know what you mean."

"Oh, I think you do," Keane countered. "There's not another soul around. You've been careful to keep yourself in a crowd for days."

Jo blinked rain from her lashes. She admitted ruefully that it had been foolish to suppose he wouldn't notice her ploy. She saw he carried no umbrella either, nor did he bother with a hat. His hair was darkened with rain, much the same color that one of her cats would be if caught in an unexpected shower. It was difficult, in the murky light, to clearly make out his features, but the rain could not disguise his mockery.

"That's an interesting observation, Mr. Prescott," Jo said coolly. "Now, if you don't mind, I'm getting wet." She was surprised when she remained in his hold after a strong attempt on her part to pull away. Frowning, she put both hands against his chest and pushed. She discovered that she had been wrong; under the lean frame was an amazing amount of strength. Infuriated that she had misjudged him and that she was outmatched, Jo raised her eyes again. "Let me go," she demanded between clenched teeth.

"No," Keane returned mildly. "I don't believe I will."

Jo glared at him. "Mr. Prescott, I'm cold and wet and I'd like to go to my trailer. Now, what do you want?"

"First, I want you to stop calling me Mr. Prescott." Jo pouted but she kept silent. "Second, I'd like an hour of your time for going over a list of personnel." He paused. Through her windbreaker Jo could feel his fingers unyielding on her arms.

"Is there anything else?" she demanded, trying to sound bored.

For a moment there was only the sound of rain drumming on the ground and splashing into puddles. "Yes," Keane said quietly. "I think I'll just get this out of my system."

Jo's instincts were swift but they were standing too close for her to evade him. And he was quick. Her protest was muffled against his mouth. Her arms were pinioned to her sides as his locked around her. Jo had felt a man's body against her own before—working out with the tumblers, practicing with the equestrians—but never with such clarity as this. She was aware of Keane in every fiber of her being. His body was whipcord lean and hard, his arms holding the strength she had discounted the first time she had seen him. But more, it was his mouth that mystified her. Now it was not gentle or testing; it took and plundered and demanded more before she could withhold a response.

Jo forgot the rain, though it continued to fall against her face. She forgot the cold. The warmth spread from inside, where her blood flowed fast, as her body was molded to Keane's. She forgot herself, or the woman she had thought herself to be, and discovered another. When he lifted his mouth, Jo kept her eyes closed, savoring the lingering pleasures, inviting fresh ones.

"More?" he murmured as his hand trailed up, then down her spine. Heat raced after it. "Kissing can be a dangerous pastime, Jo." He lowered his mouth again, then nipped at her soft bottom lip. "But you know all about danger, don't you?" He kissed her hard, leaving her breathless. "How courageous are you without your cats?"

Suddenly her heart raced to her throat. Her legs became rubbery, and a tingle sprinted up her spine. Jo recognized the feeling. It was the way she felt when she experienced a close call with the cats. Reaction would set in after the door of the safety cage locked behind her and the crisis had passed. It was then that fear found her. She studied Keane's bold, amber eyes, and her mouth went dry. She shuddered.

"You're cold." His voice was abruptly brisk. "Small wonder. We'll go to my trailer and get you some coffee."

"No!" Jo's protest was sharp and instantaneous. She knew she was vulnerable and she knew as well that she did not yet possess the experience to fight him. To be alone with him now was too great a risk.

Keane drew her away, but his grip remained firm. She could not read his expression as he searched her face. "What happened just now was personal," he told her. "Strictly man to woman. I'm of the opinion that lovemaking should be personal. You're an appealing armful, Jovilette, and I'm accustomed to taking what I want, one way or another."

His words were like a shot of adrenaline. Jo's chin thrust forward, and her eyes flamed. "No one *takes* me, one way or another." She spoke with the deadly calm of fury. "If I make love with anyone, it's only because I want to."

"Of course," Keane agreed with an easy nod. "We're both aware you'll be willing when the time comes. We could make love quite successfully tonight, but I think it best if we know each other better first."

Jo's mouth trembled open and closed twice before she could speak. "Of all the arrogant, outrageous…"

"Truthful," Keane supplied, tossing her into incoherency again. "But for now, we have business, and while I don't mind kissing in the rain, I prefer to conduct business in a drier climate." He held up a hand as Jo started to protest. "I told you, the kiss was between a man and a woman. The business we have now is between the owner of this circus and a performer under contract. Understood?"

Jo took a long, deep breath to bring her voice to a normal level. "Understood," she agreed. Without another word she let him lead her across the slippery lot.

When they reached Keane's trailer, he hustled Jo inside without preliminaries. She blinked against the change in light when he hit the wall switch. "Take off your coat," he said briskly, pulling down her zipper before she could perform the task for herself. Instinctively, her hand reached for it as she took a step backward. Keane merely lifted a brow, then stripped off his own jacket. "I'll get the coffee." He moved down the length of the narrow trailer and disappeared around the corner where the tiny kitchen was set.

Slowly, Jo pulled off her dripping hat, letting her hair tumble free from where it had been piled under its confinement. With automatic movements she hung both her hat and coat on the hooks by the trailer door. It had been almost six months since she had stood in Frank's trailer, and like a woman visiting an old friend, she searched for changes.

The same faded lampshade adorned the maple table lamp that Frank had used for reading. The shade sat straight now, however, not at its usual slightly askew angle. The pillow that Lillie from wardrobe had sewn for him on some long-ago

Christmas still sat over the small burn hole in the seat cushion of the couch. Jo doubted that Keane knew of the hole's existence. Frank's pipe stand sat, as always, on the counter by the side window. Unable to resist, Jo crossed over to run her finger over the worn bowl of his favorite pipe.

"Never could pack it right," she murmured to his well-loved ghost. Abruptly, her senses quivered. She twisted her head to see Keane watching her. Jo dropped her hand. A rare blush mantled her cheeks as she found herself caught unguarded.

"How do you take your coffee, Jo?"

She swallowed. "Black," she told him, aware that he was granting her the privacy of her thoughts. "Just black. Thank you."

Keane nodded, then turned to pick up two steaming mugs. "Come, sit down." He moved toward the Formica table that sat directly across from the kitchen. "You'd better take off your shoes. They're wet."

After squeaking her way down the length of the trailer, Jo sat down and pulled at the damp laces. Keane set both mugs on the table before disappearing into the back of the trailer. When he returned, Jo was already sipping at the coffee.

"Here." He offered her a pair of socks.

Surprised, Jo shook her head. "No, that's all right. I don't need…"

Her polite refusal trailed off as he knelt at her feet. "Your feet are like ice," he commented after cupping them in his palms. Briskly, he rubbed them while Jo sat mute, oddly disarmed by the gesture. The warmth was spreading dangerously past her ankles. "Since I'm responsible for keeping you out in the rain," he went on as he slipped a sock over her foot, "I'd best see to it you don't cough and sneeze your way through tomorrow's show. Such small feet," he murmured, running his thumb over the curve of her ankle as she stared wordlessly at the top of his head.

Raindrops still clung to and glistened in his hair. Jo found herself longing to brush them away and feel the texture of his hair beneath her fingers. She was sharply aware of him and wondered if it would always be this way when she was near him. Keane pulled on the second sock. His fingers lingered on her calf as he lifted his eyes. Hers were darkened with confusion as they met his. The body over which she had always held supreme control was journeying into frontiers her mind had not yet explored.

"Still cold?" Keane asked softly.

Jo moistened her lips and shook her head. "No. No, I'm fine."

He smiled a lazy, masculine smile that said as clearly as words that he was aware of his effect on her. His eyes told her he enjoyed it. Unsmiling, Jo watched him rise to his feet.

"It doesn't mean you'll win," she said aloud in response to their silent communication.

"No, it doesn't." Keane's smile remained as his gaze roamed possessively over her face. "That only makes it more interesting. Open and shut cases are invariably boring, hardly worth the trouble of going on if you've won before you've finished your opening statement."

Jo lifted her coffee and sipped, taking a moment to settle her nerves. "Are we here to discuss the law or circus business, counselor?" she asked, letting her eyes drift to his again as she set the mug back on the table. "If it's law, I'm afraid I'm going to disappoint you. I don't know much about it."

"What do you know about, Jovilette?" Keane slid into the chair beside hers.

"Cats," she said. "And Prescott's Circus Colossus. I'll be glad to let you know whatever I can about either."

"Tell me about you," he countered, and leaning back, pulled a cigar from his pocket.

"Mr. Prescott—" Jo began.

"Keane," he interrupted, flicking on his lighter. He glanced at the tip of his cigar, then back up at her through the thin haze of smoke.

"I was under the impression you wanted to be briefed on the personnel."

"You are a member of this circus, are you not?" Casually, Keane blew smoke at the ceiling. "I have every intention of being briefed on the entire troupe and see no reason why you shouldn't start with yourself." His eyes traveled back to hers. "Humor me."

Jo decided to take the line of least resistance. "It's a short enough story," she said with a shrug. "I've been with the circus all my life. When I was old enough, I started work as a generally useful."

"A what?" Keane paused in the action of reaching for the coffeepot.

"Generally useful," Jo repeated, letting him freshen her cup. "It's a circus term that means exactly what it says. Rose's parents, for instance, are generally usefuls. We get a lot of drifters who work that way, too. It's also written into every performer's contract, after the specific terms, that they make themselves generally useful. There isn't room in most circuses, and certainly not in a tent circus, for performers with star complexes. You do what's necessary, what's needed. Buck, my handler, fills in during a slump at the sideshow, and he's one of the best canvas men around. Pete is the best mechanic in the troupe. Jamie knows as much about lighting as most shandies—electricians," she supplied as Keane lifted a brow. "He's also a better-than-average tumbler."

"What about you?" Keane interrupted the flow of Jo's words. For a moment she faltered, and the hands that had been gesturing became still. "Besides riding a galloping horse without reins or saddle, giving orders to elephants and facing lions?" He lifted his cup, watching her as he sipped. A smile lurked in his eyes. Jo frowned, studying him.

"Are you making fun of me?"

His smile sobered instantly. "No, Jo, I'm not making fun of you."

She continued. "In a pinch, I run the menagerie in the sideshow or I fill in the aerial act. Not the trap," she explained, relaxing again. "They have to practice together constantly to keep the timing. But sometimes I fill in on the Spanish Web, the big costume number where the girls hang from ropes and do identical moves. They're using butterfly costumes this year."

"Yes, I know the one." Keane continued to watch her as he drew on his cigar.

"But mostly Duffy likes to use girls who are more curvy. They double as showgirls in the finale."

"I see." A smile tugged at the corners of Keane's mouth. "Tell me, were your parents European?"

"No." Diverted, Jo shook her head. "Why do you ask?"

"Your name. And the ease with which I've heard you speak both French and Italian."

"It's easy to pick up languages in the circus," Jo said.

"Your accent was perfect in both cases."

"What? Oh." She shrugged and absently shifted in her chair, bringing her feet up to sit cross-legged. "We have a wide variety of nationalities here. Frank used to say that the world could take a lesson from the circus. We have French, Italian,

Spanish, German, Russian, Mexican, Americans from all parts of the country and more."

"I know. It's like a traveling United Nations." He tipped his cigar ash in a glass tray. "So you picked up some French and Italian along the way. But if you've traveled with the circus all your life, what about the rest of your schooling?"

The hint of censure in his voice brought up her chin. "I went to school during the winter break and had a tutor on the road. I learned my ABC's, counselor, and a bit more, besides. I probably know more about geography and world history than you, and from more interesting sources than textbooks. I imagine I know more about animals than a third-year veterinary student and have more practical experience healing them. I can speak seven languages and—"

"Seven?" Keane interrupted. "Seven languages?"

"Well, five fluently," she corrected grudgingly. "I still have a bit of trouble with Greek and German, unless I can really take my time, and I can't read Greek yet at all."

"What else besides French, Italian and English?"

"Spanish and Russian." Jo scowled into her coffee. "The Russian's handy. I use it for swearing at the cats during the act. Not too many people understand Russian cursing, so it's safe."

Keane's laughter brought Jo's attention from her coffee. He was leaning back in his chair, his eyes gold with their mirth. Jo's scowl deepened. "What's so funny?"

"You are, Jovilette." Stung, she started to scramble up, but his hands on her shoulders stopped her. "No, don't be offended. I can't help but find it amusing that you toss out so offhandedly an accomplishment that any language major would brag about." Carelessly, he ran a finger over her sulky mouth. "You continually amaze me." He brushed a hand through her hair.

"You mumbled something at me the other day. Were you swearing at me in Russian?"

"Probably."

Grinning, Keane dropped his hand and settled into his chair again. "When did you start working with the cats?"

"In front of an audience? When I was seventeen. Frank wouldn't let me start any earlier. He was my legal guardian as well as the owner, so he had me both ways. I was ready when I was fifteen."

"How did you lose your parents?"

The question caught her off guard. "In a fire," she said levelly. "When I was seven."

"Here?"

She knew Keane was not referring to their locale but to the circus. Jo sipped her cooling coffee. "Yes."

"Didn't you have any other family?"

"The circus is a family," she countered. "I was never given the chance to be an orphan. And I always had Frank."

"Did you?" Keane's smile was faintly sarcastic. "How was he as a father figure?"

Jo studied him for a moment. Was he bitter? she wondered. Or amused? Or simply curious? "He never took my father's place," she replied quietly. "He never tried to, because neither of us wanted it. We were friends, as close as I think it's possible for friends to be, but I'd already had a father, and he'd already had a child. We weren't looking for substitutes. You look nothing like him, you know."

"No," Keane replied with a shrug. "I know."

"He had a comfortable face, all creases and folds." Jo smiled, thinking of it while she ran a finger absently around the rim of her mug. "He was dark, too, just beginning to gray when…"

She trailed off, then brought herself back with a quick shake of her head. "Your voice is rather like his, though; he had a truly beautiful voice. I'll ask you a question now."

Keane's expression became attentive, then he gestured with the back of his hand. "Go ahead."

"Why are you here? I lost my temper when I asked you before, but I do want to know." It was against her nature to probe, and some of her discomfort found its way into her voice. "It must have caused you some difficulty to leave your practice, even for a few weeks."

Keane frowned at the end of his cigar before he slowly crushed it out. "Let's say I wanted to see firsthand what had fascinated my father all these years."

"You never came when he was alive." Jo gripped her hands together under the table. "You didn't even bother to come to his funeral."

"I would've been the worst kind of hypocrite to attend his funeral, don't you think?"

"He was your father." Jo's eyes grew dark and her tone sharp in reproof.

"You're smarter than that, Jo," Keane countered calmly. "It takes more than an accident of birth to make a father. Frank Prescott was a complete stranger to me."

"You resent him." Jo felt suddenly torn between loyalty for Frank and understanding for the man who sat beside her.

"No." Keane shook his head thoughtfully. "No, I believe I actively resented him when I was growing up, but…" He shrugged the thought aside. "I grew rather ambivalent over the years."

"He was a good man," Jo stated, leaning forward as she willed him to understand. "He only wanted to give people

pleasure, to show them a little magic. Maybe he wasn't made
to be a father—some men aren't—but he was kind and gentle.
And he was proud of you."

"Of me?" Keane seemed amused. "How?"

"Oh, you're hateful," Jo whispered, hurt by his careless
attitude. She slipped from her chair, but before she could step
away, Keane took her arm.

"No, tell me. I'm interested." His hold on her arm was light,
but she knew it would tighten if she resisted.

"All right." Jo tossed her head to send her hair behind her
back. "He had the Chicago paper delivered to his Florida
office. He always looked for any mention of you, any article
on a court case you were involved in or a dinner party you
attended. Anything. You have to understand that to us a write-
up is very important. Frank wasn't a performer, but he was one
of us. Sometimes he'd read me an article before he put it away.
He kept a scrapbook."

Jo pulled her arm away and strode past Keane into the
bedroom. The oversize wooden chest was where it had always
been, at the foot of Frank's bed. Kneeling down, Jo tossed up
the lid. "This is where he kept all the things that mattered to
him." Jo began to shift through papers and mementos quickly;
she had not been able to bring herself to sort through the chest
before. Keane stood in the doorway and watched her. "He
called it his memory box." She pushed at her hair with an
annoyed hand, then continued to search. "He said memories
were the rewards for growing old. Here it is." Jo pulled out a
dark green scrapbook, then sat back on her heels. Silently, she
held it out to Keane. After a moment he crossed the room and
took it from her. Jo could hear the rain hissing on the ground
outside as their eyes held. His expression was unfathomable as

he opened the book. The pages rustled to join the quiet sound of the rain.

"What an odd man he must have been," Keane murmured, "to keep a scrapbook on a son he never knew." There was no rancor in his voice. "What was he?" he asked suddenly, shifting his eyes back to Jo.

"A dreamer," she answered. "His watch was always five minutes slow. If he hung a picture on the wall, it was always crooked. He'd never straighten it because he'd never notice. He was always thinking about tomorrow. I guess that's why he kept yesterday in this box." Glancing down, she began to straighten the chaos she had caused while looking for the book. A snatch of red caught her eye. Reaching for it, her fingers found a familiar shape. Jo hesitated, then drew the old doll out of the chest.

It was a sad piece of plastic and faded silk with its face nearly washed away. One arm was broken off, leaving an empty sleeve. The golden hair was straggled but brave under its red cap. Ballet shoes were painted on the dainty feet. Tears backed up behind Jo's eyes as she made a soft sound of joy and despair.

"What is it?" Keane demanded, glancing down to see her clutching the battered ballerina.

"Nothing." Her voice was unsteady as she scrambled quickly to her feet. "I have to go." Though she tried, Jo could not bring herself to drop the doll back into the box. She swallowed. She did not wish to reveal her emotions before his intelligent, gold eyes. Perhaps he would be cynical, or worse, amused. "May I have this, please?" She was careful with the tone of the request.

Slowly, Keane crossed the distance between them, then cradled her chin in his hand. "It appears to be yours already."

"It was." Her fingers tightened on the doll's waist. "I didn't know Frank had kept it. Please," she whispered. Her emotions were already dangerously heightened. She could feel a need to rest her head against his shoulder. The evening had been a roller coaster for her feelings, climaxing now with the discovery of her most prized childhood possession. She knew that if she did not escape, she would seek comfort in his arms. Her own weakness frightened her. "Let me by."

For a moment, Jo read refusal in his eyes. Then he stepped aside. Jo let out a quiet, shaky breath. "I'll walk you back to your trailer."

"No," she said quickly, too quickly. "It isn't necessary," she amended, moving by him and into the kitchen. Sitting down, she pulled on her shoes, too distraught to remember she still wore his socks. "There's no reason for us both to get wet again." She rambled on, knowing he was watching her hurried movement, but unable to stop. "And I'm going to check on my cats before I go in, and…"

She stopped short when he took her shoulders and pulled her to her feet. "And you don't want to take the chance of being alone in your trailer with me in case I change my mind."

A sharp denial trembled on her lips, but the knowledge in his eyes crushed it. "All right," she admitted. "That, too."

Keane brushed her hair from her neck and shook his head. He kissed her nose and moved down to pluck her hat and coat from their hooks. Cautiously, Jo followed him. When he held out her coat, she turned and slipped her arms into the sleeves. Before she could murmur her thanks, he turned her back and pulled up the zipper. For a moment his fingers lingered at her neck, his eyes on hers. Taking her hair into his hand, he piled it atop her head, then dropped on her hat. The gestures were innocent, but Jo was rocked by a feeling of intimacy she had never experienced.

"I'll see you tomorrow," he said, pulling the brim of her hat down further over her eyes.

Jo nodded. Holding the doll against her side, she pushed open the door. The sound of rain was amplified through the trailer. "Good night," she murmured, then moved quickly into the night.

Chapter Five

The morning scent was clean. In the new lot rainbows glistened in puddles. At last the sky was blue with only harmless white puffs of clouds floating over its surface. In the cookhouse a loud, crowded breakfast was being served. Finding herself without appetite, Jo skipped going to the cookhouse altogether. She was restless and tense. No matter how she disciplined her mind, her thoughts wandered back to Keane Prescott and to the evening they had spent together. Jo remembered it all, from the quick passion of the kiss in the rain to the calmness of his voice when he had said good-night. It was odd, she mused, that whenever she began to talk to him, she forgot he was the owner, forgot he was Frank's son. Always she was forced to remind herself of their positions.

Deep in thought, Jo slipped into tights and a leotard. It was true, she admitted, that she had failed to keep their relationship from becoming personal. She found it difficult to corral her urge to laugh with him, to share a joke, to open for him the doorway to the magic of the circus. If he could feel it, she thought, he would understand. Though she could admit her interest in him privately, she could not find a clear reason for his apparent interest in her.

Why me? she wondered with a shake of her head. Turning, she opened her wardrobe closet and studied herself in the full-length glass on the back of the door. There she saw a woman of slightly less-than-average height with a body lacking the generous curves of Duffy's showgirls. The legs, she decided, were not bad. They were long and well-shaped with slim thighs. The hips were narrow, more, she thought with a pout, like a boy's than a woman's; and the bustline was sadly inadequate. She knew many women in the troupe with more appeal and a dozen with more experience.

Jo could see nothing in the mirror that would attract a sophisticated Chicago attorney. She did not note the honesty that shone from the exotically shaped green eyes or the strength in her chin or the full promise of her mouth. She saw the touch of gypsy in the tawny complexion and raven hair but remained unaware of the appeal that came from the hint of something wild and untamed just under the surface. The plain black leotard showed her firm, lithe body to perfection, but Jo thought nothing of the smooth satiny sheen of her skin. She was frowning as she pulled her hair back and began to braid it.

He must know dozens of women, she thought as her hands worked to confine her thick mane of hair. He probably takes a different one to dinner every night. They wear beautiful clothes and expensive perfume, she mused, torturing herself with the thought. They have names like Laura and Patricia, and they have low, sophisticated laughs. Jo lifted a brow at the reflection in the mirror and gave a light, low laugh. She wrinkled her brow at the hollowness of the sound. They discuss mutual friends, the Wallaces or the Jamesons, over candlelight and Beaujolais. And when he takes the most beautiful one home, they listen to Chopin and drink brandy in front of the fire. Then they make love. Jo felt an odd tightening in her stomach but pursued the fantasy to the finish. The lovely lady is experienced, passionate and worldly. Her skin is soft and white. When he leaves, she is not devastated but mature. She doesn't even care if he loves her or not.

Jo stared at the woman in the glass and saw her cheeks were wet. On a cry of frustration, she slammed the door shut. *What's wrong with me?* she demanded, brushing all traces of tears from her face. I haven't been myself for days! I need to shake myself out of this—this…whatever it is that I'm in. Slipping on gymnastic shoes and tossing a robe over her arm, Jo hustled from the trailer.

She moved carefully, avoiding puddles and any further speculation on Keane Prescott's romantic life. Before she was halfway across the lot, she saw Rose. From the expression on her face, Jo could see she was in a temper.

"Hello, Rose," she said, strategically stepping aside as the snake charmer splashed through a puddle.

"He's hopeless," Rose tossed back. "I tell you," she continued, stopping and wagging a finger at Jo, "I'm through this time. Why should I waste my time?"

"You've certainly been patient," Jo agreed, deciding that sympathy was the wisest course. "It's more than he deserves."

"Patient?" Rose raised a dramatic hand to her breast. "I have the patience of a saint. Yet even a saint has her limits!" Rose tossed her hair behind her shoulders. She sighed heavily. "*Adios.* I think I hear Mama calling me."

Jo continued her walk toward the Big Top. Jamie walked by, his hands in his pockets. "She's crazy," he muttered. He stopped and spread his arms wide. His look was that of a man ill-used and innocent. Jo shrugged. Shaking his head, Jamie moved away. "She's crazy," he said again.

Jo watched him until he was out of sight, then darted to the Big Top.

Inside, Carmen watched adoringly while Vito practiced a new routine on the incline wire. The tent echoed with the sounds of rehearsals: voices and thumps, the rattle of rigging, the yapping of clown dogs. In the first ring Jo spotted the Six Beirots, an acrobatic act that was just beginning its warm-ups. Pleased with her timing, Jo walked the length of the arena. A raucous whistle sounded over her head, and she glanced up to shake a friendly fist at Vito. He called from fifteen feet above her as he balanced on a slender wire set at a forty-five-degree angle.

"Hey, chickie, you have a nice rear view. You're almost as cute as me."

"No one's as cute as you, Vito," she called back.

"Ah, I know." With a weighty sigh, he executed a neat pivot. "But I have learned to live with it." He sent down a lewd wink. "When you going into town with me, chickie?" he asked as he always did.

"When you teach my cats to walk the wire," Jo answered as she always did. Vito laughed and began a light-footed cha-cha. Carmen fired Jo a glare. She must have it bad, Jo decided, if she takes Vito's harmless flirting seriously. Stopping beside her, Jo leaned close and spoke in a conspirator's whisper. "He'd fall off his wire if I said I'd go."

"I'd go," Carmen said with a lovely pout, "if he'd just ask me."

Jo shook her head, wondering why romances were invariably complicated. She was lucky not to have the problem. Giving Carmen an encouraging pat on the shoulder, Jo set off toward the first ring.

★ ★ ★

The Six Beirots were brothers. They were all small-statured, dark men who had immigrated from Belgium. Jo worked out with them often to keep herself limber and to keep her reflexes sharp. She liked them all, knew their wives and children, and understood their unique blending of French and English. Raoul was the oldest, and the stockiest of the six brothers. Because of his build and strength, he was the under-stander in their human pyramid. It was he who spotted Jo and first lifted a hand in greeting.

"Halo." He grinned and ran his palm over his receding hairline. "You gonna tumble?"

Jo laughed and did a quick handspring into the ring. She stuck out her tongue when the unanimous critique was "sloppy." "I just need to warm up," she said, assuming an air of injured dignity. "My muscles need tuning."

For the next thirty minutes Jo worked with them, doing muscle stretches and limbering exercises, rib stretches and lung expanders. Her muscles warmed and loosened, her heart pumped steadily. She was filled with energy. Her mind was clear. Because of her lightened mood, Jo was easily cajoled into a few impromptu acrobatics. Leaving the more complicated feats to the experts, she did simple back flips, handsprings or twists at Raoul's command. She did a brief, semi-successful thirty seconds atop the rolling globe and earned catcalls from her comrades at her dismount.

She stood back as they began the leaps. One after another they lined up to take turns running along a ramp, bounding upon a springboard and flying up to do flips or twists before landing on the mat. There was a constant stream of French as they called out to each other.

"Hokay, Jo." Raoul gestured with his hand. "Your turn."

"Oh, no." She shook her head and reached for her robe. "Uh-uh." There was a chorus of coaxing, teasing French. "I've got to give my cats their vitamins," she told them, still shaking her head.

"Come on, Jo. It's fun." Raoul grinned and wiggled his eyebrows. "Don't you like to fly?" As she glanced at the ramp, Raoul knew she was tempted. "You take a good spring," he told her. "Do one forward somersault, then land on my shoulders." He patted them to show their ability to handle the job.

Jo smiled and nibbled pensively on her lower lip. It had been a long while since she had taken the time to go up on the trapeze and really fly. It did look like fun. She gave Raoul a stern look. "You'll catch me?"

"Raoul never misses," he said proudly, then turned to his brothers. *"N'est-ce pas?"* His brothers shrugged and rolled their eyes to the ceiling with indistinguishable mutters. "Ah." He waved them away with the back of his hand.

Knowing Raoul was indeed a top flight under-stander, Jo approached the ramp. Still she gave him one last narrow-eyed look. "You catch me," she ordered, shaking her finger at him.

"Cherie." He took his position with a stylish movement of his hand. "It's a piece of pie."

"Cake," Jo corrected, took a deep breath, held it and ran. When she came off the springboard, she tucked into the somersault and watched the Big Top turn upside down. She felt good. As the tent began to right itself, she straightened for her landing, keeping herself loose. Her feet connected with Raoul's powerful shoulders, and she tilted only briefly before he took her ankles in a firm grip. Straightening her poor posture, Jo styled elaborately with both arms while she received exaggerated applause and whistles. She leaped down nimbly as Raoul took her waist to give her landing bounce.

"When do you want to join the act?" he asked her, giving her a friendly pat on the bottom. "We'll put you up on the sway pole."

"That's okay." Grinning, Jo again reached for her robe. "I'll stick with the cats." After a cheerful wave, she slipped one arm into a sleeve and started back down the hippodrome track. She pulled up short when she spotted Keane leaning up against the front seat rail.

"Amazing," he said, then straightened to move to her. "But then, the circus is supposed to be amazing, isn't it?" He lifted the forgotten sleeve to her robe, then slipped her other arm into it. "Is there anything here you can't do?"

"Hundreds of things," Jo answered, taking him seriously. "I'm only really proficient with animals. The rest is just show and play."

"You looked amazingly proficient to me for the last half hour or so," he countered as he pulled out her braid from where it was trapped by her robe.

"Have you been here that long?"

"I walked in as Vito was commenting on your rear view."

"Oh." Jo laughed, glancing back to where Vito now stood flirting with Carmen. "He's crazy."

"Perhaps," Keane agreed, taking her arm. "But his eyesight's good enough. Would you like some coffee?"

Jo was reminded instantly of the evening before. Leery of being drawn to his charms again, she shook her head. "I've got to change," she told him, belting her robe. "We've got a show at two. I want to rehearse the cats."

"It's incredible how much time you people devote to your art. Rehearsals seem to run into the beginning of a show, and a show seems to run into more rehearsals."

Jo softened when he referred to circus skills as art. "Performers always look for just a bit more in themselves. It's a constant struggle for perfection. Even when a performance goes beautifully and you know it, you start thinking about the next time. How can I do it better or bigger or higher or faster?"

"Never satisfied?" Keane asked as they stepped out into the sunlight.

"If we were, we wouldn't have much of a reason to come back and do it all over again."

He nodded, but there was something absent in the gesture, as if his mind was elsewhere. "I have to leave this afternoon," he said almost to himself.

"Leave?" Jo's heart skidded to a stop. Her distress was overwhelming and so unexpected that she was forced to take an extra moment to steady herself. "Back to Chicago?"

"Hmm?" Keane stopped, turning to face her. "Oh, yes."

"And the circus?" Jo asked, thoroughly ashamed that it had not been her first concern. She didn't want him to leave, she suddenly realized.

Keane frowned a moment, then continued to walk. "I see no purpose in disrupting this year's schedule." His voice was brisk now and businesslike.

"This year's?" Jo repeated cautiously.

Keane turned and looked at her. "I haven't decided its ultimate fate, but I won't do anything until the end of the summer."

"I see." She let out a long breath. "So we have a reprieve."

"In a manner of speaking," Keane agreed.

Jo was silent for a moment but could not prevent herself from asking, "Then you won't—I mean, you'll be staying in Chicago now; you won't be traveling with us?"

They negotiated their way around a puddle before Keane

answered. "I don't feel I can make a judicious decision about the circus after so brief an exposure. There's a complication in one of my cases that needs my personal attention, but I should be back in a week or two."

Relief flooded through her. He would be back, a voice shouted in her ear. It shouldn't matter to you, another whispered. "We'll be in South Carolina in a couple of weeks," Jo said casually. They had reached her trailer, and she took the handle of her door before she turned to face him. *It's just that I want him to understand what this circus means,* she told herself as she looked up into his eyes. *That's the only reason I want him to come back.* Knowing she was lying to herself made it difficult to keep her gaze steady.

Keane smiled, letting his eyes travel over her face. "Yes, Duffy's given me a route list. I'll find you. Aren't you going to ask me in?"

"In?" Jo repeated. "Oh, no, I told you, I have to change, and…" He stepped forward as she talked. Something in his eyes told her a firm stand was necessary. She had seen a similar look in a lion's eyes while he contemplated taking a dangerous liberty. "I simply don't have time right now. If I don't see you before you go, have a good trip." She turned and opened the door. Aware of a movement, she turned back, but not before he had nudged her through the door and followed. As it closed at his back, Jo bristled with fury. She did not enjoy being outmaneuvered. "Tell me, counselor, do you know anything about a law concerning breaking and entering?"

"Doesn't apply," he returned smoothly. "There was no lock involved." He glanced around at the attractive simplicity of Jo's trailer. The colors were restful earth tones without frills. The beige- and brown-flecked linoleum floor was spotlessly clean. It was the same basic floorplan as Frank's trailer, but here there were softer touches. There were curtains rather than shades at the windows; large, comfortable pillows tossed onto a forest green sofa; a spray of fresh wildflowers tucked into a thin, glass vase. Without comment Keane wandered to a black lacquer trunk that sat directly opposite the door. On it was a book that he picked up while Jo fumed. *"The Count of Monte Cristo,"* he read aloud and flipped it open. "In French," he stated, lifting a brow.

"It was written in French," Jo muttered, pulling it from his hand. "So I read it in French." Annoyed, she lifted the lid on the trunk, preparing to drop the book inside and out of his reach.

"Good heavens, are those all yours?" Keane stopped the lid on its downswing, then pushed books around with his other hand. "Tolstoy, Cervantes, Voltaire, Steinbeck. When do you have time in this crazy, twenty-four-hour world you live in to read this stuff?"

"I make time," Jo snapped as her eyes sparked. "My *own* time. Just because you're the owner doesn't mean you can barge in here and poke through my things and demand an account of my time. This is my trailer. I own everything in it."

"Hold on." Keane halted her rushing stream of words. "I wasn't demanding an account of your time, I was simply astonished that you could find enough of it to do this type of reading. Since I can't claim to be an expert on your work, it would be remarkably foolish of me to criticize the amount of time you spend on it. Secondly," he said, taking a step toward her—and though Jo stiffened in anticipation, he did not touch her, "I apologize for 'poking through your things,' as you put it. I was interested for several reasons. One being I have quite an extensive library myself. It seems we have a common interest, whether we like it or not. As for barging into your trailer, I can only plead guilty. If you choose to prosecute, I can recommend a couple of lousy attorneys who overcharge."

His last comment forced a smile onto Jo's reluctant lips. "I'll give it some thought." With more care than she had originally intended, Jo lowered the lid of the trunk. She was reminded that she had not been gracious. "I'm sorry," she said as she turned back to him.

His eyes reflected curiosity. "What for?"

"For snapping at you." She lifted her shoulders, then let them fall. "I thought you were criticizing me. I suppose I'm too sensitive."

Several seconds passed before he spoke. "Unnecessary apology accepted if you answer one question."

Mystified, Jo frowned at him. "What question?"

"Is the Tolstoy in Russian?"

Jo laughed, pushing loose strands of hair from her face. "Yes, it is."

Keane smiled, enjoying the two tiny dimples that flickered in her cheeks when she laughed. "Did you know that though you're lovely in any case, you grow even more so when you smile?"

Jo's laughter stilled. She was unaccustomed to this sort of compliment and studied him without any idea of how to respond. It occurred to her that any of the sophisticated women she had imagined that morning would have known precisely what to say. She would have been able to smile or laugh as she tossed back the appropriate comment. That woman, Jo admitted, was not Jovilette Wilder. Gravely, she kept her eyes on his. "I don't know how to flirt," she said simply.

Keane tilted his head, and an expression came and went in his eyes before she could analyze it. He stepped toward her. "I wasn't flirting with you, Jo, I was making an observation. Hasn't anyone ever told you that you're beautiful?"

He was much too close now, but in the narrow confines of the trailer, Jo had little room to maneuver. She was forced to tilt back her head to keep her eyes level with his. "Not precisely the way you did." Quickly, she put her hand to his chest to keep the slight but important distance between them. She knew she was trapped, but that did not mean she was defeated.

Gently, Keane lifted her protesting hand, turning it palm up as he brought it to his lips. An involuntary breath rushed in and out of Jo's lungs. "Your hands are exquisite," he murmured, tracing the fine line of blue up the back. "Narrow-boned, long-fingered. And the palms show hard work. That makes them more interesting." He lifted his eyes from her hand to her face. "Like you."

Jo's voice had grown husky, but she could do nothing to alter it. "I don't know what I'm supposed to say when you tell me things like that." Beneath her robe her breasts rose and fell with her quickening heart. "I'd rather you didn't."

"Do you really?" Keane ran the back of his hand along her jawline. "That's a pity, because the more I look at you, the more I find to say. You're a bewitching creature, Jovilette."

"I have to change," she said in the firmest voice she could muster. "You'll have to go."

"That's unfortunately true," he murmured, then cupped her chin. "Come, then, kiss me goodbye."

Jo stiffened. "I hardly think that's necessary...."

"You couldn't be more wrong," he told her as he lowered his mouth. "It's extremely necessary." In a light, teasing whisper, his lips met hers. His arms encircled her, bringing her closer with only the slightest pressure. "Kiss me back, Jo," he ordered softly. "Put your arms around me and kiss me back."

For a moment longer she resisted, but the lure of his mouth nibbling at hers was too strong. Letting instinct rule her will, Jo lifted her arms and circled his neck. Her mouth grew mobile under his, parting and offering. Her surrender seemed to lick the flames of his passion. The kiss grew urgent. His arms locked, crushing her against him. Her quiet moan was not of protest but of wonder. Her fingers found their way into his hair, tangling in its thickness as they urged him closer. She felt her robe loosen, then his hands trail up her rib cage. At his touch, she shivered, feeling her skin grow hot, then cold, then hot again in rapid succession.

When his hand took her breast, she shied, drawing in her breath quickly. "Steady," he murmured against her mouth. His hands stroked gently, coaxing her to relax again. He kissed the corners of her mouth, waiting until she quieted before he took her deep again. The thin leotard molded her body. It created no barrier against the warmth of his searching fingers. They moved slowly, lingering over the peak of her breast, exploring its softness, wandering to her waist, then tracing her hip and thigh.

No man had ever touched her so freely. Jo was helpless to stop him, helpless against her own growing need for him to touch her again. Was this the passion she had read of so often? The passion that drove men to war, to struggle against all reason, to risk everything? She felt she could understand it now. She clung to him as he taught her—as she learned—the demands of her own body. Her mouth grew hungrier for the taste of him. She was certain she remained in his arms while seasons flew by, while decades passed, while worlds were destroyed and built again.

But when he drew away, Jo saw the same sun spilling through her windows. Eternity had only been moments.

Unable to speak, she merely stared up at him. Her eyes were dark and aware, her cheeks flushed with desire. But somehow, though it still tingled from his, her mouth maintained a youthful innocence. Keane's eyes dropped to it as his hands loitered at the small of her back.

"It's difficult to believe I'm the first man to touch you," he murmured. His eyes roamed to hers. "And quite desperately arousing. Particularly when I find you've passion to match your looks. I think I'd like to make love with you in the daylight first so that I can watch that marvelous control of yours slip away layer by layer. We'll have to discuss it when I get back."

Jo forced strength back into her limbs, knowing she was on the brink of losing her will to him. "Just because I let you kiss me and touch me doesn't mean I'll let you make love to me." She lifted her chin, feeling her confidence surging back. "If I do, it'll be because it's what I want, not because you tell me to."

The expression in Keane's eyes altered. "Fair enough," he agreed and nodded. "It'll simply be my job to make it what you want." He took her chin in his hand and lowered his mouth to hers for a brief kiss. As she had the first time, Jo kept her eyes open and watched him. She felt him grin against her mouth before he raised his head. "You are the most fascinating woman I've ever met." Turning, he crossed to the door. "I'll be back," he said with a careless wave before it closed behind him. Dumbly, Jo stared into empty space.

Fascinating? she repeated, tracing her still warm lips with her fingertips. Quickly, she ran to the window, and kneeling on the sofa below it, watched Keane stride away.

She realized with a sudden jolt that she missed him already.

Chapter Six

Jo learned that weeks could drag like years. During the second week of Keane's absence she had searched each new lot for a sign of him. She had scanned the crowds of towers who came to watch the raising of the Big Top, and as the days stretched on and on, she balanced between anger and despair at his continued absence. Only in the cage did she manage to isolate her concentration, knowing she could not afford to do otherwise. But after each performance Jo found it more and more difficult to relax. Each morning she felt certain he would be back. Each night she lay restless, waiting for the sun to rise.

Spring was in full bloom. The high grass lots smelled of it. Often there were wildflowers crushed underfoot, leaving their heavy fragrances in the air. Even as the circus caravan traveled north, the days grew warm, sunlight lingering further into evening. While other troupers enjoyed the balmy air and providentially sunny skies, Jo lived on nerves.

It occurred to her that after returning to his life in Chicago, Keane had decided against coming back. In Chicago he had comfort and wealth and elegant women. Why should he come back? Jo closed her mind against the ultimate fate of the circus, unwilling to face the possibility that Keane might close the show at the end of the season. She told herself the only reason she wanted him to come back was to convince him to keep the circus open. But the memory of being in his arms intruded too often into her thoughts. Gradually, she grew resigned, filling the strange void she felt with her work.

Several times each week she found time to give the eager Gerry more training. At first she had only permitted him to work with the two menagerie cubs, allowing him, with the protection of leather gloves, to play with them and to feed them. She encouraged him to teach them simple tricks with the aid of small pieces of raw meat. Jo was as pleased as he when the cats responded to his patience and obeyed.

Jo saw potential in Gerry, in his genuine affection for animals and in his determination. Her primary concern was that he had not yet developed a healthy fear. He was still too casual, and with casualness, Jo knew, came carelessness. When she thought he had progressed far enough, Jo decided to take him to the next step of his training.

There was no matinee that day, and the Big Top was scattered with rehearsing troupers. Jo was dressed in boots and khakis with a long-sleeved blouse tucked into the waist. She studied Gerry as she ran the stock of her whip through her hand. They stood together in the safety cage while she issued instructions.

"All right, Buck's going to let Merlin through the chute. He's the most tractable of the cats, except for Ari." She paused a moment while her eyes grew sad. "Ari isn't up to even a short practice session." She pushed away the depression that threatened and continued. "Merlin knows you, he's familiar with your voice and your scent." Gerry nodded and swallowed. "When we go in, you're to be my shadow. You move when I move, and don't speak until I tell you. If you get frightened, don't run." Jo took his arm for emphasis. "That's *important*, understand? Don't run. Tell me if you want out, and I'll get you to the safety cage."

"I won't run, Jo," he promised and wiped hands, damp with excitement, on his jeans.

"Are you ready?"

Gerry grinned and nodded. "Yeah."

Jo opened the door leading to the big cage and let Gerry through behind her before securing it. She walked to the center of the arena in easy, confident strides. "Let him in, Buck," she called and heard the immediate rattle of bars. Merlin entered without hurry, then leaped onto his pedestal. He yawned hugely before looking at Jo. "A solo today, Merlin," she said as she advanced toward him. "And you're the star. Stay with me," she ordered as Gerry merely stood still and stared at the big cat. Merlin gave Gerry a disinterested glance and waited.

With an upward move of her arm, she sent Merlin into a sit-up. "You know," she told the boy behind her, "that teaching a cat to take his seat is the first trick. The audience won't even consider it one. The sit-up," she continued while signaling Merlin to bring his front paws back down, "is usually next and takes quite a bit of time. It's necessary to strengthen the cat's back muscles first." Again she signaled Merlin to sit up, then, with a quick command, she had him pawing the air and roaring. "Marvelous old ham," she said with a grin and brought him back down. "The primary move of each cue is always given from the same position with the same tone of voice. It takes patience and repetition. I'm going to bring him down off the pedestal now."

Jo flicked the whip against the tanbark, and Merlin leaped down. "Now I maneuver him to the spot in the arena where I want him to lie down." As she moved, Jo made certain her student moved with her. "The cage is a circle, forty feet in diameter. You have to know every inch of it inside your head. You have to know precisely how far you are from the bars at all times. If you back up into the bars, you've got no room to maneuver if there's trouble. It's one of the biggest mistakes a trainer can make." At her signal Merlin laid down, then shifted to his side. "Over, Merlin," she said briskly, sending him into a series of rolls. "Use their names often; it keeps them in tune with you. You have to know each cat and their individual tendencies."

Jo moved with Merlin, then signaled him to stop. When he roared, she rubbed the top of his head with the stock of her whip. "They like to be petted just like house cats, but they are not tabbies. It's essential that you never give them your complete trust and that you remember always to maintain your dominance. You subjugate not by poking them or beating or shouting, which is not only cruel but makes for a mean, undependable cat, but with patience, respect and will. Never humiliate them; they have a right to their pride. You bluff them, Gerry," she said as she raised both arms and brought Merlin up on his hind legs. "Man is the unknown factor. That's why we use jungle-bred rather than captivity-bred cats. Ari is the exception. A cat born and raised in captivity is too familiar with man, so you lose your edge." She moved forward, keeping her arms raised. Merlin followed, walking on his hind legs. He spread seven feet into the air and towered over his trainer. "They might have a sense of affection for you, but there's no fear and little respect. Unfortunately, this often happens if a cat's been with a trainer a long time. They don't become more docile the longer they're in an act, but they become more dangerous. They test you constantly. The trick is to make them believe you're indestructible."

She brought Merlin down, and he gave another yawn before she sent him back to his seat. "If one swipes at you, you have to stop it then and there, because they try again and again, getting closer each time. Usually, if a trainer's hurt in the cage, it's because he's made a mistake. The cats are quick to spot them; sometimes they let them pass, sometimes they don't. This one's given me a good smack on the shoulder now and again. He's kept his claws retracted, but there's always the possibility that one time he'll forget he's just playing. Any questions?"

"Hundreds," Gerry answered, wiping his mouth with the back of his hand. "I just can't focus on one right now."

Jo chuckled and again scratched Merlin's head when he roared. "They'll come to you later. It's hard to absorb anything the first time, but it'll come back to you when you're relaxed again. All right, you know the cue. Make him sit up."

"Me?"

Jo stepped to the side, giving Merlin a clear view of her student. "You can be as scared as you like," she said easily. "Just don't let it show in your voice. Watch his eyes."

Gerry rubbed his palm on the thighs of his jeans, then lifted it as he had seen Jo do hundreds of times. "Up," he told the cat in a passably firm voice.

Merlin studied him a moment, then looked at Jo. This, his eyes told her clearly, was an amateur and beneath his notice. Carefully, Jo kept her face expressionless. "He's testing you," she told Gerry. "He's an old hand and a bit harder to bluff. Be firm and use his name this time."

Gerry took a deep breath and repeated the hand signal. "Up, Merlin."

Merlin glanced back at him, then stared with measuring, amber eyes. "Again," Jo instructed and heard Gerry swallow audibly. "Put some authority into your voice. He thinks you're a pushover."

"Up, Merlin!" Gerry repeated, annoyed enough by Jo's description to put some dominance into his voice. Though his reluctance was obvious, Merlin obeyed. "He did it," Gerry whispered on a long, shaky breath. "He really did it."

"Very good," Jo said, pleased with both the lion and her student. "Now bring him down." When this was accomplished, Jo had him bring Merlin from the seat. "Here." She handed Gerry the whip. "Use the stock to scratch his head. He likes it best just behind the ear." She felt the faint tremble in his hand as he took the whip, but he held it steady, even as Merlin closed his eyes and roared.

Because he had performed well, Jo afforded Merlin the liberty of rubbing against her legs before she called for Buck to let him out. The rattle of the bars was the cat's cue to exit, and like a trouper, he took it with his head held high. "You did very well," she told Gerry when they were alone in the cage.

"It was great." He handed her back the whip, the stock damp from his sweaty palms. "It was just great. When can I do it again?"

Jo smiled and patted his shoulder. "Soon," she promised. "Just remember the things I've told you and come to me when you remember all those questions."

"Okay, thanks, Jo." He stepped through the safety cage. "Thanks a lot. I want to go tell the guys."

"Go ahead." Jo watched him scramble away, leaping over the ring and darting through the back door. With a grin, she leaned against the bars. "Was I like that?" she asked Buck, who stood at the opposite end of the cage.

"The first time you got a cat to sit up on your own, we heard about it for a week. Twelve years old and you thought you were ready for the big show."

Jo laughed, and wiping the damp stock of her whip against her pants, turned. It was then she saw him standing behind her. "Keane!" She used the name she had sworn not to use as pleasure flooded through her. It shone on her face. Just as she had given up hope of seeing him again, he was there. She took two steps toward him before she could check herself. "I didn't know you were back." Jo gripped the stock of the whip with both hands to prevent herself from reaching out to touch him.

"I believe you missed me." His voice was as she remembered, low and smooth.

Jo cursed herself for being so naïve and transparent. "Perhaps I did, a little," she admitted cautiously. "I suppose I'd gotten used to you, and you were gone longer than you said you'd be." He looks the same, she thought rapidly, exactly the same. She reminded herself that it had only been a month. It had seemed like years.

"*Mmm,* yes. I had more to see to than I had expected. You look a bit pale," he observed and touched her cheek with his fingertip.

"I suppose I haven't been getting much sun," she said with quick prevarication. "How was Chicago?" Jo needed to turn the conversation away from personal lines until she had an opportunity to gauge her emotions; seeing him suddenly had tossed them into confusion.

"Cool," he told her, making a long, thorough survey of her face. "Have you ever been there?"

"No. We play near there toward the end of the season, but I've never had time to go all the way into the city."

Nodding absently, Keane glanced into the empty cage behind her. "I see you're training Gerry."

"Yes." Relieved that they had lapsed into a professional discussion, Jo let the muscles of her shoulders ease. "This was the first time with an adult cat and no bars between. He did very well."

Keane looked back at her. His eyes were serious and probing. "He was trembling. I could see it from where I stood watching you."

"It was his first time—" she began in Gerry's defense.

"I wasn't criticizing him," Keane interrupted with a tinge of impatience. "It's just that he stood beside you, shaking from head to foot, and you were totally cool and in complete control."

"It's my job to be in control," Jo reminded him.

"That lion must have stood seven feet tall when he went up on his hind legs, and you walked under him without any protection, not even the traditional chair."

"I do a picture act," she explained, "not a fighting act."

"Jo," he said so sharply she blinked. "Aren't you ever frightened in there?"

"Frightened?" she repeated, lifting a brow. "Of course I'm frightened. More frightened than Gerry was—or than you would be."

"What are you talking about?" Keane demanded. Jo noted with some curiosity that he was angry. "I could see that boy sweat in there."

"That was mostly excitement," Jo told him patiently. "He

hasn't the experience to be truly frightened yet." She tossed back her hair and let out a long breath. Jo did not like to talk of her fears with anyone and found it especially difficult with Keane. Only because she felt it necessary that he understand this to understand the circus did she continue. "Real fear comes from knowing them, working with them, understanding them. You can only speculate on what they can do to a man. I *know*. I know exactly what they're capable of. They have an incredible courage, but more, they have an incredible guile. I've seen what they can do." Her eyes were calm and clear as they looked into his. "My father almost lost a leg once. I was about five, but I remember it perfectly. He made a mistake, and a five-hundred-pound Nubian sunk into his thigh and dragged him around the arena. Luckily, the cat was diverted by a female in season. Cats are unpredictable when they have sex on their minds, which is probably one of the reasons he attacked my father in the first place. They're fiercely jealous once they've set their minds on a mate. My father was able to get into the safety cage before any of the other cats took an interest in him. I can't remember how many stitches he had or how long it was before he could walk properly again, but I do remember the look in that cat's eyes. You learn quickly about fear when you're in the cage, but you control it, you channel it or you find another line of work."

"Then why?" Keane demanded. He took her shoulders before she could turn away. "Why do you do it? And don't tell me because it's your job. That's not good enough."

It puzzled Jo why he seemed angry. His eyes were darkened with temper, and his fingers dug into her shoulders. As if wanting to draw out her answer, he gave her one quick shake. "All right," Jo said slowly, ignoring the ache in her flesh. "That is part of it, but not all. It's all I've ever known, that's part of it, too. It's what I'm good at." While she spoke, she searched his face for a clue to his mood. She wondered if perhaps he had felt it wrong of her to take Gerry into the cage. "Gerry's going to be good at it, too," she told him. "I imagine everyone needs to be good—really good—at something. And I enjoy giving the people who come to see me the best show I can. But over all, I suppose it's because I love them. It's difficult for a layman to understand a trainer's feeling for his animals. I love their intelligence, their really awesome beauty, their strength, the unquenchable streak of wildness that separates them from well-trained horses. They're exciting, challenging and terrifying."

Keane was silent for a moment. She saw that his eyes were still angry, but his fingers relaxed on her shoulders. Jo felt a light throbbing where bruises would certainly show in the morning. "I suppose excitement becomes addicting—difficult to live without once it's become a habit."

"I don't know," Jo replied, grateful that his temper was apparently cooling. "I've never thought about it."

"No, I suppose you'd have little reason to." With a nod, he turned to walk away.

Jo took a step after him. "Keane." His name raced through her lips before she could prevent it. When he turned back to her, she realized she could not ask any of the dozens of questions that flew through her mind. There was only one she felt she had any right to ask. "Have you thought any more about what you're going to do with us…with the circus?"

For an instant she saw temper flare again into his eyes. "No." The word was curt and final. As he turned his back on her again, she felt a spurt of anger and reached for his arm.

"How can you be so callous, so unfeeling?" she demanded.

"How is it possible to be so casual when you hold the lives of over a hundred people in your hands?"

Carefully, he removed her hand from his arm. "Don't push me, Jo." There was warning in his eyes and in his voice.

"I'm not trying to," she returned, then ran a frustrated hand through her hair. "I'm only asking you to be fair, to be…kind," she finished lamely.

"Don't ask me anything," he ordered in a brisk, authoritative tone. Jo's chin rose in response. "I'm here," he reminded her. "You'll have to be satisfied with that for now."

Jo battled with her temper. She could not deny that in coming back he had proved himself true to his word. She had the rest of the season if nothing else. "I don't suppose I have any choice," she said quietly.

"No," he agreed with a faint nod. "You don't."

Frowning, Jo watched him stride away in a smooth, fluid gait she was forced to admire. She noticed for the first time that her palms were as damp as Gerry's had been. Annoyed, she rubbed them over her hips.

"Want to talk about it?"

Jo turned quickly to find Jamie behind her in full clown gear. She knew her preoccupation had been deep for her to be caught so completely unaware. "Oh, Jamie, I didn't see you."

"You haven't seen anything but Prescott since you stepped out of the cage," Jamie pointed out.

"What are you doing in makeup?" she asked, skirting his comment.

He gestured toward the dog at her feet. "This mutt won't respond to me unless I'm in my face. Do you want to talk about it?"

"Talk about what?"

"About Prescott, about the way you feel about him."

The dog sat patiently at Jamie's heels and thumped his tail. Casually, Jo stopped and ruffled his gray fur.

"I don't know what you're talking about."

"Look, I'm not saying it can't work out, but I don't want to see you get hurt. I know how it is to be nuts about somebody."

"What in the world makes you think I'm nuts about Keane Prescott?" Jo gave the dog her full attention.

"Hey, it's me, remember?" Jamie took her arm and pulled her to her feet. "Not everybody would've noticed, maybe, but not everybody knows you the way I do. You've been miserable since he went back to Chicago, looking for him in every car that drove on the lot. And just now, when you saw him, you lit up like the midway on Saturday night. I'm not saying there's anything wrong with you being in love with him, but—"

"In love with him?" Jo repeated, incredulous.

"Yeah." Jamie spoke patiently. "In love with him."

Jo stared at Jamie as the realization slid over her. "In love with him," she murmured, trying out the words. "Oh, no." She sighed, closing her eyes. "Oh, no."

"Didn't you have enough sense to figure it out for yourself?" Jamie said gently. Seeing Jo's distress, he ran a hand gently up her arm.

"No, I guess I'm pretty stupid about this sort of thing." Jo opened her eyes and looked around, wondering if the world should look any different. "What am I going to do?"

"Heck, I don't know." Jamie kicked sawdust with an oversized shoe. "I'm not exactly getting rave notices myself in that department." He gave Jo a reassuring pat. "I just wanted you to know that you always have a sympathetic ear here."

He grinned engagingly before he turned to walk away, leaving Jo distracted and confused.

Jo spent the rest of the afternoon absorbed with the idea of being in love with Keane Prescott. For a short time she allowed herself to enjoy the sensation, the novel experience of loving someone not as a friend but as a lover. She could feel the light and the power spread through her, as if she had caught the sun in her hand. She daydreamed.

Keane was in love with her. He'd told her hundreds of times as he'd held her under a moonlit sky. He wanted to marry her, he couldn't bear to live without her. She was suddenly sophisticated and worldly enough to deal with the country club set on their own ground. She could exchange droll stories with the wives of other attorneys. There would be children and a house in the country. How would it feel to wake up in the same town every morning? She would learn to cook and give dinner parties. There would be long, quiet evenings when they would be alone together. There would be candlelight and music. When they slept together, his arms would stay around her until morning.

Idiot. Jo dragged herself back sternly. As she and Pete fed the cats, she tried to remember that fairy tales were for children. None of those things are ever going to happen, she reminded herself. I have to figure out how to handle this before I get in any deeper.

"Pete," she began, keeping her voice conversational as she put Abra's quota of raw meat on a long stick. "Have you ever been in love?"

Pete chewed his gum gently, watching Jo hoist the meat through the bars. "Well, now, let's see." Thrusting out his lower lip, he considered. "Only 'bout eight or ten times, I guess. Maybe twelve."

Jo laughed, moving down to the next cage. "I'm serious," she told him. "I mean *really* in love."

"I fall in love easy," Pete confessed gravely. "I'm a pushover for a pretty face. Matter of fact, I'm a pushover for an ugly face." He grinned. "Yes sir, the only thing like being in love is drawing an ace-high flush when the pot's ripe."

Jo shook her head and continued down the line. "Okay, since you're such an expert, tell me what you do when you're in love with a person and the person doesn't love you back and you don't want that person to know that you're in love because you don't want to make a fool of yourself."

"Just a minute." Pete squeezed his eyes tight. "I got to think this one through first." For a moment he was silent as his lips moved with his thoughts. "Okay, let's see if I've got this straight." Opening his eyes, he frowned in concentration. "You're in love—"

"I didn't say *I* was in love," Jo interrupted hastily.

Pete lifted his brows and pursed his lips. "Let's just use *you* in the general sense to avoid confusion," he suggested. Jo nodded, pretending to absorb herself with the feeding of the cats. "So, you're in love, but the guy doesn't love you. First off, you've got to be sure he doesn't."

"He doesn't," Jo murmured, then added quickly, "Let's say he doesn't."

Pete shot her a look out of the corner of his eye, then shifted his gum to the other side of his mouth. "Okay, then the first thing you should do is change his mind."

"Change his mind?" Jo repeated, frowning at him.

"Sure." Pete gestured with his hand to show the simplicity

of the procedure. "You fall in love with him, then he falls in love with you. You play hard to get, or you play easy to get. Or you play flutter and smile." He demonstrated by coyly batting his lashes and giving a winsome smile. Jo giggled and leaned on the feeding pole. Pete in fielder's cap, white T-shirt and faded jeans was the best show she'd seen all day. "You make him jealous," he continued. "Or you flatter his ego. Girl, there're so many ways to get a man, I can't count them, and I've been gotten by them all. Yes, sir, I'm a real pushover." He looked so pleased with his weakness, Jo smiled. How easy it would be, she thought, if I could take love so lightly.

"Suppose I don't want to do any of those things. Suppose I don't really know how and I don't want to humiliate myself by making a mess of it. Suppose the person isn't—well, suppose nothing could ever work between us, anyway. What then?"

"You got too many supposes," Pete concluded, then shook his finger at her. "And I got one for you. Suppose you ain't too smart because you figure you can't win even before you play."

"Sometimes people get hurt when they play," Jo countered quietly. "Especially if they aren't familiar with the game."

"Hurting's nothing," Pete stated with a sweep of his hand. "Winning's the best, but playing's just fine. This whole big life, it's a game, Jo. You know that. And the rules keep changing all the time. You've got nerve," he continued, then laid his rough, brown hand on her shoulder. "More raw nerve than most anybody I've ever known. You've got brains, too, hungry brains. You going to tell me that with all that, you're afraid to take a chance?"

Meeting his eyes, Jo knew hypothetical evasions would not do. "I suppose I only take calculated risks, Pete. I know my turf; I know my moves. And I know exactly what'll happen if I make a mistake. I take a chance that my body might be clawed, not my emotions. I've never rehearsed for anything like this, and I think playing it cold would be suicide."

"I think you've got to believe in Jo Wilder a little more," Pete countered, then gave her cheek a quick pat.

"Hey, Jo." Looking over, Jo saw Rose approaching. She wore straight-leg jeans, a white peasant blouse and a six-foot boa constrictor over her shoulders.

"Hello, Rose." Jo handed Pete the feeding pole. "Taking Baby out for a walk?"

"He needed some air." Rose gave her charge a pat. "I think he got a little carsick this morning. Does he look peaked to you?"

Jo looked down at the shiny, multicolored skin, then studied the tiny black eyes as Rose held Baby's head up for inspection. "I don't think so," she decided.

"Well, it's a warm day," Rose observed, releasing Baby's head. "I'll give him a bath. That might perk him up."

Jo noticed Rose's eyes darting around the compound. "Looking for Jamie?"

"Hmph." Rose tossed her black curls. "I'm not wasting my time on that one." She stroked the latter half of Baby's anatomy. "I'm indifferent."

"That's another way to do it," Pete put in, giving Jo a nudge. "I forgot about that one. It's a zinger."

Rose frowned at Pete, then at Jo. "What's he talking about?"

With a laugh, Jo sat down on a water barrel. "Catching a man," she told her, letting the warm sun play on her face. "Pete's done a study on it from the male point of view."

"Oh." Rose threw Pete her most disdainful look. "You think I'm indifferent so he'll get interested?"

"It's a zinger," Pete repeated, adjusting his cap. "You get him confused so he starts thinking about you. You make him crazy wondering why you don't notice him."

Rose considered the idea. "Does it usually work?"

"It's got an eighty-seven percent success average," Pete assured her, then gave Baby a friendly pat. "It even works with cats." He jerked his thumb behind him and winked at Jo. "The pretty lady cat, she sits there and stares off into space like she's got important things occupying her mind. The boy in the next cage is doing everything but standing on his head to get her attention. She just gives herself a wash, pretending she doesn't even know he's there. Then, maybe after she's got him banging his head against the bars, she looks over, blinks her big yellow eyes and says, 'Oh, were you talking to me?'" Pete laughed and stretched his back muscles. "He's hooked then, brother, just like a fish on a line."

Rose smiled at the image of Jamie dangling from her own personal line. "Maybe I won't put Baby in Carmen's trailer after all," she murmured. "Oh, look, here comes Duffy and the owner." An inherent flirt, Rose instinctively fluffed her hair. "Really, he is the most handsome man. Don't you think so, Jo?"

Jo's eyes had already locked on Keane's. She seemed helpless to release herself from the gaze. Gripping the edge of the water barrel tightly, she reminded herself not to be a fool. "Yes," she agreed with studied casualness. "He's very attractive."

"Your knuckles are turning white, Jo," Pete muttered next to her ear.

Letting out a frustrated breath, Jo relaxed her hands. Straightening her spine, she determined to show more restraint. Control, she reminded herself, was the basic tool of her trade. If she could train her emotions and outbluff a dozen lions, she could certainly outbluff one man.

"Hello, Duffy." Rose gave the portly man a quick smile, then turned her attention to Keane. "Hello, Mr. Prescott. It's nice to have you back."

"Hello, Rose." He smiled into her upturned face, then lifted a brow as his eyes slid over the reptile around her neck and shoulders. "Who's your friend?"

"Oh, this is Baby." She patted one of the tan-colored saddle marks on Baby's back.

"Of course." Jo noticed how humor enhanced the gold of his eyes. "Hello, Pete." He gave the handler an easy nod before his gaze shifted and then lingered on Jo.

As on the first day they had met, Keane did not bother to camouflage his stare. His look was cool and assessing. He was reaffirming ownership. It shot through Jo that yes, she was in love with him, but she was also afraid of him. She feared his power over her, feared his capacity to hurt her. Still, her face registered none of her thoughts. Fear, she reminded herself as her eyes remained equally cool on his, was something she understood. Love might cause impossible problems, but fear could be dealt with. She would not cower from him, and she would honor the foremost rule of the arena. She would not turn and run.

Silently, they watched each other while the others looked on with varying degrees of curiosity. There was the barest touch of a smile on Keane's lips. The battle of wills continued until Duffy cleared his throat.

"Ah, Jo."

Calmly, without hurry, she shifted her attention. "Yes, Duffy?"

"I just sent one of the web girls into town to see the local dentist. Seems she's got an abscess. I need you to fill in tonight."

"Sure."

"Just for the web and the opening spectacular," he continued. Unable to prevent himself, he cast a quick look at Keane to see if he was still staring at her. He was. Duffy shifted uncomfortably and wondered what the devil was going on. "Take your usual place in the finale. We'll just be one girl shy in the chorus. Wardrobe'll fix you up."

"Okay." Jo smiled at him, though she was very much aware of Keane's eyes on her. "I guess I'd better go practice walking in those three-inch heels. What position do I take?"

"Number four rope."

"Duffy," Rose chimed in and tugged on his sleeve. "When are you going to let me do the web?"

"Rose, how's a pint-sizer like you going to stand up with that heavy costume on?" Duffy shook his head at her, keeping a respectable distance from Baby. After thirty-five years of working carnies, sideshows and circuses, he still was uneasy around snakes.

"I'm pretty strong," Rose claimed, stretching her spine in the hope of looking taller. "And I've been practicing." Anxious to demonstrate her accomplishments, Rose deftly unwound Baby. "Hold him a minute," she requested and dumped several feet of snake into Keane's arms.

"Ah…" Keane shifted the weight in his arms and looked dubiously into Baby's bored eyes. "I hope he's eaten recently."

"He had a nice breakfast," Rose assured him, going into a fluid backbend to show Duffy her flexibility.

"Baby won't eat owners," Jo told Keane. She did not bother to suppress her grin. It was the first time she had seen him disconcerted. "Just a stray towner, occasionally. Rose keeps him on a strict diet."

"I assume," Keane began as Baby slithered into a more comfortable position, "that he's aware I'm the owner."

Grinning at Keane's uncomfortable expression, Jo turned to Pete. "Gee, I don't know. Did anybody tell Baby about the new owner?"

"Haven't had a chance, myself," Pete drawled, taking out a fresh stick of gum. "Looks a lot like a towner, too. Baby might get confused."

"They're just teasing you, Mr. Prescott," Rose told him as she finished her impromptu audition with a full split. "Baby doesn't eat people at all. He's docile as a lamb. Little kids come up and pet him during a demonstration." She rose and brushed off her jeans. "Now, you take a cobra…"

"No, thank you," Keane declined, unloading the six-foot Baby back into Rose's arms.

Rose slipped the boa back around her neck. "Well, Duffy, I'm off. What do you say?"

"Get one of the girls to teach you the routine," he said with a nod. "Then we'll see." Smiling, he watched Rose saunter away.

"Hey, Duffy!" It was Jamie. "There's a couple of towners looking for you. I sent them over to the red wagon."

"Fine. I'll just go right on along with you." Duffy winked at Jo before turning to catch up with Jamie's long stride.

Keane was standing very close to the barrels. Jo knew getting down from her perch was risky. She knew, too, however, that her pulse was beginning to behave erratically despite her efforts to control it. "I've got to see about my costume." Nimbly, she came down, intending to skirt around him. Even as her boots touched the ground, his hands took her waist. Exercising every atom of willpower, she neither jerked nor struggled but lifted her eyes calmly to his.

His thumbs moved in a lazy arch. She could feel the warmth through the fabric of her blouse. With her entire being she wished he would not hold her. Then, perversely, she wished he would hold her closer. She struggled not to weaken as her lips grew warm under the kiss of his eyes. Her heart began to hammer in her ears.

Keane ran a hand down the length of her long, thick braid. Slowly, his eyes drifted back to hers. Abruptly, he released her and backed up to let her pass. "You'd best go have wardrobe take a few tucks in that costume."

Deciding she was not meant to decipher his changing moods, Jo stepped by him and crossed the compound. If she spent enough time working, she could keep her thoughts from dwelling on Keane Prescott. Maybe.

Chapter Seven

The Big Top was packed for the evening show. Jo watched the anticipation in the range of faces as she took her temporary position in the opening spectacular. The band played jumpy, upbeat music, leaning heavily on brass as the theme parade marched around the hippodrome track. As the substitute Bo Peep, Jo wore a demure mobcap and a wide crinoline skirt and led a baby lamb on a leash. Because her act came so swiftly on the tail of the opening, she rarely participated in the spectacular. Now she enjoyed a close-up look at the audience. In the cage, she blocked them out almost completely.

They were, she decided, a well-mixed group: young babies, older children, parents, grandparents, teenagers. They gave the pageant enthusiastic applause. Jo smiled and waved as she performed the basic choreography with hardly a thought.

After a quick costume change, she took her cue as Queen of the Jungle Cats. After that followed another costume change that transformed her into one of the Twelve Spinning Butterflies.

"Just heard," Jamie whispered in her ear as she took the customary pose by the rope. "You got the job for the next week. Barbara won't be able to handle the teeth grip."

Jo shifted her shoulders to compensate for the weight of her enormous blue wings. "Rose is going to learn the routine," she mumbled back, smiling in the flood of the sunlight. "Duffy's giving her the job if she can stand up under this blasted costume." She made a quick, annoyed sound and smiled brightly. "It weighs a ton."

Slowly, to the beat of the waltz the band played, Jo climbed hand over hand up the rope. "Ah, show biz," she heard Jamie sigh. She vowed to poke him in the ribs when she took her bow. Then, hooking her foot in the hoop, she began the routine, imitating the other eleven Spinning Butterflies. .

She was able to share a cup of coffee with Rose's mother when she returned the butterfly costume to wardrobe and changed into her own white and gold jumpsuit. Her muscles complained a bit due to the unfamiliar weight of the wings, and she gave a passing thought to a long, luxurious bath. That was a dream for September, she reminded herself. Showers were the order of the day on the road.

Jo's last duty in the show was to stand on the head of Maggie, the key elephant in the finale's long mount. Sturdy and dependable, Maggie stood firm while four elephants on each side of her rose on their hind legs, resting their front legs on the back of the one in front. Atop Maggie's broad head, Jo stood glittering under the lights with both arms lifted in the air. It was here, more than any other part of the show, that the applause washed over her. It merged with the music, the ringmaster's whistle, the laughter of children. Where she had been weary, she was now filled with energy. She knew the fatigue would return, so she relished the power of the moment all the more. For those few seconds there was no work, no long hours, no predawn drives. There was only magic. Even when it was over and she slid from Maggie's back, she could still feel it.

Outside the tent, troupers and roustabouts and shandies mingled. There were anecdotes to exchange, performances to dissect, observations to be made. Gradually, they drifted away alone, in pairs or in groups. Some would change and help strike the tents, some would sleep, some would worry over their performances. Too energized to sleep, Jo planned to assist in the striking of the Big Top.

She switched on a low light as she entered her trailer, then absently braided her hair as she moved to the tiny bath. With quick moves she creamed off her stage makeup. The exotic exaggeration of her eyes was whisked away, leaving the thick fringe of her lashes and the dark green of her irises unenhanced. The soft bloom of natural rose tinted her cheeks again, and her mouth, unpainted, appeared oddly vulnerable. Accustomed to the change, Jo did not see the sharp contrast between Jovilette the performer and the small, somewhat fragile woman in the glittering jumpsuit. With her face naked and the simple braid hanging down her back, the look of the wild, of the gypsy, was less apparent. It remained in her movements, but her face rinsed of all artifice and unframed, was both delicate and young, part ingenue, part flare. But Jo saw none of this as she reached for her front zipper. Before she could pull it down, a knock sounded on her door.

"Come in," she called out and flicked her braid behind her back as she started down the aisle. She stopped in her tracks as Keane stepped through the door.

"Didn't anyone ever tell you to ask who it is first?" He shut the door behind him and locked it with a careless flick of his wrist. "You might not have to lock your door against the circus people," he continued blandly as she remained still, "but there are several dozen curious towners still hanging around."

"I can handle a curious towner," Jo replied. The offhand quality of his dominance was infuriating. "I never lock my door."

There was stiffness and annoyance in her voice. Keane ignored them both. "I brought you something from Chicago."

The casual statement succeeded in throwing Jo's temper off the mark. For the first time, she noticed the small package he carried. "What is it?" she asked.

Keane smiled and crossed to her. "It's nothing that bites," he assured her, then held it out.

Still cautious, Jo lifted her eyes to his, then dropped her gaze back to the package. "It's not my birthday," she murmured.

"It's not Christmas, either," Keane pointed out.

The easy patience in the tone caused Jo to lift her eyes again. She wondered how it was he understood her hesitation to accept presents. She kept her gazed locked on his. "Thank you," she said solemnly as she took the gift.

"You're welcome," Keane returned in the same tone.

The amenities done, Jo recklessly ripped the paper. "Oh! It's Dante," she exclaimed, tearing off the remaining paper and tossing it on the table. With reverence she ran her palm over the dark leather binding. The rich scent drifted to her. She knew her quota of books would have been limited to one a year had she bought a volume so handsomely bound. She opened it slowly, as if to prolong the pleasure. The pages were heavy and rich cream in color. The text was Italian, and even as she glanced over the first page, the words ran fluidly through her mind.

"It's beautiful," she murmured, overcome. Lifting her eyes to thank him again, Jo found Keane smiling down at her.

Shyness enveloped her suddenly, all the more intense because she had so rarely experienced it. A lifetime in front of crowds had given her a natural confidence in almost any situation. Now color began to surge into her cheeks, and her mind was a jumble of words that would not come to order.

"I'm glad you like it." He ran a finger down her cheek. "Do you always blush when someone gives you a present?"

Because she was at a loss as to how to answer his question, Jo maneuvered around it. "It was nice of you to think of me."

"It seems to come naturally," Keane replied, then watched Jo's lashes flutter down.

"I don't know what to say." She was able to meet his eyes again with her usual directness, but he had again touched her emotions. She felt inadequate to deal with her feelings or with his effect on her.

"You've already said it." He took the book from Jo's hand and paged through it. "Of course, I can't read a word of it. I envy you that." Before Jo could ponder the idea of a man like Keane Prescott envying her anything, he looked back up and smiled. Her thoughts scattered like nervous ants. "Got any coffee?" he asked and set the book back down on the table.

"Coffee?"

"Yes, you know, coffee. They grow it in quantity in Brazil."

Jo gave him a despairing look. "I don't have any made. I'd fix you a cup, but I've got to change before I help strike the tents. The cookhouse will still be serving."

Keane lifted a brow as he let his eyes wander over her face. "Don't you think that between Bo Peep, lions and butterflies, you've done enough work tonight? By the way, you make a very appealing butterfly."

"Thank you, but—"

"Let's put it this way," Keane countered smoothly. He took the tip of her braid in his fingers. "You've got the night off. I'll make the coffee myself if you show me where you keep it."

Though she let out a windy sigh, Jo was more amused than annoyed. Coffee, she decided, was the least she could do after he had brought her such a lovely present. "I'll make it," she told him, "but you'll probably wish you'd gone to the cookhouse." With this dubious invitation, Jo turned and headed toward the kitchen. He made no sound, but she knew he followed her. For the first time, she felt the smallness of her kitchen.

Setting an undersized copper kettle on one of the two burners, Jo flicked on the power. It was a simple matter to keep her back to him while she plucked cups from the cupboard. She was well aware that if she turned around in the compact kitchen, she would all but be in his arms.

"Did you watch the whole show?" she asked conversationally as she pulled out a jar of instant coffee.

"Duffy had me working props," Keane answered. "He seems to be making me generally useful."

Amused, Jo twisted her head to grin at him. Instantly, she discovered her misstep in strategy. Keane's face was only inches from hers, and in his eyes she read his thoughts. He wanted her, and he intended to have her. Before she could shift her position, Keane took her shoulders and turned her completely around. Jo knew she had backed up against the bars.

Leisurely, he began to loosen her hair, working his fingers through it until it pooled over her shoulders. "I've wanted to do that since the first time I saw you. It's hair to get lost in." His voice was soft as he took a generous handful. The gesture itself seemed to stake his claim. "In the sun it shimmers with red lights, but in the dark it's like night itself." It came to her that each time she was close to him, she was less able to resist him. She became more lost in his eyes, more beguiled by his power. Already her mouth tingled with the memory of his kiss, with the longing for a new one. Behind them the kettle began a feverish whistle.

"The water," she managed and tried to move around him. With one hand in her hair, Keane kept her still as he turned off the burner. The whistle sputtered peevishly, then died. The sound echoed in Jo's head.

"Do you want coffee?" he murmured as his fingers trailed to her throat.

Jo's eyes clung to his. Hers were enormous and direct, his quiet and searching. "No," she whispered, knowing she wanted nothing more at that moment than to belong to him. He circled her throat with his hand and pressed his fingers against her pulse. It fluttered wildly.

"You're trembling." He could feel the light tremor of her body as he brought her closer. "Is it fear?" he demanded as his thumbs brushed over her lips. "Or excitement?"

"Both," she answered in a voice thickened with emotion. She made a tiny, confused sound as his palm covered her heart. Its desperate thudding increased. "Are you…" She stopped a moment because her voice was breathless and unsteady. "Are you going to make love to me?" Did his eyes really darken? she wondered dizzily. Or is it my imagination?

"Beautiful Jovilette," he murmured as his mouth lowered to hers. "No pretentions, no evasions…irresistible." The quality of the kiss altered swiftly. His mouth was hungry on hers, and her response leaped past all caution. If loving him was madness, her heart reasoned, could making love take her further beyond sanity? Past wisdom and steeped in sensation, she let her heart rule her will. When her lips parted under his, it was not in surrender but in equal demand.

Keane gentled the kiss. He kept her shimmering on the razor's edge of passion. His mouth teased, promised, then fed her growing need. He found the zipper at the base of her throat and pulled it downward slowly. Her skin was warm, and he sought it, giving a low sound of pleasure as her breast swelled under his hand. He explored without hurry, as if memorizing each curve and plane. Jo no longer trembled but became pliant as her body moved to the rhythm he set. Her sigh was spontaneous, filled with wonder and delight.

With a suddenness that took her breath away, Keane crushed her mouth beneath his in fiery urgency. Jo's instincts responded, thrusting her into a world she had only imagined. His hands grew rougher, more insistent. Jo realized he had relinquished control. They were both riding on the tossing waves of passion. This sea had no horizon and no depth. It was a drowning sea that pulled the unsuspecting under while promising limitless pleasure. Jo did not resist but dove deeper.

At first she thought the knocking was only the sound of her heart against her ribs. When Keane drew away, she murmured in protest and pulled him back. Instantly, his mouth was avid, but as the knocking continued, he swore and pulled back again.

"Someone's persistent," he muttered. Bewildered, Jo stared up at him. "The door," he explained on a long breath.

"Oh." Flustered, Jo ran a hand through her hair and tried to collect her wits.

"You'd better answer it," Keane suggested as he pulled the zipper to her throat in one quick move. Jo broke the surface into reality abruptly. For a moment Keane watched her, taking in her flushed cheeks and tousled hair before he moved aside.

Willing her legs to carry her, Jo walked to the front of the trailer. The door handle resisted, then she remembered that Keane had locked it, and she turned the latch.

"Yes, Buck?" she said calmly enough when she opened the door to her handler.

"Jo." His face was in shadows, but she heard the distress in the single syllable. Her chest tightened. "It's Ari."

He had barely finished the name before Jo was out of the trailer and running across the compound. She found both Pete and Gerry standing near Ari's cage.

"How bad?" she demanded as Pete came to meet her.

He took her shoulders. "Really bad this time, Jo."

For a moment she wanted to shake her head, to deny what she read in Pete's eyes. Instead, she nudged him aside and walked to Ari's cage. The old cat lay on his side as his chest lifted and fell with the effort of breathing. "Open it," she ordered Pete in a voice that revealed nothing. There was the jingle of keys, but she did not turn.

"You're not going in there." Jo heard Keane's voice and felt a restraining grip on her shoulders. Her eyes were opaque as she looked up at him.

"Yes, I am. Ari isn't going to hurt me or anyone else. He's just going to die. Now leave me alone." Her voice was low and toneless. "Open it," she ordered again, then pulled out of Keane's loosened hold. The bars rattled as he slid the door open. Hearing it, Jo turned, then hoisted herself into the cage.

Ari barely stirred. Jo saw, as she knelt beside him, that his eyes were open. They were glazed with weariness and pain. "Ari," she sighed, seeing there would be no tomorrow for him. His only answer was a hollow wheezing. Putting a hand to his side, she felt the ragged pace of his breathing. He made an effort to respond to her touch, to his name, but managed only to shift his great head on the floor. The gesture tore at Jo's heart. She lowered her face to his mane, remembering him as he had once been: full of strength and a terrifying beauty. She lifted her face again and took one long, steadying breath. "Buck." She heard him approach but kept her eyes on Ari. "Get the medical kit. I want a hypo of pentobarbital." She could feel Buck's brief hesitation before he spoke.

"Okay, Jo."

She sat quietly, stroking Ari's head. In the distance were the sounds of the Big Top going down, the call of men, the rattle of rigging, the clang of wood against metal. An elephant trumpeted, and three cages down, Faust roared half-heartedly in response.

"Jo." She turned her head as Buck called her and pushed her hair from her eyes. "Let me do it."

Jo merely shook her head and held out her hand.

"Jo." Keane stepped up to the bars. His voice was gentle, but his eyes were so like the cat's at her knees, Jo nearly sobbed aloud. "You don't have to do this yourself."

"He's my cat," she responded dully. "I said I'd do it when it was time. It's time." Her eyes shifted to Buck. "Give me the hypo, Buck. Let's get it done." When the syringe was in her hand, Jo stared at it, then closed her fingers around it. Swallowing hard, she turned back to Ari. His eyes were on her face. After more than twenty years in captivity there was still something not quite tamed in the dying cat. But she saw trust in his eyes and wanted to weep. "You were the best," she told him as she passed a hand through his mane. "You were always the best." Jo felt a numbing cold settling over her and prayed it would last until she had finished. "You're tired now. I'm going to help you sleep." She pulled the safety from the point of the hypodermic and waited until she was certain her hands were steady. "This won't hurt, nothing is going to hurt you anymore."

Involuntarily, Jo rubbed the back of her hand over her mouth, then, moving quickly, she plunged the needle into Ari's shoulder. A quiet whimper escaped her as she emptied the syringe. Ari made no sound but continued to watch her face. Jo offered no words of comfort but sat with him, methodically stroking his fur as his eyes grew cloudy. Gradually, the effort of his breathing lessened, becoming quieter and quieter until it wasn't there at all. Jo felt him grow still, and her hand balled into a fist inside the mass of his mane. One quick, convulsive shudder escaped her. Steeling herself, she moved from the cage, closing the door behind her. Because her bones felt fragile, she kept them stiff, as though they might shatter. Even as she stepped back to the ground, Keane took her arm and began to lead her away.

"Take care of things," he said to Buck as they moved past.

"No." Jo protested, trying and failing to free her arm. "I'll do it."

"No, you won't." Keane's tone held a quiet finality. "Enough's enough."

"Don't tell me what to do," she said sharply, letting her grief take refuge in anger.

"I *am* telling you," he pointed out. His hand was firm on her arm.

"You *can't* tell me what to do," she insisted as tears rose treacherously in her throat. "I want you to leave me alone."

Keane stopped, then took her by the shoulders. His eyes caught the light of a waning moon. "There's no way I'm going to leave you alone when you're so upset."

"My emotions have nothing to do with you." Even as she

spoke, he took her arm again and pulled her toward her trailer. Jo wanted desperately to be alone to weep out her grief in private. The mourning belonged to her, and the tears were personal. As if her protests were nonexistent, he pulled her into the trailer and closed the door behind them. "Will you get out of here?" she demanded, frantically swallowing tears.

"Not until I know you're all right." Keane's answer was calm as he walked back to the kitchen.

"I'm perfectly all right." Her breath shuddered in and out quickly. "Or I will be when you leave me alone. You have no right to poke your nose in my business."

"So you've told me before," Keane answered mildly from the back of the trailer.

"I just did what had to be done." She held her body rigid and fought against her own quick, uneven breathing. "I put a sick animal out of his misery; it's as simple as that." Her voice broke, and she turned away, hugging her arms. "For heaven's sake, Keane, go away!"

Quietly, he walked back to her carrying a glass of water. "Drink this."

"No." She whirled back to him. Tears spilled out of her eyes and trickled down her cheeks despite her efforts to banish them. Hating herself, she pressed the heel of her hand between her brows and closed her eyes. "I don't want you here." Keane set down the glass, then gathered her into his arms. "No, don't. I don't want you to hold me."

"Too bad." He ran a hand gently up and down her back. "You did a very brave thing, Jo. I know you loved Ari. I know how hard it was to let him go. You're hurting, and I'm not leaving you."

"I don't want to cry in front of you." Her fists were tight balls at his shoulders.

"Why not?" The stroking continued up and down her back as he cradled her head in the curve of his shoulder.

"Why won't you let me be?" she sobbed as her control slipped. Her fingers gripped his shirt convulsively. "Why am I always losing what I love?" She let the grief come. She let his arms soothe her. As desperately as she had protested against it, she clung to his offer of comfort.

She made no objection as he carried her to the couch and cradled her in his arms. He stroked her hair, as she had stroked Ari, to ease the pain of what couldn't be changed. Slowly, her sobbing quieted. Still she lay with her cheek against his chest, with her hair curtaining her face.

"Better?" he asked as the silence grew calmer. Jo nodded, not yet trusting her voice. Keane shifted her as he reached for the glass of water. "Drink this now."

Gratefully, Jo relieved her dry throat, then went without resistance back against his chest. She closed her eyes, thinking it had been a very long time since she had been held in anyone's lap and soothed. "Keane," she murmured. She felt his lips brush over the top of her head.

"Hmm?"

"Nothing." Her voice thickened as she drifted toward sleep. "Just Keane."

Chapter Eight

Jo felt the sun on her closed lids. There was the summer morning sound of excited birds. Her mind, levitating slowly toward the surface, told her it must be Monday. Only on Monday would she sleep past sunrise. That was the enroute day, the only day in seven the circus held no show. She thought lazily of getting up. She would set aside two hours for reading. Maybe I'll drive into town and see a movie. What town are we in? With a sleepy sigh she rolled onto her stomach.

I'll give the cats a good going-over, maybe hose them down if it gets hot enough. Memory flooded back and snapped her awake. *Ari.* Opening her eyes, Jo rolled onto her back and stared at the ceiling. Now she recalled vividly how the old cat had died with his eyes trusting on her face. She sighed again. The sadness was still there, but not the sharp, desperate grief of the night before. Acceptance was settling in. She realized that Keane's insistence on staying with her during the peak of her mourning had helped her. He had given her someone to rail at, then someone to hold on to. She remembered the incredible comfort of being cradled in his lap, the solid dependability of his chest against her cheek. She had fallen asleep with the sound of his heart in her ear.

Turning her head, Jo looked out the window, then at the patch of white light the sun tossed on the floor. But it isn't Monday, she remembered suddenly. It's Thursday. Jo sat up, pushing at her hair, which seemed to tumble everywhere at once. What was she doing in bed on a Thursday when the sun was up? Without giving herself time to work out the answer, she scrambled out of bed and hurried from the room. She gave a soft gasp as she ran headlong into Keane.

His hand ran down the length of her hair before he took her shoulder. "I heard you stirring," he said easily, looking down into her stunned face.

"What are you doing here?"

"Making coffee," he answered as he gave her a critical study. "Or I was a moment ago. How are you?"

"I'm all right." Jo lifted her hand to her temple as if to gain her bearings. "I'm a bit disoriented, I suppose. I overslept. It's never happened before."

"I gave you a sleeping pill," Keane told her matter-of-factly. He slipped an arm around her shoulder as he turned back to the kitchen.

"A pill?" Jo's eyes flew to his. "I don't remember taking a pill."

"It was in the water you drank." On the stove the kettle began its piercing whistle. Moving to it, Keane finished making the coffee. "I had my doubts as to whether you'd take it voluntarily."

"No, I wouldn't have," Jo agreed with some annoyance. "I've never taken a sleeping pill in my life."

"Well, you did last night." He held out a mug of coffee. "I sent Gerry for it while you were in the cage with Ari." Again he gave her a quick, intense study. "It didn't seem to do you any harm. You went out like a light. I carried you to bed, changed your clothes—"

"Changed my…" All at once Jo became aware that she wore only a thin white nightshirt. Her hand reached instinctively for the top button that nestled just above her bosom. Thinking hard, she found she could recall nothing beyond falling asleep in his arms.

"I don't think you'd have spent a very comfortable night in your costume," Keane pointed out. Enjoying his coffee, he smiled at the nervous hand she held between her breasts. "I've had a certain amount of experience undressing women in the dark." Jo dropped her hand. It was an unmistakable movement of pride. Keane's eyes softened. "You needed a good night's sleep, Jo. You were worn out."

Without speaking, Jo lifted her coffee to her lips and turned away. Walking to the window, she could see that the back yard was deserted. Her sleep must indeed have been deep to have kept her unaware of camp breaking.

"Everyone's gone but a couple of roustabouts and a generator truck. They'll take off when you don't need power anymore."

The vulnerability Jo felt was overwhelming. Several times in the course of the evening before, she had lost control, which had always been an essential part of her. Each time, it had been Keane who had been there. She wanted to be angry with him for intruding on her privacy but found it impossible. She had needed him, and he had known it.

"You didn't have to stay behind," she said, watching a crow swoop low over the ground outside.

"I wasn't certain you'd be in any shape to drive fifty miles this morning. Pete's driving my trailer."

Her shoulders lifted and fell before she turned around.

Sunlight streamed through the window at her back and poured through the thin folds of her nightshirt. Her body was a slender shadow. When she spoke, her voice was low with regret. "I was horribly rude to you last night."

Keane shrugged and lifted his coffee. "You were upset."

"Yes." Her eyes were an open reflection of her sorrow. "Ari was very important to me. I suppose he was an ongoing link with my father, with my childhood. I'd known for some time he wouldn't make it through the season, but I didn't want to face it." She looked down at the mug she held gripped in both hands. A faint wisp of steam rose from it and vanished. "Last night was a relief for him. It was selfish of me to wish it otherwise. And I was wrong to strike out at you the way I did. I'm sorry."

"I don't want your apology, Jo." Because he sounded annoyed, she looked up quickly.

"I'd feel better if you'd take it, Keane. You've been very kind."

To her astonishment, he swore under his breath and turned back to the stove. "I don't care for your gratitude any more than your apology." He set down his mug and poured in more coffee. "Neither of them is necessary."

"They are to me," Jo replied, then took a step toward him. "Keane…" She set down her coffee and touched his arm. When he turned, she let impulse guide her. She rested her head on his shoulder and slipped her arms around his waist. He stiffened, putting his hands to her shoulders as if to draw her away. Then she heard his breath come out in a long sigh as he relaxed. For an instant he brought her closer.

"I never know precisely what to expect from you," he murmured. He lifted her chin with his finger. In automatic response, Jo closed her eyes and offered her mouth. She felt his fingers tighten on her skin before his lips brushed hers lightly.

"You'd better go change." His manner was friendly but cool as he stepped away. "We'll stop off in town, and I'll buy you some breakfast."

Puzzled by his attitude but satisfied he was no longer annoyed, Jo nodded. "All right."

Spring became summer as the circus wound its way north. The sun stayed longer, peeking into the Big Top until well after the evening show began. Heavy rain came infrequently, but there were quick summer storms with thunder and lightning. Through June, Prescott's Circus Colossus snaked through North Carolina and into western Tennessee.

During the long weeks while spring tripped over into summer, Jo found Keane's attitude a paradox. His friendliness toward her was offhand. He laughed if she said something amusing, listened if she had a complaint and to her confusion, slipped a thin barrier between them. At times she wondered if the passion that had flared between them the night he had returned from Chicago had truly existed. Had the desire she had tasted on his lips been a fantasy? The closeness she had felt blooming between them had withered and blown away. They were only owner and trouper now.

Keane flew back to Chicago twice more during this period, but he brought no surprise presents back with him. Not once during those long weeks did he come by her trailer. Initially, his altered manner confused her. He was not angry. His mood was neither heated nor icy with temper but fell into an odd middle ground she could not understand. Jo ached with love. As days passed into weeks, she was forced to admit that Keane did not seem to be interested in a close relationship.

★ ★ ★

On the eve of the July Fourth show, Jo sat sleepless in her bed. In her hand she held the volume of Dante, but the book was only a reminder of the emptiness she felt. She closed it, then stared at the ceiling. It's time to snap out of it, she lectured herself. It's time to stop pretending he was ever really part of my life. Loving someone only makes him a part of your wishes. He never talked about love, he never promised anything, never offered anything but what he gave to me. He's done nothing to hurt me. Jo squeezed her eyes shut and pressed the book between her fingers. How I wish I could hate him for showing me what life could be like and then turning away, she thought.

But I can't. Jo let out a shaky breath and relaxed her grip on the book. Gently, she ran a finger down its smooth, leather binding. I can't hate him, but I can't love him openly, either. How do I stop? I should be grateful he stopped wanting me. I would have made love with him. Then I'd hurt a hundred times more. Could I hurt a hundred times more? For several moments she lay still, trying to quiet her thoughts.

It's best not to know, she told herself sternly. It's best to remember he was kind to me when I needed him and that I haven't a right to make demands. Summer doesn't last forever. I may never see him again when it's over. At least I can keep the time we have pleasant.

The words sounded hollow in her heart.

Chapter Nine

The Fourth of July was a full day with a run to a new lot, the tent raising, a street parade and two shows. But it was a holiday. Elephants wore red, white and blue plumes atop their massive heads. The evening performance would be held an hour earlier to allow for the addition of a fireworks display. Traditionally, Prescott's circus arranged to spend the holiday in the same small town in Tennessee. The license and paperwork for the display were seen to in advance, and the fireworks were shipped ahead to be stored in a warehouse. The procedure had been precisely the same for years. It was one of the circus's most profitable nights. Concessions thrived.

Jo moved through the day with determined cheerfulness. She refused to permit the distance between her and Keane to spoil one of the highlights of the summer. Brooding, she decided, would not change things. The mood of the crowd helped to keep her spirits light.

Between shows came the inevitable lull. Some troupers sat outside their trailers exchanging small talk and enjoying the sun. Others got in a bit more practice or worked out a few kinks.

Bull hands washed down the elephants, causing a minor flood in the pen area.

Jo watched the bathing process with amusement. She never ceased to enjoy this particular aspect of circus life, especially if there were one or two inexperienced bull hands involved. Invariably, Maggie or one of the other veteran bulls would spray a trunkful of water over the new hands to initiate them. Though Jo knew the other hands encouraged it, they always displayed remarkable innocence.

Spotting Duffy, Jo moved away from the elephant area and wandered toward him. She could see he was deep in discussion with a towner. He was as short as Duffy but wider, with what she had once heard Frank call a successful frame. His stomach started high and barreled out to below his waist. He had a ruddy complexion and pale eyes that squinted hard against the sun. Jo had seen his type before. She wondered what he was selling and how much he wanted for it. Since Duffy was puffing with annoyance, Jo assumed it was quite a lot.

"I'm telling you, Carlson, we've already paid for storage. I've got a signed receipt. And we pay fifteen bucks delivery, not twenty."

Carlson was smoking a small, unfiltered cigarette and dropped it to the ground. "You paid Myers for storage, not me. I bought the place six weeks ago." He shrugged his wide shoulders. "Not my problem you paid in advance."

Looking over, Jo saw Keane approaching with Pete. Pete was talking rapidly, Keane nodding. As Jo watched, Keane glanced up and gave Carlson a quick study. She had seen that look before and knew the older man had been assessed. Keane caught her eye, smiled and began to move past her. "Hello, Jo."

Unashamedly curious, Jo fell into step beside him.
"What's going on?"

"Why don't we find out?" he suggested as they stopped in
front of Duffy and Carlson. "Gentlemen," Keane said in an easy
tone. "Is there a problem?"

"This character," Duffy spouted, jerking a scornful thumb at
Carlson's face, "wants us to pay twice for storage on the fireworks.
Then he wants twenty for delivery when we agreed on fifteen."

"Myers agreed on fifteen," Carlson pointed out. He smiled
without humor. "I didn't agree on anything. You want your
fireworks, you gotta pay for them first—cash," he added, then
spared Keane a glance. "Who's this guy?"

Duffy began to wheeze with indignation, but Keane laid a
restraining hand on his shoulder. "I'm Prescott," he told him
in untroubled tones. "Perhaps you'd like to fill me in."

"Prescott, huh?" Carlson stroked both his chins as he studied
Keane. Seeing youth and amiable eyes, he felt closer to success.
"Well, now we're getting somewhere," he said jovially and stuck
out his hand. Keane accepted it without hesitation. "Jim
Carlson," he continued as he gave Keane's hand a brisk pump.
"Nice circus you got here, Prescott. Me and the missus see it
every year. Well, now," he said again and hitched up his belt.
"Seeing as you're a businessman, too, I'm sure we can straighten
all this out. Problem is, your fireworks've been stored in my warehouse. Now, I gotta make a living, they can't just sit there for free.
I bought the place off Myers six weeks ago. I can't be held responsible for a deal you made with him, can I?" Carlson gave a
stretched-lip smile, pleased that Keane listened so politely. "And
as for delivery, well…" He made a helpless gesture and patted
Keane's shoulder. "You know about gas prices these days, son.
But we can work that out after we settle this other little problem."

Keane nodded agreeably. "That sounds reasonable." He ignored Duffy's huffing and puffing. "You do seem to have a problem, Mr. Carlson."

"I don't have a problem," Carlson countered. His smile suffered a fractional slip. "You've got the problem, unless you don't want the fireworks."

"Oh, we'll have the fireworks, Mr. Carlson," Keane corrected with a smile Jo thought more wolfish than friendly. "According to paragraph three, section five, of the small business code, the lessor is legally bound by all contracts, agreements, liens and mortgages of the previous lessor until such time as all aforesaid contracts, agreements, liens and mortgages are expired or transferred."

"What the…" Carlson began with no smile at all, but Keane continued blandly.

"Of course, we won't pursue the matter in court as long as we get our merchandise. But that doesn't solve your problem."

"My problem?" Carlson sputtered while Jo looked on in frank admiration. "I haven't got a problem. If you think…"

"Oh, but you do, Mr. Carlson, though I'm sure there was no intent to break the law on your part."

"Break the law?" Carlson wiped damp hands on his slacks.

"Storing explosives without a license," Keane pointed out. "Unless, of course, you obtained one after your purchase of the warehouse."

"Well, no, I…"

"I was afraid of that." Keane lifted his brow in pity. "You see, in paragraph six of section five of the small business code it states that all licenses, permits and warrants shall be nontransferable. Authorization for new licenses, permits or warrants must be requested in writing by the current owner. Notarized, naturally." Keane waited a bit to allow Carlson to wrestle with the idea. "If I'm not mistaken," he continued conversationally, "the fine's pretty hefty in this state. Of course, sentencing depends on—"

"Sentencing?" Carlson paled and mopped the back of his neck with a handkerchief.

"Look, tell you what." Keane gave Carlson a sympathetic smile. "You get the fireworks over here and off your property. We don't have to bring the law in on something like this. Just an oversight, after all. We're both businessmen, aren't we?"

Too overwrought to detect sarcasm, Carlson nodded.

"That was fifteen on delivery, right?"

Carlson didn't hesitate but stuck the damp handkerchief back in his pocket and nodded again.

"Good enough. I'll have the cash for you on delivery. Glad to help you out."

Relieved, Carlson turned and headed for his pickup. Jo managed to keep her features grave until he pulled off the lot. Simultaneously, Pete and Duffy began to hoot with laughter.

"Was it true?" Jo demanded and took Keane's arm.

"Was what true?" Keane countered, merely lifting a brow over the hysterics that surrounded him.

"'Paragraph three, section five, of the small business code,'" Jo quoted.

"Never heard of it," Keane answered mildly, nearly sending Pete into orbit.

"You made it up," Jo said in wonder. "You made it all up!"

"Probably," Keane agreed.

"Smoothest con job I've seen in years," Duffy stated and gave Keane a parental slap on the back. "Son, you could go into business."

"I did," Keane told him and grinned.

"I ever need a lawyer," Pete put in, pushing his cap further back on his head, "I know where to go. You come on by the cookhouse tonight, Captain. We're having ourselves a poker game. Come on, Duffy, Buck's gotta hear about this."

As they moved off, Jo realized that Keane had been officially accepted. Before, he had been the legal owner but an outsider, a towner. Now he was one of them. Turning, she lifted her face to his. "Welcome aboard."

"Thank you." She saw he understood precisely what had been left unsaid.

"I'll see you at the game," she said before her smile became a grin. "Don't forget your money."

She turned away, but Keane touched her arm, bringing her back to him. "Jo," he began, puzzling her by the sudden seriousness of his eyes.

"Yes?"

There was a brief hesitation, then he shook his head. "Nothing, never mind. I'll see you later." He rubbed his knuckles over her cheek, then walked away.

Jo studied her hand impassively. On the deal, she had missed a heart flush by one card and now waited for someone to open. Casually, she moved her glance around the table. Duffy was puffing on a cigar, apparently unconcerned with the dwindling chips in front of him. Pete chewed his gum with equal nonchalance. Amy, the wife of the sword swallower, sat beside him, then Jamie, then Raoul. Directly beside Jo was Keane, who, like Pete, was winning consistently.

The pot grew. Chips clinked on the table. Jo discarded and was pleased to exchange a club for the fifth heart. She slipped it into her hand without blinking. Frank had taught her the game. Before the second round of betting, Jamie folded in disgust. "Should never have taken Buck's seat," he muttered and frowned when Pete raised the bet.

"You got out cheap, kiddo," Duffy told him dolefully as he tossed in chips. "I'm only staying in so I don't change my standard of living. Money'll do that to you," he mumbled obscurely.

"Three kings," Pete announced when called, then spread his cards. Amid a flutter of complaints cards were tossed down.

"Heart flush," Jo said mildly before Pete could rake in the pot. Duffy leaned back and gave a hoot of laughter.

"Attagirl, Jo. I hate to see him win all my money."

During the next two hours the cookhouse tent grew hot and ripe with the scents of coffee and tobacco and beer. Jamie's luck proved so consistently poor that he called for Buck to relieve him.

Jo found herself with an indifferent pair of fives. Almost immediately the betting grew heavy as Keane raised Raoul's opening. Curiosity kept Jo in one round, but practicality had her folding after the draw. Divorced from the game, she watched it with interest. Leaning on her elbows, she studied each participant. Keane played a good game, she mused. His eyes gave nothing away. They never did. Casually, he nursed the beer beside him while Duffy, Buck and Amy folded. Studying him closely, Pete chewed his gum. Keane returned the look, keeping the stub of his cigar clamped between his teeth. Raoul muttered in French and scowled at his cards.

"Could be bluffing," Pete considered, seeing Keane's raise. "Let's raise it five more and see what's cooking." Raoul swore in French, then again in English, before he tossed in his hand. Taking his time, Keane counted out the necessary chips and tossed them into the pot. It was a plastic mountain of red, white and blue. Then, he counted out more.

"I'll see your five," he said evenly, "and raise it ten."

There was mumbling around the table. Pete looked into his hand and considered. Shifting his eyes, he took in the generous pile of chips in front of him. He could afford to risk another ten. Glancing up, he studied Keane's face while he fondled his chips. Abruptly, he broke into a grin.

"Nope," he said simply, turning his cards face down. "This one's all yours."

Setting down his cards, Keane raked in a very sweet pot. "Gonna show 'em?" Pete asked. His grin was affable.

Keane pushed a stray chip into the pile and shrugged. With his free hand he turned over the cards. The reaction ranged from oaths to laughter.

"Trash," Pete mumbled with a shake of his head. "Nothing but trash. You've got nerve, Captain." His grin grew wide as he turned over his own cards. "Even I had a pair of sevens."

Raoul gnashed his teeth and swore elegantly in two languages. Jo grinned at his imaginative choice of words. She rose on a laugh and snatched off the soft felt hat Jamie wore. Deftly, she scooped her chips into it. "Cash me in later," she requested, then gave him a smacking kiss on the mouth. "But don't play with them."

Duffy scowled over at her. "Aren't you cashing in early?"

"You've always told me to leave 'em wanting more," she reminded him. With a grin and a wave, she swung through the door.

"That Jo," said Raoul, chuckling as he shuffled the cards. "She's one smart cracker."

"Cookie," Pete corrected, opening a fresh stick of gum. He

noticed that Keane's gaze had drifted to the door she had closed behind her. "Some looker, too," he commented and watched Keane's eyes wander back to his. "Don't you think, Captain?"

Keane slipped his cards into a pile as they were dealt to him. "Jo's lovely."

"Like her mother," Buck put in, frowning at his cards. "She was a beaut, huh, Duffy?" Duffy grunted in agreement and wondered why Lady Luck refused to smile on him. "Always thought it was a crime for her to die that way. Wilder, too," he added with a shake of his head.

"A fire, wasn't it?" Keane asked as he picked up his cards and spread them.

"Electrical fire." Buck nodded and lifted his beer. "A short in their trailer's wiring. What a waste. If they hadn't been in bed asleep, they'd probably still be alive. The trailer was halfway gone before anybody set up an alarm. Just plain couldn't get to the Wilders. Their side of the trailer was like a furnace. Jo's bedroom was on the other side, and we nearly lost her. Frank busted in the window and pulled her out. Poor little tyke. She was holding onto this old doll like it was the last thing she had left. Kept it with her for I don't know how long. Remember, Duffy?" He glanced into his hand and opened for two. "It only had one arm." Duffy grunted again and folded. "Frank sure knew how to handle that little girl."

"She knew how to handle him, more likely," Duffy mumbled. Raoul bumped the pot five, and Keane folded.

"Deal me out the next hand," he said as he rose and moved to the door. One of the Gribalti brothers took the chair Jo had vacated, and Jamie slipped into Keane's. Curious, he lifted the tip of the cards. He saw a jack-high straight. With a thoughtful frown, he watched the door swing shut.

★ ★ ★

Outside, Jo moved through the warm night. With a glance at the sky, she thought of the fireworks. They had been wonderful, she mused, stirring up the stars with exploding color. Though it was over and a new day hovered, she felt some magic remained in the night. Far from sleepy, she wandered toward the Big Top.

"Hello, pretty lady."

Jo looked into the shadows and narrowed her eyes. She could just barely make out a form. "Oh, you're Bob, aren't you?" She stopped and gave him a friendly smile. "You're new."

He stepped toward her. "I've been on for nearly three weeks." He was young, Jo guessed about her own age, with a solid build and sharp-featured face. Just that afternoon she had watched Maggie give him a shower.

Jo pushed her hands into the pockets of her cut-offs and continued to smile. It appeared he thought his tenure made him a veteran. "How do you like working with the elephants?"

"It's okay. I like putting up the tent."

Jo understood his feeling. "So do I. There's a game in the cookhouse," she told him with a gesture of her arm. "You might like to sit in."

"I'd rather be with you." As he moved closer, Jo caught the faint whiff of beer. He's been celebrating, she thought and shook her head.

"It's a good thing tomorrow's Monday," she commented. "No one's going to be in any shape to pitch a tent. You should go to bed," she suggested. "Or get some coffee."

"Let's go to your trailer." Bob weaved a little, then took her arm.

"No." Firmly, Jo turned in the opposite direction. "Let's go to the cookhouse." His advances did not trouble her. She was close enough to the cookhouse tent that if she called out, a dozen able-bodied men would come charging. But that was precisely what Jo wanted to avoid.

"I want to go with you," he said, stumbling over the words as he veered away from the cookhouse again. "You look so pretty in that cage with those lions." He put both arms around her, but Jo felt it was as much for balance as romance. "A fella needs a pretty lady once in a while."

"I'm going to feed you to my lions if you don't let me go," Jo warned.

"Bet you can be a real wildcat," he mumbled and made a fumbling dive for her mouth.

Though her patience was wearing thin, Jo endured the kiss that landed slightly to the left of bull's-eye. His hands, however, had better aim and grabbed the firm roundness of her bottom. Losing her temper, Jo pushed away but found his hold had taken root. In a quick move, she brought up her fist and caught him square on the jaw. With only a faint sound of surprise, Bob sat down hard on the ground.

"Well, so much for rescuing you," Keane commented from behind her.

Turning quickly, Jo pushed at her hair and gave an annoyed sigh. She would have preferred no witnesses. Even in the dim light, she could see he was furious. Instinctively, she stepped between him and the man who sat on the ground fingering his jaw and shaking the buzzing from his ears.

"He—Bob just got a bit overenthusiastic," she said hastily and put a restraining hand on Keane's arm. "He's been celebrating."

"I'm feeling a bit enthusiastic myself," Keane stated. As he made to brush her aside, Jo clung with more fervor.

"No, Keane, please."

Looking down, he fired a glare. "Jo, would you let go so that I can deal with this?"

"Not until you listen." The faint hint of laughter in her eyes only enraged him further, and Jo fought to suppress it. "Keane, please, don't be hard on him. He didn't hurt me."

"He was attacking you," Keane interrupted. He barely resisted the urge to shake her off and drag the still seated Bob by the scruff of the neck.

"No, he was really more just leaning on me. His balance is a trifle impaired. He only tried to kiss me," she pointed out, wisely deleting the wandering hands. "And I hit him much harder than I should have. He's new, Keane, don't fire him."

Exasperated, he stared at her. "Firing was the least of what I had in mind for him."

Jo smiled, unable to keep the gleam from her eyes. "If you were going to avenge my honor, he really didn't do much more than breathe on it. I don't think you should run him through for that. Maybe you could just put him in the stocks for a couple of days."

Keane swore under his breath, but a reluctant smile tugged at his mouth. Seeing it, Jo loosened her hold. "Miss Wilder wants to give you a break," he told the dazed Bob in a tough, no-nonsense voice that Jo decided he used for intimidating witnesses. "She has a softer heart than I do. Therefore, I won't knock you down several more times or kick you off the lot, as I had entertained doing." He paused, allowing Bob time to consider this possibility. "Instead, I'll let you sleep off your—enthusiasm." In one quick jerk, he pulled Bob to his feet. "But if I ever hear of you breathing uninvited on Miss Wilder or any other of my female employees, we'll go back to the first choice. And before I kick you out," he added with low menace, "I'll let it be known that you were decked by one punch from a hundred-pound woman."

"Yes, sir, Mr. Prescott," said Bob as clearly as possible.

"Go to bed," Jo said kindly, seeing him pale. "You'll feel better in the morning."

"Obviously," Keane commented as Bob lurched away, "you haven't done much drinking." He turned to Jo and grinned. "The one thing he's not going to feel in the morning is better." Jo smiled, pleased to have Keane talk to her without the thin shield of politeness. "And where," he asked and took her hand for examination, "did you learn that right jab?"

Jo laughed, allowing Keane's fingers to interlock with hers. "It would hardly have knocked him down if he hadn't already been tilting in that direction." Her face turned up to his and sparkled with starlight. In his eyes an expression she couldn't comprehend came and went. "Is something wrong?"

For a moment he said nothing. In her breast her heart began to hammer as she waited to be kissed. "No, nothing," he said. The moment was shattered. "Come on, I'll walk you back to your trailer."

"I wasn't going there." Wanting to put him back into an easy mood, she linked her arm with his. "If you come with me, I'll show you some magic." Her smile slanted invitingly. "You like magic, don't you, Keane? Even a sober, dedicated lawyer must like magic."

"Is that how I strike you?" Jo almost laughed at the trace of annoyance in his voice. "As a sober, dedicated lawyer?"

"Oh, not entirely, though that's part of you." She enjoyed feeling that for the moment she had him to herself. "You've also got a streak of adventure and a rather nice sense of humor. And," she added with generous emphasis, "there's your temper."

"You seem to have me all figured out."

"Oh, no." Jo stopped and turned to him. "Not at all. I only know how you are here. I can only speculate on how you are in Chicago."

His brow lifted as she caught his attention. "Would I be different there?"

"I don't know." Jo's forehead wrinkled in thought. "Wouldn't you be? Circumstances would. You probably have a house or a big apartment, and there's a housekeeper who comes in once—no, twice—a week." Caught up in the picture, she gazed off into the distance and built it further. "You have an office with a view of the city, a very efficient secretary and a brilliant law clerk. You go to business lunches at the club. In court you're deadly and very successful. You have your own tailor and work out at the gym three times a week. There's the theater on the weekends, along with something physical. Tennis maybe, not golf. No, handball."

Keane shook his head. "Is this the magic?"

"No." Jo shrugged and began to walk again. "Just guesswork. You don't have to have a great deal of money to know how people who do behave. And I know you take the law seriously. You wouldn't choose a career that wasn't very important to you."

Keane walked in silence. When he spoke, his voice was quiet. "I'm not certain I'm comfortable with your little outline of my life."

"It's very sketchy," Jo told him. "I'd have to understand you better to fill in the gaps."

"Don't you?"

"What?" Jo asked, pausing. "Understand you?" She laughed,

tickled at the absurdity of his question. "No, I don't understand you. How could I? You live in a different world." With this, she tossed aside the flap of the Big Top and stepped into its darkness. When she hit the switch, two rows of overhead lights flashed on. Shadows haunted the corners and fell over the arena seats.

"It's wonderful, isn't it?" Her clear voice ran the length of the tent and echoed back. "It's not empty, you know. They're always here—the troupers, the audience, the animals." She walked forward until she stood beside the third ring. "Do you know what this is?" she asked Keane, tossing out her arms and turning a full circle. "It's an ageless wonder in a changing world. No matter what happens on the outside, this is here. We're the most fragile of circuses, at the mercy of the elephants, of emotions, of mechanics, of public whims. But six days a week for twenty-nine weeks we perform miracles. We build a world at dawn, then disappear into the dark. That's part of it—the mystery." She waited until Keane moved forward to join her.

"Tents pop up on an empty lot, elephants and lions walk down Main Street. And we never grow old, because each new generation discovers us all over again." She stood slender and exquisite in a circle of light. "Life here's crazy. And it's hard. Muddy lots, insane hours, sore muscles, but when you've finished your act and you get that feeling that tells you it was special, there's nothing else like it in the world."

"Is that why you do it?" Keane asked.

Jo shook her head and moved out of the circle of light into the dark and into another ring. "It's all part of the same thing. We all have our own reasons, I suppose. You've asked me that before; I'm not certain I can explain. Maybe it's that we all believe in miracles." She turned under the light, and it shimmered around her. "I've been here all my life. I know every trick, every illusion. I know how Jamie's dad gets twenty clowns into a two-seater car. But each time I see it, I laugh and I believe it. It's not just the excitement, Keane, it's the anticipation of the excitement. It's knowing you're going to see the biggest or the smallest or the fastest or the highest." Jo ran to the center ring and threw up her arms.

"Ladies and gentlemen," she announced with a toss of her head. "For your amazement and astonishment, for the first time in America, a superabundance of mountainous, mighty pachyderms led in a stupendous exhibition of choreography by the Great Serena." Jo laughed and shifted her hair to her back with a quick movement of her hand. "Dancing elephants!" she said to Keane, pleased that he was smiling. "Or you listen to the talker in the sideshow when he starts his spiel. Step right up. Come a little closer." She curled her fingers in invitation. "See the Amazing Serpentina and her monstrous, slithering vipers. Watch the beautiful young girl charm a deadly cobra. Watch her accept the reptilian embrace of the gargantuan boa. Don't miss the chance to see the enchantress of the evil serpent!"

"I suppose Baby might sue for slander."

Jo laughed and stepped up on the ring. "But when the crowds see little Rose with a boa constrictor wrapped around her shoulders, they've gotten their money's worth. We give them what they come for: color, fantasy, the unique. Thrills. You've seen the audience when Vito does his high wire act without a net."

"A net seems little enough protection when he's balancing on a wire at two hundred feet." Keane stuck his hands in his pockets and frowned. "He risks his life every day."

"So does a police officer or a fire fighter." Jo spoke quietly and rested her hands on his shoulders. It seemed more necessary than ever that she make him understand his father's dream. "I know what you're saying, Keane, but you have to understand us. The element of danger is essential to many of the acts. You can hear the whole audience suck in their breath when Vito does his back somersault on the wire. They'd be impressed if he used a net, but they wouldn't be terrified."

"Do they need to be?"

Jo's sober expression lightened. "Oh, yes! They need to be terrified and fascinated and mesmerized. It's all included in the price of a ticket. This is a world of superlatives. We test the limit of human daring, and every day it changes. Do you know how long it took before the first man accomplished the triple on the trapeze? Now it's nearly a standard." A light of anticipation flared in her eyes. "One day someone will do a quadruple. If a man stands in this ring and juggles three torches today, tomorrow someone will juggle them on horseback and after that there'll be a team tossing them back and forth while swinging on a trap. It's our job to do the incredible, then, when it's done, to do the impossible. It's that simple."

"Simple," Keane murmured, then lifted a hand to caress her hair. "I wonder if you'd think so if you could see it from the outside."

"I don't know." Her fingers tightened on his shoulders as he buried his other hand in her hair. "I never have."

As if his thoughts centered on it, Keane combed his fingers through her hair. Gradually, he pushed it back until only his hands framed her face. They stood in a pool of light that threw their shadows long behind them. "You are so lovely," he murmured.

Jo neither spoke nor moved. There was something different this time in the way he touched her. There was a gentleness and a hesitation she had not felt before. Though they looked directly into hers, she could not read his eyes. Their faces were close, and his breath fluttered against her mouth. Jo slid her arms around his neck and pressed her mouth to his.

Not until that moment had she realized how empty she had felt, how desperately she had needed to hold him. Her lips were hungry for his. She clung while all gentleness fled from his touch. His hands were greedy. The weeks that he had not touched her were forgotten as her skin warmed and hummed with quickening blood. Passion stripped her of inhibitions, and her tongue sought his, taking the kiss into wilder and darker depths. Their lips parted, only to meet again with sharp new demands. She understood that all needs and all desires were ultimately only one—Keane.

His mouth left hers, and for an instant he rested his cheek against her hair. For that moment Jo felt a contentment more complete than she had ever known. Abruptly, he drew away.

Puzzled, she watched as he drew out a cigar. She lifted a hand to run it through the hair he had just disturbed. He flicked on his lighter. "Keane?" She looked at him, knowing her eyes offered everything.

"You've had a long day," he began in an oddly polite tone. Jo winced as if he had struck her. "I'll walk you back to your trailer."

She stepped off the ring and away from him. Pain seared along her skin. "Why are you doing this?" To her humiliation, tears welled in her eyes and lodged in her throat. The tears acted as a prism, refracting the light and clouding her vision. She blinked them back. Keane's brows drew together at the gesture.

"I'll take you back," he said again. The detached tone of his voice accelerated all Jo's fury and grief.

"How dare you!" she demanded. "How dare you make

me…" The word *love* nearly slipped through her lips, and she swallowed it. "How dare you make me want you, then turn away! I was right about you from the beginning. I thought I'd been wrong. You're cold and unfeeling." Her breath came quickly and unevenly, but she refused to retreat until she had said it all. Her face was pale with the passion of her emotions. "I don't know why I thought you'd ever understand what Frank had given you. You need a heart to see the intangible. I'll be glad when the season's over and you do whatever it is you're going to do. I'll be glad when I never have to see you again. I won't let you do this to me anymore!" Her voice wavered, but she made no attempt to steady it. "I don't want you to ever touch me again."

Keane studied her for a long moment, then took a careful drag on his cigar. "All right, Jo."

The very calmness of his answer tore a sob from her before she turned and ran from the Big Top.

Chapter Ten

In July the troupe circled through Virginia, touched the tip of West Virginia on their way into Kentucky, then moved into Ohio. Audiences fanned themselves as the temperatures in the Big Top rose, but they still came.

Since the evening of the Fourth, Jo had avoided Keane. It was not as difficult as it might have been, as he spent half the month in Chicago dealing with his business. Jo functioned. She ate because eating was necessary in order to maintain her strength. She slept because rest was essential to remaining alert in the cage. She did not find any enjoyment in food nor was her sleep restful. Because so many in the troupe knew her well, Jo struggled to keep on a mask of normalcy. Above all, she needed to avoid any questions, any advice, any sympathy. It was necessary, because of her profession, to put her emotions on hold a great deal of the time. After some struggle and some failure, Jo achieved a reasonable success.

Her training of Gerry continued, as did his progress. The additional duty of working with him helped fill her small snatches of spare time. On afternoons when no matinee was scheduled, Jo took him into the big cage. As he grew more proficient, she brought other cats in to join Merlin. By the first week in August they were working together with her full complement of lions.

The only others who were rehearsing in the Big Top were the equestrian act. They ran through the Thread the Needle routine in the first ring. Hooves echoed dully on tanbark. Jo supervised while Gerry sent the cats into a pyramid. At his urging, Lazarus climbed up the wide, arched ladder that topped the grouping. Twice he balked, and twice Gerry was forced to reissue the command.

"Good," Jo commented when the pyramid was complete.

"He wouldn't go." Gerry began to complain, but she cut him off.

"Don't be in too much of a hurry. Bring them down." Her tone was brisk and professional. "Make certain they dismount and take their seats in the right order. It's important to stick to routine."

Hands resting on hips, Jo watched. In her opinion, Gerry had true potential. His nerves were good, he had a feeling for the animals, and he was slowly developing patience. Still she balked at the next step in his training: leaving him alone in the arena. Even with only Merlin, she felt it too risky. He was still too casual. Not yet did he possess enough respect for the lion's guile.

Jo moved around the arena, and the lions, used to her, were not disturbed. As the cats settled onto their pedestals, she once more moved to stand beside Gerry. "Now we'll walk down the line. You make each do a sit-up before we send them out."

One by one the cats rose on their haunches and pawed the air. Jo and Gerry moved down their ranks. The heat was becoming oppressive, and Jo shifted her shoulders, longing for a cool shower and a change of clothes. When they came to Hamlet, he ignored the command with a rebellious snarl.

Bad-tempered brute, thought Jo absently as she waited for Gerry to reissue the command. He did so but moved forward as if to emphasize the words.

"No, not so close!" Jo warned quickly. Even as she spoke, she saw the change in Hamlet's eyes.

Instinctively, she stepped over, nudging Gerry back and shielding his body with hers. Hamlet struck out, claws extended. There was a moment of blind heat in her shoulder as the skin ripped. Swiftly, she was facing the cat, holding tightly onto Gerry's arm as they stood just out of range.

"Don't run," she ordered, feeling his jerk of panic. Her arm was on fire as the blood began to flow freely. Keeping her movements quick but smooth, she took the whip from Gerry's nerveless hand and cracked it hard, using her left arm. She knew that if Hamlet continued his defiance and attacked, it was hopeless. The other cats were certain to join in a melee. It would be over before anything could be done. Already, Abra shifted restlessly and bared her teeth.

"Open the chute," Jo called out. Her voice was cool as ice. "Back toward the safety cage," she instructed Gerry as she gave the cats their signal to leave the arena. "I've got to get them out one at a time. Move slow, and if I tell you to stop, you stop dead. Understand?"

She heard him swallow as she watched the cats begin to leap off their pedestals and file into the chute. "He got you. Is it bad?" The words were barely a whisper and drenched in terror.

"I said go." Half the cats were gone, and still Hamlet's eyes were locked on hers. There was no time to waste. One part of her brain heard shouting outside the cage, but she blocked it out and focused all her concentration on the cat. "Go now," she repeated to Gerry. "Do as you're told."

He swallowed again and began to back away. Long seconds dragged until she heard the rattle of the safety cage door. When his turn came, Hamlet made no move to leave his seat. Jo was alone with him. She could smell the heat, the scent of the wild and the fragrance of her own blood. Her arm was alive with pain. Slowly, she tested him by backing up. The safety cage seemed hundreds of miles away. The cat tensed immediately, and she stopped. She knew he would not let her cross the arena. Outrunning him was impossible, as the distance between them could be covered in one spring. She had to outbluff him instead.

"Out," she ordered firmly. "Out, Hamlet." As he continued to watch her, Jo felt a trickle of sweat slide down between her shoulder blades. Her skin was clammy with it in contrast to the warmth of the blood that ran down her arm. There was a sudden, vivid picture inside her head of her father being dragged around the cage. Fear tripped inside her throat. There was a lightness fluttering in the top of her head, and she knew that a moment's terror would cause her to faint. She stiffened her spine and pushed it away.

Speed was important. The longer she allowed the cat to remain in the arena after his cue, the more defiant he would become. And the more dangerous. As yet he was unaware that he held her at such a sharp disadvantage. "Out, Hamlet." Jo repeated the command with a crack of the whip. He leaped from the pedestal. Jo's stomach trembled. She locked every muscle, and as the cat hesitated, she repeated the command. He was confused, and she knew this could work as an advantage or a curse. Confused, he might spring or retreat. Her fingers tightened on the stock of the whip and trembled. The cat paced nervously and watched her.

"Hamlet!" She raised her voice and bit off each syllable. "Go out." To the words she added the hand signal she had used before he was fully trained to voice command.

As if rebuffed, Hamlet relaxed his tail and padded into the chute. Before the door slid completely closed, Jo sank to her knees. Her body began to quake fiercely with the aftershock. No more than five minutes had passed since Hamlet had defied Gerry's command, but her muscles bore the strain of hours. For an instant her vision blurred. Even as she shook her head to clear it, Keane was on the ground beside her.

She heard him swear, ripping the tattered sleeve of her blouse from her arm. He fired questions at her, but she could do no more than shake her head and gulp in air. Focusing on him, she noticed his eyes were unusually dark against his face.

"What?" She followed his voice but not the words. He swore again, sharply enough to penetrate the first layer of her shock. He pulled her to her feet, then continuing the motion smoothly, lifted her into his arms. "Don't." Her mind struggled to break through the fog and function. "I'm all right."

"Shut up," he said harshly as he carried her from the cage. "Just shut up."

Because speaking cost her some effort, Jo obeyed. Closing her eyes, she let the mixture of excited voices whirl around her. Her arm screamed with pain, but the throbbing reassured her. Numbness would have terrified her. Still she kept her eyes shut, not yet having the courage to look at the damage. Being alive was enough.

When she opened her eyes again, Keane was carrying her into the administration wagon. At the sound of the chaos that followed them, Duffy strode through from his office. "What the…" he began, then stopped and paled beneath his freckles. He moved quickly forward as Keane set Jo in a chair. "How bad?"

"I don't know yet," Keane muttered. "Get a towel and the first-aid kit."

Buck had come in behind them and, already having secured the items, handed them to Keane. Then he moved to a cabinet and located a bottle of brandy.

"It's not too bad," Jo managed. Because her voice was tolerably steady, she screwed up her courage and looked down. Keane had fastened a rough bandage from the remains of her sleeve. Though the flow of blood had slowed, there were streaks of it down her arm, and too much spreading from the wound to be certain how extensive the cuts were. Nausea rocked in her stomach.

"How do you know?" Keane demanded between his teeth as he began to clean the wound. He wrung out the towel in the basin Buck set beside him.

"It's not bleeding that badly." Jo swallowed the queasiness. As her mind began to clear, she frowned at the tone of Keane's voice. Feeling her stare, he glanced up. In his eyes was such fury, she pulled away.

"Be still," he ordered roughly and gave his attention back to her arm.

The cat had delivered only a glancing blow, but even so, there were four long slices in her upper arm. Jo set her jaw as pain ripped through her. Keane's brusqueness brought more hurt, and she fought to show no reaction to either. The aftermath of fear was bubbling through her. She longed to be held, to be soothed by the hands that tended to her wound.

"She's going to need stitches," Keane said without looking at her.

"And an antitoxin shot," Buck added, handing Jo a generous glass of brandy. "Drink this, honey. It'll help settle you."

The gentleness in his voice nearly undid her. He laid his big hand against her cheek, and for a moment she pressed against it.

"Drink now," Buck ordered again. Obediently, Jo lifted the glass and swallowed. The room whirled, then snapped into focus. She made a small sound and pressed the glass to her forehead. "Tell me what happened in there." Buck crouched down beside her as Keane began to apply a temporary bandage.

Jo took a moment to draw air in and out of her lungs. She lowered the glass and spoke steadily. "Hamlet didn't respond, and Gerry repeated a command, but he stepped forward. Too close. I saw Hamlet's eyes, and I knew. I should have moved faster. I should have been watching him more carefully. It was a stupid mistake." She stared into the brandy as she berated herself.

"She stepped between the boy and the cat." Keane bit off the words as he completed the bandaging. Rising, he moved to the brandy and poured. Not once did he turn to look at Jo. Hurt, she stared at his back before looking back at Buck.

"How's Gerry?"

Buck urged the glass back to her lips. A faint tint of pink was creeping into her cheeks. "Pete's with him. Got his head between his knees. He'll be fine."

Jo nodded. "I guess I'll have to go to town and have this seen to." She handed the glass to Buck and wondered if she dare attempt to rise yet. With another deep breath, she glanced at Duffy. "Make sure he's ready to go in when I get back."

Keane turned from the window. "Go in where?" His face was set in hard lines.

In response, Jo's voice was chilled. "In the cage." She turned her eyes to Buck. "We should be able to have a short run-through before the evening show."

"No." Jo's head snapped up as Keane spoke. For a long moment they stared at each other with odd, unreasonable antagonism. "You're not going back in there today." His voice held curt authority.

"Of course I am," Jo countered, managing to keep the combination of pain and anger from her words. "And if Gerry wants to be a cat man, he's going in, too."

"Jo's right," Buck put in, trying to soothe what he sensed was an explosive situation. "It's like falling off a horse. You can't wait too long before you get back up, or you won't ride again."

Keane never took his eyes from Jo. He continued as if Buck hadn't spoken. "I won't permit it."

"You can't stop me." Indignation forced her to her feet. The brisk movement caused her arm to protest, and her struggle against it showed momentarily in her eyes.

"Yes, I can." Keane took a long swallow of brandy. "I own this circus."

Jo's fists tightened at his tone, at his careless use of his authority. Not once since he had knelt beside her in the cage had he given her any sign of comfort or reassurance. She had needed it from him. To masquerade its trembling, she kept her voice low. "But you don't own me, Mr. Prescott. And if you'll check your papers and the legalities, you'll see you don't own the lions or my equipment. I bought them, and I maintain them out of my salary. My contract doesn't give you the right to tell me when I can or can't rehearse my cats."

Keane's face was granite hard. "Neither does it give you the right to set up in the Big Top without my permission."

"Then I'll set up someplace else," she tossed back. "But I

will set up. That cat will be worked again today. I won't take the risk of losing months of training."

"But you will risk being killed," Keane shot back and slammed down his glass.

"What do you care?" Jo shouted. All control deserted her. The cuts were deep on her emotions as well as her flesh. She had passed through a terror more acute than she had known since the night of her parents' death. More than anything else, she wanted to feel Keane's arms around her. She wanted to know the security she had felt when he had let her weep out her grief for Ari in his arms. "I'm nothing to you!" Her head shook quickly, tossing her hair. There was a bubble of hysteria in her voice, and Buck reached out to lay a hand on her shoulder.

"Jo," he warned in his soft, rumbling voice.

"No!" She shook her head and spoke rapidly. "He hasn't the right. You haven't the right to interfere with my life." She flared at Keane again with eyes vivid with emotion. "I know what I have to do. I know what I *will* do. Why should it matter to you? You aren't legally responsible if I get mauled. No one's going to sue you."

"Hold on, Jo." This time Buck spoke firmly. As he took her uninjured arm, he felt the tremors shooting through her. "She's too upset to know what she's saying," he told Keane.

There was a mask over Keane's face which concealed all emotion. "Oh, I think she knows what she's saying," he disagreed quietly. For a moment there was only the sound of Jo shuddering and the splash of brandy being poured into a glass. "You do what you have to do, Jo," he said after drinking again. "You're perfectly correct that I haven't any rights where you're concerned. Take her into town," he told Buck, then turned back to the window.

"Come on, Jo." Buck urged her to the door, slipping a supportive arm around her waist. Even as they stepped outside, Rose came running from the direction of the midway.

"Jo!" Her face was white with concern. "Jo, I just heard." She glanced at the bandage with wide, terrified eyes. "How bad is it?"

"Just scratches, really," Jo assured her. She added the best smile she could muster. "Buck's going to take me into town for a couple of stitches."

"Are you sure?" She looked up at the tall man for reassurance. "Buck?"

"Several stitches," he corrected but patted Rose's hand. "But it's not too bad."

"Do you want me to come with you?" She fell into step beside them as Buck began to lead Jo again.

"No. Thank you, Rose." Jo smiled with more feeling. "I'll be fine."

Because of the smile, Rose was able to relax. "I thought when I heard…well, I imagined all sorts of terrible things. I'm glad you're not badly hurt." They had reached Buck's truck, and Rose leaned over to kiss Jo's cheek. "We all love you so."

"I know." Squeezing her hand, Jo let Buck help her into the cab of his truck. As he maneuvered from the lot, Jo rested her head against the back of the seat and shut her eyes. Never could she remember feeling more spent, more battered.

"Hurt bad?" Buck asked as they switched to an asphalt road.

"Yes," she answered simply, thinking of her heart as much as her arm.

"You'll feel better when you're patched up."

Jo kept her eyes shut, knowing some wounds never heal. Or if they did, they left scars that ached at unexpected times.

"You shouldn't have gone off on him that way, Jo." There was light censure in Buck's voice.

"He shouldn't have interfered," Jo retorted. "It's none of his business. *I'm* none of his business."

"Jo, it's not like you to be so hard."

"Hard?" She opened her eyes and turned to Buck. "What about him? Couldn't he have been kinder, shown even the barest trace of compassion? Did he have to speak to me as if I were a criminal?"

"Jo, the man was terrified. You're only looking at this from one side." He scratched his beard and gave a gusty sigh. "You can't know what it's like to be outside that cage, helpless when someone you care about is facing down death. I had to all but knock him unconscious to keep him out of there until we got it through his head that he'd just get you killed for sure. He was scared, Jo. We were all scared."

Jo shook her head, certain Buck exaggerated because of his affection for her. Keane's voice had been hard, his eyes angry. "He doesn't care," she corrected quietly. "Not like the rest of you. You didn't swear at me. You weren't cold."

"Jo, people have different ways—" Buck began, but she interrupted.

"I know he wouldn't want to see me hurt, Buck. He's not heartless or cruel." She sighed as all the force of anger and fear washed out of her body and left her empty. "Please, I don't want to talk about him."

Buck heard the weariness in her voice and patted her hand. "Okay, honey, just relax. We'll have you all fixed up in no time."

Not all fixed up, Jo thought. Far from all fixed up.

Chapter Eleven

As the weeks passed, Jo's arm lost its stiffness. She healed cleanly. The only traces were thin scars that promised to fade but not disappear. She found, however, that some spark had gone out of her life. Constantly, she fought against a vague dissatisfaction. Nothing—not her work, not her friends, not her books—brought about the contentment she had grown up with. She had become a woman, and her needs had shifted. Jo knew the root of her problem was Keane, but the knowledge was not a solution. He had left the circus again on the very night of her accident. Nearly four weeks later he had not returned.

Three times Jo had sat down to write him, needing to assuage her guilt for the harsh things she had said to him. Three times she had torn up the paper in frustration. No matter how she rearranged the words, they were wrong. Instead, she clung to the hope that he would come back one last time. If, she felt, they could part as friends, without bitterness or hard words, she could accept the separation. Willing this to happen, she was able to return to her routine with some tranquility.

She rehearsed, performed, joined in the daily duties of circus life. She waited. The caravan moved closer to Chicago.

Jo stood in the steaming Big Top on a late August afternoon. Dressed in a leotard, she worked on ground exercises with the Beirot Brothers. It was this daily regimentation that had aided in keeping her arm limber. She could now move into a back walk-over without feeling any protest in her injured arm.

"I feel good," Jo told Raoul as they worked out. "I feel really good." She did a quick series of pirouettes.

"You don't keep your shoulder in shape by dancing on your feet," Raoul challenged.

"My shoulder's fine," she tossed back, then proved her point by bending into a handstand. Slowly, she lowered her legs to a forty-five degree angle, bringing one foot to rest on the knee of the opposite leg. "It's perfect." She executed a forward roll and sprang to her feet. "I'm strong as an ox," she claimed and did a quick back handspring followed by a back flip.

She landed at Keane's feet.

The cascade of emotions that raced through her reflected briefly in her eyes before she regained her balance. "I didn't— I didn't know you were back." Instantly, she regretted the inanity of the words but could find no others. The longing was raw in her to hurl herself into his arms. She wondered that he could not feel her need through the pores of her skin.

"I just got in." His eyes continued to search her face after his hands dropped to his sides. "This is my mother," he added. "Rachael Loring, Jovilette Wilder."

At his words, Jo's gaze moved from his face. She saw the woman beside him. If she had seen Rachael Loring in a crowd of two thousand, she would have known her for Keane's mother. The bone structure was the same, though hers was more elegant. Her brows were golden wings, flaring out at the end, as Keane's did. Her hair was smooth, brushed up and away from her face with no gray to mar its tawny perfection. But it was the eyes that sent a jolt through Jo. She had not thought to see them in anyone's face but Keane's. The woman was dressed simply in an unpretentiously tailored suit that bespoke taste and wealth. There was, however, none of the cool, distant polish that Jo had always attributed to the woman who had taken her son and left Frank. There was a charm to the smile that curved in greeting.

"Jovilette, such a lovely name. Keane's told me of you." She extended her hand, and Jo accepted, intending a quick, impersonal shake. Rachael Loring, however, laid her other hand atop their joined ones and added warmth. "Keane tells me you were very close to Frank. Perhaps we could talk."

The affection in her voice confused Jo into a stumbling reply. "I— Yes. I—if you'd like."

"I should like very much." She squeezed Jo's hand again before releasing it. "Perhaps you have time to show me around?" She smiled with the question, and Jo found it increasingly difficult to remain aloof. "I'm sure there've been some changes since I was here last. You must have some business to attend to," she said, looking up at Keane. "I'm sure Jovilette will take good care of me. Won't you, dear?" Without waiting for either to respond, Rachael tucked her arm through Jo's and began to walk. "I knew your parents," she said as Keane watched them move away. "Not terribly well, I'm afraid. They came here the same year I left. But I recall they were both thrilling performers. Keane tells me you've followed your father's profession."

"Yes, I…" She hesitated, feeling oddly at a disadvantage. "I did," she finished lamely.

"You're so young." Rachael gave her a gentle smile. "How terribly brave you must be."

"No…no, not really. It's my job."

"Yes, of course." Rachael laughed at some private memory. "I've heard that before."

They were outside now, and she paused to look thoughtfully around her. "I think perhaps I was wrong. It hasn't really changed, not in thirty years. It's a wonderful place, isn't it?"

"Why did you leave?" As soon as the words were spoken, Jo regretted them. "I'm sorry," she said quickly. "I shouldn't have asked."

"Of course you should." Rachael sighed and patted Jo's hand. "It's only natural. Duffy's still here, Keane tells me." At the change in subject, Jo imagined her question had been evaded.

"Yes, I suppose he always will be."

"Could we have some coffee, or some tea, perhaps?" Rachael smiled again. "It's such a long drive from town. Is your trailer nearby?"

"It's just over in the back yard."

"Oh, yes." Rachael laughed and began to walk again. "The neighborhood that never changes over thousands of miles. Do you know the story of the dog and the bones?" she asked. Though Jo knew it well, she said nothing. "One version is that a roustabout gave his dog a bone every night after dinner. The dog would bury the bone under the trailer, then the next day try to dig it back up. Of course, it was fifty miles behind in an empty lot. He never figured it out." Quietly, she laughed to herself.

Feeling awkward, Jo opened the door to her trailer. How could this woman be the one she had resented all of her life?

How could this be the cold, heartless woman who had left Frank? Oddly, Rachael seemed totally at ease in the narrow confines of the trailer.

"How efficient these are." She looked around with interest and approval. "You must barely realize you're on wheels." Casually, she picked up the volume of Thoreau which lay on Jo's counter. "Keane told me you have an avid interest in literature. In language, too," she added, glancing up from the book. Her eyes were golden and direct like her son's. Jo was tossed back suddenly to the first morning of the season when she had looked down and found Keane's eyes on her.

It made her uncomfortable to learn Keane had discussed her with his mother. "I have some tea," Jo told her as she moved toward the kitchen. "It's a better gamble than my coffee."

"That's fine," Rachael said agreeably and followed her. "I'll just sit here while you fix it." She settled herself with apparent ease at the tiny table across from the kitchen.

"I'm afraid I haven't anything else to offer you." Jo kept her back turned as she routed through her cupboard.

"Tea and conversation," Rachael answered in mild tones, "will be fine."

Jo sighed and turned. "I'm sorry." She shook her head. "I'm being rude. I just don't know what to say to you, Mrs. Loring. I've resented you for as long as I can remember. Now you're here and not at all as I imagined." She managed to smile, albeit ruefully. "You're not cold and hateful, and you look so much like…" She stopped, horrified that she had nearly blurted out Keane's name. For a moment her eyes were utterly naked.

Rachael smoothed over the awkwardness. "I don't wonder you resented me if you were as close to Frank as Keane tells me. Jovilette," she said softly, "did Frank resent me, too?"

Helpless, Jo responded to the hint of sadness. "No. Not while I knew him. I don't think Frank was capable of resentments."

"You understood him well, didn't you?" Rachael watched as Jo poured boiling water into mugs. "I understood him, too," she continued as Jo brought the mugs to the table. "He was a dreamer, a marvelous free spirit." Absently, she stirred her tea.

Consumed with curiosity, Jo sat across from her and waited for the story she sensed was coming.

"I was eighteen when I met him. I had come to the circus with a cousin. The Colossus was a bit smaller in those days," she added with a reminiscent smile, "but it was all the same. Oh, the magic!" She shook her head and sighed. "We tumbled into love so fast, married against all my family's objections and went on the road. It was exciting. I learned the web routine and helped out in wardrobe."

Jo's eyes widened. "You performed?"

"Oh, yes." Rachael's cheeks tinted a bit with pride. "I was quite good. Then I became pregnant. We were both like children waiting for Christmas. I wasn't quite nineteen when I had Keane, and I'd been with the circus for nearly a year. Things became difficult over the next season. I was young and a bit frightened of Keane. I panicked if he sneezed and was constantly dragging Frank into town to see doctors. How patient he was."

Rachael leaned forward and took Jo's hand. "Can you understand how hard this life is for one not meant for it? Can you see that through the magic of it, the excitement and wonder, there are hardships and fears and impossible demands? I was little more than a child myself, with an infant to care for, without the endurance or vocation of a trouper, without the experience or confidence of a mother. I lived on nerves for an entire season." She let out a little rush of breath. "When it was over, I went home to Chicago."

For the first time, Jo imagined the flight from Rachael's point of view. She could see a girl, younger than herself, in a strange, demanding world with a baby to care for. Over the years Jo had seen scores of people try the life she'd led and last only weeks. Still she shook her head in confusion.

"I think I understand how difficult it must have been for you. But if you and Frank loved each other, couldn't you have worked it out somehow?"

"How?" Rachael countered. "Should I have taken a house somewhere and lived with him half a year? I would have hated him. Should he have given up his life here and settled down with me and Keane? It would have destroyed everything I loved about him." Rachael shook her head, giving Jo a soft smile. "We did love each other, Jovilette, but not enough. Compromise isn't always possible, and neither of us were capable of adjusting to the needs of the other. I tried, and Frank would have tried had I asked him. But it was lost before it had really begun. We did the wisest thing under the circumstances." Looking into Jo's eyes, she saw youth and confidence. "It seems cold and hard to you, but it was no use dragging out a painful situation. He gave me Keane and two years I've always treasured. I gave him his freedom without bitterness. Ten years after Frank, I found happiness again." She smiled softly with the memory. "I loved Frank, and that love remains as young and sweet as the day I met him."

Jo swallowed. She searched for some way to apologize for a grudge held for a lifetime. "He—Frank kept a scrapbook on Keane. He followed the Chicago papers."

"Did he?" Rachael beamed, then leaned back in her chair

and lifted her mug. "How like him. Was he happy, Jovilette? Did he have what he wanted?"

"Yes," Jo answered without hesitation. "Did you?"

Rachael's eyes came back to Jo's. For a moment the look was speculative, then it grew warm. "What a good heart you have, generous and understanding. Yes, I had what I wanted. And you, Jovilette, what do you want?"

At ease now, Jo shook her head and smiled. "More than I can have."

"You're too smart for that," Rachael observed, studying her. "I think you're a fighter, not a dreamer. When the time comes to make your choice, you won't settle for anything less than all." She smiled at Jo's intent look, then rose. "Will you show me your lions? I can't tell you how I'm looking forward to seeing you perform."

"Yes, of course." Jo stood, then hesitated. She held out her hand. "I'm glad you came."

Rachael accepted the gesture. "So am I."

Throughout the rest of the day Jo looked for Keane without success. After meeting and talking with his mother, it had become even more imperative that she speak with him. Her conscience would have no rest until she made amends. By showtime she had not yet found him.

Each act seemed to run on and on as she fretted for the finish. He would be with his mother in the audience, and undoubtedly she would find him after the show. She strained with impatience as the acts dragged.

After the finale she stood at the back door, unsure whether to wait or to go to his trailer. She was struck with both relief and alarm when she saw him approaching.

"Jovilette." Rachael spoke first, taking Jo's hands in hers. "How marvelous you were, and how stunning. I see why Keane said you had an untamed beauty."

Surprised, Jo glanced up at Keane but met impassive amber eyes. "I'm glad you enjoyed it."

"Oh, I can't tell you how much. The day has brought me some very precious memories. Our talk this afternoon meant a great deal to me." To Jo's surprise, Rachael leaned over and kissed her. "I hope to see you again. I'm going to say goodbye to Duffy before you drive me back, Keane," she continued. "I'll meet you in the car. Goodbye, Jovilette."

"Goodbye, Mrs. Loring." Jo watched her go before she turned to Keane. "She's a wonderful person. She makes me ashamed."

"There's no need for that." He tucked his hands into his pockets and watched her. "We both had our reasons for resentments, and we were both wrong. How's your arm?"

"Oh." Jo's fingers traveled to the wound automatically. "It's fine. There's barely any scarring."

"Good." The word was short and followed by silence. For a moment Jo felt her courage fail her.

"Keane," she began, then forced herself to meet his eyes directly. "I want to apologize for the horrible way I behaved after the accident."

"I told you once before," he said coolly, "I don't care for apologies."

"Please." Jo swallowed her pride and touched his arm. "I've been saving this one for a very long time. I didn't mean those things I said," she added quickly. "I hope you'll forgive me." It wasn't the eloquent apology she had planned, but it was all she could manage. His expression never altered.

"There's nothing to forgive."

"Keane, please." Jo grabbed his arm again as he turned to go. "Don't leave me feeling as if you don't forgive me. I know I said dreadful things. You have every right to be furious, but couldn't you—can't we be friends again?"

Something flickered over his face. Lifting his hand, he touched the back of it to her cheek. "You have a habit of disconcerting me, Jovilette." He dropped his hand, then thrust it into his pocket. "I've left something for you with Duffy. Be happy." He walked away from her while she dealt with the finality of his tone. He was walking out of her life. She watched him until he disappeared.

Jo had thought she would feel something, but there was nothing; no pain, no tears, no desperation. She had not known a human being could be so empty and still live.

"Jo." Duffy lumbered up to her, then held out a thick envelope. "Keane left this for you." Then he moved past her, anxious to see that all straggling towners were nudged on their way.

Jo felt all emotions had been stripped away. Absently, she glanced at the envelope as she walked to her trailer. Without enthusiasm, she stepped inside, then tore it open. She remained standing as she pulled out the contents. It took her several moments to decipher the legal jargon. She read the group of papers through twice before sitting down.

He's given it to me, she thought. Still she could not comprehend the magnitude of it. *He's given me the circus.*

Chapter Twelve

O'Hare Airport was an army of people and a cacophony of sound. Nearly losing herself in the chaos of it, Jo struggled through the masses and competed for a cab. At first she had merely gawked at the snow like a towner seeing his first sword swallower. Then, though she shivered inside the corduroy coat she had bought for the trip, she began to enjoy it. It was beautiful as it lay over the city, and it helped to turn her mind from the purpose of her journey. Never had she been north so late in the year. Chicago in November was a sensational sight.

She had learned, after the initial shock had worn off, that Keane had not only given her the circus but a responsibility as well. Almost immediately there had been contracts to negotiate. She had been tossed into a sea of paperwork, forced to rely heavily on Duffy's experience as she tried to regain her balance. As the season had come to a close, Jo had attempted a dozen times to call Chicago. Each time, she had hung up before Keane's number could be dialed. It would be, she had decided, more appropriate to see him in person. Her trip had been postponed a few weeks due to Jamie and Rose's wedding.

It was there, as she had stood as maid of honor, that Jo had realized what she must do. There was only one thing she truly wanted, and that was to be with Keane. Watching Rose's face as their vows had been exchanged, Jo had recalled her unflagging determination to win the man she loved.

And will I stay here? Jo had demanded of herself thousands of miles away from him. No. Her heart had begun to thud as she had mapped out a plan. She would go to Chicago to see him. She would not be turned away. He had wanted her once; she would make him want her again. She would not live out her life without at least some small portion of it being part of his. He didn't have to love her. It was enough that she loved him.

And so, shivering against the unfamiliar cold, Jo scrambled into a cab and headed across town. She brushed her hair free of snow with chilled fingers, thinking how idiotic she had been to forget to buy a hat and gloves. *What if he isn't home?* she thought suddenly. *What if he's gone to Europe or Japan or California?* Panic made her giddy, and she pushed it down. *He has to be home. It's Sunday, and he's sitting at home reading or going over a brief—or entertaining a woman,* she thought, appalled. *I should stop and call. I should tell the driver to take me back to the airport.* Closing her eyes, Jo fought to regain her calm. She took long, deep breaths and stared at the buildings and sidewalks. Gradually, she felt the tiny gurgle of hysteria dissipate.

I won't be afraid, she told herself and tried to believe it. *I won't be afraid.* But Jovilette, the woman who reclined on a living rug of lions, was very much afraid. *What if he rejected her? I won't let him reject me,* she told herself with a confident lift of her chin. *I'll seduce him.* She pressed her fingers to her temples. *I wouldn't know how to begin. I've got to tell the driver to turn around.*

But before she could form the words, the cab pulled up to

a curb. With the precision of a robot, Jo paid the fare, overtipping in her agitation, and climbed out.

Long after the cab had pulled away, she stood staring up at the massive glass-girdled building. Snow waltzed around her, sprinkling her hair and shoulders. A jostle from a rushing pedestrian broke the spell. She picked up her suitcases and hurried through the front door of the apartment buildings.

The lobby was enormous, with smoked glass walls and a deep shag carpet. Not knowing she should give her name at the desk, Jo wandered toward the elevators, innocently avoiding detection by merging with a group of tenants. Once inside the car, Jo pushed the button for the penthouse with a nerveless forefinger. The chatter of those in the elevator with her registered only as a distant humming. She never noticed when the car stopped for their departure.

When it stopped a second time and the doors slid open, she stared at the empty space for ten full seconds. Only as the automatic doors began to close did she snap out of her daze. Pushing them open again, she stepped through and into the hall. Her legs were wobbly, but she forced them to move forward in the direction of the penthouse. Panic sped up and down her spine until she set down her bags and leaned her brow against Keane's door. She urged air in and out of her lungs. She remembered that Rachael Loring had called her a fighter. Jo swallowed, lifted her chin and knocked. The wait was mercifully brief before Keane opened the door. She saw surprise light his eyes as he stared at her.

Her hair was dusted with snow as it lay over the shoulders of her coat. Her face glowed with the cold, and her eyes were bright, nearly feverish with her struggle for calm. Only once did her mouth tremble before she spoke.

"Hello, Keane."

He only stared, his eyes running over her in disbelief. He was leaner, she thought as she studied his face. As she filled herself with the sight of him, she saw he wore a sweatshirt and jeans. His feet were bare. He hadn't shaved, and her hand itched to test the roughness of his beard.

"What are you doing here?" Jo felt a resurgence of panic. His tone was harsh, and he had not answered her smile. She strained for poise.

"May I come in?" she asked, her smile cracking.

"What?" He seemed distracted by the question. His brows lowered into a frown.

"May I come in?" she repeated, barely defeating the urge to turn tail and run.

"Oh, yes, of course. I'm sorry." Running a hand through his hair, Keane stepped back and gestured her inside.

Instantly, Jo's shoes sank into the luxurious pile of the buff-colored carpet. For a moment she allowed herself to gaze around the room, using the time for the additional purpose of regaining her composure. It was an open, sweeping room with sharp, contrasting colors. There was a deep brown sectional sofa with a chrome and glass coffee table. There were high-backed chairs in soft creams and vivid slashes of blue in chunky floor pillows. There were paintings, one she thought she recognized as a Picasso, and a sculpture she was certain was a Rodin.

On the far right of the room there was an elevation of two steps. Just beyond was a huge expanse of glass that featured a spreading view of Chicago. Jo moved toward it with undisguised curiosity. Now, inexplicably, fear had lessened. She found that once she had stepped over the threshold she had committed herself. She was no longer afraid.

"It's wonderful," she said, turning back to him. "How marvelous to have a whole city at your feet every day. You must feel like a king."

"I've never thought of it that way." With half the room between them, he studied her. She looked small and fragile with the bustling city at her back.

"I would," she said, and now her smile came easily. "I'd stand at the window and feel regal and pompous."

At last she saw his lips soften and curve. "Jovilette," he said quietly. "What are you doing in my world?"

"I needed to talk to you," she answered simply. "I had to come here to do it."

He moved to her then, but slowly, with his eyes on hers. "It must be important."

"I thought so."

His brow lifted, then he shrugged. "Well, then, we'll talk. But first, let's have your coat."

Jo's cold fingers fumbled with the buttons and caused Keane to frown again. "Good heavens, you're frozen." He captured her hands between his and swore. "Where are your gloves?" he demanded like an irate parent. "It must be all of twelve degrees outside."

"I forgot to buy any," Jo told him as she dealt with the heavenly feeling of his hands restoring warmth to hers.

"Idiot. Don't you know better than to come to Chicago in November without gloves?"

"No." Jo responded to his anger with a cheerful smile. "I've never been to Chicago in November before. It's wonderful."

His eyes lifted from her hands to her face. He watched her for a long moment, then she heard him sigh. "I'd nearly convinced myself I could be cured."

Jo's eyes clouded with concern. "Have you been ill?"

Keane laughed with a shake of his head, then he pushed away the question and became brisk again. "Here, let's have your coat. I'll get you some coffee."

"You needn't bother," she began as he undid the buttons on the coat himself and drew it from her shoulders.

"I'd feel better if I was certain your circulation was restored." He paused and looked down at her as he laid her coat over his arm. She wore a green angora sweater with pearl buttons and a gray skirt in thin wool. The soft fabric draped softly at her breasts and over her hips and thighs. Her shoes were dainty and impractical sling-back heels.

"Is something wrong?"

"I've never seen you wear anything but a costume or jeans."

"Oh." Jo laughed and combed her fingers through her damp hair. "I expect I look different."

"Yes, you do." His voice was low, and there was a frown in his eyes. "Right now you look as if you've come from college for the holidays." He touched the ends of her hair, then turned away. "Sit down. I'll get the coffee."

A bit puzzled by his mercurial moods, Jo wandered about the room, finally ignoring a chair to kneel beside one of the pillows near the picture window. Though the carpet swallowed Keane's footsteps, she sensed his return.

"How wonderful to have a real winter, if just for the snow." She turned a radiant face his way. "I've always wondered what Christmas is like with snow and icicles." Images of snowflakes danced in her eyes. Seeing he carried two mugs of coffee, she rose and took one. "Thank you."

"Are you warm enough?" he asked after a moment.

Jo nodded and sat in one of the two chairs opposite the sofa.

The novelty of the city made her mission seem like a grand adventure. Keane sat beside her, and for a moment they drank in companionable silence.

"What did you want to talk to me about, Jo?"

Jo swallowed, ignoring the faint trembling in her chest. "A couple of things. The circus, for one." She shifted in her chair until she faced him. "I didn't write because I felt it too important. I didn't phone for the same reason. Keane..." All her carefully thought-out speeches deserted her. "You can't just give something like that away. I can't take it from you."

"Why not?" He shrugged and sipped his coffee. "We both know it's always been yours. A piece of paper doesn't change that one way or the other."

"Keane, Frank left it to you."

"And I gave it to you."

Jo made a small sound of frustration. "Perhaps if I could pay you for it..."

"Someone asked me once what was the value of a dream or the price of a human spirit." Jo shifted her eyes to his helplessly. "I didn't have an answer then. Do you have one now?"

She sighed and shook her head. "I don't know what to say to you. 'Thank you' is far from adequate."

"It's not necessary, either," Keane told her. "I simply gave back what was yours in any case. What else was there, Jo? You said there were a couple of things."

This was it, Jo's brain told her. Carefully, she set down the coffee and rose. Waiting for her stomach to settle, she walked a few feet out into the room, then turned. She allowed herself a deep breath before she met Keane's eyes.

"I want to be your mistress," she said with absolute calm.

"*What?*" Both Keane's face and voice registered utter shock.

Jo swallowed and repeated. "I want to be your mistress. That's still the right term, isn't it, or is it antiquated? Is *lover* right? I've never done this before."

Slowly, Keane set his mug beside hers and rose. He did not move toward her but watched her with probing eyes. "Jo, you don't know what you're saying."

"Oh, yes, I do," she cut him off and nodded. "I might not have the terminology exactly right, but I do know what I mean, and I'm sure you do, too. I want to be with you," she continued and took a step toward him. "I want you to make love to me. I want to live with you if you'll let me, or at least close by."

"Jo, you're not talking sensibly." Sharply, Keane broke into her speech. Turning away, he thrust his hands into his pockets and balled them into fists. "You don't know what you're asking."

"Don't I appeal to you anymore?"

Keane whirled, infuriated with the trace of curiosity in her voice. "How can you ask me that?" he demanded. "Of course you appeal to me! I'm not dead or in the throes of senility!"

She moved closer to him. "Then if I want you, and you want me, why can't we be lovers?"

Keane swore violently and grabbed her shoulders. "Do you think I could have you for a winter and then blithely let you go? Do you think I could untangle myself at the start of the season and watch you stroll out of my life? Haven't you the sense to see what you do to me?" He shook her hard with the question, stealing any breath she might have used to answer him.

"You make me crazy!" Abruptly, he dragged her against him. His mouth bruised hers, his fingers dug into her flesh. Jo's head spun with confusion and pain and ecstasy. It seemed centuries since she had tasted his mouth on hers. She heard him groan as he tore himself away. He turned, leaving her to find her own balance as the room swayed. "What do I have to do to be rid of you?" His words came in furious undertones.

Jo blew out a breath. "I don't think kissing me like that is a very good start."

"I'm aware of that," he murmured. She watched the rise and fall of his shoulders. "I've been trying to avoid doing it since I opened the door."

Quietly, Jo walked to him and put a hand on his arm. "You're tense," she discovered and automatically sought to soothe the muscles. "I'm sorry if I'm going about this the wrong way. I thought telling you outright would be better than trying to seduce you. I don't think I'd be very good at that."

Keane made a sound somewhere between a laugh and a moan. "Jovilette," he murmured before he turned and gathered her into his arms. "How do I resist you? How many times must I pull away before I'm free of you? Even the thought of you drives me mad."

"Keane." She sighed and shut her eyes. "I've wanted you to hold me for so long. I want to belong to you, even for just a little while."

"No." He pulled away, then forced her chin up with his thumb and forefinger. "Don't you see that once would be too much and a lifetime wouldn't be enough? I love you too much to let you go and enough to know I have to." Shock robbed her of speech. She only stared as he continued. "It was different when I didn't know, when I thought I was—how did you put it? 'Dazzled.'" He smiled briefly at the word. "I was certain if I could make love to you, I could get you out of my system. Then, the night Ari died, I held you while you slept. I realized I was in love with you, had been in love with you right from the beginning."

"But you…" Jo shook her head as if to clear it. "You never told me, and you seemed so cold, so distant."

"I couldn't touch you without wanting more." He pulled her close again and for a moment buried his face in her hair. "But I couldn't stay away. I knew if I wanted to have you, to really have you, one of us had to give up what we did, what we were. I wondered if I could give up the law; it was really all I ever wanted to do. I discovered I wanted you more."

"Oh, Keane." She shook her head, but he put her from him suddenly.

"Then I found out that wouldn't work, either." Keane turned, paced to the window and stared out. The snow was falling heavily. "Every time you walked into that cage, I walked into hell. I thought perhaps I'd get used to it, but it only got worse. I tried leaving, coming back here, but I could never shake you loose. I kept coming back. The day you were hurt…" Keane paused. Jo heard him draw in his breath, and when he continued, his voice was deeper. "I watched you step in front of that boy and take the blow. I can't tell you what I felt at that moment; there aren't words for it. All I could think of was getting to you. I wonder if Pete ever told you that I decked him before Buck got to me. He took it very well, considering. Then I had to—to just stand there and watch while that cat stalked you. I've never known that kind of fear before. The kind that empties you out, body and soul."

He lapsed into silence. "Then it was over," he continued, "and I got to you. You were so white, and you were bleeding in my arms." He muttered an oath, then was silent again. He shook his head. "I wanted to burn the place down, get you away, strangle the cats with my bare hands. Anything. I wanted to hold you, but I couldn't get past the fear and the unreasonable anger at having been helpless. Before my hands stopped shaking, you were making plans to go back into that damnable cage. I wanted to kill you myself then and be done with it."

Slowly, Keane turned and walked back to her. "I saw it happen again every time I closed my eyes for weeks afterward. I can show you exactly where the scars are." He lifted a finger and traced four lines on her upper arm precisely where the claws had ripped her skin. He dropped his hand and shook his head. "I can't watch you go in the cage, Jo." He lifted his hand again and let it linger over her hair. "If I let you stay with me now, I wouldn't be able to let you go back to your own life. And I can't ask you to give it up."

"I wish you would." Solemn-eyed, Jo watched him. "I very much wish you would."

"Jo." Shaking his head, he turned away. "I know what it means to you."

"No more than the law means to you, I imagine," she said briskly. "But you said you were willing to give that up."

"Yes, but…"

"Oh, very well." She pushed back her hair. "If you won't ask me, I'll have to ask you. Will you marry me?"

Keane turned back, giving her his lowered brow frown. "Jo, you can't…"

"Of course I can. This is the twentieth century. If I want to ask you to marry me, then I will. I did," she pointed out.

"Jo, I don't…"

"Yes or no, please, counselor. This isn't an easy question." She stepped forward until they stood toe to toe. "I'm in love with you, and I want to marry you and have several babies. Is that agreeable?"

Keane's mouth opened and closed. He gave her an odd smile and lifted his hands to her shoulders. "This is rather sudden."

Jo felt a wild surge of joy. "Perhaps it is," she admitted. "I'll give you a minute to think about it. But I might as well tell you, I won't take no for an answer."

Keane's fingers traced the curve of her neck. "It seems I have little choice."

"None at all," she corrected. Boldly, she locked her arms around him and pulled his mouth down to hers. The kiss was instantly urgent, instantly searching. Joined, they lowered to the rug and clung. For a long, long moment, their lips were united in a language too complex for words. Then, as if to reassure himself she was real, Keane searched the familiar curves of her body, tasted the longed-for flavor of her skin.

"Why did I think I could live without you?" he whispered. His mouth came desperately back to hers. "Be sure, Jo, be sure." Roughened with emotion, his voice was low while the words were spoken against her lips. "I'll never be able to let you go. I'm asking you for everything."

"No. No, it's not like that. Hold me tighter. Kiss me again," she demanded as his lips roamed her face. "Kiss me." She wondered if the sound of pleasure she heard was his or her own. She had not known a kiss could be so intimate, so terrifyingly exciting. No, she thought as she soared with the knowledge that he loved her. He wasn't asking everything, he was giving it.

"I'm leaving something behind," she told him when their lips parted, "and replacing it with something infinitely more important." She buried her face in the curve of his neck. "When you realize how much I love you, you'll understand."

Keane drew away and stared down at her. At last he spoke, but it was only her name. It was a soft sigh of a sound. She smiled at it and lifted a hand to his cheek. "If there's a way to compromise…"

"No." She shook her head, remembering his mother's words. "Sometimes there can't be a compromise. We love each other enough not to need one. Please, don't think I'm making a sacrifice; I'm not." She smiled a little and rubbed her palm experimentally over the stubble of his neglected beard. "I don't regret one minute of my life in the circus, and I don't regret changing it. You've given me the circus, so I'll always be a part of it." Her smile faded, and her eyes grew serious. "Will you belong to me, Keane?"

He took her hand from his cheek and pressed it to his lips. "I already do. I love you, Jovilette. I'll spend a lifetime loving you."

"That's not long enough," she said as their lips met again. "I want more. I want forever."

With slow, building passion, his hands moved over her. Taking his time, he loosened the buttons on her sweater. "So beautiful," he murmured as his lips trailed down her throat and found the gentle swell. Jo's breath caught at the new intimacy. "You're trembling. I love knowing I can make your skin tremble under my hands." His lips roamed back to hers before he cradled her in his arms. "I've wanted to be with you, to hold you, just hold you, for so long. I can't remember not wanting it."

With a sigh washed with contentment, Jo snuggled against him. "Keane," she murmured.

"Hmm?"

"You never answered me."

"About what?" He kissed her closed lids, then tangled his fingers in her hair.

Jo opened her eyes. Her brows arched over them. "Are you going to marry me or not?"

Keane laughed, rolled her onto her back and planted a long, lingering kiss on her mouth. "Is tomorrow soon enough?"

★ ★ ★ ★ ★

#1 *New York Times* and *USA TODAY* bestselling author

NORA ROBERTS

presents two classic stories about the kind of love
that arrives like a storm and changes everything....

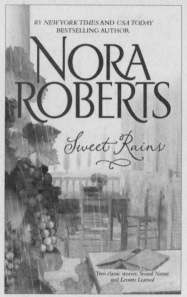

Sweet Rains

Coming soon wherever books are sold!

"Compelling and dimensional characters, intriguing plots,
passionate love stories—Nora Roberts...romance at its finest."
—*Rendezvous*